"ROSIE,

Thistle called to the queen of Chicory.

"Go away!" Rosie yelled back from the flower directly above Thistle's head. Only it wasn't a flower. Rosie had curled up in a ball, letting her petal gown mimic the adjacent blossoms.

"Rosie, this is important. Mabel is sick. She sent me here to protect you all until she can come home again."

"We know. Go away. We don't need you."

"Yes, you do."

"What can you do? You're a woodland Pixie, as wild as a Dandelion. We're a civilized garden tribe."

"Ask anyone in this district how well I tend gardens," Thistle shot back, affronted. "A Pixie is a Pixie. We all listen to plants of any variety to learn what they need to thrive." She shifted her gaze, seeking signs of movement or flashes of color.

"Rosie, where is your tribe?" Thistle asked suspiciously.

"None of your business."

"It is my business if they are all off fighting valley Pixies, or . . . or . . ." Stars above, could they be attacking the Pixies in The Ten Acre Wood, Thistle's tribe?

Not that Alder, her king and philandering lover, didn't deserve to be thrown off his throne. His own tribe was the only one with the right to do that.

Thistle didn't know for sure. She needed to talk to Alder. Not likely to happen while she was exiled to a human body.

"We're at war, Thistle," Rosie said in that superior way of hers. "And there's nothing you can do about it. We all know where your loyalties lie. And it isn't in my garden."

# CHICORY UP

Irene Radford

**DAW BOOKS, INC.**

Donald A. Wollheim, Founder

375 Hudson Street, New York, NY 10014

Elizabeth R. Wollheim

Sheila E. Gilbert

Publishers

www.dawbooks.com

First Printing, May 2012
1  2  3  4  5  6  7  8  9

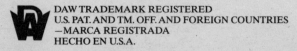

# CHICORY
# UP

# Prologue

CHICORY PEERED THROUGH THE LACY fronds of a bracken fern. His blue wings fluttered in unease. The pond at the center of The Ten Acre Wood looked full and healthy, as it should on the first day of summer vacation. A fat bullfrog croaked, slugs inched along the verge, birds sang in glorious morning greetings, and dozens of Pixies flitted about. Presiding over them all, the Patriarch Oak, full of sprouting mistletoe, invited climbers. Children should flock here from every Pixie territory for miles around.

Dawn had come and gone hours ago. The sun burned off the last traces of dew from the blooming foxgloves and the depression in the middle of lupine leaf clusters.

"Perfect," he murmured to his charges. A bit of pride made his chest swell. Finally, Queen Rosie had entrusted this vital work to him, Chicory, a ditch weed of a Pixie. *But a loyal and trustworthy ditch weed*, he reassured himself.

"Are they here yet? I don't see any children? Where are they?" Dandelion Five chittered in excitement.

"Hush," Chicory hissed at all seven of his charges. "We have to be quiet. This isn't our territory. But it's the best place for Pixies to make friends with children. That's important. Our most important work."

"Hush yourself. Never known you to keep your mouth shut for more than three heartbeats," Dandelion One sneered.

*Dandelions!* Too dumb to remember orders, and so many of them, impossible to tell them apart. That was why they had numbers instead of individual names. He was sure that other Pixie tribes had *a* Chicory, *a* Rose, *a* Foxglove, one of each, but only one. Every tribe had a horde of Dandelions. Often a dozen or more. They bred so fast no one could keep track of them all. Few bothered to look close enough to determine male from female.

Just then, three boys tromped noisily along the path from the park to the south. They probably thought they were moving quietly in their game of Pirate Treasure, or Cowboys and Indians, whatever adolescents played this year. To Pixie senses they thrashed and stomped, their whispers almost as loud as shouts.

"They look like eleven-year-olds," Chicory guessed. "Just about the age boys give up believing in Pixies," he continued in whispered tones. "Our job is to make sure they continue believing and let us stick around as friends to help them through the most difficult years of their lives."

"Impossible. Once they give up believing, it's useless to try and change their minds," Dandelion Eight said, crossing her arms and hunkering down into the leaf litter.

"Not impossible. Just difficult. That's why it's so important we do this."

"I'm tired. Let's go home," Dandelion Twelve whined. He was the youngest and smallest of the lot, probably too young to do the job. But old enough to learn about stubborn adolescent boys.

The boys in question each picked up a stout stick and swiped the tops off of the towering foxgloves. The round redheaded boy with lots of freckles and ears sticking out to the sides took a proper stance and stabbed with his mock sword. "Take that, you traitor to the Boy Scout oath," he pronounced as he lunged into a mass of sword ferns.

"Boy Scouts are lame," said the skinny, dark-haired boy with swarthy skin. He spoke with the inflection of another language holding primary place beneath his words.

"My Aunt Mabel says Boy Scouts are the best training for the Police Academy. I want to be a policeman when I grow up," the redhead continued in his superior tones.

"Cops are bullies," the youngest of the boys whispered shyly. "My dad says never trust a cop."

"Are not!" Red insisted. He turned his stick toward the other two, as if ready to run them through with a real sword. "You two aren't really my friends. You're bad boys. Disrespectful boys. Just like Aunt Mabel said." The last came out in a disappointed whisper.

"Cops are pigs!" Dark-hair placed his hands on his hips and stood as tall as he could, almost a full Pixie length taller than Red.

"Who'd let you be a cop?" Shy Boy asked. "You're too fat to pass the physical."

Chicory itched to dash in and calm the hostility. Boys should play, not fight. Their battles should train them to defend themselves, not hurt each other.

"Take it back!" Red screamed at his fellows. He cast aside his stick and launched himself through the air at the skinny boy. They tussled, rolling in the mud until Red landed half in the water. He howled in distress. Skinny sobbed and crawled through the muck to drier ground.

"Chicken, Bryon? Giving up 'cause Ian hurt you?" the dark-haired one taunted. "What kind of name is Ian anyway? Sounds like a wimp. Fights like a wimp, too."

"Go away, Luis," Red—er—Ian spat. He, too, crawled away from the mud.

*Names are important*, Chicory reminded himself. Have to remember the names so he'd know who they truly were.

"Can't hold your own in a fight?" Luis titled his head back and roared with laughter.

The indigenous Pixies congregating within the tree shadow giggled, too. Anything for a laugh, not caring who got hurt.

"They're so careless they're halfway to becoming Faeries," Chicory snarled.

He glared at the fun-loving, wild tribe of Pixies. Still, he held his troop of Dandelions back. The time had not yet come to intervene. Maybe it would not appear today.

All of the Pixies stilled. The entire Ten Acre Wood seemed to hold its breath.

Then Chicory heard the measured tread of another human intruder. An older boy, perhaps fifteen, sauntered into the clearing. His unwashed blond hair flopped heavily into his eyes and curled over the collar of his cracked leather jacket.

"Why's he wearing leather on a warm day like today?" Dandelion Three asked. Sensibly, she kept her voice low, barely more than the whisper of the breeze.

"Because he thinks it makes him look important," Chicory whispered back.

"Stupid human. Importance comes from how you act and how many people you help," Dandelion One recited one of the first lessons of Pixie.

"He hasn't figured that out yet," Chicory said. He didn't like the way the other tribe slunk off into the shadows. This was their territory. Why weren't they driving off this boy, or befriending him?

"It's not nice to fight." Leather Jacket slid the words out, like nasty oil on top of a puddle.

"Huh?" the younger boys replied almost in unison.

"If you want to be special—and important—I can show you how." Leather Jacket sidled up to Luis, the apparent leader of the trio, the one who stood aside from the fight but egged on the kids with his taunts.

All three boys looked up to the older one, eyes wide, expressions questioning.

"I've got some extra pixie sugar, special flavors all wrapped up tight in pretty paper tubes. I'm willing to share."

"Never take candy from a stranger," Red said, but not very convincingly. He heaved himself to his feet, then offered a hand up to Bryon.

"Lemme see," Luis demanded, not moving from his aggressive stance.

Leather Jacket pulled his left hand out of his pocket and slowly opened his fingers to reveal four brightly striped paper tubes, each wrapped in the clear stuff humans loved for protecting food.

All three younger boys leaned forward, peering closely at the neon pink, chocolate brown, and blinding green. "What is it?" Luis asked before the others.

Red edged backward a half step, unsure.

"Special sugar dust. Only cool guys get to eat them. I kinda like your attitude, Luis. You should be able to handle the chocolate one. It's more special than the strawberry or the lime. I'm keeping the blueberry for myself."

Luis grimaced as if he didn't truly understand the boy.

"I mean, you look big enough, and smart enough to take good advantage of this candy. But if you're afraid...." Leather Jacket started to close his hand and return the contents to his pocket.

"I'm not afraid of nothin'," Luis protested. His hand darted out and grabbed the strawberry-pink one.

"Me, too!" Bryon chimed in. He slid his hand up to take one, like a snake slithering through the grass. He latched onto the lime.

"Not so fast, Bryon." Leather Jacket trapped the youngest boy's hand within his own. "Red's bigger than you. He hasn't taken his yet. I bet he's worthy of the chocolate."

"And I'm not going to take one." He looked to Luis and wrinkled his nose. "They smell funny. You've probably left them out in the sun, and they've spoiled."

"Not at all, my friend. I made these up special just this morning." Leather Jacket stretched his arm so that the brown-and-gold paper was right under Red's nose.

Chicory caught a strong whiff of mushrooms beneath the cloying sweetness of chocolate. "I don't like this at all. We've got to do something." he whispered. "Those mushrooms are dangerous. The sugar just covers up the taste so the boys won't notice what they're eating."

The Dandelions cringed away from him. "Wh ... what can we do?"

"I don't know ..."

"Will this help?" Dandelion Seven flew quickly to a hawthorn bush in full bloom. Deftly, he broke off one of the thorns, about half as long as he was.

"Yeah, that'll work." Chicory fetched his own weapon from the obliging shrub.

"Wow, that's the biggest butterfly ever," Bryon turned lazy circles staring up at a purple-and-green Pixie who dared come out of hiding to inspect the candied mushroom powder.

"Dragonfly. Dragons wheeling on the wind, spouting clouds instead of fire," Luis added, wobbling his own circles.

Bright candy colors smudged the corners of their mouths

and around the edges of their noses. They'd sniffed the mushrooms.

*Too late.* Chicory chided himself. *We waited too long in indecision.*

"Eat it!" Leather Jacket demanded of Red.

"No. You can't make me." Ian took off for the path toward the open park. But his tennis shoes squelched with water, leaking mud with every step, slowing him down. His round body wasn't fit enough for a fast sprint.

"You guys are stupid. Not cool. I should have stayed friends with Chase and Dick, not you losers." Ian stumbled and sobbed in his desperation to get away.

Before he could fully right himself, Leather Jacket jerked out a long leg. Ian tripped and sprawled full length in the underbrush, sobbing. Leather Jacket leaped on his back and tried to stuff the chocolate powder into the younger boy's mouth. Ian clamped his teeth and shook his head. Leather Jacket grabbed a fistful of red hair and pulled sharply upward.

Ian howled in pain, only to have the candy jammed into his now open mouth.

"Pixies to the rescue!" Chicory called, brandishing his makeshift sword. Without checking to see if the Dandelions followed him, Chicory dove toward the intruder. He grinned fiercely when the point of his thorn struck the boy in the cheek and drew blood, a bright red dot.

Flipping into a backward summersault, the Pixie snagged a hank of greasy hair and pulled.

Leather Jacket slapped one hand to his injured cheek, the other to the top of his head, releasing Ian. "Ow!"

Chicory didn't bother chortling in victory. He flew in for another stab, and another. Each time he yanked out a few more hairs and tossed them into the pond.

After the fifth strike, Leather Jacket was hopping around, trying to avoid his attacker. Ian got to his feet and hastened away, his mouth agape in horror. "Bad drugs. This is what bad drugs do to you. I don't see real Pixies. I never have. Aunt Mabel's 'Pixies' are just warped hallucinations from her heart medicine," he said, cringing away from the blossoming red spots on his enemy's face. Then he ducked out of sight. "I'll never eat chocolate or candy again. I'll never, ever take any kind of drugs again!"

Chicory took a moment to check on the Dandelions. They mimicked his actions, darting in and out, attacking Luis and Bryon, not Leather Jacket. The boys' faces were now masses of dripping red splotches—worse than any case of teenage acne.

The purple Pixie the boys had previously admired joined in the attack, giggling all the while.

Oh, well. At least those boys had learned never to take candy from a stranger. Chicory hummed a sprightly tune to reinforce the lesson. *Dum dum, do do, dee dee dum.*

He stopped in mid-phrase as Leather Jacket shrank, shedding his clothes and mask of greasy dirt. A bright Gold Faery with green edges emerged and flew away.

"Had to be a Faery. Too big to be a Pixie," Chicory reassured the Dandelions. But the creature had woven, grasslike wings and the softer, rounder features of a Pixie.

Oh, well, best forget it. The kids had learned a lesson, and that was all that was important.

*Dum dum, do do, dee dee dum.*

# One

*Twenty years later.*

"DUM, DEE DEE, DO DUM DUM," Thistle Down hummed her own special music as she bent over the darkest red rose in the garden. The rose swayed in time with her song as if a light breeze stirred through the dawn air on this damp October morning. With the plant duly lulled into cooperation, she flicked a cotton swab around the inside petals.

"Got it!" she chortled, holding up the swab, now covered in rich pollen. "Now to find a likely partner. You know you all want to help me create a purple rose, the same color my hair used to be."

The rose responded by piercing her finger with a long thorn where she still held the stem.

"Ouch!" she protested, sucking her wound. She tasted a single drop of crimson blood, the same color as the rose. "You had no call to do that. You're just being selfish by keeping all that lovely pollen to yourself. If I were still a Pixie, you'd gladly share so I could have a good meal."

The rose stood tall and proud, not at all repentant.

"Or maybe you prefer to feed treacherous Faeries instead of honest Pixies," she accused.

Another thorn jabbed her butt.

"Ouch. There was no need for that, you nasty rose." But the plant stood straight and silent denying her accusation. It hadn't reached behind her.

She swung around. A flutter of movement without substance drew her eye in wild spirals up and down, back and forth, and around and around. Thistle spun about trying to follow the blue blur. Her head couldn't keep up, sending her into dizzy wobbles. She staggered around the side yard, arms out, trying to find her balance while avoiding the fake tombstone Halloween decorations.

If only she had her Pixie wings back, she'd right herself quite readily.

The stabbing pain came again. She jumped, slapping her hand over her wounded bottom.

"Stop it!" she yelled at the blue blur that was now joined by a bright yellow-and-red one. "Slow down so I can see you when you attack me."

A sly giggle erupted from somewhere behind her, in the vicinity of the last of the dahlias.

She focused on how the tall blossom-heavy stalks swayed and nodded. Her head stopped spinning at last, just before she encountered the witch's cauldron suspended by a tripod over a fake fire. The witch mannequins hadn't yet gravitated from attic to yard; otherwise she'd have crashed into them and sent the entire display sprawling.

One last deep breath, then she closed her eyes and re-opened them looking for the *thing* out of place. There! She spotted the Pixie, a splotch of not-quite-right golden yellow with purply-red streaks against the greenery. A dashing fellow all decked out in sunset colors. His translucent faded brown wings took the form of multiple sheaves of grass woven together. Their edges looked limp and curled in odd places with a few holes crusted in red around the edges. That did not look healthy.

She didn't recognize him. He wasn't from one of the local tribes.

The blue blur zoomed in on the yellow fellow, a long spike from a hawthorn tree held out like a sword.

"Chicory?" She followed the blue-garbed male. He'd lost his multi-petal cap, and a thin trail of red blood dripped down his left arm.

Thistle slid her hand around him, capturing him easily. A sure sign that the wound slowed him down.

"Let me go," Chicory protested. He wiggled and

squirmed, jabbing at her tiredly with his thorn sword. The point barely pricked her palm.

"Chicory, what ails you?"

"Seeking refuge at the hands of a human," the yellow fellow's voice sounded a bit ragged and breathless as it slid up and down an atonal scale in squeaks and slurs. Not musical at all. More like that awful noise teens called "Rock."

"I was captured," Chicory protested to his opponent. "At least I'm not hiding from the finer soldier."

"Soldier? What's this about? Pixies have no soldiers, no armies. We do not war among ourselves," Thistle said.

"What's she talking about? Talking about? She's no Pixie. No Pixie." The yellow male peeked out from behind the heavy flower head that nearly mimicked his own colors.

"She used to be our own Thistle Down," Chicory yelled back. Then he lowered his voice to a whisper, "Walk me closer, Thistle. I'll stab him from behind."

"No, I won't. Now explain yourselves. Why are you fighting, and who is this stranger? He's not from any of the tribes and gardens in Skene Falls."

"No, he's from the valley." Somewhat recovered from his exertions, Chicory stood taller and brandished his sword again.

"If he's from the valley . . ."

"He's Snapdragon, another of Milkweed's relatives, out to avenge her disgrace. And he's trying to steal our queen."

"Milkweed." Anger churned through Thistle. "The woman who stole my mate."

"I thought Alder betrayed you by making the silly white trollop his queen. But she never took a mating flight with him once she discovered how many females he had flown with already—including you. And now this intruder thinks he should have a mating flight with our Rosie to compensate, or something."

"Whatever." Thistle wished the story of Alder's betrayal would die an ignoble death instead of becoming part of Pixie mythology.

"Milkweed ended the marriage treaty, marriage treaty, but Alder won't let my sister go home! Go home!" yelled the yellow fellow.

Huh? He sounded like Dusty's computer, pausing and resetting. That meant something. Something important. But Thistle couldn't remember what.

"Excuse me, miss," a tentative voice came from the other side of the rose hedge.

Thistle looked up hastily, holding Chicory behind her, as fiercely as possible to keep him from zooming over to see who interrupted his argument with Milkweed's relative.

"Can I help you?" Thistle asked.

"Um . . . I'm a bit lost." A teenage girl stepped to the side so that she was visible between the deep-red rose and a cream-colored one with pink-fading-to-yellow edges. She looked cold, shivering in her thin T-shirt and faded jeans. She carried a limp pink backpack on one shoulder. Something about her lank, dark blonde hair hanging in ringlets reminded Thistle of someone.

"Where do you need to go?" Thistle shifted her hold on Chicory as he jabbed her palm with his sword. The shape of the girl's chin and the set of her brow also looked familiar. Who?

"I'm looking for Mabel. Um . . . I think her last name's Gardiner. Mabel Gardiner, yeah that's it." The girl child, just barely bursting into womanhood, leaned forward between the roses, peering at the Queen Anne style house with the huge wraparound porch and conical tower that dominated the corner lot.

*Curious*, Thistle thought. Maybe she was just cold and damp enough to need to get indoors quickly.

Not long after dawn, Mabel might not have left home for work.

"Lemme see," Chicory whispered, momentarily distracted from his fight with the yellow Pixie. "She might be one of Mabel's waifs. I need to know . . ."

Thistle closed her hand around Chicory once more.

"Tenth Street and Maple Drive. Small cottage with a white picket fence, and a climbing rose over the gate," Thistle said.

The girl looked blank.

"Two blocks that way to Maple Drive, then another three uphill."

"Oh, okay." The girl took one last look at the hot pink house with purple-and-green trim, shifted her backpack to the other shoulder, and hurried away.

"Curious," Thistle mused again. She let her gaze follow the girl.

Chicory used her distraction to squirm free and zipped toward his opponent. Like most Pixies, he had no memory and less concentration.

"You should follow the girl," Thistle called to him.

"What girl? This is more important!" he yelled fiercely as he thrust his sword deep into the yellow dahlia.

Yellow and red sprang up just in time. His wings fluttered erratically, the red veins deepening in color and spreading outward. Chicory followed his every loop around the plastic skeleton hanging from a tree branch. They soared above the cauldron, and dove through the tombstones. Both of their wickedly sharp, miniature swords flashed and jabbed.

"Stop it!" They both ignored Thistle's plea. "Stop it. Pixies don't fight each other. That's what humans do."

"Wrong," both Pixies yelled back at her. "Wrong, wrong, wrong," Snapdragon repeated.

"What do you mean? We're supposed to befriend those in need of a friend. That girl needs help. Pixie help."

"Whatever," Chicory muttered, still absorbed in his murderous task.

"There hasn't been a war among Pixies in . . . in . . . for as long as any of us can remember."

Chicory stabbed again. He pushed his reach too far. His wings couldn't keep up with his body and he tumbled toward the grass.

Thistle dove to catch him in her hands, sliding on the dew-slick lawn until her head fetched up against the plywood-and-plaster grave marker for William Shakespeare—conveniently the death date was left blank. According to Juliet, Thistle's hostess and her best friend's mother, the Bard would never die as long as his plays were performed and read.

Green stains spread all along the side of Thistle's gray sweatshirt and blue jeans. Her body stung everywhere she made contact with the ground.

At the last second, she caught Chicory by the wingtip between two fingernails. His feet dangled an eyelash width above the longest tip of the lawn that had been cut the day before.

"Lemme go!" Chicory protested. He wiggled and stabbed at her with his thorn.

"Not until you tell me why you and that stranger are trying to kill each other."

"Because that's what Pixies do! What Pixies do!" Snapdragon chortled. "Just ask the Dandelions. Just ask the Dandelions."

"No, we don't kill each other," Thistle protested. "We have marriage treaties among our kings and queens to prevent that. And Dandelions will follow anyone rather than make a decision on their own." Evidenced by a troop of them winding a maze among the garish Halloween decorations.

"The peace treaty giving supervision of the Patriarch Oak to your tribe, Thistle, is broken, and so are all the marriage treaties between the valley and ridge tribes. Even my queen Rosie has shredded her agreement with Milkweed's brother Hay," Chicory panted. "But this crazy guy won't accept that."

"The Ten Acre Wood treaty was imposed by the Faeries. Faeries, Faeries, Faeries. It created an artificial peace," yellow and red sneered. "Hold him still, still, still, while I run him through! Run him through." He dove with his own hawthorn sword extended.

Thistle rolled out of the way. Faery snot! That guy was fast.

"Why didn't you extend the treaty after we saved the Patriarch Oak from fire two months ago? The peace worked for *generations*, Faery imposed or not," she insisted, gasping for breath as she dodged the battle. "Rosie is better off without that conniving sneak Hay, but the other marriages are good and solid."

"Because we don't know how to do big treaties." Chicory bravely continued to harass his enemy and her from his precarious position. "You're the only Pixie who thinks about such things, Thistle. And you aren't a Pixie anymore."

Snapdragon howled as if in pain and dove directly for Thistle's eye. She ducked and rolled again, feeling the whoosh of his flight sting her ear. His sword grazed the tombstone, leaving a long white gash in the gray plaster.

It had to be Shakespeare's marker. Juliet was so not going to like that. Not one bit.

# Two

**P**OLICE SERGEANT CHASE NORTON finished signing in at the dispatch desk of headquarters behind City Hall in downtown Skene Falls. He looked over the duty assignments. So far nothing out of the ordinary. He was free to go on patrol. As long as he didn't acknowledge the backup of paperwork on his desk, maybe he could skip it a while longer.

"Sergeant Norton," Mabel Gardiner called. She sat right in front of him. She didn't have to speak so loudly, like she was calling to him from across the street, or had gone deaf since eight last night.

"Why so formal, sweetheart?" He grinned at her. She called him more intimate endearments despite the forty-year difference in their ages, and her seniority in the department. Mabel had anchored the department for so long, no one could remember her not being there. Nor would anyone allow her to retire in case she decided two as a civilian she could inform the town where all the bodies were buried, who had skeletons in their closet, and who was sleeping with whom.

Her army of Pixie spies helped her maintain an aura of omniscience. But only a few in town, like Chase, knew about that.

"Did you see this?" She passed him a single sheet of paper with a picture dominating the center of the page.

"Child missing," he sighed. He'd seen too many of these notices over the years.

"Not just any CM." She rattled the paper to draw his attention.

"Pretty fourteen-year-old runaway from Seattle area," he acknowledged.

"Not just any missing fourteen-year-old. Look at the name." Mabel sounded impatient with him.

"Alessandra Langford." He paused to think about that. Familiar name. . . ."Sandy Langford? Left town at the end of my junior year in high school. Didn't she date Dick Carrick for a while?" Oh, yeah, Dick had dated her. Chase had doubled with them a couple of times with a variety of girls. He always felt like a third wheel when Dick was with Sandy.

"Sandy went to school with you and Dick. Dick took her to the junior prom."

"Sheesh! Do you remember every date every student had in the last fifty years?"

Mabel ignored that. "Mother goes by Sandy. Her daughter is Alessa."

Something bothered him about that. Fourteen-year-old daughter. He and Dick had graduated fourteen years ago. Junior prom the previous May. . . .

"My thoughts exactly," Mabel smirked. Had she read his mind?

"Sandy wasn't the type." Except with Dick. They fogged up the windows of the car more than once.

"There is no 'type' to teenage pregnancy."

"Langford. She kept her maiden name. Why?"

"Probably never married. What is unusual is that she managed to keep her daughter this long without family support."

"Her parents?"

Mabel shrugged. "Never really knew them even though their house is on my block. I don't run with the golf-and-country-club set. Their too-big-to-take-care-of house—the Corbett mansion—has been empty more often than not since they left town a couple of years *after* Sandy left town. A missing or runaway report with her name never crossed my desk until now."

"They used to go to church with my folks. You think they threw her out?"

"Possible. Happens more often than we want to think. More concerned with their status at the country club than their daughter's welfare. Her disgrace is their disgrace times ten."

"So what am I supposed to do?" Chase asked, studying the picture. He had a feeling about that sandy-blonde hair and the set of the stubborn chin. "I can't track every runaway picture that crosses your desk."

"Just keep your eyes out for her while patrolling rather than finishing your paperwork. Her mother is one of ours. Six months since Alessa was last seen in Seattle. If she's headed this way, there's a good chance she's looking for relatives and a place to come in from the cold about now."

Chase laid the paper down on Mabel's desk. He'd memorized the picture.

"Keep it, sweetie. I want this one to turn out right."

"We all want them *all* to turn out right."

"But this time we have a vested interest in that child."

"Do we tell him?"

"Not yet, sweetheart. Not until we know if she's in town and possibly looking for him. Sandy should have told him fifteen years ago but didn't. Maybe for a reason." She looked around cautiously, nodded slightly to indicate Chief Beaumain sauntering down the hall from his office with a report he looked ready to hand to Chase. "My special friends will tell me if there's a new kid in town in need of shelter."

Dick Carrick vaulted over the low gate set in the middle of a sagging picket fence across the back of his parents' property. He had to push aside a dangling scarecrow to get through, which made him stumble on the flagstone path. "Damn. I should have taken up running years ago, not last month," he groaned as he righted himself. "Or Mom could grow up and cut back on the excess decorations."

The exercise only marginally burned off Dick's frustration. He still thought about Thistle far too often. Yearned for her, went out of his way to watch her throughout the day.

Panting from the mile he'd jogged, he dragged himself up wooden steps to the back porch. A note in the middle of a

funereal wreath made of black silk roses on the screen door
reminded him to tidy himself at the set tub. Mom had a way
of making him feel ten again. Dutifully he stuck his head
beneath the faucet and let the tepid water drench his hair.
While he toweled off, he contemplated the cracks in the old
cement sink.

A lot of memories from four generations of Carricks
were invested in this back porch. He couldn't remember if
the Queen Anne style monstrosity had been built when his
great-great-grandmother was alive or if it came later. He
did remember kissing Sandy Langford here when they were
fifteen. Sandy didn't quite live up to Thistle as a kisser, but
she came mighty close. He remembered being sent into the
garden to cut long-stemmed flowers: roses, dahlias, and carnations—Mom insisted on calling them gilly flowers as was
popular in Shakespearean times—and then placing them
into buckets of water in this sink. Later his Mom would
take them inside and arrange them into vases (with the soft
British a) for a party.

Mom hadn't entertained at all since she and Dad came
home from Stratford-upon-Avon six weeks ago. As much as
he hated her formal dinners and elegant tea parties, he almost wished she'd gather her friends in the parlor once
more.

Anything to turn her mind away from her latest obsession. His sister Dusty's wedding. Not even the town All
Hallows Eve celebration and resulting overdecorating distracted her from her exuberant wedding plans. She'd even
forgotten to quote her much-beloved Bard every other sentence.

He shook his head, spraying water like a dog. "Hey,
Mom, what's for breakfast?" he asked as he stepped onto
the black-and-white tiles of the kitchen floor. Then he
stopped short, flushing with embarrassment.

"Desdemona Carrick, if you continue to eat like that,
you won't be able to fit into your wedding gown," Mom
said, hands on hips, staring down at her only daughter. "I'm
paying a great deal of money to have a custom design made
for you."

Dusty sat at the long farm table that filled most of the big old kitchen. She hung her head over a plate of scrambled eggs and hash browns with a huge cup of coffee clutched in her hand. She never drank coffee until she got engaged to Dick's best friend Chase Norton. Now she drank it black and strong enough to etch a spoon, just like Chase did.

"Mom, she has an appetite for the first time since she was nine," Dick intervened. "Let her eat. She's too skinny as it is." Dick moved to stand between his mother and his sister.

"You don't need to protect me, Dick," Dusty said quietly.

Dick turned around and looked her in the eye, raising an eyebrow in question.

> *"My daughter!*
> *O my ducats! O my daughter!*
> *Fled with a Christian!*
> *O my Christian ducats!*
> *Justice! The law! My ducats, and my daughter!*
> *A sealed bag, two sealed bags of ducats,*
> *Of double ducats, stol'n from me by my daughter!"*

Mom wailed, quoting from *The Merchant of Venice*.

"*The Merchant of Venice*, Shylock, act two," Dusty sighed.

Mom no longer tested her children with quotes from the Bard, but she still spouted his immortal prose whenever she could. Apropos of the situation or not.

"If I'm too fat for the wedding gown Mom chose, then I'll just have to find a different one that fits better. Which I'll pay for myself." A smile tugged at the corner of Dusty's mouth, but her eyes looked wounded.

"Desdemona!" Mom screeched. "I don't believe my daughter would ever be so impolite. And as for you, Benedict . . ."

"Get over it, Mom. Your little girl grew up this summer. She's going to get married and move out in December. You won't be able to pick at her and keep her in swaddling clothes much longer."

"I'm right here, Dick. Please don't speak about me as if I weren't," Dusty said.

"Sorry, Sis."

"Well, you two can finish this argument without me," Dusty said firmly. "I'm going to work. Do you need Thistle today, Mom? I could use her help down at the museum. We're still marking the paths for the haunted maze through The Ten Acre Wood. We need to make sure they vary a bit from last year—make it more interesting." Dusty carried her plate and cup to the sink and rinsed them. Almost half her breakfast went down the garbage disposal.

"Thistle is working in the garden today," Mom replied on a pout. "Your friend is a true genius with flowers. The roses have never bloomed so well so late in the year. If anyone can get a winning, truly purple bloom for next year's Rose Festival that will best Mabel Gardiner's entry, it'll be Thistle Down. She and I have considered hiring her out to some of the neighbors who have problems with their roses. If you two would stop protecting her from reality, I could keep her in well-paid work most of the year."

*Take your own advice, Mom, and let go of Dusty*, Dick thought.

Right on cue, Thistle limped in from the back porch. She kicked off her damp sneakers at the door (required of all of them by Mom since the days of Dusty's protective isolation during chemo for childhood leukemia) and slumped into the nearest chair. She propped an elbow on the table and rested her forehead on her palm. The other hand she cradled limply against her chest.

Dick's pulse sped at the way her sweatshirt outlined her firm breasts when she pressed her hand so tightly between them.

"What's wrong?" he asked, kneeling beside her. One hand smoothed her long dark hair, so dark it almost had natural purple highlights, away from her face, noting a deep scratch on the slightly pointed tip of her ear. He looked for signs of other injury. Truly he did. Just because caressing her felt so good. . . .

Dick knew how to look for injury. He'd survived two years of medical school and came out with a Masters in biochemistry. He also kept up his Emergency Medical Technician license.

"Have you finished collecting rose pollen for the hybrid experiment?" Mom asked.

Dick looked at his sister, wondering why she wasn't helping him take care of her friend. Dusty continued standing at the sink, head down, saying nothing. He knew her thoughts. She could only deal with one crisis at a time. That's how the entire family had gotten through Dusty's cancer. At the moment, Mom triggered all her instincts to run and hide in the basement of her museum. Her eyes focused on the tiny diamond ring on her left hand, as if that symbol of her love for Chase and their coming wedding was a lifeline to sanity.

Even after the local doctors had said she had beaten the cancer and could resume a normal life, Mom had continued the habit of overprotection, homeschooling, preservative-free eating, and isolation from any germ that might dare enter the home.

Dick was as guilty as their mother. His bone marrow had helped cure Dusty. He had a responsibility to take care of her.

But Thistle needed him more than Dusty right now.

"Let me see your hand, Thistle," Dick said gently, prying the clenched fingers away from her palm. He swallowed his gasp at the sight of a three-inch hawthorn spike stuck in the thick flesh below the thumb. A steady trickle of fresh blood flowed across her palm into his. There was more on her left earlobe, like a piercing gone bad.

"What did you do?" Mom asked, reaching for the first aid kit just inside the pantry door. "Or rather, where have you been, dear? We don't have any hawthorn trees in our yard."

Mom never called Dusty "dear." She called her daughter "Baby" or her full name "Desdemona."

"The closest hawthorn is in the corner of The Ten Acre Wood where it meets the end of the gravel road," Dusty said. She moistened a paper towel and handed it to Dick. "Thistle, you swore you'd never go back there after the fire," she added more quietly.

"I didn't go there," Thistle breathed. "I won't. I can't." She fixed Dick with a pleading stare. "I must." She mouthed the last phrase.

Dick knew in his heart she had to return. Pixie was in her blood, her heritage, her entire life until her exile last August. She'd never settle for staying human.

She'd never settle for him as her mate.

He'd never settle for less than Thistle as a mate. Even Sandy Langford, his first sexual partner, paled in comparison.

He started cleaning her wound, the only thing he knew how to do at the moment, wishing the mending process extended to his heart.

# Three

"YOU CAN GO BACK TO THE TEN ACRE wood any time you want," Dick whispered to Thistle as he swabbed her wound clean with an alcohol prep pad.

His touch sent comforting vibrations all through Thistle. The alcohol didn't burn her nose and she barely noticed when he pulled the long thorn out of her hand.

"I can't go back unless I go back as a . . ." She looked cautiously at Juliet. Dick's mother had moved on to rewashing the dishes Dusty had washed earlier. "Unless I go back as I truly am," she admitted on a whisper. That opened a new ache in her heart.

She desperately needed to feel air beneath her wings, gather her tribe close as they curled up in a hollow log to hibernate for the winter, shed the cares and woes of humanity for a life lived in the moment, for the moment, and little else.

She needed to do all she could to stop the silly war among the tribes.

Dick lifted her chin with a gentle finger. "Don't cry, Thistle. I know it hurts."

She knew he meant her loss of Pixie rather than the puncture on her hand.

"But there are compensations. You can have me."

They both gasped at the issue they'd been waltzing around since that hot August morning she'd landed buck naked in Memorial Fountain at the height of rush hour, grown to full human size, minus her wings, her lavender skin, and purple hair. And most of her magic. If she'd felt alone and exiled then, she felt even more so now.

Except . . .

"Dick, I don't know. There are things I must do that I can only do as . . ."

Dick looked over his shoulder at Juliet. "Let's go upstairs to the bathroom. I want you to soak your hand in antiseptic," he said for the benefit of his mother.

"Does she need to see a doctor?" Juliet asked, still fussing with things at the sink. "Not that Thistle can afford to see a doctor. We really need to find her a good job with benefits, or at least enough work so that she can afford to buy insurance. Without the good insurance your father has from the school district, Dusty's cancer would have bankrupted us. You know if we could get your sister declared handicapped, she could stay on our insurance. The coverage the county gives her for the museum job isn't worth the premiums."

"Chase has good insurance through the police union." Dick grabbed Thistle's hand and dragged her up the back stairs before Juliet could deny that Dusty would ever actually go through with the wedding.

"She's just like old Foxglove," Thistle whispered on a giggle to Dick when they reached the upstairs hall. "Can't believe any of the little ones could possibly grow up and not need her anymore."

"That about sums it up." Dick ducked into the bathroom, still holding Thistle's hand.

She had to admit his touch made her feel all warm and cuddly, powerful enough to do anything she wanted to, yet very willing to melt into his arms and let him take away her worries and care.

He ran water into the sink and fished around beneath it for a bottle of something that smelled sharp and acidic. Not for a second did he let go of her hand.

Thistle wrinkled her nose. "Do I really need to soak in that? Wouldn't a little honey and a bandage work just as well?"

"Maybe for a Pixie. Honey does have certain antibiotic

properties. So do some spiderwebs. But this I *know* will work for a human body." Gently, Dick guided her wounded hand into the basin of water.

Thistle jerked it out again. "That's hot. And it stings."

"A little discomfort now will save a whole passel of trouble later." He pushed her hand back into the water and held it down with both of his hands.

Thistle squirmed until the water cooled a bit.

"Dick, what did you mean back in the kitchen when you said . . . when you said that I could have you if I had to give up Pixie?" She inched closer to him. His sweaty body smelled healthy and alive—as well as little rank—but that was as natural as the stubble on his face, a shade darker than his tawny blond hair.

"Thistle, you have to know that I've been in love with you since I was fourteen and you kissed me. My first kiss," he said softly, turning his head away.

"I know." With her free hand she turned his chin back to face her.

"And . . . and. . . ." He looked away again.

She rose up on tiptoe and kissed his cheek.

"Don't do that," he ground out.

"Why?"

"Because it makes me . . . because I only want to kiss you more and once I start, I might not stop."

"What's wrong with that?"

"Thistle, I won't pretend I haven't had several partners, starting with Sandy Langford and moving on to Phelma Jo Nelson and . . . more than a few others before I realized you are the only woman I truly want. When you and I make love, we will make a commitment. Sex for me, now, is a commitment, not a game." He gulped.

"I know."

"Thistle, what if the spell breaks and you suddenly become a Pixie again? Will you choose to go back to The Ten Acre Wood and a near immortal and carefree life? Or will you choose me?"

Something deep inside Thistle broke. "Dick, I honestly don't know which choice I'd make. I love you. I have since the first time you befriended me when you were five."

"I saved you from Phelma Jo putting you in a canning jar with a wolf spider." They both grinned. "And I saved you from Chase gluing your wings together with dog drool."

"You were special then and you still are. But I love Pixie. I loved being a Pixie. Yet there is trouble brewing, and I don't know the beginning or the end. I have commitments to my people."

"I can't ask you to make a choice. It has to be your decision."

"I've tried to go back. Truly I have. I've tried every bit of magic I know. I've stood at the edge of the wood and wished with all my heart. But I can't break the spell. I even asked Chicory and his brothers to throw Pixie dust on me, and it didn't work. If I can't ever go back, then I want to be with you."

"I can't take the chance that you'll just disappear on me one day. You said there are things in Pixie you need to do, that you can only do as a Pixie. You have to commit one way or another. All or nothing. Let me bandage your hand. Then I need to shower and get to work."

His touch became impersonal and distant, like a medical professional. Like he put on a different personality, a mask she couldn't peek under to find his true feelings.

"Owwww, owwww, owww!" Chicory screeched.

"Oh, hush. It's just a scratch. You're hardly bleeding," said Mabel Gardiner. She dabbed at his arm with a piece of gauze that stunk of sharp chemicals.

"You're making it worse," he sobbed.

"No, I'm not. This is alcohol, and it will kill any germs from dirt and stuff."

"You're killing me."

"Don't be such a drama queen."

"Queen? Queen! I'll have you know I'm not a queen. I'm as manly as any male you can name. Just ask Daisy."

Mabel rolled her eyes and shook her head hard enough for her tight curls to bob about. Chicory was the only one of her Pixies who knew that she indulged in bizarre rituals and concoctions to keep her hair tightly curled and white with pink-and-blue highlights, instead of gray and limp.

"I know, Chicory. I know. Drama queen means something else entirely. Now tell me how you got hurt."

"It's not important." Chicory hung his head. When Mabel said nothing, he peeked at her through his lowered lashes.

She sat back in her cushy chair at the police department dispatch desk and folded her arms. "Talk or I'll feed you to the stray cats behind the jail."

Chicory clamped his mouth shut on the words he wanted to say.

"You owe me truth, little man."

"I owe you a manicured garden."

"Is that all you're going to say?"

"That's all I *can* say. My arm still hurts. Can you put it in a sling?" He pouted and looked up at her in his best imitation of Peter Pan innocence.

"Only if you'll talk, and go looking for this child." She shoved a piece of paper toward him.

"It's too close. I have to fly to get proper focus and perspective." The black-and-white nose in the photo was as big as he was.

Mabel held out her palm for him to climb onto, then raised him high enough that the flat photo took on more recognizable lines, shades, and shadows. "Maybe," he said, twisting his neck to look at the image from all angles, including upside down. "Hard to say. The picture is flat. People aren't. Pixie eyes don't translate."

"This is not good, Chicory." Mabel shook her head, pushing the picture out of the way and returning Chicory to the desktop. "You lost your hat. I know how important your hat is as a symbol of your magic. You were due two new petals added to the crown for your help with the Masque Ball in August." She shifted topics but still held the cotton swab too close to the bloody scratch on his arm.

"I loved my hat. And I can't make a new one until next summer when chicory flowers bloom again." This time he let his lip tremble.

"So you aren't talking."
Chicory blinked rapidly as if fighting tears.
"Okay. I'm bringing in reinforcements."
"You wouldn't!"
"You bet your sweet patooty, young man."

# Four

DUSTY PULLED HER WOOL COAT TIGHTER around her as she paced the paths around the Skene County Historical Society Museum. Where were all the Pixies? They should be flitting about, gathering the last bits of pollen, nuts, and berries to tide them over the winter, or absorbing the stray shafts of low sunlight that filtered through the broken clouds.

A bevy of yellow-winged critters flew arrow-straight out of the woods, each holding a hawthorn spike directly in front of them, like spears or swords. They held a tight phalanx formation.

"So that's what Thistle wouldn't talk about this morning." She pushed her glasses higher on her nose to see them better. Dandelions, probably. They could thrive in any weather.

"Hey wait a minute!" she called. "Where are you going?"

The Pixies kept going, not turning their heads to the side or drifting away from the group, so focused they buzzed right by her ear. The last one in line flew close enough to scrape her face with his weapon. She ducked just in time to avoid a nasty wound.

Not normal Pixie behavior. Memory of blood trickling down Thistle's palm with the plant spike deeply embedded in her hand made her shudder.

"Dandelions," she muttered in disgust. "Put a thought in their heads and there's not room for anything else until they finish what they're doing."

She turned her attention back to her original chore of

inspecting the preparations for the All Hallows Festival. But not before making a mental note to prod Thistle with the news of a Dandelion army on the march—er—flight. She remembered everything she made notes about.

The children's haunted maze started here, in the middle of the knot garden—low-growing edible herbs that had all gone dormant for the season. Then the path progressed around the carriage barn for a brief foray into The Ten Acre Wood, and back out again. The intricate bow of black-and-orange plastic ribbon that Thistle had created showed up fine in daylight. What about after dusk with flashlights?

She noted some new cobwebs around the display of broken-down wagons in the long shed. Hideously appropriate for the season.

Hmm, if she brought out her brooms and conservation tools, she could delay having to deal with giving tours of the museum.

"Stop that!" she told herself.

"Stop what?" Chase asked, coming up behind her and wrapping his arms around her.

She melted into his warmth, letting his strength make her burdens seem more manageable.

"Stop thinking up excuses to hide," she murmured, turning so that she buried her face in his Kevlar-protected chest. She had to be careful to fit her arms above his utility belt with the array of weapons and tools for enforcing the law.

"That's my girl." He bent and brushed his lips across hers gently. "I know it's hard to break a lifetime of bad habits, but you are doing a marvelous job." He held her close a moment. "I've got time for coffee before I go on patrol if you've got some made inside. There's a missing child report I'd like you to look at."

"What child?"

"Someone you may or may not know. But you could set some Pixies to looking for her."

"Then let's go inside where it's warm and less damp. I do have coffee. I started a pot the moment I arrived, hoping you'd show up." She looked up, way up, to engage his gaze. "Chase, can we elope?"

"Huh?" He put a couple of inches between them, looking her full in the eyes. "I thought you wanted a big wedding so the planning would help get you used to the idea that you aren't a spinster hiding in your parents' house or the basement of the museum."

"Mom came home from Stratford-upon-Avon."

"Oh. How bad is it?" He grimaced.

She urged him back to the pioneer home that now housed the historical collections of the region. "Bad," she said.

"I know Juliet Carrick can be an out-of-control bulldozer when she gets an idea in her head."

"That about describes it."

"How bad?" He pulled her to a halt, hands on her shoulders.

"I told her that neither you nor Dick would wear tights to the wedding, nor padded tunics and lace ruffs. Dad won't either. He's threatening not to come home from University of Nevada. What does he need with another degree? For gosh sakes, he retired from teaching last summer. You'd think he's collected enough degrees."

"Have you? You don't even have to leave home to gather another MA or even a Ph.D with the Internet offering accredited classes.

"Well, now that you mention it . . . there is a class on archaeology specializing in Native basketry of the Pacific Northwest that could lead to a whole new field of study for me. I already have an idea for a thesis, might even be enough material for a dissertation . . ."

"Your father told me he wants to turn the old house into a bed and breakfast when you and Dick move out. And a degree in hotel management will make doing that easier," Chase said, squeezing her shoulders hard enough to bring her attention back to him.

Dusty snorted. "He's hiding from Mom. Three months together, twenty-four/seven doing nothing but Shakespeare almost pushed him to divorce. He settled for staying away for a while, taking another degree."

"So what else is wrong?"

"About this missing child . . ."

"Later. What's wrong about our wedding and your mother?"

"The gown is white."

"At least that much is traditional."

"It's a beautiful white-on-white brocade with just a hint of gold thread," she said trying to sound hopeful.

"But . . .?"

"Full farthingale hoop, corset, and cartwheel lace neck ruff."

They groaned in unison.

"How much of our honeymoon money do I need to spend to bribe the dressmaker?" he asked as they wiped their shoes off on the front doormat before entering the museum. Dusty exchanged her walking shoes for house slippers. Wearing shoes inside was one habit from her childhood she hadn't bothered trying to change. Though she did it now to avoid cleaning mud off the floors.

She paused to breathe deeply of the smells of old dust, lemon oil, and beeswax. Just a hint of mold underneath the familiar warmth of her museum. *Hers.* Truly hers now that Joe, her old boss, had taken a teaching job at the community college.

Mold? Time to check the new heat pump to make sure it was handling the moisture of a typical Oregon autumn. The fund-raising Masque Ball last August hadn't been totally ruined by the fire in The Ten Acre Wood. She'd found matching grant money to replace the ancient and near useless boiler and steam heat.

"I don't know if Abigail can be bribed," Dusty replied to his question. "She and Mom have been working together for a long time, costuming various events. It's more like a calling to them than historical reenactment."

"Sometimes I wish your mother could be sent back in time to 1600 and really experience how inconvenient, painful, and smelly life in Shakespeare's theater must have been. You don't suppose Thistle has that kind of magic? Or maybe some of her Pixie friends?"

Dusty shook her head. Laughter began bubbling inside her like fine champagne. Chase always made her see the lighter side of life.

"Let's elope," she said, really hoping he'd agree. Though the heavy silk wedding gown on display in "Bridget's Bridal

Boutique" window enticed her. The heavenly silk draped
like a waterfall, clung and swirled in all the right places. And,
expensive though it was, it cost only about half of what
Mom's dressmaker charged. Add the price of that gorgeous
brocade and lace, and Bridget's gown was a downright bargain.

"I get off at three Tuesday afternoon. That's tomorrow.
Soon enough for you?" Chase consulted his calendar embedded in his smart phone. "We can drive to Vancouver, Washington, get a license, waive the three-day waiting period, get
married, and be home before anyone notices we aren't having dinner down at the Old Mill Bar and Grill," Chase said.

"Yes!" She studied her own whiteboard calendar that
took up most of one wall of the enclosed porch. Tuesday
stared back at her accusingly as if it deserved five things
scheduled like the rest of the days of the month. "Any later
and we'd have to wait until after Halloween. I'm scheduled
for meetings and activities every day, morning and evening.
I can have M'Velle close up for me tomorrow. With her
work-study program, she's spending almost as much time
here as I do."

"On one condition."

Dusty froze in the act of pouring Chase a cup of coffee.
"I'm not going to like your condition, am I?"

"You have to tell your mother what we are doing and
why."

Dusty swallowed the thick lump in her throat, trying to
banish the heaviness in her chest and the panicky sweat on
her back.

"You know you have to do it, Dusty. Otherwise you
might as well hide in the basement for the rest of your life."

Phlema Jo Nelson stared at the handsome man in her office
doorway. Broken sunshine slanted in through the windows,
catching him in a golden aura. From his blond hair, the
color of ripened wheat, to the luster of his pale skin, he
basked in her admiration.

His habitual outfit of brown tweed jacket, beige slacks,
and pale green shirt looked decidedly worse for wear. And

he'd lost his shoes and socks somewhere. His dishabille made him utterly contemptible. He'd make an admirable addition to the hideous scarecrow decorations on Main Street and every front yard in town.

"Haywood Wheatland. So they let you out of jail. How'd you make bail?" she asked on a sneer. Contempt almost outweighed the fear that crawled from her belly to her mind in a gibbering mass of goo.

Never again. She'd vowed never again to let anyone control her—not her mother, foster parents, teachers, two ex-husbands, and definitely not this mentally damaged man.

Not again.

"I escaped the prison you cast me into," Hay said. "As I knew, I knew, I knew I would once the iron sickness wore off. Wore off. Though jailhouse food, though jailhouse food nearly killed me, all those preservatives and artificial additives, artificial additives," he dismissed her words with a grandiloquent bow worthy of Dusty Carrick's obsessive-compulsive mother. Any other man who bent at the waist over one extended foot and circled his wrist with a flourish would get laughed out of town. Haywood Wheatland made it look natural, polite, and . . . could it be . . . respectful.

Phelma Jo snorted at her own thought. Hay didn't respect anyone, maybe not even himself. After all, he lived under the delusion that he was half Faery and half Pixie.

He belonged in this half-crazy town that celebrated every holiday as if magic truly existed and otherworldly critters flitted about making everyone's life special.

No one had made Phelma Jo's life special, except maybe herself. To be honest, there had been two foster families that tried to make up for years of abuse and neglect from her mother and other foster parents.

Too little, too late. She'd dragged herself out of the gutter to the top of the financial heap and intended to stay there.

"Still got that computer virus, I see." She rolled her eyes.

"No matter. No matter."

"I'm calling the police. You are an escaped prisoner." She reached for the phone and punched in the first digit. Mabel would answer. Mabel knew everything about everyone in town. But she didn't hold Phelma Jo's past over her head. Mabel Gardiner was the only one in town who had honestly helped her without asking for anything in return. She still helped teens who'd fallen through the cracks.

"Ever stop and think of the irony, the irony, that Dick Carrick, one of the two people in this town you need to destroy, destroy socially, socially, and financially, is the one who testified you were under the influence of a date rape drug, date rape drug when you set fire to The Ten Acre Wood?" Hay straightened up and lounged one hip easily against her desk. "His testimony set you free of arson charges, testimony set you free of arson charges, and got me locked up."

Phelma Jo froze before she could move her fingers again. Slowly, she set the headset back in its cradle. "Yes, I am aware of the irony of the situation. But since it was you who administered the drugs, I have no wish to continue this conversation."

"Want revenge?" he asked on a short, sharp laugh that sounded almost like the bark of a lawnmower hitting a stick. No pause and repeat in that simple phrase. He must be really concentrating on what he wanted to say to break through his personal static.

"Revenge? On you. Yes. On Dick and Dusty? Still thinking about it." She picked up the phone again. "Dusty has formally apologized for some nasty remarks she made when we were kids that escalated into a fifteen-year feud. I accepted her apology."

"But you haven't, you haven't forgiven her, her, her."

Hay stayed her hand with one of his own. "Think about it. I can help you regain your status in this town as a person to contend with, to contend with, not just another victim, victim, victim."

The words resonated with more than just his personal stutter and reset.

"This town needs to know you are not vulnerable. You could run for mayor again without whispered references to the *arson* scandal."

Phelma Jo stared at the hand that covered her own. The nails looked ragged and inflamed around the quick. "Real estate sales are up, and so are my commissions," she said flatly. "I can recover on my own."

"Are sales up because more people come to you thinking they'll con you into a better deal—which they won't— which they won't—or because the economy as a whole is better and property is moving again?"

She didn't want to think about either prospect. Clients should come to her because she owned the biggest and most powerful real estate brokerage in the county.

"Dusty is engaged to Police Sergeant Chase Norton. She's untouchable," Phelma Jo admitted. The habit of the feud was hard to break. A lifetime of resentment still lingered, even though the incident had led to good outcomes for both of them.

School officials finally acknowledged that Phelma Jo's mother's boyfriend was abusing her and put her into a decent foster home. For a while.

As for Dusty: the cuts and scrapes she received when Phelma Jo fought back against her hurtful taunts didn't heal. That led to an early diagnosis of leukemia and a cure.

"Dusty has enough problems with her mother planning an Elizabethan extravaganza, Elizabethan extravaganza of a wedding," Hay almost laughed.

Phelma Jo's day brightened. "Dusty will always be a victim until she learns to stand up for herself. She's wallowed in sympathy for her cancer until she can't break the habit. Getting revenge on her is too easy. A hollow victory. And she has apologized."

"But Dick Carrick and his paramour Thistle are vulnerable. Think of the triumph, think of the triumph, of stealing Dick away from her. Thistle will have to leave town, leave town in total humiliation. Then you can break off the relationship with Dick, very publicly, with all of his dirty laundry, dirty laundry aired. All of it, going back to all the girls he loved and left in high school. Loved and left in high school. He got one of them pregnant and now his daughter is looking for him. You could ruin everything for him. Publicly. Scandalously."

"A daughter, hmmm. I wonder which one of his light-o-loves." She tapped her chin a moment, thinking and planning, knowing where to look for the girl, if she was indeed in town. But she didn't want Hay to know just how interested she was in that bit of information.

"Thistle is just that . . . a ditch weed with stickers. She sticks to everything she touches and stays there, no matter how hard you try to weed her out." Phelma Jo never had learned to trust the woman so bent on "befriending" everyone in her wake.

"You leave Thistle to me. I'll see that she runs away and never comes back. The Faeries have offered a reward for her if she ever returns to Pixie. I intend to collect. You go play with Dick. Go play with Dick."

"And where will you be? You're a fugitive from justice."

"I'll be where they least expect to find me, right under their noses. I am half Faery after all. They'll never think to look for me in my true form." He laughed, long and loud. The notes of his amusement rose to a shrill hysteria.

Phelma Jo wondered if jail had driven him mad.

He was insane before jail drove him deeper into a surreal world of his own making. Half Faery indeed.

He disappeared through her door in a cloud of dull gold glitter that should have sparkled but didn't.

Casually she dialed 911 and reported seeing an escaped fugitive. She feared what he would do to her this time. The backup county dispatcher ate it up.

# Five

CHASE'S SHOULDER RADIO CRACKLED before
Dusty could reply to his condition for eloping. Oh, how
he wished she'd comply. He wanted nothing more than to
marry her as soon as possible. They should have eloped before her parents came home from three months in England.
And her father, the moderating force in the family, took off
for Las Vegas to acquire yet another degree. What was it,
his third Masters? Or was it his fourth?

"Norton here," he said into the mike, keeping his eyes on
Dusty.

"That you, Chase?" Mabel asked. She sounded vague
and disoriented. Not at all like the Mabel who'd kept the
police department organized and on the ball since before
Chase was born.

"Who else would answer when you call this frequency?"
he asked. "Gotta go," he mouthed to Dusty. "I'll call you."

He backed out of the employee workroom tacked onto
the back of the old house, careful not to trip on the lip into
the main part of the museum.

"Sergeant Norton, Mrs. Spencer over on Seventh reports
some vandalism to her hawthorn tree."

"I know where Mrs. Spencer lives." The elderly lady had
taught fourth grade to almost everyone in town. She'd only
retired on her eightieth birthday because the state threatened to revoke her teaching certificate if she didn't.

"What's that about a hawthorn tree?" Dusty asked, following Chase toward the door.

"That you, Dusty?" Mabel asked.

"Yes. What about the hawthorn?"

"Around dawn, neighbors reported strange activity shaking the tree from within. When Mrs. Spencer went out to check, half the branches had been stripped of leaves and thorns."

"Thistle got a thorn stuck in her hand this morning. She never left our yard, and we don't have a hawthorn," Dusty said.

"I'll take it from here, Dusty." Chase dropped a quick kiss on her brow and lengthened his stride toward the door. "Think about what we discussed."

Dusty paced him, nearly running to keep up.

"Chase, let her finish talking," Mabel admonished him. "Chicory reports strangers in his territory. He came limping in this morning with a torn wing and a cut on his arm. He lost his hat, too. That's hard to imagine. Hats are important to ... to his family."

"I'll check out Mrs. Spencer's yard; then come in for a chat. Dusty, can you get away to join us in about an hour?" Chase tried to take control of the situation, knowing he'd get nowhere fast without Dusty and Mabel's cooperation.

"Let me make a few phone calls to get a volunteer to cover for me. We might get some customers, but that isn't likely on a school day in October with showers in the forecast. After school, though, we'll get older kids wanting to scout out the haunted maze before it's haunted."

"Chase, did you show Dusty the CM poster?" Mabel sounded more like herself, less weak and vague. "The kid might follow other teens into the maze."

"Not yet. You show her when we get there."

"Hope we aren't too late on that one."

Chase didn't like the unease in Mabel's warning. He hated the thought of any CM facing the dangerous reality of life on the streets. "Dusty, bring Thistle. We'll probably need her for a couple of things," Chase said, dashing out the door. He easily loped the three blocks to Mrs. Spencer's. This trip reminded him of the day last summer when he'd been summoned to a break-in at the stubborn old lady's house. The seemingly indestructible teacher had mistaken the furnace control for the fan and nearly died from heat stroke. Chase had found Thistle administering rudimentary first aid before she, too, collapsed from the heat. As she crumbled to the floor, he'd seen a shimmering outline of Pixie wings in the shape of double Thistle leaves.

That was the first day in his journey toward believing in the tiny creatures. Now he wondered if he was on the way to becoming their champion or their nemesis.

Thistle sat defiantly, in the hard straight chair in a tiny conference room just beyond the gate Mabel zealously guarded. She crossed her arms, keeping her bandaged hand hidden. Dusty sat across from her at the long table in an equally uncomfortable chair.

They stared at each other, trying to out-stubborn the friend across the table. Dusty had dragged Thistle away from the edge of The Ten Acre Wood on the east side, at the end of the gravel road. Thistle had spent nearly an hour calming her mind, seeking the center of the magic she used to command with a flick of a Pixie finger. Her meditative trance had allowed her to feel the itch between her shoulder blades where her wings used to lift her above the tug of the Earth with a thought.

She almost, *almost*, shrank back to her normal Pixie size.

Almost. Then Dusty had interrupted with her demands to attend this meeting at the police station. The trance was gone. The will to return to Pixie mixed with her need to stay with Dick and her friends as a human.

Which was right for her?

Chicory stretched out on the table to his full length of four inches. He clutched his left arm so that anyone who could see him noticed the white sling, but not his tousled blue hair that was no longer covered by his cap of darker blue flower petals. He moaned as if the world was about to end.

Thistle was afraid he might be right. If Pixies battled each other across tribal lines, then the balance of nature had twisted and toppled.

Mabel bustled in, followed by Chase. "Now that we have a bit of privacy, we can get to the bottom of this," she said, fixing each person with a stern gaze. But her eyes wandered a bit and lost focus. She looked paler than usual. Her police auxiliary uniform had lost its crispness and hung on her as if two sizes too big. If she'd been one of Thistle's elderly friends, the ones who paid her to check on them twice a day to make sure they ate, let the dogs out, and didn't leave the stove on, Thistle would have reported her to the free clinic.

Thistle turned sideways so she wouldn't have to subject herself to Mabel's strange gaze. She had a way of worming information out of reluctant witnesses, belligerent drunks, and mischievous teenagers.

"First order of business," Chase said, fishing a much folded piece of paper out of his thigh pocket. He placed it on the table so that both she and Chicory could see the face in the photograph. "Have any of you seen this girl around town?"

Chicory stared at it cross-eyed. "Maybe. Not sure. My attention was elsewhere when I caught a glimpse of girl that might look like her if her hair was longer and dirtier, and she was damp and bedraggled all over."

Thistle nodded agreement. "She asked me for directions to your house, Mabel."

Chase and Mabel exchanged a look that could have meant many things. None of them good by the frown on the old lady's face.

"Next we need to know why Pixies are stealing hawthorn spikes from Mrs. Spencer's tree."

"Hawthorns are shrubs, not trees," Chicory said. "Their berries are sweet to Pixies but not to humans."

"What is going on, Thistle?" Dusty asked gently. She reached her hands across the table like she wanted to touch her.

Thistle squirmed and pushed her chair back a few inches until it hit the wall.

Dusty frowned. Thistle hated to disappoint her friend. Of all the people in Skene Falls that Thistle had befriended, Dusty had believed in Pixies longest. Well, except maybe for Dick. But Dick was a boy, not a girl's best friend forever. Like Dusty.

"Nothing is going on that concerns you," Thistle finally

said. She kept her gaze on the cracks in the floor, tracing them endlessly around each square. *Not a lie. I'm not telling a lie*, she reminded herself.

So why did she feel hot and faint?

"But it does concern us, Thistle. It affects you and our dear friends who make our gardens flourish. Therefore, we hurt when you hurt," Mabel insisted. She tried to straighten Chicory's wingtips. They defied her attention, continuing to curl at the edges. A sure sign that Chicory ailed. Still he leaned into Mabel's caress, his moans becoming lighter, more rhythmical, like a cat purring.

"Stop that," she whispered to Chicory. "You aren't a cat. Cats are evil. They hunt us and eat us."

"Cats hunt *Pixies*. You aren't a Pixie anymore, Thistle," Chase said sternly.

Thistle recognized the pattern of their comments. She'd seen the same thing on the television last night. They called it Good Cop/Bad Cop. Clearly, Chase had elected the Bad Cop role.

Thistle looked at Chicory. Chicory returned her gaze. They were in agreement.

"Pixie business stays within Pixie," Thistle said. *Definitely not a lie*. She still didn't feel well.

"Not when my roses are drooping and getting the blight from lack of attention by Chicory and his tribe," Mabel insisted. "Rosie's in a snit about something and not holding up her end of the bargain; gardening for sanctuary. So spill it, Chicory, or I'll deed the place to my nephew. He'll have it subdivided and sold to developers within a week."

"You wouldn't!" Chicory gasped.

"Try me." Who was the good cop and who the bad now?

"We'll . . . we'll sue," Chicory replied. "We've owned those two acres longer than you have."

"Legally, you don't exist." Chase crossed his arms, then leaned back in his chair, tipping the front legs off the ground. "There is nothing you can do to stop the exchange of land."

"I'd need to run it all by the historical preservation committee first," Dusty added.

"What about your will, Mabel?" Chicory asked. He

stood straight and faced Mabel. His defiant posture lacked a little authority because of the sling and the droopy wing edges.

"I changed it once. I'll change it again." Her eyes started to roll upward and her breathing became labored.

For a moment Thistle thought the old lady might pass out.

Chase noticed, too. He leaped up and pressed his fingers to Mabel's wrist, testing her pulse the same way Dick had taught Thistle. "Mabel?" he asked.

"What? Oh, oh, oh," Mabel sputtered coming back to herself with a jerk.

"Mabel, your pulse is rapid and faint. You are having trouble breathing. I'm calling for an ambulance," Chase said, reaching for his radio.

"No, you aren't. I'm perfectly fine."

"Mabel, listen to him," Thistle said. "I know the signs. You aren't all right." She clasped the woman's hands, shocked that they felt cold enough to send a whole tribe of Pixies into hibernation.

Mabel's head wobbled forward. "Thistle, promise me you will take care of my house and garden while I'm sick?" she whispered. "You'll decorate for Halloween like everyone else in town."

"Yes, of course."

"You'll notify Chase of unusual visitors? Chase and no one else."

"Certainly. I won't let anyone damage your property or steal your belongings.

"Don't let my nephew try to sell it."

"I won't. I promise."

"Chase, write it up and let me sign it. Thistle is my authorized house sitter and gardener until . . . until . . ."

"There's no until, Mabel," Thistle insisted. She moved to stand beside the older woman and wrapped her arm about her shoulders. Thin shoulders. Thistle felt more bone than muscle beneath the uniform shirt. "The doctors will patch you up and you'll be home in no time."

Chase thrust his little shirt-pocket-sized notebook under Mabel's hands along with a pen. "Sign at the bottom. Dusty and I will witness it. The ambulance will be here any minute."

As if to punctuate his statement, a siren wailed in the near distance. Dusty ran to the front of the building to direct them.

Mabel slowly scratched something on the paper with the pen, as if it weighed more than she did. "Locked drawer. Desk. Here. Papers."

"Don't try to talk, Mabel. We'll take care of everything." Thistle removed the pen from Mabel's suddenly limp hand and returned it and the notebook to Chase.

He quickly signed his own name beside Mabel's.

"Read the papers. Today. Dusty, Chase, one of you read them today," she insisted.

The EMTs arrived, wheeling a portable bed with them and carrying huge suitcases full of equipment. Dick hastened behind them.

Thistle nearly collapsed with relief. Dick would make sure everything was okay. She could depend upon Dick to take care of her and her friends.

# Six

CHICORY WATCHED IN HORROR as too many humans gathered around Mabel, affixing strange masks to her face, inserting needles bigger than he was into her arm, and speaking too rapidly into mechanical devices. He trembled all over. His wings fluttered but refused to gather air.

"I need to go with her," he whispered.

"Leave that to the humans. You'll just be in the way," Thistle whispered back.

"No, I won't. I promise I won't touch anything. I won't play any tricks either. But I need to be with Mabel. She needs to know that her tribe is watching out for her."

"Chicory, you need to go back to your tribe and tell them what has happened. They need to know about Mabel." Thistle grabbed hold of his tunic to keep him from flying off. "You need to gather your Pixies close so you can protect your territory. With the war on, others will see you as vulnerable without Mabel."

"You're right." Chicory hung his head, feigning acceptance. "Thanks for the warning."

She nodded abruptly and followed the humans out of the little room, leaving him alone.

In one swift movement he ripped off the sling, noting briefly that the wound had already healed clean. He had full freedom of both arms. Energy returned with a surge of power to his wings.

He rose quickly to the level of the window, took his bearings, and headed for the sky. Mabel always left the glass open a bit so Pixies could come and go.

Crack! His head felt ready to explode. "Who shut the damn window!"

*Dum dee dee do dum dum.* Thistle's music chimed between his ears, replacing the discordant clanging caused by violent contact with the glass.

"I'll get you for that trick, Thistle."

"Yes, you will. But not today. Now go home. You can use the front door. No one is looking at anything but Mabel."

Grumbling and spitting, Chicory made his way slowly from doorjamb to chair back to shadowed corner until he found a jail cell with a window open enough for him crawl through. He had to ease his way between the iron bars to avoid devastating burns, but he made it clear without interference. From this back exit he flew straight up the cliff beside the waterfall, catching a much needed drink from the gushing spray, made a quick diversion around The Ten Acre Wood through the museum grounds and then over rooftops and sleepy gardens to Rosie's territory.

He found his queen and seven of her family dancing from dead blossom to dead blossom. No one had bothered snapping off the sodden flower heads when they failed to bloom after the autumnal rains came hard and frequent. No one had tidied the leaf mulch or raked the lawn—which needed mowing.

The All Hallows parade of ghostly founding fathers and pumpkin-headed zombies and hay wagons full of cornstalks and children with painted faces, was supposed to pass right in front of Mabel's garden. She hadn't decorated, and the Pixies had left it looking abandoned.

What to do? What to do?

Instead, the Pixies in charge of things pranced about in joy.

"What's happening?" Chicory asked, snagging Daisy's wingtip.

"Queen Rosie is taking Snapdragon as a mate." She clapped her hands and bounced upward, dragging him with her. "They're having a mating flight from the big sycamore on All Hallows Eve." She pointed to the massive old tree in the back lot that ran between the backyards along the entire block of houses. An iron fence separated and protected the back lot from intruders—Pixie and human. Rosie had banished the Dandelions to the wild stretch.

As they watched, Rosie slowed her celebration to include the big yellow-and-red fellow. They spiraled down into a cupped bloom of a late blooming hybrid tea rose. Rosie's pink froth disappeared into the vibrant petals of the same color.

"I thought they were going to take a mating flight," Chicory snorted. "Shouldn't they wait until then?"

"They're just napping. Rosie likes naps. Winter is coming and we are all sleepy," Daisy said, her eyes still shining with happiness shared.

"I noticed," Chicory said. Once more he surveyed the signs of neglect. Maybe the garden reflected Mabel's gradual decline in health. If so, then the Pixies needed to double their efforts, to make sure the garden gave back to Mabel some of their energy so she could heal.

"Wake up, Rosie. Wake up. Mabel's sick! Her humans have taken her to a hospital," he cried, shaking the rose stem as fiercely as he could.

"Wh . . . what?" Rosie lifted her pink head above the rim of petals. She blinked sleepily, nearing hibernation.

"Mabel's taken sick. Her heart doesn't work right. I think the valley Pixies poisoned her. We have to go kill them. All of them!" Chicory screamed.

"Don't be ridiculous," Vermilion said on a yawn. She was Rosie's daughter, from her first mating flight with another rose. "Why would any Pixie want to poison a human?" She stretched and curled back into her bed, as lazy as her mother.

"Because all the valley tribes are as insane as Haywood Wheatland," Chicory explained impatiently. That name clicked in the back of his head like he had forgotten something important. Later. He'd remember later. "We've no time to lose. We have to attack now while they are still laughing at their trick." He dragged on the limp arm of Bleeding Heart, a dark pink-and-green fellow who'd crept in from a nearby copse that got felled for new houses. Rosie had made room for him and only him in the tribe. Sixteen Pixies went homeless or broke up their family to nest elsewhere. Chicory had secreted five of them in the wild stretch among the Dandelions. Rosie never crossed the iron fence.

"We've got swords in the hawthorn of our own back corner. We've got to arm ourselves and go after the enemy," Chicory insisted.

"You bore me, Chicory. It's nearly noon. Every respectable Pixie is either napping or eating," Rosie declared.

"But the valley Pixies aren't respectable!"

"And neither are you. You've lost your cap. Now go away."

"No, Rosie. We can't afford to ignore the valley Pixies. Not now when Mabel is sick and our land is vulnerable. We are open to attack unless we strike first."

"Snapdragon, be a good boy and throw this noisy stinkbug into the cellar!"

"Not the cellar, Rosie. I'll die in the cellar." Chicory gulped nervously. "Pixies are bonded to Earth and Water. If we go underground, we get absorbed. Then we *die!*"

"Just like my Haywood might have died in the horrid old pioneer jail the night of the fire," Rosie dismissed him.

Snapdragon rose up from his place beside Rosie and latched onto Chicory's arm with both hands. Dull-yellow Pixie dust cascaded all around. Chicory's head reeled with the need to obey the big Pixie he'd tried to kill this morning.

Rosie's new lover towered over him.

"How'd you get so big?" Chicory gulped, wiggling free of the enthrallment. But only his mind worked. His body was still trapped by the more powerful magic of the intruder.

"Family secret, secret, secret," Snapdragon replied, tightening his grip. His holey, dull yellow-and-red wings flapped hard enough to throw up a strong breeze. Rosie's flower shook so violently she had to grab hold of the edges of her petal to keep from falling out.

The shape of Snapdragon's face, the half-rotten scent of his pollen, and the odd fan shape of his wings triggered a memory. "I know you," he whispered.

"No, you don't. Don't, don't, don't. And you won't be around to remind the humans where you've seen me. I have special plans, special plans for you and for them, them, them. We'll start with the cellar, cellar, cellar."

The words echoed ominously inside Chicory's head.

"Cellar!" Snapdragon crowed. With that, he grabbed Chicory by collar and belt and threw him through a small open window into the crushing darkness.

The last thing Chicory heard before passing out was the loud thud of the window slamming shut.

Phelma Jo ran her fingernail idly along the mortar between two bricks on the outside of a building on Main Street.

*Mine!* she thought. She'd had a few anxious days last summer when she thought she'd have to take out a second mortgage on this magnificent historical building to make bail for arson. But then Dick Carrick had come to her rescue and testified that Haywood Wheatland had kidnapped her and doused her repeatedly with a date rape drug to guarantee her compliance in his malicious plans to destroy The Ten Acre Wood.

The judge had dropped the arson charges against her. She hadn't had to come up with exorbitant bail money, but she had to drop out of the election race for mayor and she'd lost three important commercial clients. Otherwise, her financial portfolio and real estate holdings had remained intact. She'd recover from the scandal and run again for mayor in four years.

She loved this building for its charm and grand old elegance that fit the townscape perfectly. In a favorite daydream she had lived here when the building was new. Would her life have been less painful one hundred years ago?

Not with her mother and the string of abusive boyfriends and less-than-loving foster homes. One hundred years ago she wouldn't have Mabel Gardiner to point her toward opportunities to take control of her life. Hundreds of other teens who fell through the cracks of the legal system would have suffered as well without Mabel.

Wailing sirens right next to her jarred her out of her musing.

She watched a flurry of EMTs exit an ambulance and

dash into the police station behind old City Hall. Probably just another loser of a drunk choking on his own vomit. Like her mother.

"None of my business." She turned away to examine the bricks and mortar at the corner of the building while she waited for an insurance inspector. Old structures required a lot of maintenance and her insurer made sure Phelma Jo kept the building up to code, the real code, not the variance one she'd bribed the outgoing mayor of Skene Falls to issue her for some other properties. She rented commercial space to eight businesses, and four apartments in this four-story building. The oldest commercial building in a town filled with historical homes and businesses.

"I own you," she caressed the rough brick. "I won't let them take you away from me." Her modern properties didn't satisfy her the way this old place did. She didn't even mind the expense of keeping it up. Owning something historic in this town moved her up onto the same social rung as Dick and Dusty Carrick.

"Thinking of the devil!" Dick's smart red BMW convertible rushed past her. He skewed into a parking space right beside the ambulance and dashed into the station.

"Well, maybe this crisis is my business after all. Dick needs to rescue someone. Now that his sister is engaged to Chase Norton, the town Eagle Scout is at loose ends. I wonder what it will take to divert him . . ."

"I thought I was the town Eagle Scout," mused a tall man with flaming red hair and a mask of freckles across his face. His bright green eyes twinkled.

Phelma Jo closed her gaping jaw with a snap. Haywood Wheatland paled in comparison to this drop-dead gorgeous hunk of male.

"And you are?" she asked, standing as tall as she could. Even in sensible two-inch heels, the top of her head barely reached his chin. Unconsciously, she smoothed her glossy dark hair, certain that it had to be bristling.

"Ian McEwen, building inspector for Triple Giant Insurance." He handed her a business card. "If you are Phelma Jo Nelson, then I think we met one summer when we were kids. Mabel Gardiner is my aunt."

Phelma Jo inspected the card, rubbing her thumb across the embossed lettering to make sure the ink didn't smear. It looked authentic. He had a hard hat and industrial length measuring tape attached to his belt, and a clipboard tucked under his arm.

"I know Mabel. She's never mentioned you."

"I . . . um . . ." He blushed a brilliant shade of red that clashed with his hair. "We lost contact at the end of the last summer I lived with her. She objected to my choice of friends and I objected to . . . some of her rather strange stories about Pixies."

Phelma Jo snorted in agreement. "I've heard some of her crazy stories. And I am Phelma Jo Nelson. I own the building." She made a show of checking a note on her smart phone. The name matched the notice she'd received. "What do you need from me to get in and get out as quickly as possible without disrupting my tenants?"

"Access to the roof, the basement, the circuit breakers, heat plant, and a sample of the plumbing. Then I'll determine what else I need to see based on what I do or do not find." He flashed a grin. She noticed a twisted front tooth and a bit of an overbite. Not as pronounced as her own.

She smiled back, revealing her own crooked teeth. Unlike Dusty and Dick, neither Phelma Jo's mother nor a string of foster parents could afford braces for her teeth. Now that she had the means to have them fixed, she flaunted the constant reminder of her humble beginnings.

She felt an instant kinship with Mr. McEwen.

"This way. If you don't mind, I'll watch while you work. I don't allow strangers the run of my buildings."

"If you insist. But *I* have to insist *ÿ*ou wear a hard hat, too. Never know what kinds of bugs, snakes, and low hanging pipes will ambush you."

"I don't scare easily, Mr. McEwen. I have my own hard-hat at the entrance to the basement boiler room."

# Seven

**D**USTY ESCAPED TO THE BASEMENT of the museum in the late afternoon. M'Velle, the high school senior who worked after morning classes, had the tours covered. She also knew how to redirect the kids who wanted a preview of the haunted maze through The Ten Acre Wood — either to plan their own ambushes or avoid tricks by other kids. An hour before closing they shouldn't have more than the odd family or individual paying to see the inside. At this time of day, most stragglers contented themselves with the outdoor exhibits, especially the pioneer jail. Kids loved climbing in and out, marveling at the dirt floor sunk three feet below ground level. She knew they'd be disappointed when it was locked up during the weekend evening festivities.

She carried under her arm the fat legal-sized envelope from Mabel's desk and the missing child poster of a girl she'd never seen but would keep an eye out for. Why had Mabel insisted that Dusty and Chase read the envelope's contents today? Surely nothing could be more important than getting Mabel to the hospital. The EMTs had fixed an oxygen mask over her face and ended her repeated demands for Dusty to read these papers.

No one objected when Chase removed them from Mabel's reception and dispatch desk. The entire police department was in a bit of an uproar, not knowing how to replace the woman who had always been there as dispatcher, information officer, mother hen, and organizer. On top of that, a big accident on the interstate had demanded the attention of every spare officer, including Chase.

"Chase is too busy to handle this. So I guess I have to read and report," she mumbled. Somehow, Mabel's urgency and the locked drawer suggested a demand for privacy. Dusty never did see how Chase managed to open the lock without a key. She wasn't sure she wanted to know.

She cleared and cleaned a light table of fragile potsherds and bits of iron from an archaeological dig conducted by community college students. Page by page, she laid out the documents without reading any, until she could view them all. This was her work pattern, get an overview of all the artifacts, then examine each one more closely.

The top page acknowledged the property at Mabel Gardiner's address to be a historical house of significance to the city of Skene Falls and therefore it could not be torn down or the exterior altered in such a way as to detract from the architecture typical of its building date of 1883. The document went on to describe the home as the original carriage house and gatekeeper dwelling for a now derelict mansion on the corner of that block known as the Corbett House.

"That old? I hadn't realized the foundations dated that far back." Dusty had reviewed and filled out enough applications for historic designation as part of her Masters degree to recognize that nothing varied from the usual.

She moved on to the next paper. The Last Will and Testament of Mabel Louise Gardiner. Dusty's gaze riveted on the document. She felt as if she was invading the privacy of a respected elder statesman—er—stateswoman? Still, Mabel had demanded Dusty and Chase read the documents in their entirety.

She checked the date. Two months before, the day of the Masque Ball and the day Chase had proposed to Dusty. She raised her eyebrows in wonder. The old woman—no one in town knew exactly how old—had an agenda more complex than Dusty figured. She wound her way through the legalese, familiar with the format from historical documents. Wills said a lot about people and ways of life in previous eras. So did household inventories, and Mabel had a complete one attached to the will.

"Oh, my!" Dusty gasped as she read the first bequest. "This can't be."

She read it again. Then she whipped out her cell phone. No signal in the basement.

She moved to stand beneath one of the high windows at ground level. Still no signal. Too many clouds.

Biting her lip, she put all the papers back in the envelope, wound the string around the button to close it and carried it upstairs to her office.

She heard voices from the second-story bedrooms. M'Velle must be doing a tour. Quickly, Dusty checked the downstairs exhibits starting with the original log cabin space that was now the front parlor and then all the mismatched additions. No one else wandered about, not even the volunteers who came in each afternoon to dust and vacuum. She made a quick call from her office phone to the little house across the park grounds that served as gift shop and ticket sales.

"No guests waiting for a tour," Meggie, the other high school work-study student reported. "Though I'm having trouble with my costume for the parade. I just can't see myself as the ghost of a missionary wife. Can't I do something more interesting, Dusty?"

"Not unless you want to be the ghost of the town Madame. But I think Mrs. Shiregrove has dibs on that job."

Meggie grumbled something and hung up.

Dusty slipped into her office at the back of the building, adjacent to the enclosed sun porch that had become the employee lounge and work space. She flipped the lock on the door and sat at her desk. She'd reorganized the office and cleared out a lot of half-finished projects once Joe had left. The place actually felt like an office now instead of a cluttered closet.

She hated to think what his new office in the faculty wing of the community college looked like. His two daughters, aged four and six, kept their room tidier than he did.

Three deep breaths later she found the courage to open her cell phone again. The landline tempted her, but that was an open line with many extensions in the lounge and the gift shop, as well as the upstairs hall.

"Norton," Chase answered. He sounded distracted and harassed.

"Chase, is this a bad time to talk?"

"Yeah, kinda. I've got traffic backed up for two miles. Can't get an ambulance or tow truck in. Gonna have to use life flight. And I need the Jaws of Life to get to the last victim. We think he's dead, but can't be sure until we get enough space to reach an arm in and feel for a pulse."

"I won't keep you. But call me as soon as you have half a minute. Mabel's papers are . . . interesting."

"Yeah, sure. Later." He hung up in a hurry, barely getting the last syllable through his teeth.

Thistle stood at the gate in the white picket fence. She scanned all of Mabel Gardiner's front yard in search of her quarry. This town had a lot of picket fences. She smiled as she remembered childish flying games learning to skip from point to point. . . .

She had to forget that part of her life. For now. The highest calling was to befriend those in need. Her friend Mabel needed her to stay here, in a human body, while she was sick.

Thistle adjusted the backpack full of her clothes and toiletries slung over one shoulder. Enough for five days before she'd have to learn how to use the laundry. Hopefully, Mabel didn't keep the noisy machines in the basement. Thistle might be human now, but she still feared underground. If the earth didn't absorb and kill her, her fear of underground might.

Roses spilled over the fence almost the entire length. Even this late in the year, hybrids and old-fashioned blossoms mixed their colors and heady fragrance with abandon. Thistle let the perfume invade every one of her senses. If she still had her wings, she'd be drunk in six heartbeats. How did the local Pixies manage to fly a straight line, let alone infiltrate the entire town spying for Mabel?

An arch stretched over the gate providing a trellis for delicate, pink climbing roses. Their abundance of petals hid a myriad of secrets, including at least one Pixie.

"Rosie, may I enter your garden? Mabel sent me," she called to the queen of Chicory's tribe. Since becoming human she didn't have to ask. But it never hurt to be polite.

"Go away!" Rosie yelled back from the flower directly above Thistle's head. Only it wasn't a flower. Rosie had curled up in a ball letting her petal gown mimic the adjacent blossoms.

"Rosie, this is important. Mabel is sick. She sent me here to protect you all until she can come home again."

"We know. Go away. We don't need you."

"Yes, you do."

"What can you do? You're a woodland Pixie, as wild as a Dandelion. We're a civilized, garden tribe."

"Ask anyone in this district how well I tend gardens," Thistle shot back, affronted. "A Pixie is a Pixie. We all listen to plants of any variety to learn what they need to thrive." She shifted her gaze, seeking signs of movement or flashes of color.

All quiet. A few insects fluttered about, gathering the last bits of pollen before hibernating for the winter or dying.

"Rosie, where is your tribe?" Thistle asked suspiciously.

"None of your business."

"It is my business if they are all off fighting valley Pixies, or . . . or . . ." Stars above, could they be attacking the Pixies in The Ten Acre Wood, Thistle's tribe?

Not that Alder, her king and philandering lover, didn't deserve to be thrown off his throne. His own tribe was the only one with the right to do that.

Thistle didn't know for sure. She needed to talk to Alder. Not likely to happen while she was exiled to a human body.

"We're at war, Thistle," Rosie said in that superior way of hers. "And there's nothing you can do about it. We all know where your loyalties lie. And it isn't in my garden."

"I understand you are angry because you had to dismiss your betrothed, the one the humans called Haywood Wheatland. But you have to know that my loyalty is to all Pixies, no matter which garden, woodland, or meadow they inhabit," Thistle insisted, surprised that she truly believed her own words.

"Impossible!" Rosie spat. But she uncurled enough to

peer at Thistle, incredulous at this unique idea. "Pixies only look as far as their own tribe and territory."

"Pixies came together once to set up a treaty to protect the Patriarch Oak and make it available to all. We did that when the Faeries went underhill to avoid having to deal with humans. The cowards ran away, leaving Pixies on their own. We deal with humans all the time and we thrive." Thistle reached up and held her palm out for Rosie to settle on. "We need to band together to protect what is ours."

The pink Pixie ignored the offer of friendship. "Your king broke the treaty."

"Alder may have closed The Ten Acre Wood trying to keep Faeries out as well as Pixies in. The new discount store up on the next ridge is threatening the Faery sanctuary. Haywood Wheatland is half Faery. He misunderstood his orders to clear the wood of all Pixies. He thought he had to clear the wood!"

"Haywood is more admirable than Alder. He tried to *do* something, rather than run away. That is a cowardly Faery trait. Maybe Alder is the half Faery mutant, not Haywood."

"Alder *is* an idiot, but he's not stupid. I'm well rid of him. And if Milkweed was smart, she'd dump him in the pond and leave on her own."

"Alder won't let her." Rosie stepped away from the twisted canes of the climbing rose to step onto Thistle's hand. "He's holding her prisoner."

"Then we need to mount a rescue operation. And rearrange things so that we all work together."

"How? No one has done such a thing since the time of the Faeries. No one will believe it can be done." Rosie fluttered her wings in agitation.

"Then you and I will have to put our heads together along with Chicory and his brothers and figure out a way."

"But ... but ..."

Thistle eased through the gate and beneath the arch while she talked.

"But Pixies can't think ahead. Our lives are here, right now, and nothing more."

"Then let me do the thinking. Please, Rosie. This is important. Life for Pixies is changing. We have to *think*, not just react. All the tribes will listen to you, and I'll advise you. You will be important. More important than just one queen among many. That's something no one can give you. You have to earn it. And to earn it, you have to *think*."

"Let me sleep on this. It's almost sunset. Time for me and mine to hide from the night. You may stay in Mabel's house for now."

"I will. I promise." With a smile, Thistle raised her hand and let Rosie fly away. She took a moment to twirl and bask in the glory of the beautiful garden Mabel had provided for her friends. A sadly neglected garden, but still beautiful in its own ramshackle way.

# Eight

CHASE RUBBED HIS HANDS ACROSS HIS face and through his hair, trying to scrub away some of his fatigue.

He stared at his key for a long moment trying to remember what it was for and how to use it. The sounds of ripping metal, the cries of the injured, the wails of the grieving, and the angry honking of horns still rang in his ears. Three of the drivers in the chain reaction accident swore they'd seen a miniature man dressed in yellow, with splotchy red-and-gold wings crash into their windshields.

"He flew right at me, then paused in front of the window to make sure I saw him. I had to swerve to avoid hitting him!" They all dictated variations of that statement. One woman said that when the flying man paused, he flickered in and out of view, "Kind of like a computer monitor saving and resetting. Blink and you miss it."

All of them had passed the sobriety and Breathalyzer tests. Chase hadn't dared admit to anyone but himself that a Pixie had been at work. But which one? He had a few ideas about that even before he got the call that Haywood Wheatland had escaped county jail. He'd been spotted in Phelma Jo's office.

Chase shivered, suddenly chilled to the bone.

Then he opened the door of his tiny apartment. The heavenly aroma of garlic and tomatoes with herbs and stuff he never bothered to use when he cooked for himself greeted him. The chill faded, his stomach woke up, and his mind began to work again. Sort of.

"Dusty, is that you?" It had to be. No one else had a key to his apartment.

"Supper's ready. Get washed up while I put everything on the table," she called back from the galley kitchen that flowed into his dining/living room space.

"What kind of organic concoction that tastes like cardboard has she thrown together?" he asked himself as he splashed cool water on his face. Then he stumbled to the small round table that separated the kitchen from the living room. He only had two chairs. She occupied one. He took the other, eyeing the pile of whole wheat pasta and tomato sauce with some kind of ground meat—organic turkey he'd bet—on his garage sale china plates. He'd bet the parmesan was a variation of soy cheese, too. More cardboard.

"Eat this," Dusty said gently, shoving the plate closer to him. "You'll feel better."

"I'm too tired to eat," he mumbled. Dusty's healthy, organic diet—ingrained while she endured chemo as a child—had looked and smelled better than he thought it would. As tired as he was, he just couldn't summon a bit of appetite for the food he suspected would be tasteless.

"Why don't we run down to the café. My sister will fix us dinner. She's changed the menu. There's Desdemona's Delight, a veggie sandwich on whole wheat bread with soy cream cheese. And she added some gluten-free stuff. She wants to broaden the customer base to include people who think they can't eat out."

"No. You need to eat now, not an hour from now when we get served at Norton's."

Dusty had come to take care of him. He couldn't ever remember her doing that. The Universe needed to take care of Dusty.

"You'll sleep better if you eat something and take a shower," she coaxed.

"One bite," he agreed, too tired to fight her. When had the shy little girl he'd teased unmercifully become so strong?

*Last summer when Thistle had begun working her magic on the town.* What would happen to them all if malevolent magic and mayhem from the yellow Pixie with gold-and-red wings replaced the gentle, good-humored nurturing from Thistle Down?

A second bite followed the first, then a third, and pretty soon he was soaking up the last of the sauce with a piece of garlic toast—whole grain bread with soy parmesan and, he was sure, organic butter.

"This is really good. I never thought your natural diet would have any taste at all."

Dusty still picked at her meal. She'd never been a big eater.

"What's the matter? Don't like your own cooking?" he asked, stealing her extra piece of bread.

"No, I like my cooking. And I like to cook, when Mom will let me. I'm looking forward to having my own kitchen and someone to cook for."

"Then what's bothering you?" Chase looked around for something to drink, something with more substance than the herbal tea she had prepared for herself. He pushed back his chair, intent on making coffee. The chair legs scraped loudly on the vinyl.

Dusty looked up startled, almost like a deer caught in a car's headlights.

"Don't bolt on me, Dusty." He covered her hand with one of his own to reassure her. And just to hold her hand, a privilege he hadn't gotten used to yet.

"Chase, I read Mabel's papers," she said quietly.

"And?"

"Let me show you." She dashed across the room and retrieved the manila envelope from the folding table beside his recliner.

He guessed he'd have to get some better furniture when she moved in after the wedding. God, he wanted that to happen soon, not two months from now. With All Hallows approaching and an insane Pixie on the loose, he didn't know when or if they'd get the time to elope.

Dusty made a point of spreading the papers out on the table in neat piles. "Read them, starting with this while I clean up." She tapped a single sheet with the Historical Preservation District letterhead.

The homely sounds of Dusty moving around the kitchen,

water running, and the refrigerator door opening and closing settled his mind. He could get used to hearing her hum in the background.

*Dum dee dee do dum dum.*

Thistle's music.

With a brighter frame of mind he turned to the second packet, and the third, and finally the will.

He sat staring at it for a long time with his mouth hanging open. Finally, Dusty removed the papers from his hands and replaced them with a steaming mug of coffee.

"Drink, then speak," she directed.

"She's giving us the use of her house for ten years or until our family outgrows the place, whichever comes first."

"I gaped so long I caught three flies before I could think straight enough to call you. But you were busy with the accident on the freeway."

Chase followed directions, sipping the scalding coffee. He relished the first jolt of caffeine, then sipped again and again, feeling more alive with each mouthful. "The accident was caused by a Pixie. I've got three eyewitnesses, but they'll probably claim it was post-traumatic stress that made them say it," he choked out around a burning hot mouthful. After three long gulps of air, he sipped again. His brain churned and settled into almost recognizable patterns. "The trust agreement making the house and land into a city park and museum after we vacate is as convoluted as the city charter."

"More so. I've read every incarnation of the town charter up through incorporation of the city. I've kept up on all the changes the City Council has made over the last one hundred sixty-five years. Especially the parts the citizens didn't get to vote on," she mused, shuffling the papers around until the will sat in front of Chase.

"Mabel is one savvy lady," Chase admitted as he began plowing through the document again. After he'd made sense of the first paragraph, Dusty impatiently flipped over two pages and pointed to the bequests.

"The nephew gets all the furniture and bric-a-brac, a lot of them antiques that have been in the family for generations, and quite valuable. He can't contest the will on the grounds that he was left out," she said to clarify the next paragraph.

"And if he does contest it, he gets nothing," Chase added, amazed at how quickly she absorbed the complex language.

"But look at the house and gardens."

He did. That took another half mug of coffee to fully comprehend. "Am I just tired or does the language duplicate itself?"

"You are tired, but yes, the language repeats in several permutations so there is little if any way to misinterpret it. No loopholes."

"At least we don't have to worry about this just yet. Have you heard anything about how Mabel is faring?" Chase pushed aside the papers and grabbed Dusty's hands.

"I'm not next of kin, the nephew is, so the hospital won't tell me anything other than that she's in guarded condition. Whatever that means."

"It means she won't be coming home anytime soon. Can Dick weasel more information out of them?"

"I haven't asked. As long as Thistle resides in the house under Mabel's direction, the nephew has to wait for Mabel to die to take any action." Dusty bit her lip and looked over her shoulder for a place to hide, or run away. "That's why she made you sign as witness to her wishes."

"I know that expression, my dear. What aren't you saying?" Chase held onto her hands, not letting her slip away.

"There's one more piece of paper you need to see."

Chase held the envelope up so the opening faced the table. He shook it. Nothing more fell out.

"I hid it."

"Dusty?"

"In my purse. I really needed to think about it before I showed you."

"What is it?"

"Power Of Attorney for you and me over all decisions on Mabel's house, property, and personal possessions. There is also a separate clause for a Medical Power of Attorney and a living will for no extreme measures to prolong her life. I think we need to go to the hospital first thing and present it to whoever has control over these things." She looked away again. "Chase, that is a responsibility I don't feel qualified to take on. It should go to her nephew."

"It should. But she obviously doesn't trust him. I don't even know if he lives in town. I think I'd remember a name like Ian McEwen, though I may have played Little League with him one summer. Haven't seen him since. We'll be better off filing all this with Mabel's lawyer and having him contact the hospital with these directives."

"I'm all for historic preservation," Ian McEwen told Phelma Jo over a glass of wine at the Greek restaurant on Main Street. "Some of these old buildings, like yours, and the block building housing this place, are architecturally significant. Modern developers could learn a lot from them. But some of the houses in this town are unsound, and unsafe."

Phelma Jo nodded rather than speak around a mouthful of dolmades — spiced, ground lamb wrapped in grape leaves and served with a heavenly tomato sauce.

"Take my aunt's house for example."

"And you said your aunt is Mabel Gardiner?" she asked cautiously.

"Mabel Gardiner, on Tenth and Maple Drive. That's right"

"Mabel. The police dispatcher. I — um — know the house."

Phelma Jo had a client who wanted to buy it for the two-acre lot. Trouble was he'd have to bulldoze the house to get access to the long strip of land between backyards. The stubborn old lady wouldn't listen to an offer, even one that would have set her up nicely in a river-view condo with housekeeping for the rest of her days.

She had other reasons, very good reasons, other than stubbornness for keeping the house. Her belief in Pixies wasn't the only one either.

"Yes. She's my aunt. My mother's much older sister, who never married. She helped raise me after my dad died. Spent my summers here in Skene Falls. Did you know Mabel's seventy-eight and still working?"

"I've only guessed at her age. She keeps that as secret as the source of her inside information on everyone in town."

"Too stubborn to quit."

Phelma Jo could think of a dozen reasons to keep working. Topmost on the list was that Mabel knew where all the bodies were buried—literally—and who had which skeletons in their closet. Anyone with anything to hide was afraid to cross her. Including the mayor and the chief of police.

"What about her house?" she prodded. Like it or not, Phelma Jo also had a vested interest in keeping that house intact. If it needed repair, she'd see to it. Tomorrow, bright and early.

"Cracks in the foundation. I try to keep an eye on the place from a distance, so I can't say for sure."

"Why the distance?" He'd said something about a disagreement when he was young, but surely they'd patched up their differences since then.

"After my last summer here, she broke off all contact with my mother and me. When I finished college and moved out on my own, I tried calling and writing, but she never answered the phone or the notes. After a while, I gave up. But I still love her, worry about her."

"That's too bad, losing your contact with family and all." The right words to say, although Phelma Jo never regretted losing touch with her alcoholic mother and her mother's abusive boyfriends. Phelma Jo had never known who her father was. Her birth certificate had a big blank spot where his name should be. All she did know of her past was that her mother had been sixteen, pregnant, and a runaway when she landed in Skene Falls.

"Yeah. I'm Aunt Mabel's only family. I hate to see her alone and lonely."

Phelma Jo covered up her anger by breaking off a forkful of baklava. He had a family, dammit. He should work harder at maintaining it. She envied him even this broken relationship with a woman who gave love right, left, and sideways to kids who desperately needed it.

"This baklava is heavenly," he said taking a cautious bite. "I'm glad this place doesn't serve chocolate. I hate chocolate."

"Who doesn't like chocolate?" Phelma Jo asked, truly surprised.

"I don't. Haven't since I was a kid." Something in his eyes hinted at an old pain. Maybe his childhood hadn't been much happier than her own, except when he was with his aunt. Losing her might have led to disaster after disaster with his mother. Especially if his father went missing rather than died.

"Too many calories in chocolate anyway. I was fat until I was ten or so. Soon as I gave up stuffing my face with chocolate because it was supposed to make me feel better, I lost weight and my skin cleared up. Except for these." He pointed to the spray of freckles across his nose.

"Then I guess we won't order chocolate cake at the Old Mill when we go tomorrow night." She shrugged. "And I like the freckles. They are distinctive."

"Thanks. I stand out in a crowd, that's for sure." They laughed together. "Though Aunt Mabel says that a face without freckles is like a sky without stars. Old Celtic blessing." He grinned hugely.

Phelma Jo returned his smile and wondered how long it had been since she'd truly laughed *with* someone.

"I miss Aunt Mabel," he said quietly.

Phelma Jo reached across the table to touch his hand in sympathy. "Now that you're back in town, I'm sure you can mend your relationship with her."

"She's so lonely she makes up stories about a band of Pixies that live in her garden and how they need protection. I think she's suffering from more than a bit of dementia," Ian said quietly, as if afraid to admit to a weakness in his only relative.

What was with this town and their obsession with Pixies? Haywood Wheatland, Thistle Down, Dick and Dusty Carrick, and venerable old Mabel. Must be something in the water.

But it would explain a lot of things about Mabel and her spy network if it were true.

"I've tried to get the city out to do a full inspection on Aunt Mabel's house, but all I get is bureaucratic double-speak," Ian continued, seemingly without noticing Phelma Jo's interest.

"In this city you won't get a better response. Everyone is afraid of her."

"That's what I thought. And why I moved here from Portland last month; besides a lot of my work is gravitating here. I want to be closer to her. When we finish eating, I'm going up to the house. Try again to get her to listen to reason and have the house thoroughly inspected and either repaired or demolished."

"Do you want company?" Phelma Jo kept her hand atop his and squeezed gently. "I've known Mabel a long time. Maybe I can get her to stop and listen before throwing us both out."

"That's very nice of you. And a good idea."

"Happy to help." And she was. "Mabel is special. She deserves to have her family back."

Suddenly Phelma Jo realized that Mabel was her family, too. The only real family she'd ever had. Despite her self-serving, defensive mask, she needed Mabel in her life as much as Ian did.

# Nine

"THISTLE, CAN WE TALK?" Dick asked over his cell phone. He sat in his car across the street from Mabel Gardiner's driveway, the convertible roof pulled up to guard against the nighttime chill and drizzle.

"Why, Dick?" Thistle replied.

Through the windows, with the blinds open, he watched her move from the living room to the kitchen, carrying the old-fashioned rotary dial phone with her, tangling her feet in the long cord. Cell phones, computers, and remote controls went haywire when she was around. But she could manage the old-fashioned analog devices.

She'd explained it once. Pixies were bound to Earth and Water. Modern digital technology was aligned with Air. Faeries could manipulate them because they were bound to Air and Fire.

Half-breed mutants like Haywood Wheatland had access to all four elements. That was how he'd recruited a gang of computer gamers and gotten them addicted to Fire and blowing things up, like carnival rides and cell phone towers.

Dick shuddered with dread at the thought that Haywood Wheatland had come back into town.

"Thistle, please, I've had an awful day helping with the accident on the freeway and I need to tell you some things. Some important things."

"Okay. You can come in. The front door is unlocked."

"You shouldn't do that, Thistle. It's not safe to leave blinds up after dark and doors unlocked," he said as he got out of his car and hit the remote lock. When he heard the satisfying beep and click and saw the single flash of the headlights, he sprinted across the street.

Thistle hung up before he reached the front walkway. But she was there, opening the front door, backlit by the hall light with an aura of gold. He closed his eyes a moment, wanting to fix the image in his mind before reality intruded and robbed him of this magical moment. His Thistle waiting for him at the end of the day.

His Thistle.

"That's not safe either," he said, not as sternly as he should. "Opening the door before you know it's me waiting for you and not some thug."

"I knew it was you. You just called me. Besides, I always know when you are near."

"How . . . ?"

"I just know. It's part of who you are and what I am."

"Like we're bound together by magic?" he asked, stepping close, not quite daring to cross the threshold.

"Something like that." She looked up at him with those gorgeous violet eyes set deeply in her pale face, surrounded by a cloud of hair so dark it held purple highlights.

"Thistle, I . . ."

"Come in out of the chill," she said, stepping back and looking at the dusty All Hallows decorations she'd piled in the hallway; resin grave markers, requisite scarecrows, a flying witch, and face pieces to tack onto a tree. She'd need help setting up the battery-operated movements of the mouth and eyebrows, and the motion sensor that triggered recorded spooky sentences. He almost laughed at how the sentences always seemed appropriate to the age of the trick-or-treaters who passed by the tree. Tots and grade schoolers got Mabel's gentlest voice: "Do you want to play in my garden? Come and meet my Pixies. Pixies love to play tricks." A semi-spooky chuckle followed that. Older kids got invitations to follow the ghosts into the grave and beware the vampire hiding among the roses.

The moment Thistle firmly closed the door and flipped the deadbolt, he gave in to temptation and gathered her

into his arms. His fingers dug into her back with desperation as he claimed her mouth with his own.

She readily melted into him, her arms wrapping around
his neck and keeping him close.

Electric tingles coursed through his blood. Behind his
closed eyes, sparkling purple lights burst into fireworks. He
wanted nothing more than to continue kissing her, exploring her mouth, her cheek, her ear, and her nape with his
tongue.

The tingle of gossamer wings across her back sent new
vibrancy through him.

Gravity fell away. They drifted in a haze of light, warmth,
comfort, and a merging of souls.

In the background he thought he heard the chiming of a
dozen Pixies laughing and applauding them.

She pulled away from him abruptly.

Reality dropped him back to the ground like a plunge
into ice water.

"What is that all about, Dick? This morning you rejected
me because you were afraid of losing me." She hung her
head, letting the magnificent mass of hair fall forward, ob-
scuring her face, robbing him of contact with her expressive
eyes.

"Thistle, I . . ." He had to gulp back the emotions that
choked him. "Thistle, I love you. You know that. Today I
had to help untangle a massive accident on the freeway. I
saw a lot of pain. Lives cut short, others altered irrevocably;
all in a horrible moment of speed and loss of control. I realized the same thing could happen to me, or you, or Dusty,
or anyone I care about without warning."

"Life for humans is transitory. That's why everything you
do, or don't do, is important. Because you have so little time,
you have to live every moment to the fullest before you
die." She paused and looked up at him. The sharp angles of
her face filled out a bit, the uptilt of her eyes faded to round,
and the points at the tops of her ears smoothed. Any trace
of her wing energy dissolved.

In that moment her humanity showed through more
than ever.

"Pixies are reduced to games and pranks because we have nothing else to fill near eternity."

A half-heard conversation at the accident scene flashed across Dick's memory. He pushed it aside. The time was not right. He had to get something else off his chest first.

"Thistle, will you marry me?"

"Dick, are you sure? What if . . . what if . . . ?"

"I know I will hurt for a very long time if your curse is lifted and you *choose* to go back to Pixie. But I would gladly trade a few years, or weeks, or even days, with you as my wife than to never have you beside me at all. Please, Thistle, will you make my world complete for as long as we are granted? Marry me?"

"Yes."

Dusty watched Chase sleep. He'd drifted off in his recliner in mid-sentence. His even breathing fell into a comforting counterpoint to her heartbeat. Strain and worry lines on his face smoothed out. An endearing bit of thick blond hair flopped across his forehead. The ends fluttered ever so slightly with each breath.

She wanted to smooth it back away from his face, but was afraid she'd wake him. He needed rest.

There was something incredibly intimate about watching a man sleep; watching a *beloved* sleep. In some ways she imagined it was more intimate than sex. She'd wait until after the wedding to find out for certain. Did she have to? She loved Chase more than she thought possible when she'd had a teenage crush on him. More than she imagined when he kissed her the first time.

That first kiss had been fueled by anger and desperation on his part, fear and self-doubt on hers. He'd left her right after, both of them bewildered and needing more, but the time wasn't right. When the time was right, she'd taken the bold leap to kiss him. In public. In front of all their friends and many acquaintances at the Old Mill Bar and Grill.

Her love grew with every passing day until she wondered why she needed months to prepare her mind for their wedding night. She felt ready now.

She chuckled. She was ready, but he was sound asleep.

Chase shifted and grumbled something in his sleep. The worry lines came back for a moment. He gripped his crossed arms fiercely, as if cold. She found an old quilt at the foot of his bed and brought it over to wrap around him. He clutched the binding and settled again, easier in his dreams now.

"There's one more thing I need to do before I go home," she whispered, almost wishing she still had something in the kitchen she could scrub first. Chase had not invested in a lot of furniture, and lived rather casually, but he wasn't a slob. Thank goodness. He even cooked after a fashion. Dick, on the other hand, had a lot of improving to do before he settled down.

A few minutes on the Internet produced a phone number with a local exchange. Dusty dialed it using Chase's landline, an unlisted number that showed anonymous on any caller ID. Part of being a cop, protecting his privacy and possibly his life when out of uniform.

"McEwen," a man said in a distracted voice.

"Is this Ian McEwen, Mabel Gardiner's nephew?" Dusty asked politely.

"Yes." Hesitant now.

"This is Dusty Carrick, a friend of Mabel Gardiner. I'm sorry to inform you that your aunt, Mabel Gardiner has been admitted to Mercy General Hospital, the cardiac unit." Dusty tried to keep her voice neutral, and dispassionate. Considering the terms of Mabel's will, she didn't want Mr. McEwen to think she had deliberately delayed informing him of Mabel's condition.

"Who are you?" McEwen demanded.

"I'm a friend of your aunt's. I just inquired about her condition and the nurses wouldn't tell me anything because I'm not next of kin. I've been trying to track you down most of the day." A lie. She hated blurring the truth. What would he think of her when he found out the truth?

*Stop that!* she yelled at herself. She had to stop expecting other people to judge her. The opinion of strangers shouldn't impact her life.

But this man wouldn't be a stranger for long.

"The police department where she works did not have you listed in her emergency contact information," she continued. That, at least, was the truth. "I had to get your name from her lawyer." That, too, was sort of the truth. His name was on the papers Mabel's lawyer had drawn up.

"What did you say your name was?" She heard a snap, like a seat belt releasing and the snick of a car door opening. His home phone must forward to his cell. "How bad is she?"

Then came the soft murmur of a feminine voice in the background. He wasn't alone. Dusty realized she didn't know if he was married or anything about him. What if he had children who needed to learn about Pixies by playing in their Great Aunt Mabel's garden?

"I'm sorry, I don't know anything about Mabel's condition. The hospital won't tell me anything." Dusty avoided giving her name again. He'd find out soon enough and be blisteringly angry. "I was with her this morning when she had a cardiac episode. At least that's what the EMTs called it. I know she'll want to see you."

"I'm on my way to Mercy now. If she asks, who should I tell her called me?"

Dusty hung up.

# Ten

THISTLE MELTED INTO DICK'S ARMS AGAIN, eager to explore this new and special relationship.

"This is it for me, Thistle," Dick whispered while nibbling at her ear. "True Pixie love."

"Um." Thistle surrendered to his next kiss rather than correct him.

Pixies were fluid in their partnerships until a mating flight. That one experience of absolute trust signaled the beginning of a forever love. Of course Pixies lived in the moment, for the moment, rarely thinking ahead to consequences. Unlike Elves and Faeries who schemed and manipulated in endless games to ease the boredom of eternal life. For the past few months Faeries had manipulated Pixies to give up The Ten Acre Wood—protected and cherished by humans—because the Faery hill was threatened by new construction. Those manipulations, led by Haywood Wheatland and his fascination with Fire, had become dangerous to humans and Pixies. They couldn't be allowed to continue.

She wished the Faeries would turn their attention to important things like mating flights. Unlikely. They'd never been interested in partners beyond a few moments of pleasure. Creating mayhem was more fun for them.

After a while, when Pixies grew bored with their mates, they could choose to end the relationship and find someone new and more exciting. Sort of like human marriages. Unless the mating flight consummated a treaty with another tribe.

She'd have no mating flight with Dick in these big wing-less bodies.

Perhaps they could invent their own ritual of glorious gliding from a great height together; totally dependent upon each other for completion.

Maybe a wedding, like the one Dusty and her mother planned was the equivalent ritual.

Dick's mobile mouth sent shivers of delight and expectation all through her in ways no Pixie had ever enticed her. She wouldn't get bored with Dick, or need to seek a more exciting mate for a very, very long time.

"When?" Dick asked as he trailed kisses along her neck, pushing aside her sloppy sweatshirt to reveal her shoulder and part of her breast. "When can we get married?" His hands reached beneath her sweatshirt to cup her breasts.

"Um. Soon."

"How soon? Like tonight?" His wonderfully sensitive hands made it hard for her to think.

She was human now. She had to think; had to look beyond this moment of pleasure. A moment of ecstasy.

What was it the actress had said in the movie she'd watched last night with Juliet? The one about a king from times long ago pursuing a woman named Anne while still married to another woman, Katherine. Something about keeping a man dangling; increasing his expectations. Anne would never become queen if she allowed Henry—that was the king's name—into her bed too soon.

"We'll have a proper wedding first," she said, suppressing a giggle of delight. She pointedly took a step away from him, though she felt instantly chilled.

Dick raised his eyebrows. She'd come to recognize the expression as one of disbelief, as well as a question. "I thought Pixies didn't indulge in large rituals for anyone but kings and queens?"

"Some Pixies hold out for a formal mating flight." She knew that Rosie had. Good thing, too, as Hay turned out to have mixed loyalties as well as bloodlines. "I'm human now. My only role model is your sister. Her wedding is her mating flight. If she waits for sex with Chase until the wedding, I wait until our wedding."

"Okay." He drew out the word into many parts. "How soon can we get married?"

"How long does it take?"

"If you want a big ceremony in a church with lots of guests and a big party afterward ..."

"Like Dusty is planning."

"Like our mother is planning for Dusty. Then it takes months to get the proper dress and wedding cake and stuff. If you don't care about such things, it will take two weeks in Oregon, three days in Washington, or we can drive to Idaho and have no wait at all."

"Let's go for the two weeks. I'd like a special dress, but not the big party. It's not like I know a lot of people."

"Two weeks," he said sadly. "I guess I can wait that long. But no longer. I had a bad scare today. I don't want to waste any of the short life I've been given."

"Tell me about it." Thistle kicked the door shut, well aware of the audience in the yard beyond, though after dark all the Pixies should be curled up in their nests fast asleep. Then she looped her arm through Dick's and led him into Mabel's parlor. A tiny room compared to the one in Juliet's home. But it was tidy, with comfortable furniture, built-in bookcases on either side of the hearth, and polished bare wood floors. A few colorful braided rugs offered a little protection from chill drafts to bare feet. She hadn't wanted to disturb the cozy neatness of the room with the decorations she'd dragged out of the attic this afternoon.

She liked the welcome feel of this home. Juliet's house could be sterile at times, especially since she came home from England. Funny, Thistle didn't remember the house feeling that way when Dick and Dusty were children. But since they'd grown up ... Juliet didn't like that much at all and her house reflected her mood.

"The strangest thing about today was the testimony I overheard after the accident," Dick said, taking a seat on the sofa and pulling Thistle down so close to him she might as well sit in his lap.

Hmmm, not a bad idea. But that could lead to deeper intimacies. She settled for stroking his face and hand with a comforting touch.

"What about the testimony?" She tried out the new word, testing each syllable until it sounded right on her tongue.

"Three separate people claimed an enraged Pixie flew right at their windshield, causing them to swerve to avoid hitting him."

Thistle's breath caught in her throat. "What color was it?" she choked out. Her blood felt as if it froze in her veins.

"Yellow with crimson splotches."

"The same Pixie I saw fighting with Chicory this morning. He's carrying the war over to humans. Did you hear that?" Thistle asked, suddenly alert to anything out of place.

"It's just the wind coming up."

"I thought I heard the back door open."

"I didn't hear anything like that." He took her face in both his hands and kissed her again. The world fell away and she knew only his touch.

Chicory smashed into the glass of the basement window. His shoulder cracked and his wing crumpled. The glass remained unmoved, opaque in its disdain of his puny efforts.

The sun had set. Chill crept out of the cement walls engulfing him in strength-robbing lethargy.

He had to get out. Quickly, before underground robbed him of life as well as strength.

Pixies died underground.

Desperate, he bounced around looking for something, anything that would give him an escape. He investigated stacks of boxes, covered racks of old clothes. Hmmm, he could curl up in that moth-eaten fur coat for warmth if he had to. The bicycle with the flat tire had too much iron to be useful. So did the broken washing machine. Mabel had a new one now, up on the enclosed back porch, with a matching dryer. But Mabel never threw anything away that might be useful someday. Maybe he could use the set of wooden barbeque skewers to dig his way out.

Nope. Dirt was part of underground. No dirt visible anyway. Just this horrible cement providing a scant barrier between him and the all-consuming Earth.

What had the nephew said last time he left a message on

Mabel's telephone? Something about cracks in the foundation.

"Foundation," he muttered. "I'm a Pixie. How am I supposed to know what a foundation is?" Foundation. Fountain. He knew what a fountain was. He often played in the sparkling spray pouring out of Memorial Fountain downtown, at the center of traffic. Cars coming from six different directions (or was it seven? He couldn't remember) had to go around it. He'd had great fun splashing water into open windows or on windshields.

Alder had thrown Thistle into Memorial Fountain last summer when he cursed her with human proportions and robbed her of her wings and clothes.

Maybe if he looked for water where water shouldn't be, he'd find a crack.

If he had the strength. If he could see.

"Can't anyone turn on a light down here?"

Light? Mabel turned on lights when she came down here. Where was the switch? Not down here. Up there, 'cause she needed to see the stairs.

He flew to the staircase, ten rickety wooden steps destined to trip Mabel one of these days. He landed on his knees on the newel post at the bottom. His wings drooped in fatigue. His back ached from landing on the cement floor when Snapdragon dropped him through the open window. He had to cling to the wood for too many long heartbeats. At last he stood on shaking legs and gathered enough air to fly up three steps.

Which window? One of them had to be open for him to get dropped through. Chicory looked around at the shadows within shadows. He just barely picked out the outline of seven rectangular panes placed evenly around the basement. Each one was only inches from ground level.

"Oh, yeah. That brain-rattling thud I heard when I landed was Snapdragon slamming the window shut. How long was I asleep after that?" Hours and hours, judging by the darkness inside and out.

He gritted his teeth and crawled up to the next step. The air seemed a bit lighter up here, easier to breathe. Slowly he heaved himself up another step and then another before his

wings recovered enough strength to take him to the topmost one.

Definitely easier to breathe now. He was probably above
ground level, but still trapped by dirt and cement.

A quick scan of the closed door and its surroundings
showed him nothing but shadows. He felt around the wood.
Blank.

Gradually the soft murmur of voices penetrated his
panic.

Someone was in the house. Had Mabel come home from
the hospital? Maybe the stray child Mabel and Chase were
looking for had found the spare key inside a fake rock.

Nope. A male voice. And an adult female. But not Mabel. Who?

The voices came closer, grew louder. Ah, Thistle. Thistle
had come to take care of the house until Mabel got better.

"Thistle, open the door!" he yelled through the keyhole
as loudly as he could. Not very loud. Underground continued to leach strength from him. Or maybe the big bruise
between his wings drained him.

He dropped down to the top step. Maybe if he yelled
into the tiny gap between door and floor, they'd hear him.

"Thistle, help me!"

The voices stopped, replace by moans and slurpy kissing
sounds.

"Great. I'm dying here and she gets all amorous. Must be
Dick on the other end of that kiss."

Chicory squished himself flatter to get more sound
through the gap.

Gap?

He slapped his forehead, jostling his thoughts back into
some kind of order. A tiny bit of light filled the gap now
that Thistle and Dick were in the kitchen. Life returned to
his wings.

Slowly, careful to fold his wings tight against his back, he
wiggled and skootched and crawled beneath the door. He
had to stop twice to catch his breath. He was above ground
now, but it was night. Any respectable Pixie would be
sleeping, tangled up with as many of his tribe as could fit

into the old birdhouse hanging from the corkscrew willow tree.

A birdhouse for gosh sakes. Exile from his own tribe, along with anyone else who displeased Rosie.

Rosie had robbed him of respectability. Her laziness and her enthrallment with Snapdragon—who used to be Hay—made her one of the worst queens in the entire history of Pixie. If Pixies bothered to remember their past while ignoring the future.

"Guess I'll have to start my own tribe by gathering together all of the exiles and displaced Pixies," he said as he popped through the gap and slid onto the linoleum floor.

Dick and Thistle continued their absorption in each other, ignoring the running water and half-filled coffee carafe, and everything else in the world except each other.

Chicory shook his head in disbelief as he crawled toward the nesting box Mabel kept in the dining room, an old wooden cigar box lined with moss and cottonwood fluff. She provided lots of little luxuries for her Pixies; never knew when they'd need shelter from a freak hailstorm or marauding cats.

With his wings wrapped around him, and his body curled into a tight ball, he slept quickly and deeply, grateful to be free and alive, but ever so lonely. Pixies weren't meant to sleep or live alone.

Once he woke up to a strange sound, a door closing quietly, like someone didn't want to disturb the household.

Probably Dick leaving and he didn't want to wake Thistle. Wait. How far had the moon progressed in its journey across the night sky? Hadn't Dick left some time ago?

Chicory was so tired he couldn't remember what he'd heard and what he'd dreamed. He turned over and pulled more fluff around him for warmth. He slept deeply and dreamlessly.

# Eleven

"MOM, ARE YOU HOME?" Dick called from the kitchen door. He kicked off his shoes, and slid into house slippers, all the while keeping a firm grip on Thistle's hand. The grin on his face wouldn't fade, no matter how much his face hurt.

Thistle's smile matched his own.

"In here," Mom called from the office off the kitchen. A couple of generations ago it had been the housekeeper's room. Now the family had installed computers and filing cabinets for everything from volunteer lists to period recipes to scraps of fabric and wallpaper for costume design.

"Is Dusty home?" he asked, scanning the room for traces of his sister.

"She's out with Chase," Mom said with a distracted air, keeping her eyes focused on her eighteen-inch computer screen in the center of her antique oak rolltop desk. Dusty's netbook was missing from the smaller writing desk in the far corner.

In other words, Dusty had not come home from work before meeting Chase. Where could they be? When Dick had last seen Chase, he'd been near to falling over with exhaustion after the accident and related paperwork.

"What do you need?" Mom still didn't look up from her database. It looked like a list of volunteers with dates of enrollment, last duties, and skill sets.

"We wanted to tell you something important, and thought it would be nice if Dusty were here, too," Thistle said. She stepped across the threshold and the computer images tilted sideways before flashing solid blue and then into pure static.

"Damn. It crashed before I could save it." Mom finally looked up, blinking rapidly as she changed her focus.

"That's one way to get her attention," Dick muttered. Then he took a deep steadying breath. "Thistle and I are getting married."

"Oh?" Mom's eyes opened wide. "Do I need to shift directions and plan a double wedding?"

Dick could almost see the wheels of calculation spinning behind her eyes.

"Can we do that?" Thistle asked.

"We could, but ... Dusty deserves her own special day with a church and big reception and the entire town in attendance. We don't want to steal any attention from her. And we don't want to wait," Dick asserted. He knew his mother and her manipulations. She'd try to get Thistle into one of those godawful Elizabethan gowns if she could. His Thistle deserved to pick out her own dress, something soft and light and floating around her as she walked.

"We don't want to wait," Thistle echoed. She took his hand and stepped closer.

He bent his head to brush her lips with his own. His blood sang in anticipation.

"I suppose then you'll be moving into Mabel's house with her," Mom sighed deeply, as if such an act would break her heart.

"No," Thistle answered. "We've decided to wait for that, too. I'll be staying at Mabel's house on my own until the wedding."

"Well, that's a relief." Mom rolled her oak chair back and stood up. "I'll call your father and see when he can get away from his classes. He should attend his own son's wedding." She stood a moment in hesitation.

Her gaze lingered on Thistle, weighing, assessing, as if measuring her for her dress, or a coffin. "I have something for you," she said as if making a life or death decision.

"Benedict, your great-grandmother left a ring to be passed down to the brides in the family. I don't remember why exactly I didn't get it from your grandmother. Probably because she was still wearing it when your father and I got married. Then Desdemona went ahead and accepted that pitiful little diamond from Chase before your father and I came home from England." Mom crouched down and unlocked the bottom left-hand drawer of the desk. She withdrew a maroon velvet box, about the size of a hardback book, cradling it in her arms as if she held her first grandchild.

"I've never seen that box before, Mom," Dick said. His heart pounded hard in his chest. Suddenly he felt too small for the emotions pouring through him. A bit of awe topped them all.

"No reason you should see it. These are literally the family jewels. Not many left. Your father and I sold a couple of pieces to pay for your sister's cancer treatments. Insurance didn't cover everything. I think the ruby choker from 1898 paid for new drains and a sump pump after the floods of 1996. Insurance didn't even try to cover it."

With the box carefully centered on the desktop, Mom opened the lid slowly, peeking in to make sure nothing else had disappeared since the last time she'd looked. Satisfied, she let the top fold back to reveal some scattered pieces of glittering jewels. Centermost, in the place of honor, sat a purple ring.

"Five top-grade round cut amethysts, totaling one half carat around a blue-white diamond of another half carat in weight, set in white gold," Mom said on a sigh. She fingered the stones gently before plucking the ring out of the crease in the lining that held it snugly upright. "You'll probably have to have it resized. Thistle has long, slender fingers. Your grandmother had short, fat ones." That sounded almost like a curse, or an accusation of totally uncivilized behavior.

Thistle's eyes went wide in wonder. She bit her bottom lip. "It's too wonderful. I shouldn't . . . I can't . . ."

"Of course you can, dear. Benedict loves you. That makes you more than worthy of wearing this ring until you pass it on to your children." Closing her eyes, she handed the ring to Dick. "Do it right, son. Down on one knee and ask properly. But if you should break up, the ring comes back. It's part of the family."

"Yes ma'am." Grinning, his heart beating loudly in his ears, he dropped into the required pose and held the ring up to the love of his life. His one, true love. Thistle Down.

"Desdemona, when you get to work, could you email me the most recent volunteer roster from the Masque Ball? My computer crashed last night and I've lost some data."

Dusty looked up from the complex schedule of school tours and teacher in-service classes at the museum starting next week, and pushed her glasses firmly up to the bridge of her nose. "Um, sure, Mom. What do you need it for? I suppose it is never too late to start work on next year's fund-raiser."

"Actually, I was thinking that when Mabel Gardiner comes home from the hospital, she's going to need help. I've downloaded a stack of low-salt, reduced-fat recipes. I thought, if each of the volunteers makes one dish and puts it in Mabel's freezer, she won't have to expend vital energy cooking."

"That's a really nice thought, Mom. I'll email you the list. But you know not everyone on the list can cook." She was thinking of Marguerite Vollans, a new bride who had never boiled an egg before marrying the sous chef at the country club. He did all the cooking for them.

"There is that. Well, maybe Marguerite and some of her friends can take turns dusting and vacuuming. These old houses generate a lot of dust."

Mom leaned into the freezer section of the refrigerator. "I'd better take something over to Thistle while she's house-sitting for Mabel. Sometimes I swear that girl was raised by wolves in the forest. She has no concept of how to take care of herself."

Too close to the truth for comfort. "I know, Mom." Dusty and Dick had concocted a story that should explain everything.

"Actually Thistle's family moved away from Skene Falls to join a cult when she was in grade school. She escaped an abusive situation with only the clothes on her back. She had no ID, no money, nothing. She doesn't even know if she has a birth certificate or where to look for one." Her glasses slid down again as she closed her netbook and prepared to leave.

"Oh, dear. No birth certificate will complicate things when she and Benedict apply for a marriage license. I hate to think what kind of brainwashing she endured. Doubtless they thought women should be barefoot and pregnant and that learning to read was a waste of time. You and Dick did a good thing giving her shelter and helping her get back on her feet. And now she's going to really be part of the family."

Mom didn't look overjoyed at the prospect. "You are all growing up and getting ready to flee the nest. I don't know what I'll do when I'm alone . . ."

"It's not like either of us is moving across country when we get married. We'll stay in town," Dusty reassured her mother.

Dick had told Dusty about the marriage when she crept up the back stairs late last night. They'd hugged and laughed together, and talked for quite a while about the joys of being in love.

"Yes, of course." Mom brightened a little. "I'm glad Dick and Thistle are getting married. I look forward to grandchildren." She looked away from Dusty rapidly, suddenly aware of her *faux pas*.

Chemotherapy had saved Dusty's life, but robbed her of the ability to bear children. Thistle was Mom's only hope of grandchildren of her own bloodline.

"Thanks, Mom, for thinking of Mabel," Dusty said, desperately searching for a change of subject. "I'm sure she'll appreciate the help, even if she does insist she can take care of herself. I've got to run. I'll send you the email as soon as I get to work." Glasses settled back where they belonged, she gathered her belongings.

"Thank you. Oh, and don't forget your fitting with the modiste at five. If we want your wedding gown done on time, we have to keep our regular appointments with Abigail. Benedict won't hear of having a custom-made dress for their quickie wedding. So you are my only chance to plan the most beautiful and proper wedding this town has ever seen."

Dusty rolled her eyes and wondered just how she was going to deal with her mother's plans for the most garish and inappropriate wedding the state had ever seen.

# Twelve

"**W**HAT IS SO IMPORTANT that you pulled me out of a board meeting?" Phelma Jo demanded of her office manager.

The middle-aged woman who had kept the real estate brokerage running smoothly for five years nodded discreetly to a gaunt man in his mid-forties who looked like the weight of the world rested on his shoulders. He sat in an exhausted slump in one of the more comfortable client chairs behind the glass partition of Phelma Jo's office.

"Oh." She marched across the suddenly subdued office that took up the entire fifth floor of a prestigious new building strategically placed at the northern edge of town. She'd built her offices here to attract both local and incoming business from the larger cities in Portland's urban sprawl.

The elegant glass-and-steel structure occupied the same block as the tumbledown four-room shack her mother had rented while Phelma Jo was young. She'd run the bulldozer herself when it came time to demolish the shack.

"Get back to work," she snarled at the real estate agents, accountants, and paralegals scattered about the busy room. She shut the glass door behind her carefully, making no noise other than the obvious click of the lock engaging. Then she reached for the sound system and turned up the light jazz filtering from speakers throughout the floor. If anyone dared listen in, they'd get more static than conversation.

"I told you never to come here, Marcus," she said quietly,

taking her high-backed throne of a chair behind the pristine glass desktop.

"This is an emergency," he replied, studying his hands as if the care lines were a map to hidden treasure. Or relief from his onerous caseload.

"What kind of emergency?"

He pulled a fat file folder from beneath his winter coat draped over the companion chair. He must have intended it to remain hidden because Phelma Jo hadn't noticed it and she always looked for a telltale folder of some kind when Marcus Wallachek contacted her.

She flipped open the manila cover and gazed at the once plump, now pinched face of a young girl. The despair in her dull eyes tugged at her heart. Fifteen years ago, this could have been Phelma Jo. Back then, social worker Marcus Wallachek hadn't the resources Phelma Jo could now give him.

Phelma Jo Nelson had to rescue herself, with Mabel's guidance, from the state and county Child Services Division when the system broke down and she fell through the cracks.

Since meeting Ian, she'd begun thinking about children of her own. Not part of her business plan until now. She made a mental note to draw up a prenuptial agreement and a will declaring a legal guardian for any children they might have together, someone they both trusted to care for the little ones so they were never subjected to the vagaries of the "protective" services of the state that sometimes set up abuse rather than eliminate it.

Her manicured fingertip tracked down the page for vital statistics. "She's sixteen and still in the seventh grade?"

"No support at home, malnutrition, borderline fetal alcohol syndrome. . . ." Marcus trailed off a familiar list of excuses.

"An IQ of eighty-seven. Can she read?"

"Some, way below age and grade level. Again, she didn't get tutoring early on. Her mother insisted upon home-schooling her until she was ten. She thinks the public school system is evil incarnate more likely to teach her precious baby how to rob a bank than earn a living. When the girl failed every one of her state mandated tests, the Court ordered her into public school. She's been playing catch-up ever since."

"I see a history of short-term foster care," Phelma Jo said hopefully. She'd had a few good foster families while her mother's boyfriend was in jail awaiting trial for sexual abuse of a minor. Her mother had checked into rehab for the duration so that she wouldn't have to think about the scandal. The majority of those who took in foster children were truly nurturing and cared about their charges.

Most of them, not all. Phelma Jo wasn't going to take any chances with her own children, if she bore any, or adopted several.

"You'll also note that the mother has sued the state five times for racial discrimination whenever the girl went into foster care—even overnight while the mother was arrested for drunk and disorderly."

Phelma Jo skimmed several pages until she found the report. The mother claimed one eighth Native American heritage. It could just as easily be Latina, African, or Mediterranean since she mentioned no tribal affiliation. The little girl—Phelma Jo preferred to keep these cases anonymous—had been found wandering the traffic lanes of a busy highway outside a bar in the middle of the day. The arresting officers hadn't thought to look for a child left outside the bar when they hauled the mother off to jail. A schoolteacher on lunch break found the child and called Children's Services. A formal complaint against the teacher had been filed for "disrupting the cultural imperative of deep poverty."

"This is nonsense!" Phelma Jo almost screamed.

"Of course it is. All of it is. But the mother has made such a nuisance of these lawsuits that overworked and understaffed Social Services decided not to push her."

Phelma Jo wiped sweat off her brow in growing agitation.

"Okay, where is the child now?"

"In my office, where I left her after a trip to the emergency room. With Mabel Gardiner in the hospital, I had nowhere else to hide her. You did hear about Mabel?"

Phelma Jo nodded briefly. She'd been with Ian when he got the call.

Growing dread left a lump in Phelma Jo's gut. Her last cup of coffee wanted a rapid exit upward. She swallowed it back and asked the next question. "What brought the girl into foster care this time?"

"The girl stayed home from school for eight days, because her mother was too drunk to be left alone. She choked on her own vomit three times. The last two of those eight days had essential testing scheduled. I got called by her teacher and went looking. I couldn't place her in foster care myself, because I got called home on a family emergency. My youngest boy had a burst appendix."

"Your family has to come first. How is Jason?"

"He's recovering nicely. The surgery went well." Marcus grimaced and stared at his hands again.

Phelma Jo didn't like the look of guilt that had flashed across his eyes just before he looked away. She flipped to the last page.

A familiar name jumped out at her.

"Why in hell are these people still allowed to foster children?"

"They are very good at hiding evidence of abuse and setting up situations of their word against that of a child known to lie."

"Lying is a means of self-preservation. Survival."

"My supervisor made the placement. She doesn't know that family like you and I do." He gulped and caught Phelma Jo's gaze with pride and defiance.

"I've got photos of the bruises this time. Fresh bruises, blood, and tissue samples. DNA. She ran to me before they could force her to shower and blur the evidence. If I have my way, the man who beat you senseless for *asking* to watch television, and this girl for not knowing which prayer to say for grace on a Tuesday when the moon is half full and Mercury is in retrograde is going to jail. His wife, who cheered him on and watched, will never again have access to children. But you know the system. A good lawyer could get them off."

"Meanwhile?"

"The girl needs a safe haven and a way out. She needs sanctuary far enough away that she can't be intimidated into changing her story. She needs a friend."

Phelma Jo gulped. "She needs a friend." The phrase resonated as no other had in the entire debacle of her life. Thistle had tried to be her friend when she was seven. But Phelma Jo had been too angry to see that. Dick and Dusty had tried to be her friends in grade school. But then Dusty had betrayed her; called her "stinky-butt" out loud in front of the entire school on the playground.

The perpetual anger that had driven Phelma Jo to succeed and survive drained away.

"You know our rules. She has to be old enough and capable of taking care of herself; to pass the GED tests and get a job," Phelma Jo said sadly. "With that low an IQ and so little education . . ."

"I know. I've got a family in Medford willing to take her, help her, get her tutoring and counseling. These are good people, already part of our network. They'll bring her back to testify if it goes to trial, and I hope it does. They *will* show her the value of telling the truth and reinforce it with love. But we have to do this now so that the foster parents and their lawyer can't trace her before the trial. We can't let them intimidate her into changing her testimony."

"Okay. I'll get you what you need. Give me twenty-four hours." Phelma Jo extracted the girl's birth certificate, fingerprint card, and photo from the pocket in the back of the folder.

Marcus took back the file and slumped out of the office, too tired to demand illegal papers any sooner than tomorrow. "Off the record, I'm taking the girl home with me tonight. No one will know where she is," he said over his shoulder.

Phelma Jo grabbed her purse and jacket. Tucking the official documents inside her briefcase, she exited without explanation. Some chores she had to take care of herself.

# Thirteen

DUSTY GAZED AT THE EXQUISITE SILK wedding gown in Bridget's Bridal Boutique window. The flow of silk cascading around the mannequin enticed her to reach through the glass and caress it.

"I never thought I'd get married at all, let alone to Chase," she said on a sigh to Thistle who eyed the dress with equal longing.

She'd wasted almost half her lunch hour drooling over the gown.

"Which is more important, the wedding or the marriage?" Thistle asked. She sounded genuinely puzzled. She looked over her shoulder toward Dick, where he sat in his car across the street, talking on his cell phone.

"The marriage," Dusty replied. "Definitely the marriage. Bonding with your husband lasts a lifetime. Or it should. The wedding lasts only a few hours, a day at most."

"But it's an important ritual to start the bonding. So why not endure your mother's idea of an ideal wedding and just get on with the marriage?"

"Because it's my mother's idea and it's grotesque."

"Juliet does grab hold of an idea and not let go. Sort of like Mrs. Spencer's dog. His teeth won't chew bones anymore but he still defends them fiercely."

"That's my mother, more obsessive-compulsive than I am. Unfortunately, Shakespeare has so much rich material to draw from that she'll never get bored and move on to something else."

"Until we give her grandchildren." Thistle held her ring up to the light. It sparkled with life and promise.

Strange how well it fit Thistle's hand, almost as if custom-made for her, no resizing needed at all.

"I don't want to think about what Mom'll do to . . . to her grandbabies." Dusty returned her attention to the dress. "It would be so much easier to elope without telling her."

"Wait a minute." Thistle grabbed Dusty's arm, keeping her from moving down Main Street. "Isn't that the meaning of elope, you run away without telling anyone?"

"In this case, Chase has made it mean go get married with minimal ceremony, but *I* have to tell Mom what we are doing and why. He's right of course. I'll hide in the basement and let her continue running my life for me if I don't."

"Oh." Thistle sounded as deflated as Dusty felt. "Well, we can't do anything right now. Juliet has gone to Portland for a meeting."

"Wedding photographers and a cake. As if we can't get good ones here in Skene Falls."

"So, let's look more closely at that dress you love, and see if we can find something glittery and light for me. Dick said he'd buy any gown I chose." Laughing, they entered the shop. Thistle paused only long enough to wave toward Dick. He waved back with half his attention still on the cell phone. Almost a distracted dismissal.

Dusty began counting up the balance in her checking and savings account. Could she possibly, maybe with a little bargaining, buy the dress she truly wanted? She had enough. But would that leave enough to add to Chase's savings for a down payment on a house? They couldn't plan on the gift of Mabel's house. She *wouldn't* plan on the old woman dying. Mabel had to get better. She just had to. And soon.

Phelma Jo drifted down Main Street in a wondrous glow of new love, the morning's trauma forgotten while she took a break. She refused to think about her illegal activities outside her home or office. If she didn't think about them, then she wouldn't slip up and mention them.

The tall man beside her, Ian McEwen, had entered her life with a clipboard and a hard hat. Now he held her hand as they strolled past shops and offices decorated with ghosts and cobwebs, witches and pumpkins, banners painted with harvest motifs hung from street lamps. Posters in every window advertised the parade and haunted maze. Outlying farms showed maps to the biggest pumpkin patches with hay rides, games, and fresh produce. The All Hallows Festival was as important a town fund-raiser as the summer Pioneer Days Festival and the Christmas Festival and the Spring Flower Festival. Actually, she thought All Hallows brought in more money and tourists than any of the others. Everyone wanted to party this time of year. Costumes and pranks only added spice to the mix.

She ignored the reminders that she'd never been allowed to dress up in costumes or go trick-or-treating as a child. All that mattered was that she and Ian walked together to file the building inspection at the courthouse, almost a couple.

She dared, for the first time in her life, to imagine a comfortable future without the drama, betrayal, and heartache of reality.

Her building, the one with Bridget's Bridal Boutique anchoring the ground-floor corner space, had passed inspection, of course. She wouldn't let it fail. A well-maintained historical building commanded higher rents than the ramshackle semi-derelicts other landlords owned.

Ian had complimented her on the state of the wiring. Then he'd asked her out to dinner. They were headed back to her penthouse condo by mutual consent when he'd gotten that damned call to rush to his aunt's side.

At first Phelma Jo had resented the interruption to *her* plans for the evening. But the more she thought about it, the more she realized Ian McEwen honestly cared about his aunt. If he showed such devotion to a woman who refused to speak to him, how much more loyalty would he show to the woman he loved?

Phelma Jo planned to become that woman.

Neither of her two previous marriages had worked because she had chosen older husbands for money and prestige. And escape from her past. Now that she had money and was earning prestige, she wanted a man that *she wanted*, not someone who could get her what she wanted.

She squeezed Ian's hand and brushed her shoulder against his. He smiled down at her but did not stop his long-legged progress toward the courthouse. He had a job to complete, and it wasn't complete until the last paperwork was filed with the city and the insurance company. Then they could go to lunch.

She liked that. He was almost as driven as she to finish a job and get it done right. Of course her definition of right didn't always mean right for anyone but her own profit.

A wasp buzzed her ear. She swatted it. A wasp in October? She froze, hoping the bug would find a more attractive target. It strafed her again.

She thought she heard someone whisper, "Dusty."

"Phelma Jo, what's wrong?" Ian asked. He still held her hand.

"Bug," she said quietly through clenched teeth.

"Don't tell me you walked through cobwebs in your basement without a second thought, but a little old fly frightens you."

"Wasp, you idiot. There is a wasp getting ready to sting me."

"This beautiful bug?" A monstrous winged creature rested on his palm and nearly filled it. "It's just a moth. Pretty thing with all that red on its wings. Unusual to have a random pattern, though. I'll have to look it up later. Moths aren't dangerous."

"Looks more like a dragonfly to me," Phelma Jo said. "A biting dragonfly."

The "moth" reared its ugly head and bit Ian's finger.

Phelma Jo watched him do it. Amazement and bewilderment stupefied her, made time slow down. She saw each movement as a series of images, like a slide show.

For half a moment she found herself back in The Ten Acre Wood on a hot summer's day stuffing a purple dragonfly into a canning jar with a wolf spider. Dick had come along and rescued her prizes. What had he said about the dragonfly?

Then she reeled back into normal time.

"Ouch!" Ian shook his hand until the "moth" dropped

away. It staggered down, then caught sufficient air under its wings to fly a rapid spiral right back to Phelma Jo's ear.

"Dusty and Thistle are in the bridal shop. Dick is waiting in his car across the street. Do your job."

She didn't know where the high-pitched words came from. Part of her dismissed them as just random buzzes from the bug.

Still, she looked across the street and saw Dick Carrick in his BMW convertible, talking on his cell phone while consulting a tablet computer. And sure enough, Dusty and Thistle had just turned from admiring the shop window display to enter the bridal boutique.

The moth flew a deliberate path across the street—at windshield level forcing three cars to screech to a halt and nearly crash. It circled the BMW and landed on the roof.

Phelma Jo's jaw dropped. It couldn't be. That moth had spoken in Haywood Wheatland's voice. He claimed to be a half-breed Pixie/Faery.

The world spun in a new orbit, robbing Phelma Jo of balance. Her peripheral vision started to close down. Cold sweat broke out on her brow and back. Suddenly, her head was too heavy for her neck to support.

"Phelma Jo!" Ian caught her. "You don't look so good, little lady." Deftly, he hoisted her in his arms and strode purposefully into a side door of the courthouse.

Shrill, discordant music clanged in Phelma Jo's mind. *Ding dang chug shplach.* But she didn't care. She snuggled into Ian's chest, blotting out the anger behind the atonal chords.

Thistle hummed lightly as she deadheaded the last of the overgrown rhododendrons in Juliet's garden. She'd found the perfect gown for her wedding at Bridget's, a figure-molding sheath of light silk with an overlay of lace that sparkled with hints of lavender glitter and tiny bits of faceted glass that looked like stars spangling a night sky. *Dum dee dee do dum dum.* She hummed her happiness, imagining how the gown would look on her in candlelight during the simple, intimate ceremony.

She looked up from her daydreams to snip off another cluster of spent flower petals.

The quiet chaos of eccentric groupings of flowers and shrubs would make a perfect Pixie haven, she mused, or a location for a wedding in a different season, when the sun shone more reliably. She paused, drinking in the moist air, smelling the clouds thickening above.

With a quirk of a smile, she waited half a heartbeat before dashing for the back porch. She beat the first raindrop by half a wingbeat. In Pixie, she could count that as a prank. Cheating rain out of a drenching was difficult.

"I love my life now," she whispered. Problems between Pixies and Faeries vanished from her mind. They didn't involve her anymore.

She gazed at the little circle of gold, amethyst, and diamond on her left ring finger. Dick's promise of marriage, he'd called it. A genuine antique, Juliet had proclaimed, with a warning to be very careful of the precious gem. It came from Juliet's mother-in-law's mother.

Thistle had trouble keeping the generations and tangled relationships straight. Music replaced the puzzle in her mind.

*Dum dee dee do dum dum.*

She spun in a circle and laughed.

"I'm glad your exile hasn't been a total misery," Alder said from somewhere near her right elbow.

"What? How? Who?" As she stammered, her former lover grew from a yellow-tinged green Pixie with mottled gray bark clothing into a graceful young man half a head taller than she was.

*Skinny wimp.* That's what humans would call him. She bit back her smile, wondering how she'd ever thought him a strong and vibrant leader.

Until she knew for sure that he'd closed The Ten Acre Wood last summer to protect the tribe from a Faery invasion, she considered him a teenager prone to temper tantrums.

Thistle turned away from him and replaced her garden tools on the shelf above the old cement sink.

"Please, Thistle, I need to talk to you." Alder stayed her hand with one of his own.

She stared at the short, slender fingers. "Your touch used to thrill me. Now it doesn't," she said flatly.

He jerked his hand away. "Please, I need your help, Thistle. Pixies need your help."

"Why should I help you? You exiled me, humiliated me. Betrayed me."

"I know. And I'm sorry for that."

"Apologies aren't enough."

"Thistle, you have to come back to The Ten Acre Wood with me."

"No, I don't."

"For the sake of all Pixies, you have to come. You are the only one among us who can end the war among the tribes."

"You should have thought about that before you closed off access to the Patriarch Oak. You should have thought about the consequences before you took me on a mating flight, promised we'd be together forever when you knew you'd marry Milkweed within the week."

"Consequences?"

"Oh, I forgot, you're just a Pixie. You *won't* think beyond the next prank. Was your betrayal just another prank?"

"Pixies don't play tricks on other Pixies. That's what humans are for. You broke that rule by getting Milkweed lost on her way to our wedding."

"Go away, Alder. I don't need or want you anymore."

"But Pixie needs *you*. You are the only one of us who can think up a treaty we can all agree to. The Faeries are watching humans destroy their hill. Now they want to claim The Ten Acre Wood as their own. They are behind this war, and unless you do something about it, those cowards will win, just by sitting back and watching us destroy ourselves. Do you want to see all of Pixie die? We've buried six this last week, all killed by other Pixies."

"There is nothing I can do." Grief and regret stabbed her heart. "You should find the Faeries a new hill so they'll leave Pixie alone."

"I removed the curse on you, Thistle. I removed it right after I cast it."

"Then why can't I get back to Pixie? I have tried."

"You could have returned anytime. All you had to do

was make being a Pixie more important than your love for humans. But you don't love humans enough. There's a lost child wandering around Rosie's territory. Your territory. And you can't even see her. Until you complete this mission, Pixie will not respond to you."

"We are all lost children, Alder, wandering in a wilderness of conflicting emotions."

"Find and help this lost child. Guide her to her proper home and family. Then you can come back to Pixie. But hurry. We are running out of time."

With that, Alder shrank back to his tiny green form and flew off, dodging raindrops that fell from the sky like tears.

Only then did she realize he had no music. All Pixies had music. Why didn't he?

# Fourteen

*DUM DEE DEE DO DUM DUM.* THISTLE hummed lightly as she applied a scrub brush and cleanser to Mabel's kitchen countertops. While the house was generally tidy and clean on the surface, a lot of corners and hard-to-reach surfaces showed signs of neglect. If she'd learned nothing else about being human while living with Juliet for six weeks, she'd learned how to clean.

Cleaning gave her an opportunity to think quietly about troubling matters; like a lost child in need of help. But she couldn't help until the child acknowledged she needed help. That was one of the rules of Pixie. She had to wait for the child to show herself. But who was she? Where was she hiding? If Thistle could figure that out, she could arrange to stumble across the girl. Alder had said it was a girl child.

She applied some extra pressure and bleach water to a particularly stubborn stain. "Ketchup and mustard." She frowned at the splotch that had become ingrained in the tile.

The colors reminded her of something. Something she knew was important but flitted about, just beyond the reach of her thoughts like cottonwood fluff. Or thistle down.

She giggled at how her name fitted the idea.

A knock on the back door interrupted her musings linking names to personalities, and how she was the only Pixie capable of long-term thoughts. Why couldn't she nail down the one that drifted on unseen currents just out of her reach?

"Hi, Dick." She greeted her fiancé with a kiss to his cheek. Oh, how she liked that word fiancé. It sounded special, just like the relationship it implied.

Before she could think further, Dick grabbed her around the waist and drew her into a longer, more intimate kiss. His mobile mouth played teasing games around her face, lingering on her eyelids and at the corner of her smile. Then he plundered her mouth with his own, his tongue dancing with hers.

"You taste good. Like cinnamon," he whispered between more light kisses. "Hungry for you." He held her tighter, his fingers digging into her back with an exciting intensity.

"I thought we were meeting Chase and Dusty at the Old Mill Bar and Grill," she protested weakly. For the first time since arriving in Skene Falls, Thistle wished she knew how to cook, so she and Dick could stay here in this cozy little house and while away the evening in each other's arms.

"We should go." He stepped away from her, settled his shoulders, and drew a long breath that expanded his chest all the way down to his bottom rib.

"Before we do . . ." Thistle placed her left hand on his chest so that they could both see the wink of the gems in her ring. She also needed to keep touching him, just feel him breathe, let his warmth infuse her hand and her life. "I have something important to tell you."

"More important than dinner with Chase and Dusty."

"This will only take a moment once I gather the right words."

"Start at the beginning. One word at a time."

Thistle gulped back her excitement. "You won't like the first part. Alder came to see me today when I was working."

"You're right. I don't like that. Was he human or Pixie? 'Cause if he was human, I'll smash his nose in." Dick clenched his fists fiercely.

"He came as a human and left as a Pixie. He left alone, though he asked me to go back to The Ten Acre Wood with him."

Dead silence.

"He said he'd lifted the curse right after he threw me out of Pixie. He said I could have gone back any time if being a

Pixie was more important to me than my human friends,"
she said all in a rush.

"He did?"

"You know what that means?"

"I hope I do."

"That I love you more than I love being a Pixie. And as
long as you love me, I will never, ever leave you!"

"Promise?"

"Promise." She held out her hand to shake his, as she'd
seen people do.

Instead, he threw his arms around her waist and lifted
her high, spinning them both until dizziness and laughter
collapsed them on the floor in a long, soul-deep kiss.

Chicory crept out of Mabel's house at first light of dawn. The
second dawn. He'd slept for most of two nights and an entire
day between. This was autumn after all, the time when Pixies usually slept more and more until they hibernated.

Now he felt like a real Pixie again, ready to greet the
dawn with something akin to joy. Joy at being alive after
cheating death.

He breathed in the fresh air of a typical autumnal morning,
chill and bright with a heavy layer of dew. The shadows stayed
long all day. Later the rain would come. Later. Not now.

He indulged in a bit of fancy flying, playing tag with arcing prisms that glistened in droplets caught in the cup of
flower petals. Freedom! He'd survived the dreaded underground and now looked forward to just being a Pixie without thinking overmuch.

Enthusiastic moans and groans coming from a white
rose with red edges interrupted his celebration of morning.
Rosie and her paramour Snapdragon greeted the day with
their own ritual.

"Oh, get a tree," Chicory grumbled. On the other hand,
he didn't want Rosie bound to that shifty character.

Shifty. Good word to describe the scoundrel. He might
be round and yellow with red splotches now, but Chicory
had no doubt that last summer he'd been long and slender
and golden, like wheat ripening in the sun.

What had caused the transformation? He'd said prison food filled with preservatives and growth hormones had made him grow. What would cause the shift in color and shape? Something dire. A poison, maybe?

Chicory knew that some plants were poison to humans. Pixies never, *ever* played tricks on people with those plants.

What would poison a Pixie?

Underground.

But Hay was half Faery—if you could believe him—he should be fine underground.

Chicory looked behind him to check his own wings. They looked whole and clean, sparkling in the slanted morning light.

"Chicory, you're alive!" Daisy squealed with delight on a whisper, as if she didn't want to wake someone. The most recent delight of his life emerged from a screen of semi-tamed wildflowers. She looked tired.

Chicory reached out and caressed the lines radiating out from her eyes. They relaxed. But a frown remained etched at the corners of her mouth, even when she smiled lovingly at him.

"I'm staying out of Rosie's way," Chicory whispered. He gestured with his head toward her bower. Then, hand in hand, he and Daisy took refuge among the overgrown weeds along the picket fence.

"Rosie is impossible," Daisy said. Fierceness tightened her wings together.

"Have she and her lover done anything about maintaining the garden, or getting the tribe ready for winter?"

"Nope. They only send our tribe out to do battle with the invaders. Then they 'nap' while waiting for them to come back. Unless Snapdragon is particularly angry. Then he leads the soldiers. He's angry more and more often."

"This is wrong. Very, very, wrong." Chicory held Daisy tightly against his chest, drawing comfort from her, and giving some back.

"I think the entire tribe knows that now. They'd like a new queen. Or king." She ran her hands along the outside of his arms, clearly indicating her choice of a new king. "But they're all afraid of Snapdragon."

"He is big. And mean," Chicory agreed. He remembered all too well the sense of powerlessness when the irate Pixie had grabbed him by collar and belt and thrown him into the deadly cellar.

*Underground*. Had five hours in the half-sunken museum jailhouse right after his arrest for helping set fire to The Ten Acre Wood poisoned Hay? Something might be different about that dirt than the protections woven into a Faery hill. But nothing could protect Pixies or Faeries from iron sickness. Chase had forced Hay into iron handcuffs that made him sick and unable to shrink back to Pixie size and escape.

"Vicious," Daisy corrected him. "He's worse than the Murphy family's three Siamese cats. Combined."

"That's bad."

"What are we going to do, Chicory?" A fat tear glistened in her golden-green eyes.

"Thistle would tell us to oust Snapdragon and Rosie."

"Thistle left for work an hour ago. Something about Mrs. Jennings needing her medications an hour before she eats."

"Yeah. I know. She doesn't think like a Pixie anymore. She looks ahead and thinks about consequences."

"What are consequences?"

"The bad things that happen after you play a prank." Daisy still looked puzzled. "Alder cursing Thistle into human form was a consequence of her making Milkweed late to her wedding."

"Oh," Daisy replied flatly. "Oooohhh!" Her eyes brightened with understanding. "If we oust Rosie and Snapdragon, they will try to hurt all of us."

"Exactly."

"So, what can we do?"

"We can leave." An idea buzzed Chicory's mind like a trapped fly beating against a closed window.

"But . . . but . . . we'd be alone!"

"Not if we take my brothers, Delph and Aster, and their girlfriends, Marigold and Buttercup, with us."

"That's—um—six." Daisy had to count on her fingers. "Is that enough for a new tribe?"

"Not quite. But it's a start. We can always add a few Dandelions."

"Wh ... where will we go?" She looked excited and frightened at the same time.

"Well, Mabel told us to trust Dusty."

"Yes. Her museum has a lovely herb garden, but it's so close to The Ten Acre Wood. Won't Alder object?"

"Of course he will. So we'll go to her home, not the museum. I don't think there's a tribe living there. Maybe long ago, but not now. There are lots of flowers and shrubs. Juliet Carrick is trying to compete with Mabel's roses in some kind of human game."

"Let's take Bleeding Heart. He's not happy here and only stays because his copse is now an ugly apartment building. Maybe Cinqefoil will follow him."

"Good idea. We'll make it known that any displaced or exiled Pixies are welcome in our new tribe. We'll be bigger and stronger than any of the others. Do you think we have to take some Dandelions, too? I don't know if Dusty's mom will appreciate Dandelions in her yard."

"Later. If we need numbers to protect ourselves from an outraged Hay. Should we ask Wisteria?" Daisy looked toward the entwined vines that made a thick trunk climbing over and around, and completely hiding, the wrought iron fence and arched gateway from the main yard to the back property.

Chicory suddenly realized that the aloof Pixie lived in close proximity to iron every day of her life. Had the poison in the metal warped her personality as Snapdragon's time in the human prison had changed him into a bloated, diseased monster?

"I don't think she'll come," Chicory whispered back to Daisy. "I haven't seen her out of her bower in ages."

Around them, the world was coming awake. Birds chattered to each other, squirrels scurried, and Pixies poked their heads above the rim of their sheltering flowers. "Has anyone actually seen Wisteria outside her plant in ... oh ... three or four summers?"

"I saw her ... um, I think it was last spring."

"We'll let her know she's welcome once we've staked out our territory over at Juliet's yard. But it has to be her decision."

"Each of us who comes has to make that decision. We won't coerce anyone. Snapdragon does that too much. He'll try to stop us," Daisy said, brow furrowed in concentration.

"I know. Which is why we are leaving with an open invitation to any Pixie who is displaced or uncomfortable or overcrowded. The lost children of our tribes. Those are the Pixies Snapdragon is recruiting for his army."

As if called by his name, Snapdragon emerged from the limp rose blossom that had been his bed with Rosie. Without a wing flip of hesitation he darted over the back fence to the wild area. Within seconds he'd marshaled the half-domesticated Pixies—mostly Dandelions—who lived back there. Nominally they looked to Rosie as their queen. Mostly they did as they pleased, when they pleased—just like weeds. A stronger queen than Rosie would have brought them to order long ago.

They formed into their ranks, making an arrow formation behind Snapdragon. Wings beating in perfect unison, they flew off toward The Ten Acre Wood.

An army ready to do battle.

Chicory felt a deep urge to line up with them, become part of the group. Fight and die together, or live and fly together. It didn't matter which.

"Chicory, snap out of it!" Daisy yelled anxiously. She grabbed his wingtip and yanked him away from the army.

Chicory shook his head to rid himself of the magic compulsion that enveloped the army. Faery *magic*. Evil and malicious, uncaring who got hurt, all to satisfy Faery desires and nothing else.

"Maybe we can stop the war if we pull all the fighters away," Daisy said softly.

"You never know." He kissed her nose and went about the process of gathering his new family. "Daisy?"

"Yes, beloved?"

"When we get settled, will you take a mating flight with me?"

"From any oak in town."

# Fifteen

CHICORY HELD UP HIS HAND, signaling to the troop behind him to stop at the back gate of Juliet Carrick's home. He sniffed cautiously. A neighbor cat had patrolled the yard within the hour and, from the smell of things, caught a mouse.

No other predators lingered.

Juliet had retreated inside after cutting a few roses, escaping the cold drizzle.

Chicory shivered. Winter was coming. Fast. He needed to find a nesting place for his little band. *His family*.

He pointed right and left, directing the Pixies to seek out places to shelter. Bleeding Heart went directly to some drooping leaves of his namesake along the border of the fence line. He began trimming brown leaf edges.

"We haven't time to groom just yet," Chicory reminded him.

"I can nest within the heart of the stems tonight." The younger Pixie looked up at him hopefully. He must miss his home plant. Mabel had some growing wild in the back lots, but Pixies had to cross that wrought iron fence to get there. Not all of them had the courage, especially newcomers.

"Tonight maybe. But that's not enough shelter for all of us through the winter." Chicory flew on. "Damn, Juliet keeps a tidy garden. Too tidy. Not even a decorative stump." He kept seeking among the fake tombstones, fake fire with a cauldron on a tripod, and dubious scarecrows. Juliet never did anything by half. Her carnations and rhododendrons had all been neatly deadheaded, probably by Thistle. A few of the roses still bloomed, but the blossoms were too tight to open and the edges looked brown and too saturated to finish blooming.

He checked the few trees for woodpecker holes. Nothing. They were all too healthy to attract the birds. Not even an old squirrel nest.

The rain came faster and harder, some of the drops as big as his head.

"Under the porch!" he called to one and all.

"But . . . but that's underground," Delph, his youngest brother protested.

"Not quite. It's *under the porch*. That's different," Chicory explained, holding two loose boards apart and counting wings as they passed into the semi-dry area out of the wind.

Daisy, bless her, found two cracked flower pots filled with dead leaves and a rotting bird's nest. Temporary, at best. His people deserved better.

Above him he heard Juliet humming Thistle's music. *Dum dee dee do dum dum.*

Thistle had lived here as a human. Of course her music permeated the house.

Hmm, what music could he give Juliet to replace that catchy little tune?

"Time to confront the owner," he whispered.

"Couldn't you just talk to Dusty? She lives here, too," Daisy said, not minding her voice.

The humming stopped abruptly in mid-phrase. "Who's there?" Juliet asked.

Chicory heard her moving around the porch. She stepped out from the sheltering overhang and peered around the yard.

"Um . . . just me," Chicory said brightly. He flew through the gaping slats and hovered directly in front of Juliet's nose. His wings beat a new tattoo: *Dum dum do do dee dee dum*.

Dick wandered into Dusty's museum. Officially, the pioneer home held the prestigious title of Skene County Historical Society Museum. Since Dusty had taken over as

curator on Labor Day weekend, everyone in town called it
Dusty's place. She spent more time here than at home. At
least she wasn't hiding in the basement anymore.

He heard a murmur of voices. Only a few words came
through. "Lawyer," and "filed," and lastly "hospital." Puzzled, he proceeded inward.

"Anyone home?" he called from the front parlor. Then
he sneezed. Didn't anyone dust this place?

"Back here," Dusty said, appearing in the doorway to the
back of the house. She wore normal slacks and a blazer today instead of pioneer costume. A telltale smudge across her
nose and cheek proved she hadn't given up her basement
haunting completely. Her glasses tipped close to the end of
her nose. She pushed them back into place before he could
get a good look at her eyes, a sure indicator of her mood and
health.

The glasses allowed her to hide almost as much as the
basement.

Dick took care to step up the extra half inch at the doorway. The original log cabin had multiple additions up, down,
side to side, and back; each at a slightly different level and
style of construction. He wouldn't refer to the hodgepodge
as architecture.

"What's up, Dick?" Chase asked from his semiperma-
nent position at the end of the long worktable in the employee lounge.

Dick grabbed a cup of coffee from the carafe Dusty kept
filled. He noted that she had tea: hot, black, and sweet. "No
coffee, Sis?" He took the chair beside Chase.

"Only at home." She flashed a grin at him while she deliberately closed a fat file folder.

"If you don't like coffee, you don't have to drink it on my
account," Chase said. He covered both of her hands with
one of his own.

"It bugs Mom."

"Enough said." Dick saluted her with his cup and took a
long swig. "Shakespeare wouldn't have drunk coffee, so neither Mom nor Dusty can."

"Shakespeare wouldn't have drunk tea, would he?

Seems to me everyone drank ale or small beer," Chase mused.

"Since when has a detail bothered my mother? Tea is very British." Dick imitated a posh English accent. "Therefore, it will substitute very nicely in her obsessive-compulsive brain."

"So what brings you to my lair on a cold October morn when sensible tourists and school groups stay home? There will be bunches of kids after school helping with the maze, or scouting it." Dusty shifted the file onto the chair beside her. Out of sight, out of mind?

Dick's curiosity spiked. If she'd left the thing alone, he wouldn't have noticed it.

"I've just come from the courthouse where I found out that Thistle and I can't get a marriage license anywhere in the country without ID."

"And Thistle has none. Technically, she doesn't exist," Chase finished the thought for him.

"Another of Peter Pan's lost children," Dick muttered. He and Chase had played Peter Pan in The Ten Acre Wood when they were six, taking turns with the Captain Hook role. Thistle made an admirable Tinker Bell substitute, keeping her own name because Tink was really a Faery— the enemy of Pixies.

"I gave Mom the spiel about Thistle being raised in a cult," Dusty said. "Can you use that to get around it?"

"No. They'd still want some kind of documentation that she was born in this country. It's worse than an illegal immigrant. At least they have birth records in their home country."

"As a duly sworn officer of the court, I can't help you," Chase said. At the same time he pulled his little notebook out of his shirt pocket, tore out a blank page, and began writing something in his slanted but neat all caps printing. He'd always had neat handwriting, even in third grade, because it was easier to keep track of details.

"Now there's a guy in Portland supplying fake IDs to migrant workers; he's so good the INS has been trying to shut him down for ten years." Chase finished writing and just tapped his pencil on the paper a moment. "If I knew how to find him, I'd have him behind bars."

"What makes this guy so good?"

"Don't know. The last border official I talked to suspected he also supplies papers to the Russian Mafia. Me, I just think he's a talented computer hacker with a huge database of infant deaths. See, he orders copies of the birth certificate when an infant dies. Then when someone needs official papers, he's got matches from all over the country of age, gender, and ethnicity."

"What about social security numbers?" Dick asked, suddenly very interested in the piece of paper Chase was folding into neat quarters.

Dusty kept her eyes on the paper, like she didn't know what her fiancé had written. Dick was willing to bet she did.

"Most cases, anyone under twenty has a number issued at birth. But if the baby dies, sometimes the paperwork doesn't get completed. Those are the ones our ID guru wants."

"How do you explain to Social Security an adult who doesn't have a number?"

"The usual. Parents were missionaries or diplomats, and the kid was raised overseas. Now the parents have died in the latest insurrection or Ebola outbreak. Paperwork is a mess; kid can't find any records but the birth certificate. Your cult story also works. No modern conveniences, brainwashing, and no records for the evil IRS or ATF officials to audit."

"Living overseas would explain any accent," Dick mused. Ideas stumbled around his mind refusing to coalesce.

"Right on." Chase made a mock pistol of his fingers and pretended to shoot. With his other hand he slid the paper beneath Dick's fingers. Then he gulped his last swallow of coffee and pushed his chair away from the table. "Gotta get back to work. See you tonight, Dusty?"

"Yes. I'll meet you about six. We can have dinner and then go visit Mabel."

"Is Mabel better?" Dick asked. He itched to look at the paper. A warning headshake from Chase made him put it into his inner suit jacket pocket.

"She's out of intensive care," Dusty said.

"Give her my best. I've got to run, too. You, baby sister, can get back to your potsherds and restoring antique underwear, or whatever it is you do when you don't have any tours."

"Paperwork and bookkeeping. Endless piles of paperwork and bookkeeping," she grunted. "I may clean and classify two Russian pots just to relax before my appointment with the dressmaker at five."

"Do that." Dick exited in Chase's wake. His hand reached for the folded paper before he'd cleared the parlor.

"Wait to read that until I am no longer in sight or hearing. I need deniability, so you might burn it as well." Chase hastened out the door and around the corner toward the broad cement steps that led down the cliff to downtown.

Dick waited until he was inside his car, the doors closed and locked, the engine idling, and the radio blasting before succumbing to the temptation of the paper.

He expected a name and number in Portland.

He never dreamed he'd read the few words Chase had written.

Phelma Jo helps teenagers hide from abusive parents and foster care.

# Sixteen

"**W**ELL IT'S ABOUT TIME ONE OF YOU showed up in my garden," Juliet said on a huff. She planted her hands on her hips and stared unblinking at Chicory.

"Um . . . you know about us?" He backed off, finding her big blue eyes beneath her reddish-blonde curls a bit too much to take in all at once. He'd heard people in town comparing her to a Queen Elizabeth I, in coloring and temperament. She certainly carried authority in that gaze.

"Of course I know about Pixies. I've been friends with Mabel Gardiner and Pamela Shiregrove for too long not to suspect something strange kept their gardens more spectacular than everyone else's. More spectacular than *mine*. It just took a little investigation to find you." Juliet held her palm flat beneath Chicory in invitation.

Cautiously he dropped his feet onto her hand, keeping his wings ready to flit off again at the first sign of danger.

"What is your name, young man?" Juliet asked. She didn't move, didn't threaten in any way.

Chicory relaxed a little. He reached up to doff his blue blossom hat to her as he bowed and realized he had none. He completed the bow anyway. "Chicory, ma'am. At your service."

"Chicory, heah. That's a mighty pretty flower I haven't been able to grow. It prefers ditches to my garden."

"That's because you haven't dug deep enough for the roots. I can help you get most anything to bloom bigger and better. Me and my tribe that is. If you let us stay."

"That's a nice offer, but I already grow award-winning flowers."

"Not as many awards as Mabel or Pamela Shiregrove. And not for your roses. Only for your gillyflowers." Oh, Chicory knew all about the rivalry among these women. His years of spying for Mabel had taught him a lot.

Juliet stiffened and started to close her fingers into a fist. Her eyes focused elsewhere and a frown deepened the lines on either side of her mouth. Chicory rose up to the level of her nose.

Instantly, she opened her fingers. "I can see some advantages. What else can you give me in return for access to *my* garden?"

"We actually need a bit more than that." Chicory put on his most winsome smile, the one that always convinced Mabel to give him an extra drop or two of honey.

"What is that, young man?"

"Shelter. Winter is coming fast and we won't survive long exposed to the weather."

"What kind of shelter?"

"Someplace warm and dry that marauding cats can't get into."

"There's a big basement . . ."

"Excuse me, ma'am, but basements are underground. That will kill us all within a day."

"How about the attic? There are vents up there so you can come and go as you need without bothering me to open a door or window for you."

"That would be perfect, ma'am."

"My name is Juliet. You may use it."

Chicory bowed again, remembering only at the last minute that he didn't have a cap to doff.

"However, you are asking a lot from me. I store a lot of valuable antiques up there. I can't have you and your people wiping your muddy boots on them. And shelter inside a home makes you renters of a kind."

"Um . . . you know that Mabel always knew everything about everyone and how to find them in an instant."

"Ye—es."

"How do you think she did that?"

Juliet raised her eyebrows while her eyes flitted right and left. "You. You and your people?"

Chicory bowed again, willing to take full credit for the work of an entire tribe, plus the half-wild ones who lived beyond the iron fence.

"Well, then. Come in and bring your . . . er . . . friends."

"Tribe, Juliet. They are my tribe. More than a family. The best friends a Pixie can have, other than special humans." He gave her a wink, secretly inviting her into his tribe.

"I'll make tea and we'll discuss this."

"With honey?" Chicory asked hopefully.

"Only a drop. I've heard that Pixies get drunk on honey."

"Does Thistle Down get drunk on honey now that she's human?" Chicory clamped his hand over his mouth, afraid more secrets would spill forth.

"Thistle, hmmm. That would explain a lot." Juliet tapped her foot. "Thistle was a Pixie and is now human."

Chicory nodded his head reluctantly, unable to lie but not quite up to speaking more truth.

"I wonder what the Bard would do with that scenario." She smiled hugely. "Well, come in. Come in all of you. We have things to discuss over tea. But no honey. I need you sober so you can scout out some people for me."

"Who would that be?" Chicory waved to Daisy who peered between the loose slats, eavesdropping shamelessly.

His tribe emerged in a flock to swoop happily toward the shelter Juliet offered.

"I need to know what my daughter is up to and why she's running away from her wedding."

Dusty walked softly down the cardiac care corridor of Mercy Hospital alone. Dick had begged off, something about another car accident. If they went to dinner, it would be after visiting hours at the hospital were over.

She buried her nose in the simple bouquet of carnations and baby's breath. She didn't like the scent of fear that overlaid the pervasive odor of disinfectant.

Sharp reminders of the weeks and months she'd spent in

the hospital as a child. Endless nights spent alone with humming equipment and nurses just out of reach, her family gone home.

She remembered pain, fatigue to the point of nausea, and fear that kept her immobile. She remembered loneliness. In a way, that had hurt more than all the other stuff, the knowledge that no matter how much she loved her family, and they loved her, they could not endure her cancer for her. She had to do it alone.

If she could get out of this visit to the hospital, she would. But she owed Mabel the courtesy of a visit.

She counted off the room numbers until she found 436 in the corner. The wide door—wide enough to accommodate portable beds, wheelchairs, and several staff—was propped open a couple of inches. Inside, a monitor beeped an uneven rhythm.

Not good.

"Mabel?" she asked cautiously as she knocked on the door.

A rough mumble came from the fragile lump beneath the covers in the semi-darkened room.

"Mabel, can I come in?"

More mumbles that sounded almost affirmative came a little louder. Dusty decided to accept that as an invitation.

"Hi, Mabel, I brought you some flowers."

"Didn't have to do that."

"I know, Mabel, but I thought they might cheer you a bit." Dusty placed the milk glass vase on the nightstand beside the bed.

"Not from my yard."

"No, I bought them from Main Street Flowers. Mike Gianelli says 'Hi' by the way. It's October and all the gardens are too soggy and past their prime to cut a decent bouquet."

"Gardens and Pixies go to sleep in winter. Is everyone okay at my house? Are the All Hallows decorations up? Will the parade go down Tenth Street this year?" A little animation lit Mabel's wan and drawn face.

She looked so wasted when just days ago she'd been plump and vibrant. Or was that months ago? Dusty thought hard, trying to remember when Mabel had last strode strongly around Skene Falls, confident and indestructible. Early last spring. By the Masque Ball in August she'd already shown signs of weight loss and a reduction in energy. The change had happened so gradually no one noticed.

Except the Pixies. She remembered Chicory and his brothers arguing about whether Mabel was sick or not the night of the ball.

"As far as I know, everyone at your house is well. Thistle is staying there, and Dick visits often. They set out the decorations yesterday afternoon. Dick did the talking tree. He and Thistle are engaged."

"Good. What about the Festival?"

"Everything is on track. Though I wish Mom would shove some of her decorations over to your yard. She overdid it a bit."

"Only a bit?" They laughed together for a moment.

"Your nephew wants to visit you," Dusty said when she thought Mabel's smile was firmly in place.

"No." The smile collapsed along with her posture. "Only you and Chase. You two are my heirs. Not *him*."

"As much as Chase and I appreciate your generosity, Mabel, it's not fair to Ian. He's your nephew. He only wants what's best for you. You aren't well. You'll need help when you leave the hospital. You may not be able to live on your own anymore."

"I'm not alone. I've got my Pixies."

"Can Rosie or Chicory call nine-one-one if you fall or have another attack? Can they cook and clean for you? Or run to the pharmacy to refill your meds?"

Mabel looked away rather than answer.

"This is something you need to think about, Mabel."

"I have thought about it. I'll die before I'll go to one of *those* places. I want you and Chase to have the house. For a time anyway. I know it's not big enough for a growing family."

"Mabel," Dusty gulped back a lump that seemed permanently lodged in her throat. "Mabel, I can't have children. The chemo stole that from me. Adoption is expensive. We're going to have to wait to save up before we can afford children." She fussed with getting her glasses back to the perfect place on the bridge of her nose to avoid showing her emotions.

"Oh, I know all about that. Don't worry, there are ways." Mabel winked broadly, like she was letting Dusty into a big secret. A secret Dusty couldn't figure out.

"I figure if you live in my house rent free for a couple of years, you'll be able to afford a nice place for yourselves and the children that come your way. Then the garden becomes a park and the house becomes a historical dwelling, part of the museum complex." She paused to breathe and clear her throat. "You can add it back into the haunted house tour Sunday afternoon and evening if you want."

Alarmed at the turn of the conversation, Dusty offered Mabel the glass of water with the bent straw. Mabel drank greedily, as if those few sentences had parched her throat desert dry.

"I've thought it out. You and Chase move into the house as soon as you get back from your honeymoon. Dick can afford to buy a house for him and Thistle."

This time her breath did not come back as easily. She persisted. Needing to say her piece.

"But I don't want the place empty for even a day before that. Mr. Ian McEwen will see that as an excuse to claim the place and sell it off to developers. Won't have that. Don't want anyone displacing my Pixies. He doesn't believe, and he runs with a rough crowd."

"I checked the registry of Historic Homes. Ian can't tear down the house. And unless he buys one of the adjacent houses, there is no access to the back lots. The land is worthless to a developer."

"Won't stop him."

"Mabel, I've talked to Ian. He really does care about you. He just wants what is best for *you*."

"No, he doesn't. He's a greedy, money-grubbing bastard. Started when he was ten, taking up with a drug runner in The Ten Acre Wood. I put a stop to that in a hurry. Not in our Ten Acre Wood. His father was just as bad. Worse, maybe. Boy's already tried to condemn the house twice because of cracks in the foundation. Rosie says there aren't any cracks. She'd know."

Dusty wondered if she would. Foundations were underground and Pixies couldn't go there. Even in human form, Thistle couldn't—or wouldn't—go into a basement.

"Mabel, I wished you'd let Ian visit you here in the hospital. Ease his mind about your well-being."

"Nope. Only you and Chase. Don't want to see anyone else, and I've told the nurses and hospital security no other visitors." She clamped her mouth shut and rolled over to face the window, her skinny back to Dusty.

# Seventeen

DUSTY SQUIRMED AS ABIGAIL, THE modiste, pinned a seam in the corset cover for her wedding garments.

"Please, Miss Desdemona, you must stand still," the woman said around a mouthful of pins. Her fake French accent took on overtones of Brooklyn with the impediment.

The next pin pricked Dusty's skin through many layers of handkerchief weight linen.

"Ouch!" She batted Abigail's hands away from the garment. A tiny dot of blood oozed through the surface of the corset cover.

"Now, look what you've done, Desdemona," her mother admonished. "If you'd just stand still, we could get this fitting finished and you could go back to your little hobby at the museum."

"Mom, my *job* is not a little hobby. I earned a Masters degree to get that job."

"But think of how much more you could do with that degree. You could teach! Imagine the joy of exposing fertile little minds to the wonders of history and literature. The years I taught school were among the best of my life."

"Mom, I am perfectly healthy now. I've been free of cancer for fifteen years. You could have gone back to teaching long ago if you really wanted to." Dusty pushed back the little worm of guilt that she had been the reason her mother had to sacrifice her career.

*She's manipulating me again. I won't give in. I won't. I*

*can't. If I give in now I'll never be free of my past. I'll always be Mom's little lost child.*

"But Dr. Martin said you need checkups for the rest of your life . . ."

"Checkups, not an invalid lifestyle. Not enough reason to keep you home." *Smothering me with your fears.* Maybe Mom was truly the one who was running away and had become lost. Lost in a fantasy world.

Dusty bit back the words that she needed to say. A lifetime of deferring to other people so she could indulge in the safety of shyness made her drop her head and tune out her mother's reprimands.

"Now, Abigail, if we soak that little stain in cold water, right now, it won't show in the least."

"My fault, Madame," Abigail said, accent back in place. "Such a tiny drop of blood. No one will see it on an undergarment. We proceed with fitting."

"If you think so, but I do want this wedding to be perfect."

"It's my wedding, Mom, not yours."

"Of course, Desdemona. I want it to be perfect for you. It's the biggest day of your life. We need to make the most of it since you can't have children because of the cancer. Now don't you think we should redecorate your room? I don't think a man as strong as Chase will want to sleep beneath a canopy of pink ballerinas. I do so love a full house." A sly smile crept over her face.

"Mom, do you even listen to yourself?"

"What? What did I say?"

"You're planning on me staying at home with you and Dad for the rest of my life. Chase and I have plans. He has an apartment . . ."

"Such a waste of money to rent a little place like that. Better he move in with us. After all, a policeman doesn't make a lot of money, and you won't go find a better paying job at the community college. You should have taken the teaching position instead of pushing Joe into it just so you could stay at your museum . . ."

"Miss Desdemona," Abigail interrupted. "I need you to try the hoops to see how they fit over the corset. Then next fitting we progress to the dress itself. Such a beautiful piece of material . . ."

Something inside Dusty burst, like an overripe peach thrown against a barn. She'd done that once with Dick and Chase when she was six. And gotten into trouble for it. But, oh, how satisfying to hear and almost feel the squish as pulp flew in all directions.

"I'd rather elope than wear this horrible contraption!" There she'd said it. She'd let her true feelings fly and go splat against her mother's face—judging by the horrified expression of gaping jaw and wide eyes, strawberry-blonde eyebrows reaching for her receding hairline.

Dusty began pulling at ties and hooks that she couldn't really reach. A dozen pins cascaded from the seams, landing on the floor with loud pings in her mother's shocked silence.

"I hate this dress. I hate the wedding you are planning. I hate thinking about living in your house the rest of my life. I hate being your fragile little doll. I want a life of my own! A wedding of my own. A home of my own."

"If you don't wear this dress . . ." Mom's voice turned quiet, precise, and menacing.

"I'll buy the one in the window of Bridget's with my own money."

"A contemporary dress won't carry near the impact of a historical recreation. You can't possibly mean that you prefer something *modern*. You're a historian. Surely you want something that reflects your personality."

"Yes, I do. And I've found the perfect dress, and it's not this one. If you like it so much, you wear it." Dusty threw the first petticoat into her mother's face and marched behind the dressing screen. "Abigail, get me out of this corset or I swear I will shred it with my fingernails." Dirty, broken fingernails after a morning in the basement cleaning, sorting, cataloging, and photographing artifacts found in a Chinook tribal midden. She knew where she belonged and who she was when she worked at the museum, in and out of the basement.

Phelma Jo tapped her foot impatiently against the floor of her Lexus—cream with gold trim. Ian was late meeting her at the Old Mill Bar and Grill. She'd been waiting since a half hour before their scheduled date of six thirty PM. It was now six forty-five. She had a clear view of the parking lot behind the building and the front entrance. He had not shown.

"No one does this to me!" she said, reaching for the key still in the ignition. "No one." Not in high school. And definitely not now. Even Dick Carrick had the good manners to call her and break off their three-date relationship rather than stand her up.

"How did I offend Ian?" She paused with her fingertips on the key chain.

A tap on her window dragged her out of her loop of self-doubt.

"Ian!" She turned the key to auxiliary and rolled down the window, delight and reassurance filling the gaps in her mind, pushing out the bad thoughts. "Is everything okay? You look tired."

"I am. Sorry to be so late, things got dicey at the office. I hate people who lie."

Phelma Jo prepared the luxury car for leaving it.

"Do you mind if we just sit for a few moments and be quiet?"

"Sure, come on in." With a flick of a button she unlocked the doors.

He slumped into the cushy leather seat beside her.

"Do you need to talk about it?" God, was that her speaking? She had no time or use for people who had to hash out their "feelings." They needed to just make a decision and get on with their lives.

She wished now that she'd told Dusty that back in second grade. No, in kindergarten. The girl annoyed her no end with her crippling shyness and constant deferral to Dick for any decision or speech. She should just get over herself and do something!

"No, I don't really need to talk about it. I just need to get all the yelling out of my head before we eat."

"Yelling doesn't sound good." Phelma frequently indulged in yelling when faced with stupid people who made mistakes, especially if the mistake cost her money.

She never yelled when her secrets were at stake. Yelling drew attention. Silence did not.

"It wasn't pretty. But it was necessary. I had to fail a building inspection because the owner produced a forged work order from a nonexistent electrician that a fire hazard of a fuse box had been replaced by a new circuit breaker. Like I wouldn't notice a false and illegal front over the old box, and dangerous pennies replacing blown fuses? He wasn't happy. My boss wasn't happy because he's going to lose a client. I wasn't happy because the man's lies are so wasteful and endangered all of his tenants as well as a whole block of wooden buildings if the thing caught fire."

Phelma Jo caught her breath. How many times in her life had she lied? She started young as a survival mechanism with a drunken mother and her abusive boyfriends. Then she'd lived with a few less-than-caring foster parents and social workers, until Marcus had taken her case and showed her ways to get around the system. Mabel had tried to teach her the value of truth, but the habit had become ingrained. When she needed out of a mercenary marriage or a way to manipulate real estate clients into giving her the best price, she lied more easily than telling the truth.

"Lies can be destructive." She patted his hand.

"Especially when they cover illegal behavior. Thanks for being here, and letting me vent. I think I needed it, though I don't usually indulge. Let's go eat."

"Yes. Let's." Phelma Jo took his arm as they crossed the street, determined to change some of her bad habits before he found out about them.

Right after she finished one last round of forged birth certificates and fingerprint cards.

"No," Phelma Jo said the next morning without looking away from Dick or muffling her words, or even hedging like she wanted to say yes but was afraid someone was listening.

"But . . . but, Phelma Jo, I know you've helped other

people get new IDs so they can hide from...." Dick pleaded. He ignored the sweat trickling down his back.

"Teenagers. I've helped teenagers who have been abused by their parents and the system. I've helped kids who have no alternatives to survive. Now get out of my office. I have work to do."

"I can pay you."

"What part of 'no' don't you understand? Thistle has lost her documentation or wants to lose her past. She's not abused." Phelma Jo swiveled her chair to face the window behind her desk.

Dick could see by her expression that she found this hard. He decided he had nothing to lose by pressing the issue.

"Phelma Jo. We are desperate. Thistle grew up in a commune ..." he spun out the story he and Dusty had concocted months ago. "She's been abused, too."

"She's an adult, perfectly capable of standing on her own two feet and figuring it out herself. Go tell that lie to a judge. Maybe he'll believe you." She began fumbling with papers, trying to end the interview.

"Phelma Jo, you owe me for keeping you out of jail after you set fire to The Ten Acre Wood."

"You told the truth. Haywood Wheatland dosed me with roofies to make me compliant to his orders. I was under the influence of a date rape drug and not responsible for my actions. What you are asking is illegal and I'll have no part of it."

"And I thought you had become reasonable, willing to be a friend." He half turned away from her in disgust.

She shuddered. "Friends. Why is this town obsessed with friends? When I truly needed a friend, your sister, my only friend, betrayed me. I have my own friends now. You and your codependent sister—God, I wish she'd just get over herself—are not among them."

"Consider yourself off the wedding invitation list, if we can ever get legally married without ID."

"Why can't you just live in sin? No one thinks twice about that anymore."

"We don't want that. We want a lasting marriage with

legitimate children. I want to be able to provide for the love of my life, which includes health insurance and tax deductions, which I can't do if we aren't legally married. But you wouldn't know anything about that."

"It won't be a legal marriage with fake ID. Go away, Dick. I don't care what you do, or how you do it. Just leave me out of it. I don't even want your money to do this."

"You haven't heard the last of this, Phelma Jo." Dick stalked out of the glass office, slamming the door so hard the frame shook. The noise drowned out any reply she made. If she bothered.

Now what?

Phelma Jo had said something . . . Go see a judge and see if he'll believe the story of the abusive cult.

Yeah. He could do that. Chase would know which judge in town was most likely to listen with a sympathetic ear and start the ball rolling to get a proper ID.

Thistle's wedding wasn't called off, just postponed a bit.

# Eighteen

THISTLE CAUTIOUSLY COUNTED THE burners on Mabel's stove, matching them to the dial at the back. "Left front." She looked at the little burner, comparing it to the size of the half-full teakettle. Too small. "Left rear." That one looked a closer match. She turned it on and carefully centered the kettle on the coils. She heaved a sigh of relief. That wasn't so hard. In a few moments she should have a nice cup of tea to refresh her between appointments with her friends.

A plan was forming in the back of her head for seeking out the lost child while she patrolled the ridge district, making sure each of the old folks had what help they needed to remain in their homes and independent a little longer.

If she were out in the cold looking for shelter, where would she go? A Pixie would find a hollow log or abandoned birdhouse. Hm. What about detached garages and attics?

A quick rap on the back door interrupted her search for the perfect cup. With a dozen to choose from, how was she supposed to know which was the perfect one? The same thing went for garages and attics.

Answering the door gave her a good excuse to postpone the decision. Decisions.

"Dick? Why aren't you at work?" she asked, throwing open the door.

"I need to talk to you," he said as he gathered her into his arms and kissed her briefly. Then he kissed her more deeply. "I could get used to this," he sighed. His hands clutched at her waist with a strange intensity.

"Me, too. But that doesn't tell me why you are here and not sitting in some doctor's office trying to sell him pills." She rested her head against his chest, content to listen to his heart and breath.

"We've run into a minor problem getting a marriage license."

"Oh?" Chills run up and down her spine. She knew she shouldn't have planned on happiness.

A lost child couldn't plan on happiness either. Thistle felt more than a little lost, between Dick's world and Pixie.

"Nothing we can't overcome, but you need to do something for me." He kissed the top of her head.

"That almost sounds ominous."

"Not really. I need you to write out, in your own hand, the story we tell about you escaping from a commune. That you have no idea if you have a birth certificate, or your parents' last name."

"But . . . but that's a lie."

"Of course it is. But if we tell the truth, a judge is more likely to lock you in an insane asylum than grant you a substitute birth certificate."

"Um . . . Pixies can't lie."

"I know that, but you aren't a Pixie anymore and you said you'd never go back. So surely you can manage to write out a story."

"I don't know. It feels so wrong. Besides, I wouldn't know what to say."

"Just try it. Please? If it doesn't work at all, I suppose I could write it and have you sign it. But it will look better if written in your own hand."

"If you think I should." Thistle broke away from Dick, scanning the kitchen for pencil and paper, and inspiration to get out of the onerous chore.

"Maybe Mabel keeps paper and pens in the desk over in the corner," Dick said. Obviously, he'd seen through her attempts at delay.

Just then the kettle began to whistle. "Dick, would you look for paper and pencil for me? Do you want a cup of tea?" She grabbed a mug at random, pleased that it was the one with sunflowers painted all over it. She liked sunflowers. Bright and cheerful, plentiful seeds that lasted a long time and fed Pixies quite well.

"No, thanks. I haven't got time," he said, his voice half muffled as he bent his head over the drawer in the plain wooden desk. It was sturdy and square in a pale wood. Dusty had called it a schoolteacher's desk.

"Got it!" Dick proclaimed waving a thick sheaf of papers and a pencil at her.

"I guess I can't put this off any longer."

"Sorry, my love. We have to do this if we want to truly and forever get married."

"For you, I'll try." Thistle placed the paper squarely on the counter and held the pencil as Dusty had taught her long ago. She stared at the blank page long and hard. "What do I write?"

"Start with 'I, Thistle Down, a resident of Skene Falls, Skene County, Oregon . . .'"

"Not so fast." That seemed easy enough if she could remember how to spell it all. Letter by letter she put the words onto the page. "Now what?"

"Do solemnly swear."

That didn't sound good. She felt the potential lie building in her tummy, spreading dark tendrils of fire upward and outward.

Dick continued to dictate the words for her. Her head grew numb. Darkness encroached from the edges, turning her vision into a narrow tunnel, like crawling into a hollow log with one end blocked with moss. Tiny points of light came through, not much else. Her chest felt heavy. She couldn't breathe. Heat robbed her of thought and connection to the four winds, and the floor.

Which way was up and which down?

"Thistle!" Dick caught her as her knees gave out.

The world righted for Thistle again. She reached up and caressed Dick's face. "I'm sorry, beloved. I can't do it. I cannot lie." Hot tears filled her eyes even as she cherished the feeling of resting her head in his lap as she stretched out on the floor. Disappointing him hurt almost as much as the lie.

"Are you okay?" he asked, running his hands delicately around her shoulders and neck, looking for something wrong. "Your skin is a little warm, but not feverish. Your eyes are clear now. What happened?"

"The lie."

"Oh."

They lingered in silence a bit.

"Drink your tea, get your senses straightened out again while I write out the statement on a separate sheet of paper. Then all you have to do is copy it letter for letter. You aren't telling the lie, I am. All you are doing is copying letters from one sheet to the other. Can you do that?" He hoisted her back to her feet and sat her at the tiny table in the window nook.

Thistle sat gratefully, sipping her tea and watching Dick as he bent over the counter. His long legs and lean back looked stiff, anxious. No more than she. "I understand that this is important," she told herself.

"It is very important," Dick replied.

"I want to be with you forever, no matter how much it hurts to tell a lie."

"You aren't lying. You are copying letters. Nothing more."

"If you say so."

Phelma Jo slumped within her dark, oversized trench coat. She pulled the hood closer about her face as she approached the pocket park, an unkempt vacant lot with a single picnic table and bench, two blocks from the elementary school.

"You're late," Marcus whispered from behind the dubious shelter of an overgrown lilac.

"My schedule isn't fluid today," Phelma Jo replied. She'd had to make lame excuses to Ian to leave their lunch date early. Lies. Lies she swore she had given up for the sake of preserving her relationship.

"Do you have the papers? The new foster parents are flying in from Medford later this afternoon. They have to have those documents to get the girl in school, to keep her safe until the trial." Marcus twisted his hands anxiously, looking right and left for observers.

"Don't whine, Marcus. This is not witness protection. It's giving children who fall through the cracks a second chance." Phelma Jo fished a packet in a plastic file protector from inside her coat and handed it to him.

He grabbed it and secreted it inside his own raincoat. "Is it all here?"

"Everything but vaccination records. I won't do those unless I know for certain the child has had them."

"That's the least of our worries. I've got to go." Without further ado, he ducked his head lower into the upturned collar of his coat and walked purposefully out of the park toward his beige sedan parked a block away.

Phelma Jo sighed in relief. Done. This last chore was done and she could get on with the rest of her life. A life she hoped she'd spend more of with Ian.

As she turned to exit in the opposite direction, toward the historic neighborhood adjacent to the museum and The Ten Acre Wood, a tall figure approached along the sidewalk.

She'd know that long and purposeful stride anywhere. Ian had followed her. Throwing her hood back she plastered a big smile across her face. A false smile that spoke as many lies as Phelma Jo Nelson lived.

"What was that all about?" Ian asked without preamble. He stopped directly in front of her. If she wished to flee without speaking she'd have to go around him.

"Just some business papers that needed delivery in a hurry," she replied keeping her smile in place. Inside, she bristled at the thought of having to explain herself to anyone. Yet she didn't want any more secrets or lies to come between her and this handsome man.

"I know Marcus Wallachek. His oldest son is in my Scout troop. He's not looking to buy or sell a house," he said flatly.

Phelma Jo met his semi-accusation with silence.

"He's a social worker," Ian continued. He sounded nervous, as if he *had* to fill the silence.

"I know."

"Phelma Jo, what is this about? Neither one of you is

likely to choose to exchange papers outside an office, let alone in this half-forgotten out-of-the-way place on a miserable day." As if to emphasize his words the wind blew a wave of chill rain in their faces.

"Believe it or not, I have business that must remain confidential."

"If you wanted confidentiality, you should have just said so. Instead, you lied to me about a dentist appointment."

Phelma Jo gulped. Nervousness had made her excuse less plausible than usual.

"You wanted secrecy, not confidentiality. You lied rather than trust me with the truth."

"Truth!" she snarled. Anger ate at her. Anger that had propelled her through life at breakneck speed to trample the ghosts of her past.

Or run away from them.

Had all her lies and manipulation been driven by a need to run away rather than to prove herself to a disapproving town?

She wouldn't think about that. She could justify every action, every lie, every less-than-truthful scheme.

"Well, Mister Holier-than-Thou, I just made it possible for Marcus to rescue a little girl who was beaten nearly unconscious by a man who uses ignorance as an excuse to enforce control over children *with his fists*. The current political climate is sympathetic toward fundamentalist Christians, so he exploits that attitude. He invents a new prayer to say for grace at each meal. Different every day, every meal. And when his foster children can't recite that prayer—because he hasn't made it up yet—he beats the devil of impiety out of them. Ten years ago the big campaign was to limit children's exposure to sex and violence on TV, to get them off their fat rear ends and turn off the set. He used the excuse that I broke house rules by asking to watch television before seven thirty or after seven thirty-eight."

"What? No man of honor would . . ."

"Wake up to reality, Mr. Eagle Scout. Not everyone has your sense of honor. Or any sense of honor. They manipulate the system. If authorities don't believe the religious crap, he counterattacks the child's accusations. He didn't beat them. They tripped or came to him wounded and bruised. He was the last foster parent I had. I ran away from him. I've taken care of myself ever since. Not every child can manage that. So Marcus and I work with a kind of underground railroad to help teens run away from the system when it breaks. Before it breaks them."

"A laudable cause. But surely there must be a way to help that isn't illegal . . ."

"There isn't. At least not that we've discovered." She made to move around him. He blocked her with a hand on her shoulder.

"Phelma Jo, there has to be a legal way, an honest way . . ."

"If there was, your aunt, Mabel Gardiner, would not have started the network. One of the reasons she's so deathly afraid you'll tear down her house is because it is a stop along the path to freedom for the teens we help."

"My aunt would never do anything illegal. She's a police dispatcher!"

"Grow up and take off your rose-colored glasses, Ian. A lot of people break the law when they see the letter of the law becoming more important than the spirit behind the law."

He gulped, his Adam's apple bobbed. Then he firmed his jaw and leveled his gaze on her. "Phelma Jo, I don't know if I can continue seeing you as long as you take this view of life."

"Fine. You either accept me for who I am, or you get lost. So get lost." She pushed him aside and marched across the street, making a point of avoiding the clearly marked crosswalk. Cheap plastic scarecrows, tied to signposts, mocked her as the wind made them wave, their lopsided grins making fun of her tears that threatened to join the rain splashing her face.

# Nineteen

CHASE PAUSED AT THE EDGE of The Ten Acre Wood in his afternoon patrol. Today's drizzle was uncomfortable. But he had a waterproof jacket and plastic cap protector. His boots would serve him in a foot of snow. Driving a cruiser around town couldn't replace the more intimate contact of foot patrol. No need to watch for traffic while seeking out potential risky behavior. No need to worry about parking the vehicle and securing it before giving chase on foot.

Normally he loved walking the streets of Skene Falls in any weather, checking on citizens, watching for vandals, and doing his best to keep his town a little safer. *A little neater!*

In the last week he'd spotted more than the usual amount of suspicious behavior: teens out of school, cars driving slowly along the same residential streets repeatedly, drunks staggering out of bars and into their cars, and Halloween decorations torn out of yards and dumped elsewhere. Dumped here.

A pile of junk lay heaped in the roadside ditch. Halloween decorations stolen from neighboring yards.

Before Mabel got sick, her Pixies reported such things early and he was able to avert crimes before they started, mostly just by making his uniformed presence known.

He'd also rousted three illegal homeless camps in the Wood in as many days.

Today he need go only as far as the drainage ditch. He counted a sodden witch cutout, at least six strings of green-and-orange lights, sheaves of leaves tied with orange and

black ribbons—now also drenched beyond usefulness—
and three of the ubiquitous scarecrows. The Pixies weren't
doing their job.

"Norton to dispatch," he called into his shoulder mike.

"Skene County sheriff's office," came the anonymous
male reply.

Damn, he wanted to hear Mabel's friendly banter. But
until she recovered, or the chief hired a new dispatcher,
they had to make do with part-timers and backup from the
county.

"Dispatch, I've got a pile of refuse discarded from the
latest vandalism reports. There's too much for me to carry
back to the station for matching with lost items. Can you
send a cruiser with a forensics tech? We might get a fingerprint or two." He gave directions.

"Officer Johnson is on the way. ETA three minutes." The
voice was so bored and monotone it might have been a recording.

Johnson was okay. Young and in need of experience, but
dedicated. "I'll be right here unless something comes up."

While he waited, his mind wandered to happier times in
his youth. A grin spread across his face in fond memories of
the adventures he and Dick had invented deep within the
forest shadows. The best parts of his life, including the first
kiss he shared with Dusty, had been spent in and around the
wood.

Lately not so much, what with the fire last August, the
homeless camps, and now this pile of yard decorations ruined by rain, and it looked like spray paint on the witch and
scarecrows. The woods drooped today as if in sympathetic
sadness. Cedar limbs, heavy with rainfall and coming winter, sagged nearly to the ground. The greens and browns of
mixed evergreen and hardwood blended together in a uniform blanket. A few bright red-and-gold leaves clung to
maple trees, granting a brief reminder of the vibrant life
within the wood that would burst forth again come spring.

Generations of children had played here. Some had befriended the Pixies who dwelled near the pond. Some, like
himself, had not discovered the magic until later.

He was glad now that knowledge of Pixie had come to

him at last. He had a new appreciation of life, of the value of friendship, and of the magic that existed under every green leaf, in the blue of the sky, of refreshing rain, and of the love of his life. Dusty.

"Soon, Dusty. Soon you will be my wife and I won't have to say good-bye at the end of the evening, only good night."

About that time Johnson arrived, alone without a tech. Together, they donned latex gloves and loaded the mess onto a tarp in the back seat. Johnson drove off. They'd exchanged perhaps six sad words about the bad attitude in the neighborhood.

Chase walked on, following the gravel road to the dead end at the edge of the cliff and the foot path that curved across a vacant lot to the historic neighborhood. A sigh escaped him as his mind spun with daydreams of spending the rest of his life with Dusty, raising a bevy of adopted children with her, of Scouts, school plays, and dozens of other activities.

A sting grazed his cheek. He slapped at it instinctively. His fingers came away wet with blood. Ducking and seeking the source, his free hand leaped to loosen his weapon from its holster.

No gun report, screams, or pounding feet.

What?

More warm blood trickled down his cheek toward his jaw. Another quick swipe with his hand revealed a long gash across his cheekbone, nearly to the ear. He might need stitches. After he found the culprit.

Another long sting across the back of his hand followed by a blur of yellowish movement. With reflexes honed by seven years on the force, martial arts, and weapons training, Chase grabbed at the blur.

Something soft fluttered against his palm and closed fingers.

He watched as a hawthorn spike flashed between his fingers. Thistle had been jabbed in the hand with a hawthorn spike several days ago. Mrs. Spencer's tree—er—shrub had been stripped of thorns.

"And who do I have here?" He raised his closed fist and peered at the tiny green boots kicking against his wrist. Yellow legs seemed to stop abruptly at the line of his finger-nails.

"Lemme out!" came a high-pitched whine, akin to a mosquito buzz.

"Wrong time of year for mosquitoes, or much insect life at all. Not enough sun to attract the last of the dragonflies. So you must hail from Pixie," Chase mused.

"You can't see me. You can't hear me," the tiny voice chanted. A bit of glittering yellow pollen, that was probably Pixie dust, drifted around Chase's fist.

"Oh, but I can see you and hear you. And I know just what to do with you. The Murphys' three cats are getting fat and lazy. They need someone like you to chase."

"Lemme go. Please. He'll kill me if I don't show up for muster. He's worse than those three cats combined!"

*Muster?* That was an odd sounding word from a Pixie.

"Who will kill you and how? I'm an officer of the law, sworn to protect all the citizens of Skene Falls. Including Pixies." Anxiety began to play lawn bowling in his middle. He didn't like the sound of this at all.

*Show up for muster.* That was a military phrase. "I can't imagine any Pixie with enough self-discipline to join an army. You guys are supposed to be more interested in fun, practical jokes, and friendship. Friendship that keeps you on the look-out for crime before it happens." Chase opened his hand just enough to grab a green sawtooth wing with two fingertips. The rest of the little fellow was all garbed in yellow, including a cap made of long slender petals. A dandelion.

"Well, Snapdragon has other ideas. And he's going to be really mad. He may throw my brothers into the cellar if I don't show up on time." The yellow Pixie shivered all over.

"Cellars are not good for Pixies." Chase shared Dandelion's chill. "But how can he throw you anywhere you don't want to go?" Chase remembered Alder throwing Thistle out of Pixie altogether. But that was different.

"He's bigger'n any Pixie I've ever heard about in leg-end and lore. And he's mean. Mean as a ground wasp. And he's not from around here, but he's in charge somehow."

"What's your tribe, Dandelion? I'll fix it so you can go home, safely."

"I used to sort of belong to Mabel. At least she sent me places to listen to you humans blather on and on and on about nothing. Mabel thought it was important, so I listened. But Mabel isn't around anymore. Maybe not coming home ever. And this guy Snapdragon saunters in, cozies up to our Queen Rosie, and now he's fighting this war against anything that goes into or comes out of The Ten Acre Wood."

"I thought Rosie was betrothed to Hay, from the valley tribes." Chase tried to puzzle through the complex relationships Thistle had explained to him. He got lost about the time Alder signed a marriage treaty with Milkweed, Hay's sister. Only Alder had taken Thistle on a mating flight the day before the wedding. Only . . .

He shook his head in bewilderment.

"Thistle says that the first rule of Pixie is that you don't play tricks on other Pixies. That's what humans are for."

"This war is not about pranks. Snapdragon threw Chicory into the cellar two nights ago and no one's seen him since. Daisy cried herself to sleep. Pixies don't cry."

"Chicory? The sarcastic blue guy who helped me fix Dusty's music box last summer? Chicory, the guy who helped Thistle's friends tickle the clouds and bring us much needed rain to fight the fire in The Ten Acre Wood?"

"Yeah, that Chicory. He was a good guy. We all liked him. Wish he could kick Rosie off her pink rose and become king."

"Somehow I don't think that will get rid of Snapdragon. What does he look like?"

"Like a snapdragon. Big, bloated, yellow with ugly red spots that look like they're eating his wings. Only they can't 'cause he can fly faster and farther than any of us. Gotta have whole wings to gather that much air. He makes us practice with our hawthorn swords by stabbing at his wings. I'm terrible at it. He moves so fast I can't see where to strike."

"I haven't heard about this Pixie before. How come?" But it sounded a lot like the description of a huge dragonfly witnesses said caused the big accident on the freeway.

"Dunno. Let me go, please. Before he gets even madder

than he already is." Dandelion opened his eyes wide and turned on a winsome expression that tugged at Chase's heart.

"I don't think I should let you help this guy."

"But . . . but . . . but my brothers?"

"What are your brothers' names?"

"Dandelion. We're all named Dandelion. Every tribe has a least a dozen of us hanging around the edges, getting in the way. So many of us you can't walk without tripping over us. We're hardy and good breeders. In winter we're the ones sent out of the nest for food, 'cause the cold doesn't hurt us until it's cold enough to snow." He puffed out his chest with pride.

"Ah." Chase smiled. That described dandelions perfectly. "If there are so many of you, then Snapdragon isn't likely to miss just one." And if they bred like weeds, two more would pop up for every one that got pulled.

"Um . . . hadn't thought about that."

"Do you know where Dusty lives?" Chase asked, an idea brightening his mind.

"Yeah, big pretty pink house with a porch that wraps nearly all the way around it?"

"That's the one, only I wouldn't call the pink pretty. It's a bit garish for my taste." Harem pink with purple-and-green trim that was supposed to complement each other and look Victorian but somehow clashed. Juliet Carrick missed the boat on color combinations.

Dandelion giggled. "That's what I think, but I'm not supposed to say so. Rosie likes those colors."

Chase opened his hand, letting the Pixie stand on his palm, no longer restrained.

"Well, I want you to gather your brothers and as many of the others as you can and go hide at Dusty's house. I don't think there are any Pixies living there and the family could use some help with the garden."

"You mean it? Our own place?"

"Yeah. But you have to continue spying on the town and report back to me. I need to know what's going on before people get hurt."

"You mean like them?" Dandelion pointed toward three

boys in the twelve-to-fifteen-year-old range sauntering down the gravel road toward the museum from The Ten Acre Wood. Each had a cigarette dangling from his mouth, and they all flicked disposable lighters on and off with their thumbs.

As Chase watched, they angled their steps toward the carriage barn, open on the south side and filled with antique wagons and carriages, all made of old, dry, and very flammable wood.

Chase didn't recognize any of the boys from the local school.

"Yeah. Like them. Now go weaken Snapdragon's army and take refuge at Dusty's." Chase watched the Pixie flap his wings with strength and energy as he rose up and took flight on an arrow-straight path toward the forest.

Chase followed at an oblique angle to intercept the hoodlums. They all had a strange dust clinging to their wet hair and shoulders. He'd noticed a similar dust coating the first car in line at the multi vehicle pileup. It looked like rusted gold. Only gold did not rust.

# Twenty

A FLICKER OF MOVEMENT OUTSIDE caught Dusty's attention. She used her pioneer costume apron (the afternoon had filled the museum with groups of older tourists and she'd changed to accommodate them) to clear her glasses of dust specks. Glasses repositioned on her nose, she squinted to look out the upstairs bedroom window that faced north, toward the carriage barn and the wall of trees behind it that marked The Ten Acre Wood. Three boys in their early teens marched toward the barn from the gravel road. Each held a disposable cigarette lighter in front of him with a straight arm. Their stance reminded her of the flag bearers in the Olympic Parade of Nations.

None of them looked right or left as they flicked their lighters. In the dull, overcast light of the early afternoon, Dusty saw tiny flames flare and retract with each flick. Panic sent her heart racing. She dropped the specially treated dusting cloth, and dashed through the maze of furniture, cradles, and antique toys for the stairs.

"Call nine-one-one!" she yelled to the volunteer about to start a tour in the front parlor. "Call the police! Call the fire department."

Dusty swung around the last banister on the ball of her foot, changing her trajectory for the front door.

"Dusty? What should I tell them?" Mrs. Sanderson called after her fleeing back.

"Vandals with lighters," Dusty panted, not pausing.

Then she was on the front porch, visitors and volunteer crowding behind her. Her training to put the safety of visitors first stopped her in her tracks. "Please, go back inside and call the authorities," she begged Mrs. Sanderson and the two couples in their early sixties.

"There's Sergeant Norton coming up behind the boys," Mrs. Sanderson pointed out.

Dusty's heart did a little flip of gratitude and love for the man. "Chase will take care of this. But you should call for backup in any case," Dusty insisted, ushering them back into the parlor.

The moment she closed the door behind them, she took off across the grass, leaping over the herb garden and skirting rhododendrons.

"Stop right where you are," Chase called to the three boys.

They kept on marching toward the carriage barn as if they hadn't heard the voice of authority behind them.

"Stop, or I'll shoot!" Chase drew his weapon with one hand, gesturing for Dusty to move out of the line of fire with the other.

She darted to the side, the third point of a triangle with the boys at the top she and Chase on opposite corners.

The boys trod forward, no longer flicking the lighters on and off. The flames held steady even in the slight wind created by their movement.

Anger at the audacity of these children threatened to overwhelm her.

Then a grinding buzz caught her attention. Keeping one eye on the boys, she searched for the source. No mistaking it for anything but a Pixie on a rampage. From the volume, it must be near. Her eye tracked a blur of yellow movement circling the boys' heads.

*Ding dang chug shplach.* A discordant blast of noise accompanied the buzz from the big Pixie. The biggest Pixie she could imagine. It must be at least six inches long, instead of the usual four.

Mouth agape, she stared for half a heartbeat that felt like an eternity. Time seemed to slow down, images coming to her in pixilated slideshow images. Chase raised his gun. The boys took one more step closer to the barn.

The Pixie taunted them all, leaving a trail of dull yellow dust tinged with flaking rust. Pixie dust?

Shouldn't it sparkle? This was not an ordinary Pixie by any stretch of the imagination.

The lead boy pulled his right arm back, ready to cast the lighter into the rattletrap flatbed farm wagon that sagged and warped in all the wrong places.

*Ding dang chug shplach.*

Dusty almost caught words along with the awful discord. Something about watching flames climb higher and higher. The words "obey me" repeated over and over.

She knew that voice. Where did she know it from?

The jerky rhythm in the almost singing told her that even if Chase managed to shoot the boy, the lighter would still fly forward.

"No!" she yelled, launching herself in a flying tackle.

Neither Chase nor Dick had been able to bring down an opponent outside the end zone with that move. Dusty drew on memories of early ballet classes, cut short by leukemia, and connected with the boy at waist level, dropping them both to the grass.

He still held the lighter in his hand. The flame floundered in the damp grass.

A shot cracked through the tense air.

She braced herself for pain. She heard a dull thud of a bullet impacting wood and dared breathe.

A quick glance showed the boys looking around in bewilderment, staring at their lighters as if they'd never seen them before.

The big Pixie with red boils on its wings had disappeared in silence.

Chase's heart nearly stopped as he watched Dusty fall simultaneously with his gunshot. He holstered the weapon as he dashed to her side. Hands and knees shaking, he knelt beside her.

"Dusty? Oh, my God. You can't be hurt. Tell me I didn't hurt you!" No blood. That was a good sign. What about the kid beneath her?

She shook her head as she roused, bracing herself on stiff arms. "I can't see."

"Where are you hurt?" Chase demanded. "Oh, God. Oh, God. What have I done to you!"

"N . . . nothing. I don't think anything's wrong other than a bullet hole either in my barn or the wagon. And I can't find my glasses to find out what you did hit." She shook her head again as if ridding her ears of an annoying sound. "Damn, that gun is loud. Louder than that horribly diseased Pixie."

Chase searched frantically about until he spotted the wire frames about three feet away. That was some tackle to send her glasses flying that far. With a touch of admiration he picked them up and handed them to Dusty. She wiped the lenses with the hem of her apron before seating them firmly on the bridge of her nose.

"Huh?" the boy on the ground muttered. "Wha . . . what happened?"

"Good question, boy." Chase checked the other two boys. They stood rock solid, still staring at their lighters as if they held alien weapons. Not exactly alien, but the weapon of choice of a deranged Pixie. "I need to know why you and your buddies were so intent on setting fire to antique exhibits within the bounds of a city park," Chase replied. He pulled Dusty to her feet, checking again for visible signs of injury. His hands lingered on her waist while his fingers clenched in relief. And guilt for endangering her. He never should have unholstered his weapon.

"I dunno," the boy replied. "We was sneaking into The Ten Acre Wood for a smoke during lunch break. Next thing I know I'm on the ground, pinned by a ninety-pound girl. Damn, she packs a wallop. I think she broke my ribs." He coughed shallowly, holding his middle. "Can I sue?" He looked up at his partners in crime. They stared in bewilderment at him. One flame guttered from lack of fuel, and the boy closed the lighter, pocketing it swiftly.

The other boy looked around for an escape, oblivious to the open flame in his hand.

"Not likely. You were in the process of committing a major crime," Chase snarled. "With those two. You are all under arrest for criminal mischief. You have the right to remain silent . . ." He probed the boy's middle with ungentle fingers while he recited the ritual words.

The boy winced a little when Chase pushed harder on his lower rib cage. No cry of pain, no attempt to roll away from the cursory examination. That told Chase the boy was faking it. A typical criminal ploy: make the victim look more guilty than the perpetrator.

"Dusty, please confiscate the lighters from the other two boys," Chase said firmly and politely. He handed her a new set of gloves and a plastic evidence bag. No sense taking a chance that the potential hoodlum had a lawyer in the family, or one who was a friend of the family. "Before they take it into their heads to finish the job they started."

A siren erupted in the distance. The deep bleep between whoops told him both fire and police hastened here. Relief and dread warred inside him. He needed help with the boys. He'd have a devil of job explaining why he fired his weapon. The paperwork alone would keep him at his desk for a week, if the captain didn't fire him on the spot.

All because of a damn Pixie gone mad with bloodlust and a fascination with fire.

# Twenty-one

THISTLE STARED AT THE EMPTY SHELF in the middle of Mabel's refrigerator. "I knew I put three slices of leftover pizza there just two days ago."

The refrigerator didn't answer.

But her tummy did. Her mouth salivated at the thought of Canadian bacon, mushroom, olive, and fresh tomato. She was hungry and needed to have some lunch soon, before Dick picked her up to go to the courthouse with that awful paper full of lies. Lies she had written.

Thinking about the lies made her stomach clench and her vision grow dark.

No longer hungry, she straightened up and closed the refrigerator door. Just because she wasn't hungry anymore didn't mean she knew what had happened to the pizza.

She sniffed cautiously, separating out the smell of old house damp, weather damp, cereal bowls soaking in the sink damp. That didn't feel right. She'd used one bowl this morning. One bowl of granola and soy milk. So why were there two bowls in the sink?

Thistle closed her eyes and stilled her body, listening to the house as it settled and shifted in the increasing wind. It sighed through a crack in the attic. Or was it a sob?

Step by step she skipped up the stairs, pausing to listen each time the boards creaked. Nothing changed as she crept past the two bedrooms, Mabel's large one and the smaller guest room where she nested, not wanting to disturb Mabel's privacy even though she wasn't home to be disturbed.

The sobs continued. Not a natural sound even in a house as old as this one.

In the middle of the landing she reached up and yanked on the cord fixed to the trapdoor. A ladder unfolded as the trap descended on well-oiled hinges. Thistle had fixed the creak and groan her fist day here when she hunted out the Halloween decorations.

Alder had said a lost child hid in her territory and that Thistle had to help her before she could go home to Pixie. In a few moments maybe the child would no longer be lost. Thistle intended to do what she could to help. But would she go back to Pixie?

Not just because it was time. She might go back if Pixie really needed her. Might. Not for sure, or forever.

Then she climbed hand over hand, no longer fearful of whoever hid up here, grateful the lost one hadn't chosen the basement as a refuge.

Thistle's hand slid on a bit of red wax on the top rung of the ladder. It hadn't been there two days ago. She'd have noticed the big splotch. She sniffed it and found a hint of cinnamon under the oily stuff that made a candle. The lost one had brought burning candles with her. Not a good idea. Fire had a way of escaping and seeking out Pixie strongholds, just because it could.

"Who . . . who's there?" came a trembling voice.

"I'm Thistle. I've come to help," she said softly, scanning the shadows in the far corners of the attic. A faint glow off in the corner went out, leaving behind the smell of something burnt.

"You . . . you can't help. No one can." Something moved in the deep corner to her left, beside a tiny window where the glow had been. The ceiling was low over there, where the roof sloped steeply toward the gutter. Someone could wedge themselves in there and pull a box or trunk in front of them and remain unseen. But not unheard.

"Maybe. Maybe not. I can listen. I'm very good at listening."

"You aren't Mabel."

"No. Mabel is sick. I'm helping her by taking care of her house—and her responsibilities." Thistle sat on the edge of the attic entrance, feet still on the fold-down ladder. Not threatening the lost one by coming too close or appearing aggressive. Slowly she looked over her shoulder into the dim corner. The light from the window suggested the outline of a head with lank, shoulder-length hair.

"It's cold up here. We can talk downstairs in the parlor. I've turned on the furnace to banish the damp."

"You won't throw me out?"

"Not if you have a good reason to stay."

"Depends on what you call a good reason."

"Are you afraid of someone?"

"Y . . . yeah."

"Then I'll do everything I can to make sure you are safe."

"You sure?"

"Cross my heart." Thistle made the gesture beloved of children for many generations to seal a promise, though she'd rather spin in a circle, asking the four winds to acknowledge her oath.

Floorboards creaked and something heavy slid across warped wood. Thistle sat very still. When she judged that her quarry approached, she turned and backed down the ladder. She held the contraption steady, waiting.

After a few moments a pair of tennis shoes, frayed at the toes, appeared on the top step. Long legs, clad in threadbare jeans, followed. Eventually, a girl just blossoming into womanhood stood beside her. Taller than Thistle by half a hand's breadth and lean, needing to fill out around her bones, shadows hollowed her cheeks and made dark pits of her blue eyes. Dark blonde hair flopped across her brow as she hung her head, surveying Thistle from beneath lowered lids. She clutched a dirty pink backpack by the straps as if afraid to be separated from her few belongings.

Thistle was willing to bet she didn't have a jacket or blanket in there; only the filthy sweatshirt from some school that she wore for warmth and protection from the elements.

"Where I come from, it's polite to share names. I've told you mine."

"Um . . . I'm Hope."

"Hope." Thistle tasted the word. "That is not the name your mother gave you. What do you hope for?"

The girl reared her head back in surprise. "How'd you know?"

"I just know. It's one of my talents. Now what do you hope for?"

"Something different. Something better."

"Sounds good to me. Let's go downstairs and get you warm."

"Can I have a cup of coffee?"

"Let me look to see if I have any. We can talk in the kitchen while I fix you something hot to drink. It's warm and cozy in there."

Hope trailed behind Thistle, still holding her backpack, her eyes darting right and left, wary as a bird trapped on the ground.

"I've never made coffee before," Thistle confessed as she pulled a red plastic jug of the grounds from the cupboard. She hated handling the artificial container. When she'd first left Pixie, anything plastic like bags or jars, or synthetic clothing burned her skin wherever it touched. As she got more and more used to her human body, and human life, the discomfort lessened. She still didn't like it.

"Where did you grow up? The woods?" Hope found the coffeemaker in a different cupboard and set about brewing a pot.

"Yes, actually." Thistle pulled the folded papers from her little purse and handed them to Hope. "This explains it. I have to leave in a few moments. We can talk more when I get back. Can I trust you here alone?"

"Of course." Hope rolled her eyes up as only a teenager could manage.

"Promise?"

"Cross my heart." The girl made the ritual gesture.

"It would help if I knew what you are running from. Or running to."

Hope hung her head and bit her lip in a gesture reminiscent of Dusty. After a long moment, she straightened up as if she'd found her courage while contemplating her toes. That posture shift also reminded her of Dusty. Except for the height, she could be a close cousin, or sister.

Or niece.

Thistle froze from the inside out at that thought.

"I'm looking for my dad," Hope said, defiant in her resolve.

"Who is your father?" Thistle didn't like the quaver in her voice.

"I . . . I've never met him. I didn't even know his name until I had this huge fight with my mom."

The sound of a car pulling into the driveway beside the house startled Hope. She took one frantic look at the back door, grabbed her pack and dashed toward the front of the house. By the time Dick knocked on the back door, Thistle heard the attic trap pulled up to conceal the girl once more.

"I know your secret now, Hope. One of them at least. We can't let you hide much longer. But you are safe for now. We'll confront your past together."

"Thank you for seeing us on such short notice, Judge Pepperidge," Dick said upon entering the richly appointed office.

"No problem, Dick." John Pepperidge waved Dick and Thistle to the straight-backed chairs in front of the desk. At forty-three he was the youngest judge in the county. He had a reputation for intelligence and fairness.

His father, George, was the only candidate for mayor of Skene Falls in November. Phelma Jo had withdrawn from the race after the scandal of the fire and logging off of The Ten Acre Wood.

"I haven't seen much of you since you and Chase dominated the high school football team," Judge Pepperidge said.

"Those were the glory days." Dick smiled, not willing to discuss his checkered academic career with this overachiever who succeeded at everything he tried.

"But you landed in a good career, in spite of yourself," John Pepperidge laughed good-heartedly. "So introduce me." He half stood and proffered his hand toward Thistle.

Dick made the introductions. Thistle blushed prettily and didn't say much. She still looked a little pale after that episode writing out her story. Her gaze remained firmly away from both Dick and the judge. That worried Dick. Lying was such a big part of modern life, he didn't know if he could follow her example. Or live up to her expectations.

For Thistle, he'd try. As soon as they got through this one huge lie about her past.

Necessary, he reminded himself.

"Now tell me what brings you here?" Judge Pepperidge asked. His eyes returned to Thistle again and again, squinting and puzzling as if he should know her but couldn't remember from where.

Dick almost laughed. Given Thistle's wide variety of friends from her Pixie days, spanning several generations, she had probably been influential in Johnny Pepperidge's life, giving a serious and studious boy the gift of laughter and not taking himself too seriously.

Dick's mirth flipped to jealousy. Had Thistle kissed the judge in his youth as she'd kissed Dick?

She patted Dick's hand reassuringly, as if she followed his thoughts.

"Thistle has no records or ID," Dick said boldly.

"I'm not an illegal alien," Thistle interrupted. "I've lived near here all my life."

The judge raised his eyebrows in question but said nothing. One of his tactics to encourage reluctant witnesses to keep talking just to fill the silence.

"Thistle's parents raised her in a religious commune. They did not believe in education for women or in electricity or plumbing or anything else modern," Dick said.

"Where were you born?" the judge asked, leaning forward and resting his elbows on his massive mahogany desk. His eyes sparked with interest.

"I . . . I don't know for sure." That was the truth. Thistle blushed and lowered her gaze. But she flicked Dick a glance to make sure she'd used the right words.

"Her mother would have been at home with a midwife or a friend, not a doctor or a hospital."

"Birth certificate?" the judge asked.

Thistle shrugged. "I wouldn't know where to look."

"If her parents recorded anything, it would have been in a family Bible," Dick filled in the blanks. He didn't want a repeat of that fainting spell. He hadn't told her of the brief glimpse of dark shadows he'd seen twining about her arms. The lie had tried to eat her.

"Where are your folks now?" Pepperidge leaned back in his chair and studied the ceiling as if it would give him the answers to his questions.

"They are behind a wall with armed guards somewhere east of here. When Thistle escaped, after a severe beating for disobedience, she left with nothing, not even clothes. She ran for days and days, barely surviving on creek water and berries," Dick added. He needed to get the story straight and convincing. Giggles and a splash of Pixie dust wouldn't help her evade answers right now.

"So, I take it, the story of you showing up in Memorial Fountain naked in the middle of rush hour on a hot August morning was the end result of your 'escape.'" Johnny Pepperidge grinned.

Dick caught a glimpse of the mischievous imp a Pixie might inspire him to be when he was a kid.

Why did the judge put imaginary quote marks around the last word?

Thistle nodded vigorously at the last statement. It came fairly close to a truth she could agree with.

"I'm interested in rooting out this commune. I will not allow freedom of religion as a defense for domestic abuse, or denying children an education in my court." He fixed Dick with a suspicious gaze.

"I've spoken to Chase Norton about it. He's our police sergeant . . ."

"I know Sergeant Norton. We've worked together on some other sticky issues. What's he doing about it?"

"I don't know exactly. Something about county tax rolls, trying to find a large piece of property on the foothills of Mount Hood owned by a shadow corporation." Dick made that up as he spoke. It sounded like a logical procedure.

"Good place to start. Have Chase call me *if* he finds anything. I doubt he will. So Thistle needs some ID?"

"Yes, sir. We want to get married; only we can't get a license without ID. I can't register her for my company benefits without a social security number," Dick pleaded.

"First step is to run her fingerprints through all data-bases, and check for social security numbers . . ."

"Chase did that when he arrested Thistle her first day in town. Both came up negative. Our family lawyer said you would be our next step. That you have some authority in cases like these."

"So, Thistle, your folks were really intent upon staying off the system's radar." The judge swung his chair around facing the wall of law books, as if they would give him inspiration. "Yes, I have some authority. I'll need a witnessed and notarized statement, preferably in your own handwriting, Thistle."

"Got it." Dick handed over the trifolded piece of Mabel's stationary.

Judge Pepperidge raised his eyebrows when he saw the monogram.

"I'm house-sitting for Mabel while she's in the hospital," Thistle volunteered in a rush. "It was the only blank paper I could find."

"I'll witness your signature and have my secretary notarize it and make a copy for your records. The original I'll push through the Bureau of Vital Statistics. This is doable, but it will take time."

"Any idea how long? We really want to get married. Legally." Dick didn't like the whining tone that came through his words.

"Are you pregnant, Thistle?" Pepperidge fixed her with a probing stare.

"No, sir. I insist that we wait to have sex until after we are married." She sat up straight and firmed her chin.

Dick almost laughed at her indignation.

"Understood." The judge winked at Dick. "I'll see what I can do to push this through. But don't make any plans for at least a month. Maybe three. Bureaucracy has its own timeline that rarely coincides with reality."

"Thank you, Judge Pepperidge," Dick said.

"Thank me on your tenth anniversary. Or name your first child after me."

# Twenty-two

THISTLE PUT THE FINAL FLOURISH at the end of her name where she signed the paper Dick had dictated for her. She had deliberately blanked the meaning of the words, concentrating on making each letter perfect. She'd slipped a couple of times, but Dick had reassured her that the mistakes made it look more authentic.

Then she'd practiced writing her name on a separate piece of paper over and over until it came naturally. She liked the way ink flowed easily from the fat fountain pen the judge had offered her for this momentous ceremony. Something about the pen added officialness and import.

Respectfully, she placed the pen back on the judge's desk. The secretary nodded to her, gathered up her logbook and seal and left without a word.

"We are going to get married." Dick patted Thistle's hand when she'd finished. "And soon. Just not as soon as we'd hoped."

"Then we'll have to make good use of the extra time and plan a lovely wedding. Maybe we should ask Dusty and Chase if they want a double wedding after all."

"Considering how Dusty is reacting to Mom's extravaganza, she just might appreciate a second bride to take some of the pressure off her," Dick chuckled.

"Heard about that," Judge Pepperidge leaned back in his chair. "The moment the rumor mill said that Juliet Carrick would require Elizabethan dress, every man in town started making other plans for that date."

"Dad squashed that as soon as the idea blossomed in

Mom's over-fertile imagination," Dick reassured him. "So far only the bride is getting stuck with an historically accurate gown, and she's balking."

"Dusty walked out of a fitting yesterday and told Juliet that if she liked the dress so much she should wear it. Now she's talking about eloping," Thistle added.

Humans seemed to think casual conversation was necessary after a ritual, like this signing thing. She thought a moment of respectful silence was better suited.

"I'll file the necessary forms today, Dick. My secretary will call you when we know more." The judge dismissed them, all parts of the ceremony concluded.

"Let's find Dusty and Chase and tell them the news," Thistle said, bouncing up and down just a little, as if trying to catch air on wings she'd lost three months ago.

"Good idea. At least we know where to find Dusty," Dick chuckled, guiding her through the offices to the corridor and grand staircase of the courthouse. "If she's not hiding in the basement, she's in her office."

"I thought she . . . she stopped hiding in the basement." Thistle nibbled her lower lip in worry. "She's grown a lot since last summer."

"True. But Mom can't find her in the basement—no cell phone signal and the tour guides have learned not to bother her down there." Dick lost a little of the happy glow on his face.

"We really need to do something to make both Juliet and Dusty reconsider the wedding plans."

"No, Thistle. Dusty needs to do that herself. We can offer her support in her decision, but she has to tell Mom herself that reenacting a Shakespeare play is not what this wedding is about."

"Does Juliet make every gathering about her own wishes rather than the true purpose?" Thistle knew a Pixie or two who did the same. Alder's bride Milkweed was one.

"Usually. But she always gets the purpose accomplished, within her own parameters."

They both giggled a bit, more to return their moods to the joy of the day than true mirth.

"It's raining pretty heavily. Do you want to drive up to

the museum?" Dick looked out from under the deep porch of the City Hall/Courthouse/Police Station. A fat raindrop plunked into his eye. He shook his head. "Definitely a day better suited to a short drive than a long walk."

"Agreed." Thistle rose up on tiptoe to kiss his cheek. "I'll wait here for you to bring the car around."

He returned the kiss briefly and dashed down the steps toward the street. His pretty car—with the top up—sat parked at the curb across the street and a block and a half down.

A deep-throated buzzing started in the back of her head. She looked around. "That sounds like a Pixie. But not like a Pixie," she mused.

The annoying sound seemed to hover and circle around a single spot, neither moving closer nor fading into the distance. From the volume of the throb of beating wings she guessed the Pixie should be at the lamppost at the foot of the steps.

Nothing. No blur of movement or flash of color alerted her. "Who?" she asked the air.

*Ding dang chug shplach.*

She covered her ears to block out the awful noise. Worse than the sirens hastening along the ridge above her.

Worse than Alder's total lack of music.

Her gaze darted restlessly about. Now she wished she'd braved the rain to go with Dick. That persistent buzz made her wince.

Dick bent slightly to unlock the car.

Another familiar figure darted across the street from the second lamppost on the right. A young woman with a dirty pink backpack. She walked purposefully, without looking right or left. Cars screeched to a halt around her. Angry drivers leaned on their horns. She ignored them, moving quickly.

Hope. Hope must have followed them.

Without a word, she tapped Dick on the shoulder. He looked up, surprise written on his face. "Who?"

Thistle saw his mouth form the word but couldn't hear it. The buzzing in her ears grew louder.

The Dick's expression cleared. "Sandy?" he asked. The girl shook her head.

Sandy Langford. The first girl he'd taken to bed.

Dick and Hope looked so much alike, with only hints of the mother's blood in the girl, a human would have to be blind not to see the relationship. Thistle's Pixie senses showed her lines of energy reaching out from both of them, trying to find the connections, to bond and bring them together.

The ugly yellow-and-rust Pixie looped around them, trying to tie those strands of energy together. He didn't need to. They reached out on their own, understanding the bonds of blood and love better than Snapdragon's artifice.

"You have brought these two together. Your job as a human is finished," Alder whispered to her. "He has no need of you now that he has found his daughter. Her mother will come back into his life soon as well."

A fat tear slid down her cheek. She brushed it away as she would a gnat. Another replaced it.

She didn't know if she rejoiced for Hope and Dick or feared that in their need to get to know each other there would be no room for her in their lives ... or that Dick would remember his love for the girl's mother.

"He loved her mother once. He loves her still. Now that he knows about his child, he will go back to her. He has no need for you to fill the empty place in his heart," Alder continued his malicious litany.

Across the street, Dick placed a heavy hand on the girl's shoulder and squeezed.

"You are evil, Alder."

"Less so than Snapdragon."

"Snapdragon, or Haywood Wheatland, or whoever he is, is more honest in his evil. He doesn't cloak his words in half-truths, doesn't pretend to be your friend when he's not."

"He's half Faery. He lies as easily as a human."

"What about you, Alder? How can you lie?"

"I am your friend, Thistle. I do not lie. I am your king. I'm only doing what is best for you. Come back to Pixie where you belong. Leave the complex emotions to the humans. Live for the day and forget about plans and consequences. Come home."

"I hate being human!"

And still Dick continued to talk with Hope, scrutinize her, look all around town, but not at Thistle. He made no move to hasten back to her with his car.

Thistle ran down the steps. Rain matted her hair and soaked her shoulders. Her shoes splashed muddy water up her slacks all the way to her knees. At the sidewalk she paused, willing Dick to look back at her, acknowledge her, take his eyes off his daughter.

She ran left, away from Dick and his child, the child he shared with a woman he'd loved long ago, still loved. The bond of that lovely child was stronger and deeper than his proposal to Thistle. She ran up the steps that climbed the cliff face.

Pixie needed her. Dick did not.

The steps seemed to grow wider and taller as she stretched from one to the other. Still she ran.

Breathless and sweating, she rounded the landing to the final flight. Her clothes were wet. She was wet to the skin. The clothes dragged against her skin, too loose and floppy to be of use.

Without thinking, she shed them and grabbed a cobweb in the corner of the stair to cover her nudity.

Onward she plunged, gathering a fallen leaf and bit of fluff from a thistle weed gone to seed.

At the last step that opened to the lawn and the knot garden behind Dusty's museum, her wings spread and her feet lifted free of the confines, the restrictions, the rules, and the heartache of being human.

She flew as fast as she could into the heart of The Ten Acre Wood.

Home.

# Twenty-three

"**W**HO DID YOU SAY YOU ARE?" Dick asked the waif standing in front of him. She'd asked him for directions and a handout. What was this world coming to that ragged teens could skip school and panhandle right in front of the courthouse.

"Do you remember Sandy Langford from high school?" She answered his question with a question, something Sandy used to do all the time. It drove him nuts.

"Sandy? Yeah, I remember her. She left town a long time ago." He dismissed the question. A strange buzz started up around his nape, making it hard to think.

"I'm her daughter."

"And?"

"Nothing. Forget it. Forget me. Everyone else does!" The girl wrenched out from under his grasp and ran full tilt toward Main Street.

His head continued to ring with a discordant whine. It might have been raucous laughter if it came from a miniature Pixie throat. No, too discordant to belong to a Pixie. Pixies chimed when they spoke, or laughed.

*Ding dang chug shplach.*

He looked around frantically and saw the bloated yellow figure with ugly red splotches on its wings, flying drunken spirals around his head. Snapdragon. The mutant Pixie-Faery half-breed everyone was talking about. "Tricked you. Tricked you all!" He wobbled away, laughing so hard he had trouble keeping air under his wings.

"Broke you and Thistle. Broke you, broke you, broke

you. She'll never be yours now. Never, ever, ever," he chortled as he disappeared among the rhododendrons beneath the courthouse windows.

Dick gave chase. He really needed to make sense of this.

Reality reared its ugly head and he remembered why he was trying to unlock his car.

"Thistle?"

No sign of her on the courthouse steps. Only a penetrating buzz like a streetlight on the fritz.

Then a renewal of the annoying laughter in the super-high soprano range that cut through the static as Snapdragon rose up from the shrubbery and wound his way higher and higher, pausing on each windowsill of the four-story building. Dick's gaze riveted on the Pixie. Something about those fungal infection splotches on the wings triggered a memory. Something about insanity and red dyes. . . .

Dick recognized the face of the large Pixie.

"Haywood Wheatland, come back here and face me like a man."

"Tricked you. Tricked you good," the Pixie sneered. "Tricked everyone." He flitted toward the roof, a little steadier than a few moments ago.

"Where's Thistle?" Dick demanded. He took the steps two at a time, hoping desperately that Thistle had taken refuge inside.

"Ring around the Rosie. Tricked you all. Trick you again. Trick Thistle better than Alder or sissy Milkweed."

Ice particles pricked Dick's veins from inside.

"Where is she? Where's my Thistle?"

"Where you'll never find her."

"You can go back to your lost love now. Thistle won't stand in your way," another Pixie voice whispered. The voice didn't chime with music like the other Pixies he knew. Nor did Snapdragon's, what passed for his music, *ding dang chug shplach*, was as ugly and out of place as he was. But this other guy was surrounded by silence.

"What the f . . ." Lost love. Sandy Langford's daughter. What was this all about?

"You don't need Thistle. You need your lost love," the whisper continued to wiggle into his mind.

Dick dashed back to his car, flung open the door, and dropped into the leather bucket seat. He'd turned on the ignition before he got settled and barely remembered to close the door before setting it into gear.

He peeled out of the parking spot and executed an impossible U-turn in the middle of the street.

How long had he talked to the girl? Not long. He hoped. Thistle couldn't have gone far on foot. But why would she leave him for talking to a lost child?

Where would she go?

The last time her world had crumbled around her, she'd called Dusty. He prayed that the love of his life would seek out her best friend again.

He took the steep road twenty miles an hour over the speed limit, gears grinding, and turned onto Center Street on two wheels. The driver of a big red pickup yelled something obscene and shook his fist as Dick cut him off.

With a screech of brakes and one wheel on the curb he parked in front of the museum in a handicap spot. "Thistle!" he called as he ran inside. "Thistle, are you here?"

Then, through the side window in the parlor, he noticed the fire engine, police cruiser, and paramedic truck. His feet sped up without conscious thought. "Chase?"

"No running inside the museum," Dusty reprimanded him as if he were a naughty fourth grader on a field trip.

"What happened? Have you seen Thistle?" He leaned forward, examining paramedic Bill Musgrave's careful application of butterfly bandages over a wickedly swollen wound along Chase's temple and cheek.

"I strongly recommend you see a doctor for this," Bill said sternly as he dabbed away blood and lymph that still oozed.

"I second that," Dick said. "That gash is already infected."

"And I agree," Dusty added.

"Later, when I've completed all the paperwork required from this little fiasco," Chase ground out. "Bad enough I'm going to be patrolling a desk for the next couple of weeks. I need to be out walking my town."

"I missed something," Dick said.

Dusty gave him a quick report.

She said nothing about Thistle in her narrative, only suggestions that Haywood Wheatland might have hypnotized the culprits. She couldn't mention Snapdragon with Bill still hovering over Chase's wound.

Dick wanted to strangle the malevolent Pixie, right here and now.

He took a deep breath to calm himself. Thistle was unhurt. Upset and uncertain, maybe. Neither Snapdragon or the other Pixie voice—he suspected Alder—had said anything about Thistle being hurt.

Then he bent and looked more closely at the wound, almost like a knife slash. They weren't telling him everything.

"Your refusal to see a physician is going on my report, Chase," Bill said. "Since you're going to be desk-bound for a while because you fired your weapon, endangering four civilians—one of them your fiancée—you might as well spend some of that time at the clinic." Bill snapped his kit closed and exited.

"What really happened?" Dick asked. He opened an alcohol swab from a pile of packets Bill had left behind, as if he knew they'd be needed.

"I got sideswiped by part of Snapdragon's army of Pixies," Chase replied. He only winced a little when Dick cleaned the wound again.

"Did they use hawthorn spikes for swords?"

"Yep."

"Um . . . I'm ordering you to get to the clinic. I'll drop you off on my way. I've got to find Thistle, fast." Worry gnawed at his gut.

"Explain?" Dusty asked, hands on hips, best schoolteacher frown on her face.

"No time for details." He hauled Chase to his feet with a firm grip on his friend's elbow. "But while we're gone, Dusty, get on the Internet or into your personal reference library and see what you can find about ergot poisoning."

"Moldy rye, Saint Vitus' dance, great for making a red dye that doesn't fade or bleed. What else do you want to know?"

"Does it affect hay or straw from grains other than rye?"

Dusty logged onto the computer in the corner of the employee lounge, fingers racing.

"I think Haywood Wheatland may have contracted it while partially underground in the old pioneer jail, where you stashed him while we fought the fire spreading to downtown last August," Dick replied. "The purple-red pustules on his wings look something like a picture I saw in a biology text years ago. Either that or a fungus. But I can't think of any fungal infection that would drive him violently insane. So, Chase, you'd better make sure the doctor irrigates that wound with lots of saline just in case Snapdragon poisoned those Pixie swords with his own disease. Come on, Chase. I have places to go and a fiancée to hunt for."

Phelma Jo stood stock-still in the parking place next to her car in front of the grade school, three blocks from her meeting with Marcus. And with Ian.

An angry car horn and a shout made her jump to the curb. The distraught woman driving a forest-green minivan muttered a string of invectives at her all the while she rammed her car into the empty spot, slammed her car door, and stalked into the grade school. Rabid birds attacking innocent children earned as many curses as Phelma Jo.

She stared at the woman blankly, her mind jumping from Ian's rejection, to the disjointed and nonsensical words, to the image of Haywood Wheatland as a weird dragonfly/moth/Pixie biting Ian's finger.

"Oh, my God!" She clamped her hand over her mouth, gaze darting right and left, up and down.

Haywood Wheatland, the boy toy she'd flaunted in front of the town last summer was some kind of miniature flying pest. Right out of some fairy tale, and it sounded like he'd attacked a child. Images flickered through her memory: stuffing a purple dragonfly into a mason jar with a wolf spider and having Dick steal it, claiming the bug was really a Pixie. Then watching the dragonfly perch on Dick's outstretched hand and morph into the tiny figure of Thistle Down as she blew him a kiss of thanks. Haywood Wheatland binding her with magic before he ran out of energy and substituted duct tape. The flitting lights that streamed out of The Ten Acre Wood ahead of the fire. The sound of chiming laughter haunting her whenever she walked around town, especially in the environs of Dusty's museum.

"I'm going crazy," she reassured herself. "I have to be. Pixies do not exist."

But she'd seen them with her own eyes.

Frantically she searched the soggy shrubbery next to the sidewalk where she suspected a deranged Pixie might hide and taunt her with the loss of someone she really cared about. No sign of the yellow bug with red splotches on its wings.

Nothing. If the creature existed outside of her mind, he'd found other people to torment.

Torment. That was a good word for the way Haywood had treated her, compelling her to set fire to The Ten Acre Wood, beloved by the entire town.

She shook her head, forcing the mind-numbing loop of questions aside. "I have too much work to do to waste time standing here in the rain." With Halloween banners and scarecrows fluttering in the breeze, mocking her very existence.

Resolutely, she got into her car and headed toward her office building on the north end of town overlooking the river and the railroad tracks.

Something deep within tugged her away from her reality toward Dusty's museum and The Ten Acre Wood. Answers. She needed answers. Answers that Dusty seemed to hold close to her chest, hidden from the world. Just as she hid herself.

"Shyness, my butt. She's a silent manipulator hoarding the town's secrets as if they were ancient artifacts." Mabel did much the same thing.

Four minutes later she parked beside the museum.

"Why is it that everyone in town ends up here sooner or later?" Phelma Jo asked the air as she entered the dark but cozy entry.

"Because this is our history. We can ground ourselves in our roots here," Dusty replied, looking up from the rocker by the hearth. Flickering electric lights of a fake fire glowed behind the glass plate of the old iron stove in the corner. She stilled the motion of the chair and stood up. Dressed in a faded calico gown with a dirt-streaked apron and looking pale, frail, and insubstantial, she could have been a ghost.

Phelma Jo stepped back, hand to her heart. She forced herself to breathe deeply, center herself in the reality of today.

In decades past, Dusty's shyness had kept her in the background, looking in on reality occasionally; otherwise living in her own world of books and history and artifacts. A metaphoric ghost.

Maybe she was just rehearsing for the after-dark tours scheduled throughout the week.

"I discarded my past. I look to the future," Phelma Jo said haughtily.

"Do you? Is that why you built your steel-and-glass, high-rise condominium and office building on the lot where your mother's shack used to stand?" Dusty stepped over the velvet rope that divided the front parlor from the entryway and casually walked to the back of the old home. "Can I get you a cup of tea, or did you want to pay admission and take the tour?" she called over her shoulder, as if she expected Phelma Jo to follow her.

"I'll take the cup of tea and a bit of your time." Phelma Jo forced aside a sarcastic retort, relying on politeness. One of her foster mothers had urged her to try politeness when anger and derision failed. Sometimes it worked.

"What do you need, Phelma Jo?" Dusty asked as she filled two mugs with hot water from a simmering electric kettle. She set them on the long worktable along with a box of tea bags, sugar packets, and spoons. "If you take milk in your tea, I think I've got some in the fridge."

"That's okay. Black is fine. With a little bit of fake sugar." Phelma Jo took a chair at the far end of the table, amazed that she didn't have to wipe dust off the seat.

"I presume you haven't come to apologize for rubbing my face in the dirt during recess in fourth grade," Dusty said, fixing her gaze firmly on Phelma Jo. She stirred a disgusting looking pale syrup into her herbal tea. Agave syrup was the name on the bottle. Who ever heard of that?

"No, I haven't come to apologize." Phelma Jo returned the stare, amazed that Dusty had finally learned to stand up for herself. She supposed that her engagement to Chase had filled her with more self-confidence than she'd exhibited in fifteen years.

"I've already apologized to you for my part of that fiasco," Dusty looked at her shoes. "We both need to admit it all turned out for the best. You got out of an abusive situation and into foster care. I got an early diagnosis of leukemia and life-saving treatment when the scrapes didn't heal."

"Agreed. But I nursed the hurt so long, as a coping mechanism, it's become very hard to let go."

"So why did you seek me out today?"

"I . . . I've seen some strange things lately. I thought you might be able to answer some questions."

"Because I'm strange?" Dusty cocked her head and hid a smile by taking a sip of her tea.

"No . . . well, yes. You always did live in a different reality from the rest of us. Living in your imagination and writing little stories about your so-called adventures."

"What did you see?"

"A bloated yellow dragonfly with red donuts on his wings and the face and voice of Haywood Wheatland. Call me crazy and send me to a shrink. But I swear that's what I saw."

"Sort of a combination of these three things?" Dusty asked, shoving her open laptop to where Phelma Jo could see the screen.

Right there on the glossy surface, in three separate windows, Dusty had arranged a picture of a dragonfly in brown and gold, a yellow-and-red snapdragon blossom, and sheaves of grain with alien reddish-purple pods instead of seeds on the tops.

"I don't see . . ."

"Close your eyes and let your memory of each image overlay on top of the other," Dusty suggested.

Phelma Jo obeyed. Slowly she visualized each item and

let them merge until . . . until she saw in her mind the nasty
bug that had bitten Ian and taunted her.

"Oh, my!" she gasped involuntarily.

"Oh, my, indeed," Dusty echoed.

"What is that?" Phelma Jo pointed to the picture of the
mutated grain.

"Ergot."

Phelma Jo cocked her head in question. "Should I know
what that means?"

"It's a poison fungus that infects damp grain. Mostly rye
and barley, sometimes wheat. In advanced cases it causes
muscle spasms, hallucinations, and insanity as a prelude to
a painful death." Dusty sounded calm and rational. Dispassionate. But her fingers tightened into fists.

"Dick and I think that when you were first arrested
when we sent you to the hospital and put Hay into the pioneer jail that is half underground, he may have been infected from the dampness in the ground. Add to that a
general body weakness and suppression of his immune system from the iron handcuffs, and he succumbed. That's why
it took him almost two months to regain enough energy to
shrink back to his normal form and fly away from jail."

"By that time he was already insane," Phelma Jo mused.
She told Dusty about her visit from Haywood the day he
escaped.

"That was the day of the big accident on the freeway. A
number of drivers reported a nasty yellow-and-red bug as
big as a small bird nearly slamming into their windshields."

"Damn," Phelma Jo said, thumping her half-empty tea-
cup onto the table.

Dusty raised her eyebrows.

"I . . . I think I saw him do the same thing downtown the
day he bit Ian."

"Downtown? Was it today? In front of the courthouse?"
Dusty leaned forward, shoulders tense with anxiety.

"No, it was a few days ago. You and Thistle had just gone
into the Bridal Shop. Dick was in his car talking on his cell
not far away."

"Do you know why Thistle ran away from Dick today?"

"No. Other than that she woke up and realized what an

unfaithful ass he can be." What had Hay said? Something about separating Dick and Thistle, humiliating them, sending Thistle back where she belonged?

Where did she belong? Sometimes she acted like she'd come from another world.

Like Pixie.

"You do know where she is! Which way did she go?" Dusty sounded breathless with anxiety.

"Not today. I haven't seen her or Dick today. But I bet if you find that horrible creature, you'll find Thistle Down." She pointed to the computer screen.

Phelma Jo and Dick seemed to be in the same boat. Separated from their loves.

That did not mean she'd take Dick back or comfort him. She wanted Ian, not a poor substitute pining for his lost love.

# Twenty-four

CHICORY INSPECTED THE SLATS across an attic opening that overlooked the porch roof of Juliet's home. All he could see beyond the roof was another house with grass that hadn't seen a mower all summer and not much in the way of shrubs. The house was smaller than Juliet's. Hmmm, a yard that truly needed a few Pixies to take care of it.

The other members of his tribe flew from corner to corner, trunk to box to rafter, exploring their new winter home.

"We usually cover the inside of that vent with plywood for the winter," Juliet said. "Cuts down on drafts. But I can leave it open if you and your tribe need to come and go. We do have a few bright and dry days in the winter." She rocked idly in an old wooden chair that creaked with each forward movement. "Of course that will increase our heating bills. I certainly hope your work in my garden is worth the trade."

"You may cover the vent." Chicory flitted from the slats to hover in front of her. He moved forward and back with each of her rocks so that he stayed the same distance from her. "When we hibernate, we only go out once in a while during the false spring in February. We can go through the house if we need to."

Her movements were making him dizzy. But he had to maintain his authority. *I'm king of my own tribe!* he chortled to himself.

"'Now is the winter of our discontent,'" Juliet muttered, eyes half closed.

"Huh?" Chicory asked. Maybe he really was too dizzy to understand his new protector.

"Just a quote from Shakespeare," Juliet said brightly. "I do love the way his words trip so blithely from my tongue."

"Who lives across the street?" Chicory asked. He had to get the conversation back to something solid, that he could keep straight in his head.

Juliet stopped rocking to look over her shoulder toward the vent. "Which house?"

"The small one with the peeling gray paint and neglected yard." Chicory took up a perch on the open drawer of a walnut wardrobe cabinet. A peek inside showed him a nest of old bed linens. Hmm, nice place to sleep away the cold weather. Just big enough for the eight of them. Four couples. By spring they'd probably have at least one baby Pixie to increase the tribe.

As king, he'd have to make sure they all took mating flights. Juliet had a big maple in the back corner, a hundred feet high at least. Plenty tall for a good long mating flight. He grew warm just thinking about it. And scared.

What if his wings weren't strong enough to support both him and his Daisy-love? What if he failed . . . ?

No. He mustn't think about that. "I'm king. I have to take care of my tribe," he muttered to himself.

"Oh, that house," Juliet scoffed. "Phelma Jo Nelson's mother rented that house for a while when the children were small. She lost her job at Norton's Diner and moved to someplace cheaper. I don't know who owns it now. But I think it recently sold. I hope the new owners take better care of it. It's an eyesore that should have been torn down ages ago."

"It needs some Pixies to take care of it." Chicory gnawed his lip. That yard needed friends. The prime duty of every Pixie was to befriend those in need. As king, he should make sure that house had friends. But his tribe was so small they couldn't take care of both yards, and Juliet offered them shelter during the winter . . .

He had no idea being king was so hard. He had to make decisions. He had to think.

He needed Thistle's help. She knew how to think and weigh consequences.

"Where's Thistle?" he asked Juliet.

"What? Oh, at Mabel's house, I guess. She moved over there a couple of days ago. Something about watching the property while Mabel is in the hospital." Juliet rose gracefully from the rickety rocker and opened the doors of the wardrobe, inspecting the dusty clothing inside. "I wonder if I could persuade Dusty to wear her great-grandmother's wedding dress since she won't wear the gown I had designed for her." She fingered a frilly gown with odd puffs and drapes. It had once been cream-colored with an overlay of lace. Now it looked gray with dust.

"You'll have to get it cleaned before you ask her," Chicory advised. "She's got her heart set on a dress in the window of the bride store downtown."

"She has. She said something about that." Juliet whirled around. A piece of lace came away in her hand with a gentle ripping sound.

Daisy and her sisters set up a worried chatter. They darted from various parts of the attic to converge near Juliet's shoulder. They picked at the torn lace and worried over ways to reconnect the delicate threads with spider silk.

"Why didn't Dusty tell me earlier?" Juliet dropped the fragment of lace. It fluttered to the ground, surrounded by girl Pixies.

Chicory watched it with a feeling of doom. The scrap fell like a Pixie who'd lost his strength in the middle of a mating flight.

"Chicory, why didn't Dusty tell me when I first started planning her wedding?" Juliet prodded. She sat back in the chair and glared at him.

"Because she's Dusty."

"What's that supposed to mean?"

Chicory bit his lip, staring at the fallen lace.

"Tell me. That's part of our bargain. You keep me informed, and I let you use my attic."

"She's afraid to speak. Afraid you'll judge her and find her lacking, just like . . . like when she was a kid."

"But . . . but she's grown up now. She's getting married."

"When was the last time you let her make a decision?"
Chicory darted for the vent, not sure he wanted to watch
Juliet think that one through.

But one day he'd have to. That was also part of being a
king.

And one day he'd have to face Rosie and Snapdragon.
That was also part of being king. His tribe wasn't safe until
the war was over once and for all.

Chase sat on the exam table in one of the three tiny rooms
in the clinic. He held an ice pack to his head over the hawthorn sword wound. A headache throbbed in the same region across his eyes to the other temple. The ice helped a
little. Getting back to work would help more.

He wanted his boots, his hat, and his weapons back.

Damn, it was humiliating to be laid low by a four-inch-
tall, worthless dandelion of a Pixie.

The sound of multiple shuffling feet and hushed voices
in the hallway gave him hope that his endless wait to be
seen by a doctor was almost up. He sat a little straighter and
set the ice pack beside him.

The commotion moved deeper into the clinic.

"I'm sure the police have called someone to deal with a
swarm of killer bees," Nurse Hazlitt said firmly.

"They wasn't bees," a much younger voice insisted with
a hint of a lisp. "Was Pixies. Pixies with swords."

"More likely a small bird infected with that killer flu virus," an adult female said.

Chase slid off the table and opened the door a crack. He
peered out, straining to hear every word. Seven children
ranging from tiny kindergartners to gangly third graders
milled about, sporting deep scratches on hands and faces
similar to the one he had.

"Nurse, I need to talk to these children," he insisted,
opening the door all the way. He half turned to make sure
the kids all saw his own war wound.

All seven clamped their mouths shut and stared up at
him with eyes wide in wonder and . . . and defiance.

Nurse Hazlitt shifted her gaze from Chase to the children and back again. "Oh, dear, this looks serious. I may have to call animal control or the CDC, or *someone*." With wide open arms she tried to herd her charges into the largest examining room at the back of the building.

Chase stalked after her in stocking feet. "I need to know where and when," he said reaching for his pocket-sized spiral notebook and a pencil. "As you can see, I know what attacked us all." He tapped the eraser end of the pencil next to his wound and wished he hadn't. The headache deepened.

From the way the littlest girl in the pack winced, Chase guessed she had a headache, too. Probably a reaction to whatever venom Snapdragon had applied to the spikes. A fat tear rolled down her cheek, catching on her upper lip. She sniffed pitifully.

"I just wanted to see the pretty Pixie," she whispered. "I didn't mean to hurt him." Her chin trembled in prelude to more tears.

"I'm sure you didn't, sweetheart." Chase went down on one knee beside her. He figured she'd tell him more than the two oldest boys with chins thrust out defiantly and lips pressed together in a narrow line. The oldest boy squinted his eyes and peered at Chase suspiciously. He remembered that look; had tried it on many times when he was that age.

He'd need the keys to the kingdom to open their mouths.

And Thistle was the only one he knew who knew how to penetrate Pixie, now that Chicory was gone. He wondered if Dick had found her yet.

"Are you going to arrest the Pixies, Mr. Policeman?" the little girl asked. Another tear threatened to spill down her cheek.

"No, sweetheart. I'm going to figure out how to fix the Pixies so they don't hurt anyone. Now you let Nurse Hazlitt take care of you, and I'll check up on you later." He trapped the tear with a finger against her cheek, then he stood up and went back to his exam room for his boots and his coat and his weapons.

"Sergeant Norton, you haven't seen the doctor yet," the nurse protested. "This is looking serious. What if the bird that attacked you all was rabid? Hell, I don't know if birds carry rabies, but they do carry a host of other nasty viruses. We have to stop this now. What if we don't find the sick bird before Halloween? We'll have to cancel the festivities to keep our children safe. And that will cost the town a whole lot of money."

"I'll come back when you and the doc aren't quite so busy. I have to find a lost Pixie."

# Twenty-five

"THISTLE!" DICK CALLED, pounding on the back door of Mabel's house. He listened carefully for any sounds of movement within. Nothing.

"Thistle!" This time he used the spare key hidden inside a fake rock beside the back steps. "Anybody home?"

Empty. Already the house had that faintly moldy smell of vacancy. The place was devoid of life. Not even a Pixie flitted by the window. The showery morning had turned to a steady autumnal downpour. Any self-respecting Pixie would have crawled into winter hibernation.

"Thistle, where have you gone?" he asked the air.

A soft, muffled sob replied. He listened, seeking direction. The sound came again. He tracked it to the dining room. Slowly he pushed open the swinging door to the small room between the kitchen and the front parlor.

He expected to find Thistle curled up in a chair crying over whatever malicious scene Snapdragon had staged downtown, and the lies he whispered into her ear. What lies?

He didn't know anything. Only that something had frightened Thistle and she'd run away.

Instead of her thick black hair, he saw only a soggy adolescent girl with raggedly cut dishwater-blonde hair. She wore jeans and a T-shirt that had seen brighter and more solid days. Her bare feet were stuffed into tennis shoes a size too small, judging by the way her big toes pushed against the worn canvas.

The girl who'd approached him downtown.

The lost look in her eyes reminded him of Dusty when she needed a buffer between her and reality.

"Who are you, really?" Dick asked, startled by the pathetic sight.

"Huh?" The girl looked up, startled, eyes wide like a deer caught in a car's headlights, needing to flee but not quite sure where to go or how to escape the monster bearing down on her.

"I won't hurt you." Dick held his hands away from his body, palms up, careful to keep his fingers open. What had his psych class in med school said about confronting frightened teenagers? A runaway by the looks of her; scared, alone, cold, and hungry. "Just tell me who you really are and why you are here?"

"Di ... did Mabel send you?" she asked, twisting her head right and left, tangled hair flying into her eyes.

"Um ... sort of," Dick replied. He stood stock-still, not wanting to frighten her into flight, but still needing to know ... to know if she was one of the runaways that Phelma Jo helped with new ID and transportation out of town.

And what she had to do with Sandy Langford.

Shit, was Mabel involved in that, too? She must be.

"Who sent you to Mabel?" Dick asked.

"Kids at the shelter. They told me to check with Mabel at the police station and where to find the spare key to the back door if she wasn't there. She wasn't there." She left a lot out of that tale.

"Mabel is in the hospital with a heart attack. I ... my girlfriend and I are house-sitting for her until she's better." That stretched the truth a bit, but also explained why Mabel had been so insistent that someone live in the house while she was away.

She needed someone to guide these kids along her underground railway.

Did Thistle know? Had Thistle met this girl already, maybe mentioned Sandy to her as a school friend of Dick's. More than a friend, actually.

"Oh." The girl's chin trembled and a new spate of tears threatened to spill from her frightened eyes.

"Look, I need to find my girlfriend right away. Have you seen her? About this tall." He held his hand level with his chin. "Black hair, purple eyes."

The girl shook her head. "The place was empty when I got here." She sniffed again and bit back more words that wanted to spill out.

If she didn't lie outright, she didn't tell the whole truth. He needed the whole truth in order to find Thistle.

"I thought this was someplace safe," the girl said around her tears.

"Normally it would be." But today was not normal. He looked closely into each corner as if he'd find Thistle hiding there, or answers, or something.

His phone chirped an alarm. "Damn!" He looked at the time, willing it to be twenty minutes, or an hour earlier. The black LED numerals on the white face ticked off more seconds in the wrong direction.

"Look, I *have* to get back to work. And I can't leave you here . . ."

"Don't kick me out. Please, I'm begging you. I . . . I can't go back out on the street again. I . . . I just can't." She wrapped her arms around herself and shivered.

"I don't know you. I don't even know your name. And this isn't my house. I can't leave you here alone."

"I won't steal anything, or break anything, I promise."

"How about I take you someplace that I promise will be safe and no one will think about looking for you there?"

She puckered her face suspiciously.

"You don't have a lot of choices here . . . what is your name?"

"I'm Hope," she said, firming her chin and looking him square in the eye, defying him to contradict her.

A made-up name, denying her true identity. Dick didn't care. He just needed to get her out of here so he could go make some money so he and Thistle . . .

Damn. Thistle was still missing. Still hurting. Unless she'd gone back to Dusty after sulking a while in private.

Dusty. Of course. He'd take this child to Dusty instead of his mom. Dusty had teenagers working for her in the afternoons. Meggie and M'Velle could help her get this waif where she needed to be, whether back home with her parents or into a shelter.

Was Sandy truly her mother?

"Come along, Hope. I've got a spare jacket in my trunk you can wear. My sister will get you help."

"Who's your sister?" Hope looked like she was digging her heels in.

"My sister presides over the heart and roots of this town, and the whole world winds up on her doorstep at some point." Even if it was just a fourth-grade history field trip.

"Dusty! I need your help."

Dusty looked up from her computer screen to find her brother stalled in the doorway and Phelma Jo staring beyond him.

"Now what?" Dusty asked. Her quiet museum and favorite place to hide from the stresses of dealing with people had become Grand Central Station today.

Maybe she should take a cup of tea into her office, lock the door, and leave the tours and ticket sales to M'Velle and Meggie.

The creak of footsteps on the floorboards upstairs reminded her that Meggie was giving the current tour. She worked better in the gift shop and M'Velle gave better tours. Which was why she insisted they swap places, to learn all the skills necessary to running this business and historical treasure.

"Um, ah, Dusty, this is Hope. I found her at Mabel's. Um, maybe Phelma Jo can help her. Or you could take her to Mom. I don't know. I've got to get back to work." He turned to flee.

"Dick, why would I take her to Mom?"

"Because, maybe if she had a waif to smother, she'd let up on you and that hideous wedding gown. Oh, and if you see Thistle, hold onto her until I can talk to her. 'Bye." He dashed out the way he'd come, leaving a miserable looking teenage girl behind.

"Another one," Phelma Jo said on a heavy sigh.

"Another one what?" Dusty asked.

The girl studied her worn shoes.

"Get her warm and cleaned up, give her something to eat. Whatever she needs. Don't worry and go all shy on us now, Dusty. She won't judge you."

"I'm not . . ."

"Yes, you are. This doesn't mean we are now or ever will be friends. If she gives you any trouble, call this guy." Phelma Jo fished a business card out of her purse and slapped it on the long table.

"Children's Services . . ." Dusty read aloud.

"I ain't going to CSD!" Hope protested, looking Dusty in the eye for the first time. Something clicked in Dusty's mind, an almost recognition between them.

"What have you got against CSD?" Phelma Jo asked. She stood directly in front of the girl, daring her to lie. Or run away.

"Kids on the street talk," Hope replied, tracing patterns on the plank floor with her big toe that threatened to burst through her tennis shoes at any moment.

"Runaway?" Phelma Jo asked. Her tone brooked no defiance.

Hope nodded.

"Don't believe everything you hear on the street, kid. Not all foster parents are evil, and not all caseworkers are so overwhelmed they don't care anymore. Marcus Wallachek is one of the good guys. He'll take care of you."

"Do you want to go home?" Dusty jumped in before Phelma Jo could intimidate the girl into running. Again.

Hope shook her head violently.

"I need to talk to Mabel," Phelma Jo said, fishing for her keys in her slacks pocket. "Maybe your mom is the best person to take her for now. I'll be in touch." She walked deliberately toward the front door.

Dusty and Hope stared at each other. "Want to talk about it?" Dusty finally broke the silence.

"No."

"I've got some instant soup and hot water if you need something to eat."

The girl's stomach growled loud enough for the Pixies in The Ten Acre Wood to hear.

"Eat while I organize my girls. Then I'll take you to my mother." And she intended to call Chase, too, the moment she got a bit of privacy.

"Sergeant Norton, where do you think you are going?" Police Chief Beaumain stood squarely in the doorway to Chase's office.

Caught in the act. Chase had only stopped in long enough to check the recording of the 911 call from the school. Now he either had to stay put or run over his boss. Beaumain had earned his place as chief, and the respect of his force, with hard, honest work, and diligence above and beyond the call of duty.

"Sir, I'm needed up . . ."

"You are needed behind that desk filling out the eighty-five pages of report required for firing a weapon in the line of duty." Beaumain didn't budge.

If they were on the football field, Chase could have easily tackled the shorter man. Bulldog Beaumain had earned his own reputation on the gridiron and would have taken Chase down with him.

"Sir, there's a situation uphill. Swarms of killer bees or infected birds or something else with wings are attacking children on the school playground."

"Heard about it. Called the state Ag department. They are on it."

"But, sir . . ."

"No buts about it. Nurse Hazlitt called me. Since you refused treatment of your wound, she advised you stay put. I need to collect your weapons and your badge until we sort out this mess." He held out his hand.

Chase hesitated, reluctant to give up his gun, stick, and Taser to anyone.

"Norton, do I have to lock you up?"

"No, sir." Reluctantly, Chase unsnapped his holster, withdrew his service pistol, and handed it to the boss grip first.

Beaumain held out his other hand.

Scowling, Chase handed over the nonlethal weapons as well.

"What about the knife in the ankle sheath and the derringer in your boot?"

"Not service issued, sir."

"I know that. Not authorized either, but sometimes necessary. I have to take them, too."

Chase growled something impolite. "Leaving me naked."

"I know, I know. But the sooner you finish the paperwork, the sooner we can put you back on active duty."

"It will still take two weeks to convene a hearing."

"Fine time for a honeymoon. After you complete the reports." Beaumain turned to leave, laden with Chase's weapons and backups. "Oh, and Nurse Hazlitt is sending down an EMT to wash out that wound with saline and decide if you need stitches or not. It looks unnaturally swollen to me. I'd hate to clear you of overstepping your authority only to have you laid out flat on sick leave."

Chase flopped into his desk chair and buried his face in his hands. His fingers touched the swelling along the thorn scrape. He winced as pain stabbed the full length of the cut. Beaumain was right. He needed medical attention.

After he made some headway on his report. He should call Dusty. He needed to call her just to hear her voice. Maybe he wouldn't feel so naked if she held his hand.

Maybe they should just elope and spend the next two weeks on their honeymoon.

"Ms. Carrick had an emergency at home," M'Velle said when he called the museum.

Dusty didn't answer her cell.

Chase threw his pen across the room, grabbed the keys to his pickup, and headed out. Paperwork would wait. There was always a backlog of paperwork no matter how much he worked on it. Finish one report and three more cropped up.

Dusty's emergency, no matter what it was, was more important.

# Twenty-six

"**W**ILL YOU INTRODUCE ME TO TITANIA and Oberon?" Juliet asked as she rocked to and fro. She fiddled with bits she'd torn from a silk flower and a needle and thread.

Chicory had to shake his head to break free of the hypnotic rhythm of her rocking and the flick of her needle. He took a sip of cooling tea from the doll-sized cup his new protector had set out for him. Scattered about the front parlor, his tribe nodded and drifted drowsily.

"Ms. Juliet, I'm afraid I can't do that," he said and stuffed a cookie crumb into his mouth so he wouldn't have to say anything more.

"They are real! I knew it. The Bard couldn't have drawn such wonderful verbal portraits of them if they weren't." Juliet stopped rocking, leaning forward to peer at Chicory over the tops of her glasses.

> "*I know a bank where the wild thyme blows,*
> *Where oxlips and the nodding violet grows*
> *Quite over-canopied with luscious woodbine,*
> *With sweet musk-roses, and with eglantine:*
> *There sleeps Titania some time of the night,*
> *Lull'd in these flowers with dances and delight;*
> *And there the snake throws her enamell'd skin*
> *Weed wide enough to wrap a fairy in.*'"

"You really should get trifocals, Ms Juliet. That way you

wouldn't have to adjust your glasses constantly." Chicory tried to change the subject.

"You're almost as good at diverting me as Benedict," Juliet said, returning to her rocking. She took a sip of her own milky tea. Her eyes crossed a little bit in contemplation.

Chicory stifled a yawn.

" 'Enjoy the honey-heavy dew of slumber.' That's from *Julius Caesar*," Juliet said. "No more honey for you in your tea."

Chicory shook himself awake. He knew he had obligations to Juliet in return for the freedom of her attic, but stars and storms above, didn't she realize that Pixies needed their naps? Especially this time of year.

"Why is it difficult for the king of a Pixie tribe to introduce his patron to the king and queen of Fairies?"

Chicory took another sip of tea. Some of the sugar and caffeine wiggled into his brain, waking him up. A little. A very little.

"Because Pixies and Faeries don't get along. They have their realms. We have ours. As long as we don't cross borders, everything is fine."

"William Shakespeare got it right, though, didn't he?"

"Mostly."

"Only mostly? What did he do wrong?"

"Faeries went underhill. They're cowards, refusing to share the world with unbelieving humans. Pixies stayed above ground and won over enough people to help us thrive. Lovely people like you. Faeries only come out when called, or to manipulate people and Pixies in their never-ending games. They think it's great fun to make us do dumb and ugly things, hurtful things to each other, like puppets on their magic strings." Anger at the current Faery king heated his blood and twisted his tummy into livid knots. The old guy, whoever he was, would rather kill and disrupt Pixies throughout the town so he could claim The Ten Acre Wood as home. No way would a Faery bother going to the trouble of finding a new home of his own. No, he had to steal The Ten Acre Wood. He'd build a new hill and destroy all that was sacred about the treasured place.

"We play tricks on humans, but only so they'll learn something—even if that is only to not take themselves so seriously. We *don't hurt* our friends. And we can only go underground to die. Takes a lot, I mean a whole lot, of magic for either race to survive in the other's realm." He shuddered with cold and dread, remembering how Snapdragon had so casually thrown him into Mabel's basement.

"Oh, well. Another time, perhaps. For now, here's a new cap for you." She held out a frothy blue thing. "See, I've worked a bit of gold thread into the top of it because you are a king."

Chicory's heart swelled almost to bursting with pride and gratitude. "Th-thank you, Ms. Juliet," he whispered around the lump in his throat. He bowed properly.

She slipped the cap of silk flower petals onto his head. It fit perfectly.

"May I look in the mirror?" he asked.

"Of course."

Joyfully, Chicory rose up and flew straight toward the big mirror stretched over the mantel. He turned this way and that to admire the new cap. "Oh, Ms. Juliet, it is perfect. Just perfect! I'm a proper king now."

"Of course you are, dear. The crown does not make a king, but a king makes a crown."

"What's that from?"

"I don't know." Juliet looked up startled. "Did I say something profound on my own? Without quoting the Bard? I didn't know anyone could do that."

Chicory suppressed a giggle.

"Mom? Are you home?" Dusty called from the kitchen.

"Do you need to disappear?" Juliet whispered to him.

"No, ma'am. Dusty knows all about Pixies. She and Thistle are best friends from long ago."

The sound of two sets of footsteps crossing the kitchen linoleum floor made both Chicory and Juliet sit up a little straighter. Chicory whistled to his tribe to wake up and get ready to hide.

Daisy flitted up toward the molding on the high ceiling then down to the double door opening between the parlor and the formal dining room and hung upside down, her dainty feet hooking over the ornate wooden frame that hid sliding doors. She loosed a quiet whee-oo whistle. "Caution."

Chicory took up his post on the corner of the coffee table but did not totally relax. His tribe took refuge in the velvet drapes and on the mantel, looking like cute porcelain statuettes.

"Experts at hiding in plain sight," Juliet said sotto voce. "No wonder you survived so long."

"Mom, I need your help," Dusty said from the doorway. Her gaze riveted upon Chicory. Then her eyes opened wide and her mouth formed a silent "oh." "You're not dead?"

Chicory barely heard her words. He flipped a jaunty wave as he peered over her shoulder at the scrawny girl who hovered in the dining room, eyes downcast but warily searching the room.

"Help with what, Desdemona?" Juliet asked. She, too, surveyed the newcomer with curiosity and wariness.

"Desdemona? How weird is that?" the girl sneered.

"Mom, Hope here is another stray that Dick picked up and dumped in my lap. She's cold, tired, and hungry, and I have to get back to work."

"Not so fast, Desdemona," Juliet said, holding up a hand to halt her daughter. "Explain, please."

"Sheesh, she doesn't want me any more than my stepfather." Hope turned on her heel and headed back the way she came.

Dusty snaked out a hand and caught her T-shirt. They all heard the fabric tear.

Hope's shoulders slumped in defeat.

"I didn't say that." Juliet rose from her rocking chair, set her cup and saucer on the table, and approached the girl cautiously. "I asked for more explanation. Now who are you and why are you one of Benedict's strays?" She threw her hands in the air in one of her dramatic poses. She really should have taken up the theater. "When and why Benedict graduated from wounded birds and battle-hardened feral cats to lost girls I'll never know. But I took in the animals he tamed, fed them, cleaned up after them, and grew to love them. I might even do the same for you. But you need to justify your place in my house first."

The girl looked up her. Something like respect flashed in her eyes before she dropped her gaze again and spotted Chicory.

Gulp. No sense trying to hide now.

"Dusty, are you here?" Chase came in through the back door—no one seemed to use the front—and across the kitchen to the dining room in direct line of sight with the entire tableau. "M'velle said you had an emergency . . ." He stopped short, seeing first Hope and then Chicory.

"Shit, this is a trap. You tricked me!" Hope rounded upon Dusty with accusations on her lips. "You lied to me. I said no police and you said fine. Now *he's* here." She looked as if she'd run right around Chase and out into the cold rain.

Time to earn his keep. Chicory flew up and over Dusty's head to settle into a hover directly in front of Hope's nose. "I'm the only one around here who gets to play tricks. These people may be weird, but they are honest."

Her eyes rolled up in her head, and she collapsed at Juliet's feet.

Dusty dropped to her knees to check the girl's neck pulse. A steady beat throbbed against her fingertips.

Chase crouched beside her. "What is going on here?" he whispered.

"I wish I knew," she replied.

Hope stirred and moaned. Her eyelids fluttered.

"Take it easy, Hope. I think the warm house after the outside chill, and an empty tummy were just too much for you."

"I'll make some more tea while you sort this all out," Mom said. "Chicory, perhaps you and your tribe had best come with me. We don't want to shock the girl any more than you already have." She casually stepped over the waif and retreated to the kitchen. A flurry of winged creatures followed her.

Dusty counted eight Pixies, led by Chicory's blue form.

"What's going on here, Dusty?" Chase asked again.

"I don't rightly know," she replied. "From the few things Hope said, I'm guessing that she's a runaway who's been living on the street rather than a reject from foster care. Dick found her at Mabel's."

"Mabel's house. Everything weird starts at Mabel's house." He eased his back against the doorjamb, stretching his long legs across the access to the parlor. As he rested his head against the jamb, he scrunched up his eyes in pain.

"Headache?" She shifted to gently rub his temple.

"Ah, that feels good." He leaned into her hand.

Dusty twisted around to rub both his temples. "What did the doctor say about your wound?" She figured she knew what he'd say. Stubborn male.

"Didn't stick around long enough to see him. The elementary school sent seven kids down with similar wounds to mine. Our old pal Snapdragon has expanded the war."

"Oh. Then why are you here?"

"Running away from the headache of the report I have to file in order to get a hearing so I can get my weapons and my badge back. Life was easier before I believed in Pixies."

"You lot are crazy, you know," Hope said quietly.

"Cheer up. It gets crazier the longer you stay," Dusty said on a giggle. "While I get the first aid kit, I suggest you check out the book of Shakespeare quotations in the bookshelf beside the fireplace. A lot easier and quicker than reading the complete works. It is wise when dealing with my mother to sprinkle at least some of the better known quotes through any conversation."

Two minutes later when she returned with wet washcloths smeared with soap, a bottle of antiseptic with gauze pads, bandages, and aspirin, she found Chase and Hope in mirrored poses, sitting on the floor, backs against the wall, and knees drawn up to their chests, clasped firmly in place with knotted hands.

She knelt beside Chase and jerked the sagging butterfly bandage away from the seeping wound. She didn't like the pinkish color of the fluid, but she supposed his body was doing its best to flush out any toxins from the hawthorn sword.

"I'm taking you back to the clinic," she announced.

He cringed away from the sting of the soap. "I've got too many things to do."

"It will give you an excuse to avoid that horrible report a little longer."

"Yeah, I suppose."

"And I'm staying with you until the doctor either clears you or sends you to the hospital."

"What about me?" Hope asked. Her chin sank deeper into the cleft between her knees.

"Mom may give you a headache, but she'll feed you, keep you warm, and protect you for a reasonable amount of time."

"What about the Pixies? Should I take my hallucinations seriously?"

"Life will be a lot easier around here if you do," Chase said. "I didn't believe either until I had the evidence thrust in my face a few months ago. Which reminds me — has anyone seen Thistle? I figure she'll have more answers than anyone."

"Thistle? Is that the gal Dick was looking for at Mabel's house?" Hope asked. Her eyes darted from side to side, avoiding making contact with either of them.

"Yes," Dusty answered. "I'm not sure what happened between them, but it must be bad if she's not here or at Mabel's."

"What about the people she helps? She's never missed a day checking on the old folks," Chase said.

"I'll have Mom call around. But this is looking bad."

"Don't tell me this Thistle person is a Pixie, too," Hope sighed.

"Not anymore," Chicory replied, flitting in from the kitchen. "Juliet says . . . she says to come and have some peanut butter and crackers. Dinner will be ready in an hour and 'Who rises from a banquet with the same appetite as when he sat down?' Or something like that." He whipped around, ready to return to the kitchen.

"Chicory, why aren't you dead?" Chase called after him.

"Who told you that?"

"Fellow named Dandelion."

"Which Dandelion? There are dozens of them in every tribe. Except mine. I haven't added any yet."

"I'm not sure, but he was following Snapdragon. I diverted him here. Wouldn't be surprised if he and his brothers are hiding in the back garden right now. But that doesn't answer my question. Why did he think you were dead?"

"We-ellll — "

"Spit it out," Dusty ordered.

"Snapdragon threw me into Mabel's basement, and everyone knows that underground is death to Pixies."

"So why aren't you dead?" Dusty asked, curiosity piqued.

"I am not hearing this conversation," Hope said, shaking her head. "I'm outta here." She rolled to her feet.

"Only as far as the kitchen, young lady!" Dusty ordered. "But I can guarantee the conversation in the kitchen is weirder."

Hope slid down to resume her place on the floor.

"Talk, Chicory," Chase said. "You talk a lot most of the time."

"Okay, okay, okay. I managed to crawl up the stairs. That got me above the worst of the death fumes. Then I slipped under the kitchen door and slept it off in one of the nesting boxes Mabel keeps around the house."

"Did Thistle see you? She'd have helped, you know," Dusty said.

Chicory blushed, that is if a blue Pixie could blush. His skin looked darker blue.

"She and Dick were making out, hot and heavy in the kitchen. I don't think she cared about me and my doom at that point."

"So whatever happened between Thistle and Dick took place today," Dusty mused. "He left the house whistling at eight this morning," she went on to explain. She was starting to worry about her best friend.

"That's very interesting, Chicory," Chase interrupted her thoughts. "So how'd you end up here? Inside. Entertaining my future mother-in-law?"

"It started to rain. I asked for refuge and she gave us the

attic. Now, if you don't mind, you all are wanted in the kitchen, and I need to see if the Dandelions are willing to join my tribe. I'm the new king, see, and it's my responsibility. And Daisy wants a mating flight." He flew out, darting up and down in a complicated spiral, sort of skipping with excitement.

Dusty wanted to rejoice with Chicory about how he'd run away from a bad situation and found a much better one. But all she could think about was how Thistle should be here to rejoice with him.

Chicory halted at the swinging door to the kitchen—now politely propped open for him—"Oh, and if you can't find a way to help the waif, there's a really old tradition that allows us to absorb her into Pixie. Only there are so many of them nowadays that we don't have enough magic left for all of them. Thistle should know how to do it since she's changed from one to the other."

# Twenty-seven

**P**HELMA JO SAT IN THE HARD, uncomfortable visitor's chair in Mabel Gardiner's hospital room. The old woman had been moved from critical care to a semiprivate room—though the bed closest to the door was unoccupied at the moment. Mabel reclined against the raised head of the bed, her knees propped up by the strange contortions of the mattress and frame. She wore a pretty pink quilted silk bed jacket and someone had combed her lank hair.

A single pink rose stood upright in a cheap milk glass vase, decorated with pink ribbons. Something about that lopsided rosebud bothered Phelma Jo. The shape was out of sync with everything, neither straight nor curved, just sort of lumpy without reason.

"We have a new runaway, Mabel. I can't handle this. I can't help you anymore."

"Tell me about the runaway. Where is she?"

"How'd you know it was a girl?"

"Just guessing. Girls give up the street life faster than the boys. It's only October. The boys will tough it out until the second frost. Usually late November." Mabel picked at the soft blanket covering her to the waist. Her gaze kept drifting to the rosebud.

"Is your gossip network still intact?" Phelma Jo asked. She, too, looked at the flower. If she tilted her head just so, and let her eyes cross a bit, the lump could almost be a tiny pink Pixie.

No. She refused to go there. The day had been too weird

already. She needed a heavy dose of normal. Sending run-aways and teens who'd fallen through the cracks of the foster care system on the road to safety was normal. Mabel, as head of the network of helpers, was normal. Hospitals were normal.

Pixies, like Haywood, or Snapdragon or whatever he called himself this week, or that pink lump, were definitely not normal.

"I still hear things. But I don't like what I hear, and I don't always trust the messengers." Mabel sighed and turned her attention back to Phelma Jo. "Tell me about the runaway. I've had Chase, and some others, looking for one girl in particular."

"I don't know much. Dick found her in your house, took her to his sister with orders to pass her along to their mother. I don't know if I trust Juliet Carrick . . ."

"Juliet's is a good place for a while. She's obsessive but not dangerous. She was a teacher before Dusty got sick, so she knows kids and won't put up with bullshit. Until we get the girl to open up and talk about her past, we'll let Juliet focus on her. We can't know where to send the girl until we know what she's running from. Juliet will make her talk to save her sanity. What's her name?"

"She calls herself Hope. I think she grabbed the name out of the air to avoid telling us who she really is. We can't track her past without her real name."

"If I had my computer and police database, I could start checking faces on the milk carton. Match her up with Child Missing reports. Or you could ask Chase to show you the MC poster. If it's the same girl, I know how to find . . . relatives."

"Are you going to be well enough to go back to work?" That was really why Phelma Jo had come. She needed to pass on her job of forging papers to someone. There was a guy in Portland who was pretty good. But he wasn't committed to the lost and abused children. The network needed someone who had been there and knew how desperately these teens needed a way out of the system.

But if Mabel no longer anchored the underground railway, who would? Phelma Jo couldn't. Shouldn't. Wouldn't.

"I don't know if I'll be able to work again, even part-time, or as a volunteer," Mabel said quietly. "The doctors are surprised I've recovered this much."

"Are they treating you well?" Phelma Jo quickly ran through a list of investments she might transfer for quick cash. I can set you up in a private facility with state of the art . . ."

"No. Save your money for the kids. I'll be all right. Just not what I used to be. I worry about my house and my garden. Is Thistle taking care of everything?" Her gaze wandered back to the rose.

Phelma Jo thought she heard a tiny sniffle. Was tough, pragmatic, ornery, and insightful Mabel crying?

"Thistle and Dick had a big fight this morning. She took off. As of an hour ago, Dick couldn't find her."

"Oh, dear. That is not good news." Mabel cocked her head, as if listening. "You really do need to match the runaway to the poster. Quickly."

*Thistle has gone back to Pixie.*

Had Phelma Jo really heard the rose talking?

She closed her eyes and fought a wave of disorientation. Heat flushed her face. At the same time her hands grew cold and clammy.

"I refuse to believe this," she said emphatically.

"Wake up, sweetie. You can't deny the evidence of your eyes much longer," Mabel chuckled. "There is trouble in Pixie right now. My Rosie has come to her senses. But the rest of them . . ." Mabel shrugged. "Thistle going back to Pixie may be the best thing right now. If she can't straighten them out, no one can. But we have to leave Pixie business to the Pixies. That's one of the rules. Get the girl talking so that we can find the best place for her. Don't move her from Juliet's, though. She really needs to be there. The entire Carrick family needs her there."

"Dick loves Thistle. He's really hurting right now." Phelma Jo stalled, thinking about Thistle being a Pixie. About any Pixies mucking up her town.

"He'll get over it. Dick always gets over his momentary fascinations with a woman."

"Not this time. This is the real thing for him," Phelma Jo admitted.

Just like she was aching in her mid-region because Ian had rejected her.

"If Thistle is gone, we need someone inside my house until I get home. Can't let that fussbudget nephew of mine tear it down for a few cracks in the foundation. Tell Dusty and Chase they can have the house now and not wait until they are married. That will at least get Dusty out of the way of her mother's obsessions."

"I can get an unbiased building inspection. Maybe we can fix the house, make it safe again, without tearing it down," Phelma Jo offered, wondering why she was so suddenly willing to take care of Mabel. She needed to take care of herself. Only herself. She'd spent a lifetime doing that, not caring about anyone who threatened her or got in her way on her convoluted path to financial security and independence.

*What about emotional security?* the tiny voice asked. *You need to love and be loved, just like the rest of the world.*

"No, I don't!" Phelma Jo pushed her chair back and rose. "I'll check back tomorrow with news about Hope."

"Phelma Jo," Mabel said softly.

"What?" she asked, cranky and bewildered and lonely.

"You've buried your past pretty deep. One of these days you are going to have to confront it in order to move on." Was that Mabel talking or the pink Pixie hiding in the rose?

Phelma Jo shook her head to free it of that fantasy. "What do you mean? Everyone in town knows my past."

"Yes, and you have fought hard to overcome it. That doesn't mean you've dealt with it," Mabel replied, still plucking at the blanket.

Phelma Jo turned on her heel and left the craziness that surrounded everyone she talked to lately.

Dick ran his hands through his hair and tiredly leaned his elbows on the steering wheel. "Where are you hiding, Thistle?" he asked the air.

No answer. Of course she didn't answer. Something had frightened her. Like any Pixie, she'd hide until she felt safe again.

What had done this to her? To them?

Snapdragon. But why?

One last house. He'd checked with all of the old folks Thistle visited twice a day to make sure they ate, took their medications, let the dogs out, had the heat or fans set at the right temperature. Sometimes she washed the dishes for them or cleaned up when they'd dropped things, or made messes of themselves. None of her elderly friends could continue to live alone without Thistle. The community paid her to do what came naturally to someone born in Pixie: to befriend those who needed them.

He dragged himself out of his car and up the walkway to Mrs. Spencer's front door. Mrs. Spencer had taught his fourth grade class. Most everyone in town had had her for a teacher at some point. Now in her eighties, the entire town had a vested interest in keeping her happy, healthy, and safe. She'd been Thistle's first client.

A white-muzzled mutt with floppy ears bounced against the front window beside the door. Horace barked enthusiastically to welcome him.

"Who needs a doorbell when you have a door dog?" He grinned and rang the bell.

"Yes?" asked a leggy brunette about his own age, wearing pressed designer jeans, a purple silk shirt, and a chunky necklace of gold and raw crystals about her neck. She opened the door as far as the security chain allowed. "Dick Carrick? Is that you?" She pushed the door closed just enough to release the chain, then flung it open again. In one deft movement she grabbed Horace's collar and pulled up the hooked latch of the screen door. "Come on in. What brings you here?"

"Hannah Fleming?" Dick had to search his memory for the name of the woman he'd dated occasionally over the years. How long since he'd dug out his little black book and called her?

Not since Thistle came back into his life. Maybe not for a couple of months before that.

"Of course I'm Hannah. It's only been six months since we went to that party to open the new wing at Mercy Hospital."

Dick walked past her into the small front room made smaller by an eclectic collection of chairs, tables, and sofas from half a dozen decades in the past. "Mrs. Spencer?" he asked rather than pursue his checkered past.

"My grandmother. She's in the back room napping. Do you need her for something special?"

"No, no, don't disturb her. I was just wondering what time Thistle checked on her this morning."

"Thistle? Oh, you mean the dark-haired girl. I don't know that she came at all today. The dishes were still dirty and the laundry not done when I got here about noon. I wondered at the time if she'd been keeping the schedule we pay her for."

Dick sniffed for any trace of Thistle's unique perfume. She always smelled like fresh flowers. This room smelled of closed air and damp dog. The damp dog plopped his butt onto Dick's shoe, wagging his tail expectantly. "What do you need, pup?" He bent to scratch the dog's ears.

"Hmf, he's hardly a pup. In dog years he's older than Nanna," Hannah said. "And he just went out, so he's just playing you for more attention."

"Is that so, Horace? Didn't Thistle let you out this morning?"

Horace whined.

Dick couldn't speak Dog as well as Thistle, but he got the distinct impression that Horace's ears swiveled forward at mention of Thistle. "I miss her, too." Dick crouched to Horace's level. "Where is she, boy?"

Horace whined plaintively.

"I guess she never made it here today," Dick sighed, standing again with one last ruffle of the dog's ears.

"You're worried about her, Dick," Hannah said. "That's a new one for you." She plopped down into one of the overstuffed chairs that almost swallowed her. She crossed her legs at the knee, twitching her foot like a cat flicks its tail in agitation. "Actually, I'm surprised you remembered my name. But then you dated me a total of six times since our junior year in high school. That makes me your longest and most regular relationship." More twitching of her foot.

"Don't remind me. I have a lot of past indiscretions to make up for. I guess I was just waiting for the right woman to come along. I haven't wanted to date anyone but Thistle since the day I met her. We're engaged, planning a Valentine's Day wedding." That should be long enough to get her paperwork in order.

If he could find her, talk to her, figure out what was going on.

Hannah raised her eyebrows. "Dick Carrick becoming faithful? Is hell freezing over?"

Dick cringed. "Yeah, well, we had a little disagreement, and now I can't find her to explain."

"I'm still in touch with Sandy Langford," she said out of the blue.

"Sandy?" That was the second time today—or was it the third—that Sandy's name had come up. Dick tried to picture a face to go with the name. All he came up with was the girl he'd found in Mabel's house. "What's she up to? I haven't seen her at any of the class reunions."

"She's a dental hygienist in Seattle. You should contact her."

"Why?" He wanted answers and wanted them now.

"Just do it. I think she needs to hear from you."

"Sorry. I've got enough on my plate right now. I have to find Thistle. Thanks for your time, Hannah, and please give my best wishes to your grandmother." He let himself out. Horace tried to follow him, but Hannah grabbed the dog's collar.

At the last second, Dick turned back. "If I can't find her, can I borrow Horace to track her?"

"Wow, you do have it bad, Dick. Yeah, you can borrow Horace if she hasn't come home by tomorrow. But call Sandy tonight. It's important."

As important as a missing daughter, perhaps?

"If Thistle doesn't come home by tomorrow, I'm reporting her missing to the police."

Which gave him a better idea. Chase knew how to trace

people who were lost or even those who didn't want to be found. Chase had access to bloodhounds trained to track people.

But those anonymous tracking dogs didn't love Thistle like Horace did.

# Twenty-eight

"CHASE, I'VE BEEN THINKING," Dusty said softly, holding his hand as they waited for a clinic doctor to see him.

"Is that dangerous thinking or just Dusty being the smartest person in town thinking?" He rested his head in his hands, elbows on knees.

She rubbed his temples some more, the only relief from his headache he seemed to get. The aspirin hadn't touched it.

"I'm thinking about Thistle and what happened between her and Dick.

Chase sat up. Dark circles ringed his eyes. He looked wounded. She wished the doctor would come soon and give him something for his pain.

"What about Thistle and Dick?" he asked.

"If he hasn't found her yet, maybe she went ... home."

"Is that possible?" Chase dropped his head again.

"I don't know. But I think I should take a look in The Ten Acre Wood when I go back to lock up the museum."

"Not alone, Dusty. Please don't go into a dark and abandoned forest after dark alone. I don't care how important the errand, the place isn't safe after dark."

"This is The Ten Acre Wood we're talking about. It's a city park. Every kid in town plays there. The haunted maze is nearly set up for All Hallows. There are dozens of people in and out."

"Not after dark. It may be a park, but only so we can protect it from developers. There are no streetlights, no po-

lice patrols. But there are a lot of places for vagrants and
petty criminals to hide. You're vulnerable. Promise me
you'll wait until daylight, or take Dick with you, or wait for
me." He grabbed her hand and squeezed tightly.

"That's a good idea. I'll take Dick with me. If Thistle is
there, she might listen to him."

"What if she can't come back?" he asked. "We don't
know how that . . . um . . ." he looked up at the receptionist
behind her glass partition. "We don't know anything about
this transfer of power thing. What if she's used up all her
ability to shift in going back?"

"I don't know. But I have to try. She's my friend and she's
hurting. My brother is hurting. I have to help them."

"So do I. She's the solution to all these. . . ." He pointed
to his still seeping wound.

Just then the nurse opened the door to the examination
rooms at the back of the building. "We're ready for you,
Chase. No more waiting."

"I've heard that one before," he muttered as he winced
and levered himself upright.

"I'll be right here when you're done," Dusty said. The
moment the door closed behind him, she whipped out her
cell phone and called her brother.

Thistle dropped onto a mushroom sticking out of a fir tree
trunk. The cream base with pale-green-and-rust swirls through
it looked familiar. She needed a bit of a nap. But it was so cold.
She wrapped her arms around herself and shivered.

Her fingertips brushed against the silky membrane of
her wings.

She froze in uncertainty. Wings. She'd grown her wings
again.

A hasty glance around, surveying the size of the trees,
the breadth of the sword ferns, and the cushiony platform
beneath her, sent new chills through her.

"I'm back in Pixie," she whispered. The sinking feeling of
watching Dick with his daughter, of their energy reaching
toward each other, drained all emotion from her. In her
blind, instinctive run from the truth, that Dick had always

loved Sandy Langford, had sired a daughter with her, leaving Thistle an inadequate stopgap, she must have shed her human form and her clothing. Now she had returned to her natural self.

And she was cold and alone. "No Pixie should sleep alone," she whispered. "I'm home. But is this really home?"

"And about time you showed up," Alder said, hovering in front of her. His leaf-shaped wings beat a rapid tattoo. He'd donned scraps of real leaves and bark to guard against the autumnal chill and dripping rain.

Thistle scooted back on her mushroom until her back rested against the rough bark, her wings spread out beside her.

"What? How?"

"If you don't know that you finally figured out who you are and where you belong, then you are in sad shape. You might not come out of it until spring. We're setting up a bower in a hollow log on the other side of the pond. A cat and a raccoon got into a fight last night and left plenty of fur behind to make it all nice and snug and warm for the winter," Alder said. He looked longingly at Thistle's mushroom. "May I join you?"

"No." She continued to shrink against the tree but made sure she was in the middle of the resting place with no room for him on either side.

"Thistle, this is me, Alder. Your friend and your king. You don't have to be afraid of me."

"I did last summer when you kicked me out of Pixie." A surge of anger warmed her a bit. But her teeth still wanted to chatter in uncertainty. No, make that out-and-out dread. She didn't want to be here.

But if she returned to her friends. . . .

Dick bonding with his daughter, with the ghost of his memories of the girl's mother standing beside them.

She didn't have the courage to go back to that.

Pixies avoided the complex emotions humans reveled in.

Faeries manipulated those emotions, then sat back in their safe home underhill and watched people hurt from the inside out until the pain engulfed their entire personality.

Pixies ignored the pain in favor of pranks that sometimes startled people back into proper laughter.

"Thistle, you've come back to me. That's what's important. You can trust me."

"No, I can't. You betrayed me. You betrayed your wife. You betrayed your tribe and left it vulnerable to this war with Snapdragon. I can't trust you. And I didn't come back to you."

"That's exactly what Milkweed says. But if you didn't come back to me, then why did you come back?" He flew a little circle around the tree, up and down, to stretch his wings. Hovering was hard work.

Thistle squirmed a bit, wondering if she was so very tired because she wasn't used to flying or if she just wanted to sleep away all her problems and wake up tomorrow morning with no worries or concerns.

Or memories.

"I'm surprised you are still king, Alder."

"There is no one else the tribe trusts. Except maybe you. And I don't know why that is. You aren't even a real Pixie anymore, just another human refugee running away from life. I thought we'd stopped taking those people in."

He shrugged his shoulders and flitted off toward the pond and the center of The Ten Acre Wood.

A spatter of raindrops followed his path across the open clearing.

Thistle huddled closer to her tree trunk. She needed to find shelter. That hollow log lined in cat-and-raccoon fur, with the warmth and companionship of a dozen other Pixies sounded good.

"I'll find my own bower. Someplace Alder won't dare invade. He may be king of the tribe. But he's not *my* king. Not anymore. And he's not a proper king or Pixie because he doesn't have any music." She dropped down to ground level and began her search for sanctuary. A cold and lonely sanctuary without Dick to hold her close.

"Thistle!" Dick called into the deep shadows of The Ten Acre Wood. From the glow of the nearest streetlight he made out the rounded shapes of sword ferns and the tall spikes of foxglove gone to seed. Beyond that, he caught vague suggestions of towering fir trees, spindly alders, and an occasional bushy maple, or maybe they were cotton-woods. He didn't know.

"Thistle, please come home," Dusty pleaded from beside him.

They both took a cautious step forward, keeping their flashlights pointed low to show the way, and to keep the glow from blinding them to small movements above ground level. Bracken ferns brushed against their legs. Dick stepped on a dry stick that cracked loudly. Dusty jumped at the sudden noise, so like the report of a gun.

Dick wrapped an arm around her shoulders. "It's been a long day for both of us," he whispered. "We'll go home soon. But we have to try this."

"Yes, we do. I'm okay. Just jumpy. And I think I need to stay with Chase tonight. He's not well. Stripped of his gun and badge, he's as alone in the wilderness as Thistle."

Dick nodded sharply. "I'm not the one to judge you. Let's just hope Mom is so engaged with . . . with the girl she doesn't notice you're missing." What if Hope truly was Sandy Langford's daughter? What if the girl had sought him out for a reason; sought *him*, not shelter at Mabel's.

"There's the Hanging Tree Judge Pepperidge set up for the maze." Dusty flicked her light at the sturdy maple with a noose dangling from a branch ten feet up.

"Look! Did you see that?" He followed a flicker of movement along the tops of the ferns. For just a second, he thought he saw a glimmer of purple reflecting the street-light and the last of the dying sun.

"Yes. We have to follow her." Dusty broke away from the safety of the path. She tromped through the ground cover, heedless of blackberry vines snagging her jeans and cedar boughs slapping her face. Dick followed her toward the cliff on the west edge of the woods. A fifty-foot drop to down-town Skene Falls.

"Careful." Dick grabbed her hand and hauled her back. The encroaching darkness shifted his perceptions. How far away was the cliff? He heard the rush of water where the pond drained into a creek and spilled over the edge. Eons of drainage had eaten away at the volcanic rock making an inward curve in the wandering cliff.

Dusty shone the weak beam of her flashlight in the direction they'd seen the flicker of movement.

"That thing is so old it's barely bright enough to show your next step." He pointed his own flashlight higher; it illuminated a broad swath of the forest.

Another flicker with a hint of lavender just at the perimeter of the light.

"Thistle, please come back," Dusty called. "You're my friend. You can trust me."

The movement hovered for a few seconds.

"Thistle, I need you," Dick added his own plea. "I never meant to hurt you. Whatever I've done, I apologize. We can talk about this. Help me understand what's wrong, please."

Dick held himself as still as possible, waiting, hoping his words penetrated through the walls of distrust between human and Pixie.

"I love you, Thistle. Only you."

Another flicker in the light. He thought he saw something tiny move hesitantly toward them. It wound and braided a trail around the path of light, never encroaching close enough to do more than confirm to his eye that something was out there and moving closer.

His chest ached until he released his breath and drew it back in.

"Thistle, as your friend, I beg you, come home to us," Dusty whispered, repeating her litany of friendship. Nothing was more sacred to a Pixie than friendship.

Dick didn't dare speak again. If he did, he might start crying and he wouldn't be able to stop until he held his beloved in his arms once more.

A faint giggle drifted through the air like tiny chimes singing to the wind. *Dum dee dee do dum dum.*

Thistle's song.

*Soon.*

Dick risked a little smile. "I love you," he whispered. Maybe he only thought the words. He wasn't sure.

The flicker of lavender and green took on definition,

green wings in the shape of double thistle leaves, a pouf of dark purple hair, and a tiny figure, paler than the rest of her. Something gauzy draped about her body and trailed behind her.

*Thistle, my love.* Dick didn't know if he said the words out loud or not. The pounding of his heart in his ears drowned out all other sound.

Another lovely little giggle and a twist of Dusty's curls lifted in the air.

Dusty raised her hand to touch her hair. The Pixie shot up to the tree canopy.

"Thistle, come back!" he called.

"Idiot," Dusty said with disgust. "She has something important to do first. She said she'd come back soon."

"What could be more important than us being together?"

"The safety of her people. Freedom from Faery manipulation. Protection of this sanctuary from both humans acting under manipulation and Faeries doing the manipulating. Maybe if you thought like a Pixie and tried to stop construction of the discount store on top of a Faery hill, or found another hill for them that isn't in The Ten Acre Wood, she'd come back to you sooner."

She stamped her foot and stalked back toward the lights around her museum.

"She must honor you as a friend, Dusty. She played a trick on you."

"But she has work to do. Help her do that if you truly love her."

# Twenty-nine

"CAN I HAVE A LITTLE PRIVACY HERE?" Hope spat at Chicory. She looked away from him into the flame of a candle lantern atop the chest of drawers beside the doorway. The flame, protected by a glass chimney, held her attention longer than anything else had all day.

Chicory back-winged until he could perch on the desktop two feet from where the girl stood in the middle of the turret attic. A single bed, with drawers beneath it snugged under one window. A cedar chest became a window seat under another. The third window at the center was really a door that led to a tiny landing. The door to the spiral staircase had long since sagged off its hinges and been moved to somewhere else in the house.

She hadn't bothered to turn on the overhead light, content with the softer glow of the candle.

"I notice you chose this out-of-the-way cubby with windows on three sides with no curtains. You could have had the guest room that has only one small window covered in thick drapes and shades. I'd say you're more interested in the view than privacy." Chicory smirked at her.

"There's privacy and then there's privacy." Hope dropped onto the chest, propped her elbow on the windowsill, and stared out at the night. The candle reflected in the glass looked as if it was a comforting presence right beside her. Streetlights illuminated the neighborhood in dim yellow puddles of light. Thick, old trees shaded large portions of the sidewalks and yards. The moon tried to shine through the thinning clouds but couldn't yet compete with the electric lights. Tomorrow would be clear and frosty, though. Respectable Pixies needed to be indoors, or within a snug bower by now.

The kind of night when predators stalked and cats ruled.

Chicory crossed his knees and hugged himself tight. He'd made the right decision to seek refuge inside for the winter. Even though that refuge came with the obligation to drink tea with his hostess and stay up long past his bedtime. He suppressed a yawn.

"Why'd you run away?" he asked

"None of your business."

"If you can't tell me, an imaginary Pixie, then who are you going to tell?"

"I thought Mrs. Carrick said that the highest calling of a Pixie is to befriend those who need a friend most. Friends don't pry." She flipped around to face the other direction, out of direct line of sight with Chicory.

He flitted over to the adjacent windowsill. She didn't have to look directly at him, but he was close enough to read her expressions.

"Eventually, you're going to have to tell someone where you came from and why you ran away. That's one of the rules Mabel set up. We can't help you unless you talk." He mimicked her pose, elbow on knee, hand on chin, gaze on the view outside.

A freshening wind pushed a tree branch against the windowpane. It rattled like it wanted in, along with the night predators.

Hope jumped back, startled.

"It's cold out there tonight. And going to get worse as we head into winter. Stars and storms above, I'm glad I don't have to worry about staying out of the weather and finding a hollow log that will keep me dry. Even then, logs have a tendency to leak. I hear cardboard shacks underneath bridges aren't much better," Chicory continued casually.

"It's not my fault," Hope insisted. "Mom and I were doing just fine by ourselves. Then she had to fall in love and get married. Everything changed. She didn't need me anymore, and *he* didn't want me in the first place. I hope they're happy." Hope shooed him off the windowsill and threw herself down on the narrow bed.

She couldn't hide the trembling of her limbs. Or her chin.

"That's a start, Hope. We'll talk more tomorrow. Or you can talk to Juliet. She won't judge you. She's one of the good guys."

"I've heard that before." She turned toward the wall and pulled up the quilt, still fully clothed with her shoes on and her backpack between her and the wall, as if she needed to protect her few belongings from theft or to be prepared to run at a moment's notice.

"You'll be more comfortable if you put on the nightie Juliet loaned you, and brush your teeth."

"Go away. I'm asleep."

"Not yet, but you will be. When you wake in the morning, all warm and safe, maybe then you'll talk."

"Go away." She turned her face to the wall, eyes clenched shut.

Chicory giggled a bit and hummed his song: *Dum dum do do dee dee dum.*

Hope breathed a little easier.

He set his wings to a softer rhythm on a count of three. *Dum du-um, do do dee, dee du-um.* A nice song, that. He drifted with the music, until he almost fell asleep in mid-flight. He blew out the candle and slowly retreated down the spiral staircase to the second floor of the house and the enclosed staircase up to his own section of the attic.

Refugees. He had to remind himself that this might feel like home already to him, but he and Hope were both refugees. Refugees running away from one home to something better. She hadn't accepted the concept of home yet. Until she did, she'd keep running and never find more than temporary sanctuaries.

Hesitantly, Dusty knocked on the door to Chase's apartment. The time had come to make her own decisions and stop hiding what she truly wanted behind her shyness.

"Who's there?" he mumbled around a yawn.

She sensed a shadow behind the spy hole as he peered out.

"Dusty? What are you doing here? What's wrong?"

It took all of her courage to remain there and wait for him to undo deadbolts and security chains. Then he yanked the door open and gathered her into his arms, holding on to her as if his life depended on keeping her close.

"What's wrong?" he asked again.

She ran a glance over him, noting sleep-heavy eyes, jeans hastily donned, bare feet and chest, and tousled blond hair. "Nothing is wrong with me," she whispered into his chest, letting the fine hairs tickle her cheek. His warmth after the chill night in The Ten Acre Wood, his presence after witnessing Dick's loneliness, and her love for him banished her anxiety and fear. "I . . . I came to check on you. To stay with you. You shouldn't be alone right now."

His hands clenched onto her arms as he closed his eyes and gritted his teeth. "I'm okay. Woozy from the pain pills, still sore around the six stitches, depressed that I have that monster report to complete before I can go back to work, but my eyes are crossing and I can't concentrate. Other than that, I'm okay. You don't have to stay. I know you wanted to wait . . . But, God, it's hard to let you go."

"Then don't let go." She shuffled her feet, manipulating them backward into the apartment without letting go.

"Do you know what this means?"

"Yes." She stood on tiptoe and brushed her lips across his. "But if you need sleep more than sex, I understand. I'm prepared to sleep in the recliner. But I need to watch over you as much as you need not to be alone."

"I've felt so alone and lost. When I watched you fall after I fired my weapon, my heart nearly stopped with fear that I'd hurt you. I feel so guilty. I might have killed you." He buried his face in her neck.

"You didn't hurt anyone. You did your job trying to protect historical treasures that are really only piles of rotting lumber and not worth the trouble of housing."

"That doesn't change the fact that I fired my weapon at civilians."

"Hush, my love. I know. Neither one of us has to be

alone or lost anymore. Or if we are lost, we'll be lost together." She kicked the door closed. "As long as I have you, I can even put up with my mother's wedding plans. Our marriage is more important than her dream wedding."

Thistle shivered in the dawn light. Carefully she peeked out from beneath the leaf litter where she'd made her bed. "This will not do. I have to find a better place."

Would nesting with the rest of the tribe be any better? Less lonely, and warmer certainly. But she'd have to put up with Alder.

Time to do something about that. She'd learned a few things last night when Dick and Dusty came to find her. But she hadn't grown big again. There was something she had to do as a Pixie before she *could* go back.

She quenched her thirst on some raindrops caught in the cup of a lingering foxglove blossom. She even found a few grains of pollen left inside, overlooked by hummingbirds and Pixies alike.

A little closer to the wetlands around the pond she found a salal berry, translucent red, fully ripe, and delicious. Enough to feed her for the entire day.

The carefree life of a Pixie filled her with a hint of joy. If it weren't so cold. But her mind kept whirling. She needed to do something about Alder. She needed to stop Snapdragon from bringing war to the tribes. She needed to send Milkweed home or make her flatten her wings for Alder.

That was something she could do before winter sleep overtook her. Hmmm, if she could get into the museum, Dusty would let her hide in the basket filled with yarn balls beside the electric fire in the upstairs parlor.

But first things first. Milkweed had to make a decision. Or have one made for her. Thistle knew how to get the poufy white-and-gold Pixie moving.

She whistled up her friend, the varied thrush. Unlike their cousins the robins, these brightly striped yellow-and-black birds hung around for the winter. The lady bird took a perch in a vine leaf maple at the edge of the clearing. The bright orange-and-yellow leaves made her look dull and drab, unnoticeable to any cats lurking below the scrubby little tree.

Thistle smiled and stroked the bird's soft neck feathers. "Why don't you have a name?" she whispered.

The bird cocked her head and chirruped something about not needing a name.

True conversation didn't work with birds. They'd earned the insult "birdbrained." This one understood Thistle well enough and made her needs known. Other than that, they exchanged meaningless coos and shifts of body to indicate wants and approvals.

Thistle continued stroking the bird as she whispered her plan.

The bird trilled her agreement.

Thistle smiled and flitted off to find her tribe. A wisp of white tipped with gold wandering between the Patriarch Oak and the mist above the waterfall showed her precisely where the sort-of-queen of the tribe spent her morning. Only an idiot bathed in the frigid air when she should be looking to add more clothing to keep her warm and dry.

Milkweed shook herself dry and looked around. Morning sunlight slanting through the trees turned the mist into arcing rainbows. The delicate prisms caught in a perfectly symmetrical spiderweb strung between two slender alder trees. A big, spotted brown garden spider crouched in the middle, waiting to pounce on the first bug—or Pixie—to fall within the trap of the web.

Milkweed dove head first toward the web, wings tucked back, billowing white hair streaking behind her. Nothing but the best silk for that queen, Thistle mused.

She back-winged and watched the spider scuttle up the support strand as the Pixie stole her home out from under her.

Milkweed laughed as she draped the strands over her shoulders, and around her wing base. The individual threads twined together, looping and sticking in all the right places to form an elegant gown that trailed behind her.

It reminded Thistle of the beautiful wedding gown in the store window that Dusty so admired.

Thistle shook off the reminder. She didn't want Milkweed appearing the least bit bridal. She wanted her gone. For the health of the tribe, Milkweed had to go.

A bit of breeze pushed spray from the waterfall over Milkweed. Water droplets caught on the gossamer gown. A stray shaft of sunlight made them sparkle like the diamonds in Thistle's ring. She stared at the gems a moment in wonder. Why hadn't she lost it when she shrank to Pixie size? It should have stayed big and fallen off her finger. It should have abandoned her.

Instead, it reminded her quite painfully that a piece of her heart remained in the human world, a bit of her humanity glared at her.

She tugged at the gold band. It stuck on her slender finger, bonding with her skin, refusing to even turn.

"Oh, Dick, I will never be free of you and my love for you." The import of Dick coming to look for her hit her. The ring carried Dick's promise to love her forever. She'd accepted that promise along with the ring. Even if she remained a Pixie, Dick would still love her. Above all others. He'd sought her out, not gone running to the mother of his child.

A flutter of movement brought her attention back to Milkweed. Thistle shook her head to clear her mind of bright images and memories of Dick holding her hand, kissing her, making her feel complete, cherished, no longer lonely. Her gaze fixed upon Alder hovering in front of his queen.

"Fly with me, Milky," he whispered, reaching his arms around her in a tight embrace.

Milkweed laughed, high and shrill. "Thistle came back. You'll be flying with her half a day after I flatten my wings for you. Think again."

Before Thistle could shout a protest, the sunlight caught Alder's aura. Bright red-and-orange flames spiked through his life energy.

"Fire!" Thistle gasped. "He's not fully a Pixie. Fire repulses us. That is a Faery element. We are the stuff of Earth and Water."

That explained a lot. But it also raised more questions.

# Thirty

D USTY HUMMED CONTENTEDLY as she counted out the cash in the register drawer. The number of bills and coins matched the list perfectly. In the locked cubbyhole beneath the counter she found the bank deposit from yesterday's receipts properly itemized and ready to go. She sighed and smiled inwardly. Meggie and M'Velle had done their jobs well.

Everything was right with the day. Chase was back at his desk diligently writing the lengthy report explaining why and how he'd fired his weapon. Her mother had cast an accusatory glance at her when she went home to shower and change early this morning, but miracle of miracles, she'd said nothing about being out all night.

Pixies scattered about the kitchen probably helped. And so did having a new obsession: Hope.

Thistle was still missing, and Dick hadn't made an appearance yet. Dusty was almost glad she didn't have to confront her brother and Hope together about the Missing Child poster Chase had shown her. That was something they needed to work out on their own.

Dusty wasn't going to let any of that bother her today. She and Chase loved each other. Truly and completely. That was all that was important.

In the back of her mind she made a list of essentials she could leave at Chase's apartment tonight . . .

The bells above the front door of the little house that acted as a gift shop and ticket sales, as well as an interesting part of the county history, jingled sweetly. She looked up to

find M'Velle yawning in the doorway. She wore a professional looking wool plaid skirt, blouse, and boat neck
sweater.

"You're here early," Dusty said.

"Parent-teacher conferences. No school. I figured you'd
need some help with the decorations and stuff for the flashlight tours this weekend." She yawned again, shaking her
head as if to clear it of morning cobwebs. The beads in her
tightly braided black hair clanked together, adding a new
layer of life music to the little door bells.

"Did I ever tell you how much I appreciate you and
Meggie, and how well you do your jobs?" Dusty came
around the counter and hugged the taller girl.

"Sometimes. And I really appreciate the glowing recom-
mendation you gave me for my college app." M'Velle
hugged her back.

"And you do know that if you ever have a problem, get
into trouble, or fight with your folks that you can come talk
to me. You don't have to run away." A niggle of uncertainty
crept into Dusty's voice.

"Of course. We're friends." M'Velle frowned. "Though
there was a time in middle school when I was almost ready
to hit the road and seek my fortune away from this town
and the bullies that hung around the convenience store
across from the school."

"I'm surprised Mr. Tyler didn't run them off."

"Sergeant Norton did that. He was the first adult to tell
me that black skin is as beautiful as white, and that I was
smart enough not to let stupid high school dropouts intimidate me. You started tutoring me about the same time, and
I figured out that you both were telling me I can do anything if I only try."

"And study hard to get the best education you can,"
Dusty added.

"Yeah, that, too." M'Velle stepped aside. "Mind if I get a
cup of coffee in the lounge?"

"Sure, go ahead. I have a few things to do here: restock
some books and candy, fill the bird feeders in the park. I'll
let you finish up the decorations here while I work on
stringing cobwebs in the downstairs parlor."

"Um . . . what brought on the effusive emotional display, if you don't mind me asking?"

"That girl, Hope." And Chase, but M'Velle didn't need to know that.

"The runaway," M'Velle said flatly. "She's not talking yet?"

"Nope."

"Want me to give it a try?" M'Velle didn't look too happy at the prospect.

"Let's give my mother a while longer. I'm just having trouble wrapping my mind around the concept of finding life at home so intolerable she needed to run away."

"And yet you did the same thing, hiding in the basement for so many years."

"That's different."

"Is it?" M'Velle left without waiting for an answer.

Dusty had to stop and think. She still wanted to play with artifacts and documents down in the basement rather than confront the people who scared her. Her heart raced, and she broke out in a cold sweat at the thought of giving tours or speaking up in town meetings. But she did it. Chase and Thistle had helped her find the confidence to stop running away from reality. With Chase by her side, reality might not be so bad after all.

Why should she worry how other people judged her when Chase approved of her in so many wonderful ways?

The bell jangled again. Harsher this time. Dusty pulled herself out of her thoughts. She looked up, expecting M'Velle.

Phelma Jo stood in the doorway, feet planted, arms straight at her sides, chin thrust out belligerently.

"What's wrong?" Dusty asked. Her mind raced through a dozen horrors that might bring Phelma Jo to her doorstep this early.

"Nothing is wrong. What makes you say that?" Phelma Jo relaxed her clenched fists and stiff neck enough to look around the tiny gift shop.

"You just looked terribly angry or unhappy. I was sure you had bad news." Dusty fiddled with a stack of chapbooks and pamphlets she needed to put on the spinning display, proud that she had written two of the short books about local history and points of interest.

"Well, I guess it might be bad news. Mayor Seth told me to tell you there's a town meeting in City Hall at noon to discuss the recent attacks by rabid birds or something. We may have to cancel the All Hallows Festival."

"Birds don't carry rabies. They carry West Nile or the bird flu virus."

"Whatever."

"Have there been more attacks?" Dusty asked anxiously. She bit her lip, remembering the six stitches on Chase's temple and the migraine that left him almost blind. She didn't want to think about the seven children who'd ended up at the clinic yesterday.

The basement sounded so very inviting.

She firmed her shoulders and chin, determined to face this.

"A teacher and two boys walking to school this morning got stabbed. The teacher may lose an eye. The boys should be okay, but they'll have scars," Phelma Jo said. For the first time in a long time she looked a little lost, vulnerable.

"This is bad."

"Yeah," Phelma Jo replied. "A bunch of parents are refusing to allow their kids outside on the playground, or to walk to school. And they certainly aren't going to let them go trick-or-treating next Tuesday. The whole town is going to lose a big bunch of money if we cancel the parade on Saturday and the haunted maze in The Ten Acre Wood."

"Thank you for stopping by, Phelma Jo. Tell Mayor Seth that I'll be there. Perhaps if we have to cancel outdoor activities we can move some of them to the high school gym."

"Whatever." The familiar, forthright, and always angry Phelma Jo returned. "Draw up some plans and bring them. Oh, and take down all the bird feeders. They attract potentially dangerous birds." She slammed the door as she left. The bells lost all sense of musicality.

"Pixies eat the millet more than the birds do," Dusty protested to an empty room. "And birds aren't the problem. Rogue Pixies are." She desperately hoped that Thistle found a solution soon.

Phelma Jo looked around the crowded Council room in
City Hall. She counted three, no four, camera crews from
the local affiliate news programs, including Bill Tremaine,
the senior and most respected of all the anchormen. More
news people sat in the front row on either side of Tommy
"Digger" Ledbetter from the Skene Falls *Post*—identifiable
by their open notepads and huge cameras. Only a few of the
one hundred folding chairs were left unoccupied. Twenty-
some people stood against the marble walls. Angry frowns
and worried brows dominated the room.

She frowned, too, for a different reason. She pushed her
way through the crowd, not caring how many toes she
stepped on, or whose ribs she elbowed.

"Mind if I sit here?" she asked Dusty, nodding toward
the empty seat beside her.

"I was kind of saving it for Chase." Dusty left her purse
on the aisle seat.

"If he's this late, he deserves to stand." Phelma Jo picked
up Dusty's dainty little purse and deposited it in her lap.
Then she sat, smoothing her slacks to keep the crease clean
and crisp and even.

"There's an empty chair over there." Dusty pointed to
the opposite side of the room. "I've never known you to
pass up an opportunity to flirt with a handsome man."

Phelma Jo deliberately refrained from looking at the tall
red-haired man who kept his eyes on the dais, waiting for
Mayor Seth and the City Council to emerge from the back
room. "I prefer not to sit next to, or converse with *that*
handsome man." She couldn't help but look at his profile,
though. The spray of freckles across his nose softened the
strong lines of his jaw and drew attention away from his
slightly protuberant ears.

Dusty raised her eyebrows in question.

"That's Ian McEwen, Mabel's nephew. The one who
wants to tear down the house you and Chase are about to
inherit," Phelma Jo whispered.

"I've been wanting to meet him. I need to explain some
things about Mabel. She really needs her family right now."

"She needs to know that you and Chase will respect her wishes," Phelma Jo returned. "The property needs protection. For a variety of reasons. Preservation of a historical house and grounds is only part of it."

Just then the door to the back room opened and City Councilman George Pepperidge strode out alone. Solemnly, he took the chair to the right of center on the dais. With great ceremony he lifted the gavel in front of the mayor's seat and rapped the table twice.

The room quieted instantly.

"Ladies and gentlemen, most of you know that I'm running for mayor next month, unopposed," Councilman Pepperidge began.

Phelma Jo's face burned. She'd planned to run against George in the election, until the scandal of Haywood Wheatland and the fire in The Ten Acre Wood had terminated her plans.

Postponed, not terminated, she reminded herself.

Dusty's hand covered her own and squeezed lightly in mute sympathy.

Phelma Jo held her breath. This was what it had felt like when Dusty was her friend back in grade school. Before the awful incident of name-calling and flying fists.

Then Dusty withdrew her comforting touch before Phelma Jo could reject it. Confusion warred with her anger and embarrassment.

"Mayor Seth is not well today. His latest stroke preys upon his strength. So I called this emergency meeting and will preside over the discussion," George continued.

"What are we doing about those rabid birds?" a man called from the center of the room.

Front and center, Digger scribbled notes. Five cameras around him flashed.

"It's not safe to walk outside anymore. Our kids are in danger," a woman yelled from the back of the room.

The room erupted in sound. The cameras, single shot and video, caught it all.

"We are working with animal control and the medical community on that," George held up his hand for order.

"What about the parade day after tomorrow? Are you

canceling that?" Digger asked. He snapped a picture with his enormous camera at the same time.

"The full City Council will make that decision later today when we've had a chance to talk to the authorities."

"Why wait?" the first man asked. "I'm not letting my kids attend. And I'm taking them out of school until this town is safe again."

"We need to get lab results from the blood samples taken from the victims," George continued. "We need to know what disease we are dealing with and which animals or birds are responsible."

"Well, I'm taking my shotgun to anything that flies through my yard or lands on a bird feeder anywhere in town," the woman sitting right in front of Phelma Jo yelled. Only she was standing now and shaking her fist.

George pounded his gavel several times to no avail. Everyone in the room had something to say and wanted to say it right now.

George pounded his gavel hard. "People, stop and think a moment. We have to look at alternatives. Safe alternatives."

"The only alternative is to kill every murdering bird in the county!"

"This town has a lot of tradition and money invested in the All Hallows Festival." George spoke above the unruly shouters.

*Good for him*, Phelma Jo thought. She was learning a lot about leadership here. Research for when she considered herself ready to take the reins and control this town.

"We on the City Council hoped to use profits from this year's festival to fund the clinic another year. Think about what we lose if the clinic closes January first when state funds run out. Just today, Ms. DuBois, our kindergarten teacher, will have some vision impairment, *but not lose her eye,* because of the prompt response of our EMTs and the close proximity of the clinic. If she'd had to be transported to Portland, even by helicopter, treatment would have been too late."

"That's good news," Dusty whispered. "I wonder why Dick didn't answer the emergency call. It's not like him to sleep through or refuse a call."

"Probably still mooning over his lost Thistle." Phelma Jo shrugged.

"Think about how much money our downtown merchants need to make this next week just to stay in business in these hard economic times," George continued. "Now I called this meeting to hear some alternatives, not blind panic."

"The only alternative is to cancel everything until we kill all those damn birds!"

Dusty pulled a sheaf of papers from the leather satchel at her feet. Her fists clenched so tight she almost tore the documents. "Where's Chase?" she asked Phelma Jo. As if Phelma Jo should know. "He promised to help with this."

"Get over yourself, Dusty, and just read the papers. Sometimes you take this shyness and vulnerability too far."

Jerkily, Dusty raised her hand in mute request to be recognized by the chair. As she should. As they all should.

"Yes, Ms. Carrick?" George said with a huge sigh of relief.

Dusty stood up, holding her papers in shaking hands. "I contacted the Audubon Society. They said that since all of the reported attacks have taken place during daylight hours we need not cancel the Haunted Maze after sunset. The likelihood of a diurnal bird continuing to attack after dark . . ."

"What's a diurnal bird? One that craps twice a day?" the woman in front of Phelma Jo sneered.

A ripple of muffled laughter went around the room.

"Oh, shut up and listen to someone who's smarter than you, Jessica Marley," Phelma Jo ordered. "Dusty may bore us to death with historical trivia, but when have any of you known her to be *wrong*? So listen to her. She's got plans that can make the best of a bad situation and save the Festival."

Across the room Ian McEwen started a round of applause. He nodded to Phelma Jo in approval.

Why did that make the whole day seem better, brighter, and worth fighting for?

# Thirty-one

CHASE WATCHED HELPLESSLY as the townsfolk at the meeting swarmed over Dusty. He quickly lost sight of her diminutive form among the mass of humanity. On the dais, George Pepperidge banged his gavel helplessly for order.

If Chase had been in uniform, he'd have a whistle. Damned regulations kept him out of uniform and off the street. Not knowing what else to do, Chase put two fingers into his mouth and blew. The shrill sound cut through the noise.

"Give the lady room to breathe, and we'll all get our questions answered," he called. A few bodies moved backward, enough to let him see the top of Dusty's head.

Resolutely, he stalked forward, elbowing people out of the way until he stood next to his fiancée. She looked up at him, bewildered and grateful and near panicked. "You okay?" he asked quietly.

"Better now that you're here." Her breathing sounded ragged, and sweat dotted her brow.

"How am I going to fit my whole diorama into the high school gym? I need three flatbed trucks," someone asked from the other side of Dusty. Two other people pressed against Chase's back.

"I said breathing room!" Without waiting for a reaction, he scooped Dusty up and sat her on the Council table facing the room. George Pepperidge peeked around her, still pounding his gavel.

"Chase, I . . ."

"Just close your eyes and visualize a white board with all your committees listed and tasks assigned to each. Draw arrows in your mind connecting things," he said quietly.

"I need a board . . ."

"No, you don't," Phelma Jo snorted. "You're the smartest person in the room. You can keep all of it in your head and still have space for historical anecdotes and Shakespearean quotes. Stop thinking about what you can't do and do it!"

Chase nodded slightly in her direction. She tossed him a grimace, complete with rolled eyes, and flounced back to a chair in the center of the first row. Slowly the crowd joined her, putting a bit of order into the unruly group.

"Who has the phone number of the school board chair?" Dusty asked quietly.

"I do," Digger Ledbetter said, pulling out his cell phone.

She closed her eyes. Chase watched her eyelids twitch as if in REM sleep, or reading the virtual white board printed on the inside.

"Digger, please call and politely request the use of the gym and the auditorium all day Saturday for our static parade. We'll discuss fees later when we have time."

"I'll get him to waive the fees." George Pepperidge held out his hand for Digger's phone to complete that chore.

"Reverend Tilbury," Dusty continued, eyes still closed. Damn, she remembered everyone in the room. "Is the basement of the Episcopal Church available for the craft fair? You're right next to the school, so visitors can visit both without moving their cars from the downtown plaza to the high school. I'm sure we can arrange some kind of donation . . ."

"Any rental fees will be donated to the clinic fund," the pastor said. "I'll make sure the basement is available. The kitchen, too."

"Impressive," George said to Chase.

"Yes, she is. When we break through the habits of shyness. She combines her mother's talent for organization with her own subtle, but diplomatically correct vulnerability, which makes people want to help."

"No, I meant you, Sergeant Norton."

"Huh?"

"You saw what needed to be done and did it. And you did it correctly because you know the people of this town and what is right for them."

"Part of my job. Which I can't do right now because of the administrative leave thing."

"What would you say if I appointed you to the vacancy on the City Council that will occur when I move from this seat to the mayor's place?"

"I'd say there are better candidates. I'm not ready."

"What other candidates?"

Chase looked around the room where most of the town's movers and shakers had gathered. "Digger Ledbetter. But he'll probably turn you down. He prefers digging news out of the murk of city life. Phelma Jo comes to mind."

"Hmphf," George snorted. "She'll run against me in four years."

"She'll run against you in four years anyway. Why not learn to work with her and let her learn that running a town is hard work, and compromises are more efficient than bulldozing her way through the issues. That she has to lead, not control."

"Something to think about. Now, about your job . . ."

"A job I can't do from a desk. Especially during the All Hallows Festival. We've got something vicious running around town stabbing innocents. I need to be out on patrol, protecting our people."

"Yes, you do. I suggest you return to your desk and complete as much paperwork as possible today. Then report to the review committee at nine tomorrow morning. Be prepared to defend your actions."

"Sir?" Hope filled Chase's chest. He'd finished the monster report this morning. Dusty had given him release from his pain and energized his thoughts back into coherency.

"Phelma Jo has taught me that sometimes a bulldozer is the right tool for the job."

"Yes, sir."

"Oh, and have you heard the rumor that Lieutenant Ledbetter, Digger's smarter older brother, has applied for a better paying job with the State Police?"

"Um . . ."

"Of course, you've heard. Nothing remains secret for long in this town."

Chase smiled and nodded rather than admit to anything. There were secrets and then there were secrets.

"You will take the lieutenant's exam on November second. That's an order. I expect you to pass and be in line for promotion when the opportunity arises."

"Yes, sir."

"You're going to need the pay raise. Dusty looks like a high maintenance kind of woman."

"Not as much as her mother."

"Got that right. I figured that out when she was sixteen and I mistakenly asked her to the senior prom." He rose and left the room on a chuckle. He paused at the back door. "Oh, and for the next couple of hours your job is to make sure Dusty is safe, happy, and not overwhelmed with people so she can get her job of saving All Hallows done right."

"On it, sir." The best job in the world.

"Then catch up on your paperwork. Stay up all night if you have to. We're going to need you on the street after that. I have a funny feeling something weird is going to happen."

"Who ever heard of a static parade?" Phelma Jo complained, three seconds after Chase left Dusty at the empty high school gymnasium. Phelma Jo got there first, not having to deal with sixteen people trying to delay her with repetitive questions.

Dusty figured now that Chase had removed her from the press of the populace he'd completed his duty to protect her.

She took four rolls of black-and-orange crepe paper streamers from Phelma Jo. "You heard about my static parade back in the town meeting when I introduced the idea."

"This town doesn't do well with new ideas."

"Tradition is good. It binds us as a community. But there are times when we have to adapt to a changing world around us."

"I suppose. You're the expert on tradition and history."

"How many times in the last twenty years, because of rain, has the All Hallows Parade been delayed or so poorly attended it was barely worth the fuel for the trucks. No rain in the gym. *Voila*, we have the parade and guarantee you won't need an umbrella to view it." Dusty swept her arms to include the big room.

"Unless the roof springs a leak," Phelma Jo reminded her. "A new roof is on the budget for next year."

"I won't let it leak this weekend," Dusty said firmly. She wondered if Pixie magic could hold off the rain as easily as they tickled clouds to release some when the town badly needed it to help quench the fire Phelma Jo had started in The Ten Acre Wood.

A chill breeze erupted from the back doors of the gym as the janitor came in with a rolling cart piled high with tarps. Dusty remembered that the Pixies were heading indoors, getting ready to hibernate, not play pranks with the weather.

Phelma Jo giggled. "I don't think you have much to say about whether it rains or not."

"The principal assured me the tarps are to protect the floor from the displays and thousands of tromping feet, not from a leaking roof." Dusty flounced deeper into the room, assessing dimensions.

"If you say so," Phelma Jo grumbled. "How'd I get roped into helping you?"

"George Pepperidge volunteered you." Dusty studied the echoing space. With the bleachers rolled back and the basketball hoops retracted, she had a lot of room to work with. "Do you think there's enough room for all the floats if we organize it like a maze and people wander up and down aisles like streets marked with paper ghost cutouts?"

"Or yellow bricks. How am I supposed to know?" Phelma Jo looked at the four rolls of streamers left in her hands. "I haven't the foggiest idea about how to do this. You'd be better off with Thistle. Or your mother."

"But you are good at keeping people on topic and delegating chores." Dusty decided she needed a map. She liked maps, especially old ones. Maps contained a lot of information if you knew how to dig them out.

"So are you, if you can do it all by email. We haven't time to wait for email and responses and endless 'thank yous' and 'will dos' before people finally sign off and do the job." A tiny smile touched the corners of Phelma Jo's lips. A little moment of agreement. Maybe they wouldn't make it all the way back to friendship, but they traveled toward companionship.

"So, Phelma Jo, find someone with a measuring tape. A big industrial-sized one. I need to know the precise dimensions of this place and the size of every display that would have been on a flatbed truck but will now be on the floor."

"That I can do." Phelma Jo whipped out her phone and flipped through the touch screen. "I don't want to work with him. Hell, I don't even want to talk to him. But he's the person you need right now." Then she spoke into the phone. "Ian, you wanted to get more involved in the community. I have the job for you. High school, now. Bring your tape measure, graph paper, and a hard hat. Report to Dusty." She hung up abruptly.

"Phelma Jo, I appreciate your help, but why are you being so cooperative?"

"I'm not sure. But it feels like the right thing to do."

An hour later Dusty blinked at the efficient map she and Ian had pieced together. Sixteen pieces of graph paper taped together spread across the floor. "It's beautiful and efficient, but we cannot, as in *ever*, put the first missionaries next to the brothel," she said, stepping away from the map and the man who had come to her rescue.

Phelma Jo had introduced him and then carefully backed off to the side, making phone calls and keeping tabs on the people coming and going, and what they dumped here in preparation for the setup tomorrow afternoon. Not once did she look at the handsome redhead. He very carefully avoided looking at Phelma Jo's station by the exterior door. She said she had a better signal there. He feigned disinterest with anything but the map and his measurements.

Dusty appreciated his precision in measurement and ability to reduce numbers to diagrams on the graph paper. He didn't have a lot of imagination and tended to see things

in black and white with no shades of gray, but he was bright
and witty and knew the town.

"The brothel was here first," Phelma Jo called as she slid
her phone shut once more. "Madame Bethany's was well
established as a place of entertainment, fence for stolen
goods, and a Shanghai holding cell three years before the
first missionary set foot in town. Seems to me the leader of
the missionaries was her best customer."

"That may be true. But we can't put them next to each
other in a public parade. This town doesn't do very well
with subtle," Dusty said.

"But that is the most efficient use of space!" Ian
protested. "And chronologically . . ."

"Ever hear of political correctness?" Dusty asked sarcas-
tically.

"He lives by political correctness, even when it's hypo-
critical," Phelma Jo spat.

"Political correctness tries to soothe clashing opinions.
As such, I see your point, Dusty. But there is no other logical place to put the missionaries. Their exhibit is small, just
the right size to tuck in here beside the saloon and its
sprawling annex." He blushed at the reference to the illegal
portions of the bar's trade.

"How about if we trade the Boy Scouts with the
brothel?" Dusty mused, looking for smaller exhibits—the
ones designed for pickups instead of flatbeds.

"Now *that* is funny," Phelma Jo said, finally deigning to
wander over and actually look at the map. "Next you'll
want to include a tribe of Pixies in the parade."

"Pixies, if I dared include them, would fit better flying
around from exhibit to exhibit rearranging the decorations
and untying aprons and shoelaces," Dusty said. But that
was an idea. She could get the elementary school children
involved. Thistle could organize the pranks. She was good
with children . . .

But Thistle was missing. And Dusty didn't have time to
entice her home.

Ian carefully averted his eyes away from Phelma Jo.

Dusty took another step back and looked at her two

companions. She didn't need Thistle's magic to see how the two sparked off each other. Their energy was definitely trying to connect, but something kept the sparks from jumping the gaps.

Their gazes locked for half a heartbeat.

"I'm out of here. I've wasted enough time and need to get back to work." Phelma Jo averted her eyes from Ian.

*Running away,* Dusty thought. Just as Thistle and Hope had run away. And Mom. Mom used Shakespeare to avoid dealing with unpleasant reality. And Dad had run away to another university rather than deal with Mom. Then there was Mabel, running away from her family rather than face the possibility that her beloved home, a sanctuary for Pixies and runaway teens, might not be perfect.

Dusty had run away to the basement too many times. At least now she was trying not to.

Did she have the courage to try and stop the pattern in those around her?

"My eyes are crossing from looking at the map. I need a break," Dusty said, more like thinking out loud. "I haven't visited Mabel yet today. Ian, do you want to come with me?"

"Dusty," Phelma Jo said, warning clear in her voice. "We have to respect Mabel's wishes. She doesn't want to see anyone but you and Chase, and maybe me."

"I don't think Mabel is thinking clearly. She needs to connect with her family. But that's something you don't have a lot of experience with."

Anger flushed Phelma Jo's face.

"Think about it, Phelma Jo. There was a time, before I screwed things up between us, when you pretended to be my sister. You wanted family so desperately you practically lived at my house. I'm sorry we lost that closeness. But surely you must see that family is what Mabel needs right now."

"I—I'd like to see my aunt," Ian said. "I've tried several times, but she closes her door to me."

"Well, I know how to open it. Come along. Phelma Jo, if you want, you can come, too."

"No way. You aren't my family, and neither is Mabel. I have work to do. Maybe I'll see you around. Maybe I'm done with being a good citizen. Let the Eagle Scout take up the slack." She flounced out the door across the gym to the interior corridor. Running away, even if she did it slowly enough to be called back.

# Thirty-two

THISTLE ROSE UP TO HOVER beside Milkweed where she basked in the fitful sunlight on a flat rock beside the pond. Most of the tribe flitted about collecting pollen and berries and seeds to hoard for the winter. The little ones gathered soft moss and shed animal hairs to line the nest. Milkweed did nothing to enhance the tribe or work with them. Neither did Alder.

"Alder, tell your bride why the Old Faery really chose you to be king?" Thistle called out so that all could hear her. Now that she looked for signs of Faery blood in Alder, she saw that he stood half a hand taller than she. His magical power pulsed through him, almost visibly stronger than any Pixie. Had it come to him simply by claiming kingship, or had it been there all along, carefully hidden and controlled?

"What is she talking about, Alder? We both know she's full of Faery lies," Milkweed protested.

"Faery lies. That explains a lot, doesn't it, Alder?" Thistle said.

"I don't know what you are saying. Perhaps the cold from sleeping alone, too close to the Earth, has addled your thinking." Alder dismissed her with a gesture.

"Look at his aura, Milkweed," Thistle commanded, as if she were ordering Suzie and Sharon, her old boss' kids to bed on the nights she babysat them. "See the fire that encircles him, fuels his magic, taints his blood."

"What ... what?" Milkweed looked a little cross-eyed.

"Lying about your family lines is enough to negate the

marriage treaty," Thistle said. "My guess is that the Old Faery in the Patriarch Oak was your grandsire, Alder. He raised you to take his place as king of this tribe. A tribe that should serve the Patriarch Oak and all Pixies, not just the few Pixies who call this wood home."

"Don't be ridiculous, Thistle. Everyone knows that Pixies and Faeries can't breed. It's all myth and legend and stories to frighten small children," Alder snorted.

A young Pixie threw a half-rotten walnut into the pond. Water sprayed upward and outward, touching Milkweed's spider silk gown.

Alder reached for Milkweed's hand to draw her away from the pond. Water, the element that could draw him in and completely absorb him, just as Earth did to Pixies.

"Milkweed, your brother, Hay, is half Faery. You know it and I know it. He is myth and legend and frightening children's story come to life," Thistle said gently. She needed this frothy white-and-gold Pixie to listen and understand. Her brain was as poufy as her gold-tipped white hair. Too easy for Pixies to dismiss and forget things that were unpleasant to think about.

"Hay's not . . . He wouldn't . . . He couldn't . . ."

"Yeah, he is, and he's proud of it. Only thing is, he has both the Faery size and loyalties. But he didn't get Faery brains. His true father, King of the underhill that is in danger of being demolished for a discount store, ordered him to clear The Ten Acre Wood of Pixies so the Faeries could reclaim it as their own. Hay decided that meant he should clear The Ten Acre Wood. That's why he manipulated Phelma Jo into buying the timber and starting to clear-cut."

Both Alder and Milkweed shuddered at the ominous idea of all these tall trees reduced to stumps.

"When the timber cutting failed, he tried to set fire to the wood. He manipulated young men with Faery mushrooms so they'd blow up construction equipment and carnival rides. Rides with lots and lots of innocent people, *children*, onboard. And now he's leading an army of Pixies to kill all of us, and the humans who get in his way."

"No. My brother would never . . . wouldn't . . . did he, truly?" Milkweed looked totally confused.

"Yeah, he did."

"So what?" Alder protested. "That was Hay. Not me. I closed the wood to keep the Faeries out."

"And where did you get the magic to do that, if not from your own Faery blood?" Thistle asked. "Is the lying, dishonorable, cruel Faery blood the reason you cannot remain loyal to any female? Is a mating flight just another thrill for you instead of a sacred ritual?"

"Well, I'm not putting up with a half Faery mate, or even a ..." Milkweed paused to count her fingers, "a quarter Faery. I'll not have my life and my children tainted by monsters!" Milkweed withdrew her hand from Alder's and back-winged across the pond toward the spray of the waterfall.

"Where will you go, Milkweed?" Alder asked, an ugly sneer on his face that stretched his ears up and his chin out, revealing his diluted heritage. "You can't go home again. You'll be disgraced. Your tribe will exile you."

"There's a varied thrush waiting for you in the silver knot garden beside the museum, Milkweed. She'll take you anywhere you want to go. Home, to another tribe, to a place where you can start a new tribe. Whatever you wish," Thistle countered. "And don't be so hasty in fearing your own tribe. If they truly love you, they will take you back, unblemished. Remember you were *right* to refuse a mating flight. You were *right* about Alder, and they were wrong."

Milkweed turned and fled.

"Milkweed, stop. Come back. I love you," Alder called. But he made no move to follow her. He'd have to pass through the water spray if he did.

"Now it's time to reveal your cowardice, your malice, and how totally wrong you are for the job of king," Thistle said. She stood on the flat rock Milkweed had just vacated and faced her tribe and the Patriarch Oak. Ritual had to be observed.

"There is no one else to be king of this tribe, Thistle. The tribe will not accept anyone else as king." He gestured widely to include the population who had stopped their chores to observe and listen. They knew the ritual even if none of them had ever participated in one.

"We must have a king to survive the coming battles with other Pixies and humans," Alder continued his oration; his defense. "There is no one else qualified to be king."

"Except, maybe, Thistle," someone said quietly. They all heard the young male voice.

"Are you ready to forsake your human friends and stay in Pixie forever?" Alder asked, more accusation than question.

The diamond-and-amethyst ring weighed heavily on Thistle's hand.

Chicory pointed out to Juliet a knot in Hope's hair that was going to have to be cut out. No amount of coaxing and brushing would loosen the strands.

"Why did you come to Skene Falls, Hope?" Juliet asked, working the comb gently through the girl's hopelessly tangled hair. "It's not like we have a lot of agencies and facilities to help the homeless and runaways."

"Um . . . I heard about Mabel helping kids in trouble." Hope refused to look at the scissors Juliet retrieved from the kitchen table, or at Chicory, even when he flew right in front of her nose and made funny faces.

"Your hesitation says more than your words do," Chicory told her. He'd dealt with human children who couldn't tell the truth if you bribed them with chocolate cake. But they usually came around after a few Pixie pranks. "I'm done tweaking your hair and tripping you, and stealing bits of your breakfast cereal. Time to come clean, kid."

"The cereal wasn't that good. You're welcome to it, little man." She crossed her arms in front of her.

Juliet snipped the knot of hair out and placed it gently into Hope's left hand. "That clump of hair is a pretty good metaphor for your life. More tangled than one of Shakespeare's plots.

*'Of what men dare do! What men may do!*
*What men daily do, not knowing what they do!'*

That's from *Much Ado About Nothing*."

"It wasn't nothing!" Hope protested. Tears glistened in her eyes as she stared at the mass of dark blonde hair in her hand.

"Something needs to be said, or Juliet is going to throw you out," Chicory said gently. He touched one of the overflowing tears. "What was so bad at home that life on the street looked better?"

"I wasn't going to stay on the street."

"Then what, or whom, were you running toward?" Juliet asked quietly. She sat beside Hope and held her hand, stroking the back of it as if petting a cat.

Nasty image. Chicory banished the idea of a cat ever polluting this friendly household.

"I came looking for my dad. My real dad. My . . . my mom grew up in this town. I thought if I could find her parents or maybe my real dad, I wouldn't have to put up with her new husband. Everything was fine with just the two of us. Why'd she have to go and get married anyway?" More tears spilled.

Chicory didn't know how to stem the flow. His middle ached for this lonely child.

"Sometimes a woman needs a man," Juliet said, still calm and sympathetic.

"Why didn't she just have sex then and forget the bastard?"

"Did he hurt you? If he did, we can make him stop. Legally." Anger touched the edges of Juliet's voice.

Chicory wanted to do more than just stop a man from hitting a child. He wanted . . . he wanted to become as violent as a human. Or a Faery.

"No," Hope said so quietly that Chicory had to strain to hear the word.

"Then what was so bad?" he asked, relieved that he could let his anger fade.

"He . . . he didn't want me. He made it quite clear that I didn't belong in that house anymore. It was my mom's house. Our house. Not his."

"We'll think about that later, Hope. If your mother grew up here, perhaps I know her parents. It is a fairly small town and I know a lot of people."

"I think they may have moved away." Hope sniffed. "I couldn't find them in the phone book. They . . . they threw my mom out when she got pregnant. Threw her away like she was trash."

"What is their name? I still might know how to find them. Or Chicory and his tribe might know. They acted as spies for Mabel for many years. They know everything and everyone."

"Sam and Polly Langford. They used to send Christmas cards to mom's aunt. She took us in and helped raise me while Mom finished school."

"Langford. Langford. Why do I know that name?" Juliet asked the air.

"Because I dated Sandy Langford our junior year," Dick said, coming down the back stairs. He looked in bad shape with his hair standing on end and he still wore his pajama bottoms and a T-shirt. He hadn't shaved.

Chicory smelled his morning breath—and it was midafternoon, well beyond the time for him to brush his teeth and clean up—from across the room.

Dick squinted his red-rimmed eyes and stared at Hope. "Oh, my God! Are you the reason Hannah Fleming told me I needed to contact Sandy? You really are her daughter."

Hope returned his stare, mouth agape and more tears streaming down her face. "I didn't know your name until that last day at home. Mom said I was as big a liar as my father. That's the first time she ever said your name that I heard."

"Your mother moved away the summer before senior year. She never wrote or called. She never told me she was pregnant, so how could I lie to her?"

"You told her you loved her," Juliet reminded him. "I heard you on the phone. "You loved her, but not enough to talk to her when she was alone and hurting because you had an essay to write for your early admission college application."

"Oh, God, did I really do that?" Dick sat in the chair across the table from Hope and buried his head in his hands.

"You most certainly did. I wondered at the time if that

was why she left town in such a hurry. Her parents moved to California the next year. I lost track of them after a holiday card came back with no forwarding address."

"I was in college by then. Sam got a better job offer or something."

"But?" Juliet asked. "What haven't you told me, Benedict?" She stood up and faced her son. Chicory could see the effort she made to control her emotions. A lot of emotions that swung back and forth like the pendulum in her long case clock in the parlor. "Are you this girl's father?"

"Um—what's your mother's phone number, Hope. I think I need to call her," Dick said, looking more awake than a moment before.

Chicory guided his hand toward the cup of tea Hope had left cooling on the table. His friend needed it more than anyone in the room at the moment.

# Thirty-three

"WHY DIDN'T YOU TELL ME, Sandy?" Dick asked after the awkward introductions had been made over the phone. Damn. He wanted to have the woman in front of him, face-to-face, to ask all the questions that piled up in a fathomless jumble in his mind.

"She's safe? Tell me again. Is Alessandra safe?" Sandy screamed hysterically over the cell phone airwaves.

"She calls herself Hope now. But there is a fourteen-year-old girl huddled in my mother's kitchen who said you are her mother." He spoke each word firmly and crisply.

"Thank God. I'll drive down tonight, right after I get off work. Don't let her run away again."

"Hold on, Sandy. Not so fast. I need to know why you didn't tell me you were pregnant. I need to know that if you come and get *our* daughter, that she will be safe with you and not run away again. Why didn't you tell me?" He nearly screamed the last sentence.

A dozen Pixies appeared in his doorway, hovering anxiously. He kicked the door shut.

The little critters retreated with an "Eeeepp!" sound.

Within seconds, a dainty white-and-green one peeked through the gap between the door and the floor.

So much for privacy. By dinnertime the entire town would know about his daughter the runaway.

"I tried to tell you. You said you loved me but were too busy with college essays or something, anything so you didn't have to talk. You lied. You threw me away as surely as my parents did."

Dick ran his hands through his hair, heavy greasy hair that desperately needed shampooing, exhausted from the emotional storms of losing Thistle and now this. His gut twisted.

"I'm sorry, Sandy. Truly sorry I didn't make time for you when I knew you'd been crying." He wasn't even sure he remembered that phone conversation. He had been busy, getting ready for his senior year, applying to colleges, planning extra science and math classes to qualify for premed. His future was on the line that summer.

He had no idea that Sandy's was too.

"I was a selfish idiot." What else was new? "You should have tried harder. Come talk to me face-to-face and not relied on the phone." Like now.

"What would you have done if I had gotten through your thick head, Dick?" Sandy sounded coldly angry now, instead of hysterical. "We were seniors in high school, for God's sake. You didn't really love me. Did you even once think about the consequences?"

"Did you?"

A long silence followed that thought. They both needed to take responsibility for those madly passionate moments when they were too young to think beyond that moment. To think with their brains instead of their hormones.

"You probably haven't even thought about me in all these years."

That hit too close to home. How often had he used the L word over the years to get sexual gratification and nothing else out of a relationship?

But he hadn't lied when he'd told Thistle he loved her. He clung to that tiny morsel of truth, praying she knew he hadn't lied that time.

"I . . . I don't know what I would have done. But I had a right to know. I had a right to help even if we didn't get married." He dropped heavily into the armchair by the window. Reality began to creep into his tattered brain.

He was a father. Hope was his daughter. Hope . . . she'd been so scared when he first found her hiding in Mabel's dining room, and he hadn't made time for her, hadn't taken an interest in her. Just like he'd treated her mother. Guilt dominated his anger and confusion.

How could he have not known she was his daughter!

"Would you have finished college, gone on to medical school if you'd known?" Sandy asked. She sounded so bloody logical. "I decided I had to take care of myself. I couldn't trust anyone else to take care of me, not my parents and definitely not an eighteen-year-old *boy*."

"It's been fourteen years, Sandy. I have a good job. I could have helped with money, with time, with something!"

"Hannah told me you dropped out of med school after two years." Now she sounded guilty. "But by then I'd finished my courses to become a dental hygienist. *I* had a good job. Alessa and I were living with my Aunt Ruth, helping her through her last illness. I didn't have *time* to think about you."

"Not even in the wee small hours of the morning when you couldn't sleep?"

"I was afraid."

"Afraid of me?"

"Afraid you'd take her away from me. Like you are trying to do now."

"I'm trying to wrap my head around the fact that I have a fourteen-year-old daughter who found life on the streets preferable to living with her stepfather."

"You have to understand, Mike and I have only been married a year."

"Hope . . . I mean Alessa doesn't like him."

"I don't think she'd like any man I brought into the family."

"Why is that? She says he didn't hurt her. But he made it clear he wanted her gone." He couldn't help the sarcasm that colored his voice and his thoughts. "Just another territorial male clearing out the nest of unwanted offspring to make room for his own?"

"No. It's not like that. I . . . I . . ."

"You what? Didn't have time for her anymore? Just like you didn't have time to give me a choice about the raising of my daughter?"

"No! I made time for her. Just her and me. But . . . but . . . there was just the two of us for so long, I may . . . I may have spoiled her a bit. She was always so good and helpful, I didn't have to enforce rules and curfews. She started acting out when Mike and I became serious. He wouldn't let her get away with breaking the rules."

The picture started to clear a bit in Dick's mind. "Before Mike, she didn't have any rules."

"Not many. We didn't need them." Sandy was crying again.

"She's as headstrong and secretive as you," he said. A smile crept across his face as he remembered some of the arguments he and Sandy had. They'd fought about everything, the color of his shirt clashed with her dress, who would drive on dates, where they should go, whose homework was more important. Until finally he'd given up calling her.

He hadn't heard from her in three weeks when she called that hot August night while he pounded away at his college application essay.

But a lot of those fights had ended in searing kisses, long make out sessions, and then finally a naked romp in the back seat of his mother's car on prom night, and a few times afterward.

"Sandy, Hope—I mean Alessa is safe, warm, and fed. She's starting to bond with my mother, her grandmother. Which is more than your parents did."

"Yeah, I know. When I refused to abort, they sent me to live with Aunt Ruth so their reputations wouldn't be tainted. Aunt Ruth never married and lived her life according to her own rules, not those set down by a church or country club."

"Can you give us a couple of days to straighten out Alessa's head before you come get her?" Dick pleaded.

"This is Thursday," she said. Then she breathed so deeply he thought she'd inhale his phone from two hundred miles away. "I'll come get her Sunday noonish. I don't need directions, I remember the way. And if you take her through the haunted maze Saturday night, don't lose her. She's good at slipping away and hiding. I couldn't take her to a mall until she was eight."

"I'll see you Sunday."

How was he going to explain all this to Thistle? If he could find her.

Was that why she'd run away? Because she'd seen Hope approach him and recognized the truth long before he did?

Thistle found a perch in the lower limbs of the Patriarch Oak. She didn't want to go any higher, or remember the time she'd climbed up with Alder. From here she could see most of the tribe as they searched for last-minute stores of berries and nuts before hibernating. Not much longer before the first frost sent them all deep into the bower where they'd snuggle and keep each other warm, tell tales of favorite pranks when the sun warmed them enough to awaken, love each other freely, and bless the birth of new Pixies in the spring.

A part of her wanted desperately to recapture that feeling of belonging and sharing, the dropping of rules, the bliss of forgetting and not worrying about tomorrow.

Another part of her watched carefully for signs of intrusion by humans and how they might damage the bower.

Already Dusty's volunteers had marked paths with orange-and-black ribbons for the festival. Bows that Thistle had tied and made special with extra loops and dangling beads.

The sun passed noon and began a rapid descent toward the horizon across the big river.

Alder flew into the clearing. He took a stand upon the flat rock across the pond from her, hands on hips, feet spread, a deep frown on his face.

She couldn't see his aura in the flat light. Now that she knew what to look for, though, his mixed bloodlines were obvious, especially in the deep darkness of his eyes that slanted upward on the outside edge, nearly colliding with the ragged green hair at his temple. His extra large and sharply pointed ears stuck through the hair as well. She wondered how he'd hidden them for so long.

Alder whistled sharply. No one paid him any attention.

They were too used to his meaningless bluster to bother abandoning their essential chores.

"Listen to me!" he screamed.

Foxglove and six Dandelions looked up.

A satisfied smile creased his face. The contempt in his posture robbed him of the handsome charm she'd once seen. Or had he cast a glamour on her so that all she saw was what he wanted her to see?

From her perch, she could almost see the waves of magic radiating out from him. She was too far away to feel more than a light tickle. But she wanted to like him, to listen to him, to let him make all the decisions, knowing they would be right.

No, they wouldn't be right. Not for her or for the tribe.

Deep inside herself, she found a bit of human resolve to push away his manipulation.

"Milkweed has left The Ten Acre Wood. She has broken the marriage treaty," he announced. "We must no longer have any dealings with her tribe in the valley. Her name will never again be mentioned by any of us."

"About time," Thistle muttered.

Obviously, the tribe agreed with her. They went back to storing their treasures inside a hollow tree north of the clearing.

"Didn't you hear me?" Alder called, not at all pleased with the easy dismissal of his tribe.

"I heard you," Thistle said. Deliberately, she reclined against the rough bark of the oak.

"But you already knew."

"So what do you want from them? Adoration?"

"Acknowledgment that something has changed within the tribe."

"But nothing has changed. Milkweed was never their queen. She rejected you within hours of arriving. What did she do here besides take baths, steal webs from spiders, and look pretty?"

Alder frowned, his brow creased in thought. Difficult thought from the depth of those furrows, deep enough to plant some mint in them if they filled with dirt.

"Time to face reality, Alder." Thistle heaved herself away from the comfort of the tree. "No one listens to you because you've made a lot of bad decisions. Milkweed was just one of them. Why listen to you, or obey you, when that only makes for more trouble? Pixies may not think ahead, or examine consequences, but they do learn if you hit them on the head often enough."

"But I have the magic to enthrall them. They have to obey me. I am their king."

"Are you? You aren't fit to be king if you have to use magic to lead them." She flew over to his rock and stood in front of him, mimicking his arrogant pose.

"Who will lead this tribe if I do not? They haven't had a true king the entire time the Old Faery presided in the Patriarch Oak. None of them know how to lead. I've been feeding them Faery mushrooms to make sure of it."

"That's why your magic is so weak! It's false magic, an illusion created by forbidden mushrooms. We all know that fungus is forbidden for a reason."

"But . . . but . . ."

"Don't worry, Alder. Someone will step into the vacancy once they've shit out the mushrooms. That's the way of Pixies. Most of us flit from day-to-day without much thought. But when we have to do something for the tribe, someone always rises to the top."

"Like I did."

"No. The Old Faery, your grandsire, thrust you up there because of your blood, regardless of your ability or intelligence."

"My blood. Exactly. I was bred to lead."

"You were bred to repeat everything the old one said. He never taught you to *think*."

"Pixies don't think. They don't need to."

"And Faeries do? No, they run away. They'd rather hide in their hill and feel superior. Then, when their hill is threatened, they don't know how to do anything but steal someone else's home. Was that your next decision? To invite the Faeries to come live here?"

"No."

Thistle glared at him, daring him to continue the lie. True Pixies couldn't lie. That's what Faeries did. And humans.

She had lied when she wrote out the story of why she didn't have a birth certificate. If she'd been a true Pixie, she wouldn't have been able to sign her name to the document, even if she had only copied Dick's words.

*Oh, Dick! What have I done?* Her tummy ached so bad she needed to bend over and wail like a lost infant.

Something kept her upright, despite her grief. Something like a human need to set wrong things right again.

"Tell me the truth, Alder. When are the Faeries arriving?"

He bit the insides of his cheeks to keep his words, and his lies inside.

"I'm guessing All Hallows Eve, the turning of the year. The tribe huddles in the bower that day and night so the hundreds of people having fun in the haunted maze won't disturb them, or step on them, or kill them. Then, in the morning, most Pixies consider winter has come and they hibernate. They won't become aware of the outside world until spring. Plenty of time for the Faeries to come in and build a new hill for themselves, leaving no room for Pixies in the wood."

Alder's eyes opened wide in wonder. "How did you know?"

"Because I think!" Anger rose up in her, making her feel bigger, stronger, righteous. She grabbed Alder's arm at the elbow and began to spin. Once around, he kept pace with her. She sped up. Twice around he stumbled. More speed. His feet left the ground, but his wings couldn't keep up.

And still she spun him until he lay flat in the air.

With a deep breath and picture in her mind she let go at the precise moment so he flew off, directly into the spray of the waterfall. Water that would destroy him if he got drenched.

"Go back to the Faeries in their hill. Where you belong."

The sound of slow, sarcastic clapping brought her to a full halt. She turned cautiously to face the Patriarch Oak.

Haywood Wheatland, now Snapdragon, stood on a middle level branch, his deformed wings and purplish red splotches weeping bloody pus clearly visible.

"Very good, my dear. You've accomplished in one day what I've been trying to do for weeks. I now have no impediments to taking over and clearing The Ten Acre Wood of every last Pixie. Including you. Soldiers, attack!" He pulled a hawthorn spike from behind him. More of the poisonous bloody pus dripped from the wickedly sharp tip.

# Thirty-four

CHICORY TWEAKED DICK'S NAPE where it peeked out beneath the pillow.

Dick slapped at the annoyance.

Chicory lifted the hem of his T-shirt and brushed past the back of Dick's waist.

"Go away!" Dick stuffed his head deeper beneath the pillow and reached to pull the sheet higher across his back.

"My job is to wake you up," Chicory whispered.

"I'm awake."

"But you aren't up. And you aren't presentable, and you aren't downstairs bonding with your daughter." This time Chicory pulled hard on Dick's hair.

"Ow!"

"You gonna get up?"

"Why should I?"

"Because there are things to do and people to see and decisions to be made."

"Give me some privacy, will ya? I liked this house better when humans were the only ones living here."

"Was that before or after Thistle joined the household?"

Dead silence.

"Thistle. She's your problem."

"Yeah, well, she ran away. I'm not sure why."

"I think you do know. She has a job to do that she can only do in Pixie. Hope just made it easier for her to go do it."

"Whatever. Go away and let me sulk in peace."

"You've sulked all day. I'd say you are sliding into depression."

"You aren't my doctor. Besides, I'm entitled."

"No, you aren't. You've had your sulk. Now it's time to do something."

"Like what? Thistle is gone and she won't ever come back. I don't know if she can come back." Dick rolled over and planted the pillow on his chest, hugging it tight as if it might replace his lost love.

"She can come back if she wants to." Chicory took a perch on the top of the lampshade on the nightstand.

"She doesn't want to."

"How do you know? Have you talked to her?"

"Yes. She wouldn't listen. She's gone back to Pixie, where she belongs. I knew that would happen eventually. I just didn't expect it so soon. I thought we had enough love between us to keep her here a bit longer."

Chicory's thoughts flew to Daisy, his own love. Did they have true, lasting love? Pixie love? Or was it just convenience that had thrown them together? He hoped it was love. Really and truly hoped that he'd found his destined life-mate.

"If she truly loved me, you'd think she'd listen to me." Dick sat up, still hugging his pillow.

"There is a way . . ." Chicory nearly choked on his audacity. He started shaking in fear. Did he have the right? Did he have the strength?

He heard Daisy's trilling laughter in the corridor beyond.

"I'm king of my tribe, I have resources I didn't have before," he said, as much to reassure himself as well as Dick. He rubbed one petal of his gold-trimmed cap, the one Juliet had made especially for him. The love and care she put into each stitch gave him a tiny bit more magic.

"Resources? Like what? I thought all you did was spread gossip and report rumors."

"We are the stuff of magic," Chicory whispered.

Dick didn't look interested.

"I can make you a Pixie for the span of one day, from sunrise to sunset." Gulp. He hoped he could.

Dick stilled. Chicory could almost see his ears twitch to hear more.

"You could go to Thistle, explain to her, not let her run away from you because you could follow her." All the way to the top of the Patriarch Oak if necessary.

"You could do that?" Dick swallowed. His throat apple bobbed as if his fears were an obstruction. He could get around them, but only with difficulty.

"It will be dangerous."

"I'd walk through hell to get Thistle back."

"Okay. I need some time to prepare." And master his own fears of wielding that much magic in one shot. It might deplete his powers all the way down to the source.

"I'll wait. A little while anyway." Dick flopped back onto the bed.

"All magic costs. I can only do this in return for a favor." Chicory thought furiously, making it up as he went along.

"How much? I've got money in the bank . . ."

"Pixies don't need money. We need friendship. Right now, Hope is my friend, and she needs her father."

Dick turned over, hiding under the pillow again.

"I can only make you into a Pixie if you do this for me. And for Hope. Get yourself cleaned up and dressed and go spend the evening with your daughter."

"How long?"

"When you wake up in the morning, all will be different." Chicory hoped so anyway.

Thistle glanced at the angle of the afternoon sun without taking her eyes off of Snapdragon. His eyes had taken on the same bloody purple hue as the pustules on his wings.

At least two hours until sunset, when all Pixies, including the ugly mutant possessing the Patriarch Oak must sleep. How had the day gotten so late? She'd lost hours between eating that salal berry in the early morning, catching her first glimpse of Alder's fiery aura, sending Milkweed home, and finally banishing Alder. And now this endless staring match with Snapdragon.

What to do? What to do?

"What would Dick do?" she whispered to herself.

"Hide!" she screamed to her tribe. "Divert them, lead them astray. Don't let them catch you."

"You'd have us desert our territory?" Foxglove, a younger version of the old Pixie who brewed concoctions and mothered the entire tribe, looked up from where she blended into the seed pods of her namesake plant.

"Just for tonight. Tomorrow I'll think of something else. Now lead the intruders astray and hide." She suited her orders by whisking off the flat rock across the swollen pond, right under Snapdragon's perch. He dove after her, hawthorn spike extended.

She managed to stay ahead of him just barely, the poisoned thorn brushing her heels.

Where to go?

The waterfall had worked with banishing Alder. She aimed straight for the thundering water and the drifting spray. In and out. The cool water refreshed and chilled her at the same time.

"You forget, Thistle Down, I am half Faery. I command all four elements!" Snapdragon sneered at her.

Faery snot!

Half Faery. Hmmmmm . . .

Faeries lied all the time. Worse than humans. Pixies couldn't lie.

Thistle took a chance and dove into the tiny pool of still water behind a rock that sat in midstream. The currents tugged at her, right and left, trying to go around the obstacle. But she and this rock were old friends; she'd basked in a ray of sunlight on many an autumn day when the dark granite absorbed heat that couldn't remain in the air. She knew every crevice and ledge on this rock. Snapdragon did not.

Thistle crawled into a deep crack feet first. The tip of her nose stuck out, nothing more.

"You can't stay hidden forever, Thistle Down," Snapdragon called from somewhere above her and toward the far bank.

She risked a peek. Her enemy flew from grass to fern, to carriage barn, to sleepy knot garden, peering deep into every shadow. His discordant music *ding dang chug shplach* made her ears ring.

"Gotta find fire. Need fire. Must burn," he sort of sang, his words slurred as if he'd drunk a whole thimbleful of honey. He flew a wavering, incoherent path. His words were meaningless. He'd be lucky to stay awake long enough to find a sheltered bed before sunset.

A giggle threatened to erupt. She was well and truly hidden. But she was also wet and cold.

The amethyst-and-diamond ring weighed heavily on her hand. She clenched her fist to keep it from falling off.

Was the ring trying to call her back to humanity and Dick? She hoped so. But she couldn't go back yet. Not yet. She had to deal with Snapdragon once and for all. Then she'd find a way to be with Dick forever.

# Thirty-five

"**W**HY'D YOU LET HIM COME WITH YOU?" Mabel asked. Her face flushed with temper. The monitor beside her hospital bed beeped faster.

"I brought your nephew because he is your only family and he deserves to know that you are healing," Dusty said matter-of-factly. Gently, she smoothed the sheet, and re-folded the top over the light blanket that covered Mabel to the waist. Then she hit the bed control to raise the head.

"Put that back down. I'm not comfortable sitting up yet," Mabel insisted, more angry than ill. Her face remained flushed. But her gaze strayed to Ian, drinking in the sight of him. "Has your mother bankrupted you yet?" she finally asked.

"Not quite," Ian chuckled and pulled up a straight chair to sit beside his aunt.

"What about the drugs? I caught you with kids that were headed down the wrong path and a known drug dealer."

"I learned my lesson. Haven't seen Bryon and Luis since I was eleven. Now I don't even take an aspirin unless the doctor holds me down and forces it down my throat."

"You can't have my house. I've got it protected as an historic building that has to be preserved." She crossed her arms and humphed. "Dusty, have you and Chase moved in yet?"

"After the wedding, if you are still unable to care for yourself. The house is still yours until *you* decide it's time you need assistance and move to something easier to care for." Dusty reassured the old woman.

Old. When had Mabel become so old? And irascible? So weak and vulnerable?

"I don't want your house, Aunt Mabel," Ian said softly. "I bought the Goddard House across the street from the Carricks and I'm intending to fix it up, maybe add on to the back or open the attic, if I ever need more room."

"You want my land . . ."

"That is my mother's idea, not mine. She thinks it's valuable. It's not."

"What do you mean it's not valuable?" Mabel speared him with the glare that had subdued noisy drunks, irate thieves, and frustrated police officers for decades.

Ian, bless him, did not back down. "I mean that there is no access to the long strip behind your house unless you bulldoze one of the houses."

"The old Corbett place next door is up for sale. It's such a mess it will have to be bulldozed."

"I think the Corbett House—your house used to be the gatekeepers' cottage and carriage house for it—is also on the historic registry," Dusty mused, thankful that she'd done her homework when she first read Mabel's will and trust documents. "Whoever buys it will have to restore it. It's a bank-owned rental at the moment and has been for sale for nearly four years. I've read three petitions from the bank to remove the historic designation so they can pull down the structure and try to develop the strip—if they could buy it from you."

"That strip running between the backyards on your block would make an excellent pocket park or community garden," Ian said. "If we move your side fence in about three feet, and borrow another three from the Corbett land, we'd have enough for a public path. If we go with the community garden route, we could even put in a locked gate. Only those with rented plots would have access," Ian continued.

"Lots of new condos and apartments are springing up as the town grows and we attract commuters. Wouldn't surprise me if the residents jumped at the chance to have a bit of garden for vegetables, and roses and such," Dusty added.

Mabel's expression softened a bit. Then her eyes narrowed in speculation. "Dusty, would you and Chase agree to making the back lot a community garden? I know you won't live there long, once you start a family, but your interests are primary."

"Mabel, Chase and I . . ." Dusty gulped and swallowed a few tears. "Since the chemo, I can't have children. Chase and I have discussed adoption, but it's so expensive, we'll have to wait several years." She turned her head away at the one great sadness in her relationship with Chase.

"You and I, and Chase too, will have a long discussion about that very shortly. In the meantime, living in my house without paying rent or a mortgage should help."

"We appreciate that. Thank you for entrusting your home to us."

"More than the house." Mabel fixed Dusty with that glare of hers until Dusty had to look up. An instant of understanding passed between them. "I expect you to tend my roses as well."

"Of course. Rosie . . . your roses are in good hands. Now about the adoption business . . ."

"Later. Now, Ian, tell me about your plans for the Goddard House, and how did you save enough for a down payment with my no-good sister spending every dime she can get her hands on?"

Dusty took that as her cue to leave. "Call me if you need a ride home, Ian," she said as she gathered her purse and keys.

"No problem. I'll walk. It's only a mile or so back to the school and my truck."

One problem solved. Six more cropping up. Dusty decided her next stop would be Chase's office. He had some explaining to do about Mabel's house and the possibility of adoption.

"Alessa, I really hope you will come see me from time to time," Dick said, elbows on the kitchen table. His daughter—wow this was his daughter!—sat across from him. She made geometric patterns with her crackers.

"I won't come back at all if you keep calling me that."

"What? Alessa? That's the name your mother called

you. Alessandra, same as her name. She's Sandy, you're Alessa."

"Yeah, but it's her name. I don't want it. I want my own. I'm Hope now."

"Okay, Hope." Dick pushed aside his fears. His basic psych classes in med school would paint all kinds of bipolar disorders on this identity issue. There was more going on here than a rebellious child running away from a new and complicated family readjustment. "I eagerly anticipate you coming to see me on holidays and maybe several weeks during the summer. That's what hope means. Looking forward to a brighter future."

"Will your fiancée hope to see me, too?"

"I think so. She's used to a big extended family." He certainly hoped Thistle was coming back. That he could persuade her they really and truly belonged together. Tomorrow. He only had a little longer to wait.

"Speaking of holidays, why has this town gone so nuts about Halloween?" With a jerk of the head she indicated the floral arrangement at the center of the table. Golden chrysanthemums, red-and-orange leaves, a miniature scarecrow, and a candle all set into a glass pumpkin bowl. "I mean, there's stuff all over town, even on Main Street and around City Hall. Every yard looks like a horror movie set with gravestones and ghosts and witches and lights and stuff. You put sound effects on a motion detector on your front gate for trick-or-treaters." She tried to sneer with adolescent superiority, but her eyes shone with a bit of anticipation.

"For a long time this town was just another rural community with a failing textile mill and a long road into Portland for any decent paying jobs. The festivals helped bring tourist dollars in and formed a community bond; gave us a reason to remain an incorporated city rather than just another suburb. We've kept up the traditions even though the new corporate owners of the mill have revived the town economy, and the freeway makes Portland seem close enough to commute."

"You guys really get into it?"

"Yes. In fact, I plan on taking you through the haunted maze in The Ten Acre Wood tomorrow or Saturday night.

My sister has organized most of it. Volunteers will represent the ghosts of some of our more notorious ancestors, including pirates, riverboat gamblers, and an ax murderer. So there are bits and pieces of history lessons thrown into the fun."

"Cool." Hope reached across the table for the matches tucked beneath the flower arrangement and calmly lit the pristine orange candle. The wick flared to life in paler colors than the flowers and leaves. She stared at it for a long time, seemingly mesmerized by the flickering blue-and-white center of the flame. The match burned down. She ignored it until she had to shake the matchstick free of fire or get burned.

An afterthought, or instinct rather than conscious decision?

Still she stared at the candle. Her face relaxed as her mind wandered.

Bits and pieces of that damnable psych course fluttered through Dick's mind like a troubled Pixie looking for a safe perch. *I'm looking for trouble where there is none.*

"We'll talk to your mom about visiting me as often as you like when she comes to get you on Sunday."

"Mom's coming here?" Hope snapped out of her trance. "No way. No how. I'm not going back. Not if *that* man is still living in her house." She shoved her chair back so hard it crashed against the floor. Then she ran out the back door without even stopping for a sweater or jacket.

"Chase Norton, you are as obsessive-compulsive as I am," Dusty said.

"Huh?" He looked up from the computer screen to find his fiancée smiling at him from the doorway of his office. Of course, the moment he looked away from the text on the screen he knew where to place a comma to make sense of the long narrative. "Have you been standing there long?"

He half stood, ready to wrap her in a long and crushing hug. Maybe add a kiss or six to the embrace. He hadn't wanted to leave her this morning when they both went to work. He didn't want to let go of her now.

"I've watched you just long enough to feel guilty about disturbing you." She moved close enough for him to grab her about her waist. He followed through with his plan.

Several breathless moments later he blindly hit the comma key, hoping the cursor was in the right place. He didn't want to spend any more time untangling his report of ejecting a man from Chase's parents' diner for drunk and disorderly when they refused to serve him a beer. They didn't serve any alcohol, but that didn't keep the man from putting his fist through a glass desert case.

"I'm ready for a break. Do you want some dinner? Ginny's supposed to have fried chicken on the special menu," he said, still clinging to Dusty.

"In a moment." She bit her lip.

"This looks like it might take a while. Why not talk about whatever is troubling you over dinner?"

"I think this needs more privacy than your family's diner."

"Don't tell me you're backing out of the wedding! I didn't hurt you last night, did I?" Panic made his heart race.

"No, silly." She giggled a bit as she playfully hit his chest. "If anything, last night made me even more eager to spend the rest of my life with you. Did you know that when you fall deeply asleep, when pain and stress fall away, your face relaxes so much that you look ten again. Like you did when I first fell in love with you."

"I look forward to discovering more about you when you are deeply asleep and I'm not exhausted and woozy from pain pills." He kissed her again.

"Mabel hinted at some things that make me hopeful about our future together."

"And what did Mabel say?" He nuzzled her neck, drinking in the faint hint of her lavender shampoo and soap.

"Something about helping us with adoptions."

His heart skipped a beat. He hadn't planned on having this discussion until after the wedding. In some ways last night was their wedding. He took a long, deep breath and released it. "Pull up a chair. You're right. This will take a bit of sorting through and needs a lot of privacy."

When she'd dragged the straight wooden chair across the

tiny room so she could sit beside him, he held her left hand in both of his on her thigh.

"Mabel runs an underground railway for teens that have fallen through the cracks of the system and need either a new identity and relocation or advocates in court for emancipation from abusive homes—their own or foster care." He blurted out the words so he didn't have time to think about it. "I'm not directly involved, but I know about it, unofficially, and sometimes direct kids to her."

"Is that why Hope was in her house when Dick found her?"

"Probably. Runaways sometimes pick up word of a safe haven on the street. Some of those girls are pregnant."

"And Mabel thinks we can convince those girls to let us adopt the child," she finished for him. Her eyes brightened with tears and her lip trembled; ever-so-hopeful but afraid at the same time. Afraid she'd guessed wrong.

"I was hoping so, but didn't want to suggest it until Mabel offered." His fingers caressed the ring on her left hand.

"But?"

He fought for the right words.

"There is always a but . . ." she prodded him.

"When a girl is desperate enough to run away, she feels unloved, unwanted, like she has no right to happiness or family. Selling herself on the street for food and shelter doesn't seem wrong. It's survival. Her body isn't hers to protect. Then a new life blossoms inside her and suddenly she feels as if this baby is the only person in the world who can love her. Like the child is the only thing in the world that is truly, solely hers. She'd rather accept meager welfare than give up the baby."

Dusty worried her lip with her teeth some more. "I think I understand. So how does that help us?"

"If we find the right girl and offer open adoption, she can visit anytime and the baby knows she's the birth mother. We'll have a better chance of being able to afford the adoption process and don't have to go overseas to adopt an infant."

Dusty flashed him a blazing smile. Her tears of hope became tears of joy, spilling down her cheeks unchecked.

He smoothed them away with a fingertip. "I hope those are tears of joy."

"They are. I want at least one baby I can raise from birth, but I'd resigned myself to adopting an older child. They need homes and loving parents, too."

"We'll talk more when we get home tonight." He kissed her again, wanted to linger, but those awful reports weren't going away. He'd made good headway through the afternoon. Not enough. He'd be here all night if he didn't let Dusty go right now.

Right now.

His cell phone rang. "Norton," he barked into the instrument of tortuous interruption.

"Chase, there's a fire at the high school gym," Dick shouted anxiously. "I just got called to meet the trucks there."

"Damn, I miss having Mabel in house. The county dispatcher tells me nothing," Chase snarled. The high school. Where the static parade was supposed to take place day after tomorrow. Someone was out to destroy the town festival. Someone with a kinship with fire.

Either Haywood Wheatland aka Snapdragon or the teens he enthralled sprang to mind.

"There's more." Dick sounded like the world was about to end.

"What?" He put the cell phone on speaker to include Dusty in the conversation.

"Hope has run away again."

"And ...?"

"She has a fascination with fire. I just confirmed it with her mother."

# Thirty-six

D ICK SHRUGGED INTO HIS HEAVY volunteer
fireman jacket one-handed, keeping Chase and Dusty
on the line. "I'm afraid . . ."

"Don't be," Chicory whispered to him. The little blue
creature circled his head, wings beating double time. "Hope
has not gone far."

"How long has Hope been gone?" Chase asked. His
voice had the vacant echoey quality of the speaker func-
tion.

"Maybe five minutes. No longer," Dick confessed.

"Then she can't be responsible for the fire. It would take
her twice that long just to walk to the school, another five
for the smoke to get noticed." Chase sounded calm and re-
assuring. Professional.

"Dick, we'll meet you there!" Dusty called. She sounded
panicky with ragged breath. After all, it was her static parade getting set up in the gym.

"Chicory says that Hope only got as far as the back
gate," Dick said. He'd believe that when he saw his daughter there and no sooner. As he spoke, he dashed out, jacket
only half on. "If you get there before I do, explain to the
chief why I'm late." He closed his phone and jumped down
the three steps to the flagstone path.

A motionless shadow within a shadow by the back gate
drew Dick like a magnet. He stepped deliberately, making
sure Hope heard his approach over the sirens climbing the
hill from downtown. "Hope, sweetie, those are fire trucks. I
have to go." He held her by the shoulders.

"You're abandoning me. Just like my mother did when she married *that* man."

"Not at all. Mom will be home from the grocery store in a few moments. You won't be alone long. And the Pixies will keep you company."

She wrenched away from his grasp. "You're just like . . ."

"Hope, listen to *me* and not your rampaging emotions that make no sense." He shook her slightly as he turned her around to make sure they made eye contact.

"What?"

"Listen, Hope. I'm an EMT with the volunteer fire department. There is a fire. I need to go. People need me to be there. I have obligations and responsibilities. I am not abandoning you."

"Can I go with you?" She looked up at him, fearful. Why was she so afraid of being alone when she'd run away from home into the solitude of life on the streets?

"Not this time." More sirens approached. "That's three trucks at least. A bad fire. People will be very busy, almost frantic to put it out quickly. I'm afraid you might get hurt because you don't know what to do, where to stand. I really don't want you hurt. You've come to mean a lot to me in just a few days."

Her eyes focused on him. "Okay. I'll wait for Grandma inside."

"Where it's warm and dry. I don't want you to catch a chill."

"I won't." She turned to retreat into the house where cheery lights beckoned with the promise of warmth and friendliness. "And thanks for explaining to me. I'm just so sick of no one telling me anything. All I want is to know why."

Dick watched her until she'd closed the kitchen door behind her. Then he turned his attention—or the half of it that wasn't lingering with his daughter—to getting to the high school and the fire as fast as possible.

"You want to talk about it, Hope?" Chicory assumed a casual pose in front of the flour canister, legs stretched along the kitchen counter, his head propped up with an elbow. He flattened his wings against the sculpted fruit design of the milk glass container. This one with pears fit him better than the grapes or apples of the sugar and tea canisters.

"Nothing to talk about," she said, head down, rearranging her cheese and crackers again. Squares this time, box of four square crackers. She moved a fifth, broken one around the outside of the design with a seemingly idle finger.

She spoke volumes without saying a word.

"How about all that 'Don't abandon me!' crap you gave Dick?"

"None of your business." Her voice sounded flat. She'd had this conversation before.

"The highest calling for a Pixie is to befriend those in need. You sound like someone mightily in need of a friend right now."

"Friends accuse you of horrible things you didn't do and then they leave. Or they tattle." She shoved her chair back, the wooden legs scraping noisily on the floor.

"Who'd I tattle to? Since when is a Pixie in a position to judge you about right or wrong? Pixies can't lie."

"Everyone lies."

"Not Pixies. We *can't*. As in 'it is physically impossible.' If we even think about lying, we curl up into a ball, turn into dust, and blow away in the slightest breeze." He thought about the trouble Thistle had writing out her statement for the judge. While it wasn't all a lie, some of it was. Her stomach cramps and dizziness had been real and debilitating until Dick wrote out the words and she copied them. Not telling a lie, just copying letters onto a page.

"I wish people were like that." Hope plopped back into her chair. Her careless movement shifted the broken cracker farther away from the square, which remained intact.

Interesting.

"So who told lies about you?"

Hope remained silent so long Chicory thought she wasn't going to answer.

"A bully at school," she whispered.

"I hate bullies. Their anger at themselves gets so tight

they can't contain it. So they let it spill onto innocents. The only way they can feel good about themselves is to make other people hurt worse than they do." Their blind anger also made bullies prime targets for pranks. But they never got the joke.

"You think so?" Hope looked up, hope filling her eyes.

"I know so. So what did the bullies at school say about you?"

"You wouldn't understand."

"Try me. I may be little—by human standards—and look like a kid, but I've been around a long time. I've watched lots of bullies, heard most of their lies."

Hope curled in on herself.

Chicory flew to the plate of crackers and stood atop the broken one off to the side. "Look at me, Hope. Talk to me. If you don't tell someone what's really going on inside your head you'll have to keep running away from it. Whatever it' is."

"It's hard." A tear snaked down the side of her nose.

"So is living on the streets, scrounging for food in dumpsters, getting cold and wet, never sleeping soundly because you can't know what danger lurks in every shadow. Always running away from yourself."

Her face worked as she alternately tried to speak and bite back the words.

"Just the first part. Just tell me what lies the bullies told about you. You know they are lies. I will know they are lies. You can trust me that much."

"This really cute guy, he's on the basketball team, and a senior, and every girl in school wanted him."

"And?" This was starting to sound a bit like the story of Alder and every girl Pixie in his tribe.

"And he asked me to the dance after the last basketball game of the season. It's a big deal every year. More so last spring 'cause the team was going into the championship playoffs."

"He made you feel special."

"Yeah. He's a *senior*, for gosh sakes. I was only a freshman. He could have asked any girl in school."

"But he chose you. Did he say why?"

"I didn't ask. I just agreed to go. Mom bought me a really pretty dress, and he gave me a corsage and everything."

"But?

"He only asked 'cause he bet some guy he could get inside my pants. He said he loved me, but I was just another virgin in his long list of conquests."

Another Alder. "Did you let him?"

"No."

"Ah. His pride couldn't take rejection. So he lied and bragged to everyone that you had succumbed to his charms. And because he's a big man in school, people believed him rather than you, even some of your friends."

"Yeah."

"Your Mom, maybe?" Hope turned her face away.

Chicory shifted tactics. When you can't get a straight answer, go for the sideways one. "This wouldn't be a big deal in Pixie, unless it involved a mating flight—that's like a wedding ceremony to humans. A mating flight is supposed to be forever."

"Sex is a big deal for humans. Especially for people as young as you, Hope," Juliet said from the back entrance to the kitchen. She had her arms full of cloth bags filled with fresh food.

"You eavesdropped! You're as bad as my mom." Hope pounded the table as she stood up, ready to flee again.

Chicory flew up directly in front of her face. She had to cross her eyes to focus on him.

"Stop!" Juliet shouted in her best schoolteacher voice.

Strangely, Hope did.

"Juliet overheard by accident. She is the one person in this whole world who can really and truly help you. So sit down and spill the rest of it," Chicory coaxed.

Mouth agape in wonder, Hope sat. Juliet joined her on the other side of the table. "I only heard the last bit, but I suspect that what hurt most was not the lies, but the people who believed the lies," she said. Her eyes focused on the candle flame that Hope had lit earlier. "Can you imagine how I felt when a gossipy old lady in my church said it was my fault that Desdemona got leukemia and almost died?"

"That's just stupid," Hope spat.

"You know that and I know that, but there were others who didn't want to believe that God could hurt me and my family by giving my child cancer. For no reason. So they had to blame a human. I'm Desdemona's mother and therefore it had to be my fault, not God's. God did it as punishment or something."

"What . . . what did you do?"

"We held our heads high, ignored the gossips, and got on with our lives, doing everything humanly possible to get Desdemona the treatment she needed. Did you know that Benedict, your father, gave his bone marrow to restart her immune system after the chemo? He, as much as anyone, or the drugs saved her life. That's when he decided to go into medicine."

"No, I didn't know."

"So who believed the lies and treated you so badly you felt like you had to run away from the family and friends who love you most?"

"Mike. Mom's husband."

Interesting that she didn't call the man her stepfather, like she should. Chicory began to see the family structure moving into place to push her aside. Did her mother know?

"What did he say?"

"He told me to get out. He said I was just trash like my mother had been. He wasn't going to have a whore for a daughter."

"I think I need to call your mother," Juliet said.

"No, please. He'll just make things worse."

"The truth never made anything worse.

"Mike won't believe you any more than he did me. And Mom listens to him now. She never, ever listens to me since he moved in."

"We have to try, Hope. If she shuns you because of a lie, then she's not worthy of being your mother. I think Benedict would have a good case to sue for sole custody of you."

"He won't want me either. He's getting married soon and he'll only have time for Thistle." Hope slumped, nearly dissolving into herself.

"Don't bet on that. I know my son. And I've come to know Thistle. They will welcome you, Benedict already loves you. Now go upstairs and wash your face. I'm guessing it will just be the two of us for dinner. But that's actually a good thing. I need a co-conspirator and you are the best candidate. And take Chicory up with you. I don't need him throwing flour all over the kitchen while I make dumplings."

"I never!"

"You do, too. Now go with Hope." She leaned down close and whispered, "Watch her. And take care of her."

Chicory nodded and flew up to Hope's shoulder. "I need a big favor, Hope."

"Like I'm in a position to help a Pixie."

# Thirty-seven

DICK STARED IN DISMAY AT THE FLAMES shooting high into the twilit sky. Smoke billowed outward in the still air.

His high school burned. The front portico shot fire and smoke out of broken windows.

This was the place where he'd taken his first biology classes and fallen in love with science. Where he'd met a string of girls, made friends, earned some trophies. The big State Championship Science Fair plaque was his.

Generations of townsfolk had attended school here. The original school from 1850 was gone; the 1922 building now housed the middle school. This one dated back only to the late 1950s, but all the accumulated trophies and memorabilia since the early days were collected here—except for the oldest stuff that Dusty had confiscated for her museum.

Gone. So much of the town's past was gone. He ached from his gut outward. He'd cherished his high school memories where he'd gloried in accolades in sports and academic awards, loved the girls, made and cemented lifetime friendships.

Fathered a daughter.

A blast of heat and noise lit the scene with the garish orange blaze of a greedy fire and new fuel. The glare and the heat drove him back. He shielded his eyes with his arm. Sweat poured down his face and back. Still he was grateful for the heavy protection of coat, helmet, pants, and boots.

He retreated behind the EMT truck coughing out smoke. Returning to reality, and adult responsibilities.

In the near distance, he heard Chase shouting directions to control traffic around the busy intersection. Firefighters shouted for more water pressure.

A comrade stumbled toward him, supporting a limp figure. "Here's our witness, he called in the alarm," Digger Ledbetter said around his own coughing spate. Dick almost didn't recognize him without his camera, notebook, and press pass.

Dick shoved an oxygen mask over the witness' face.

"Help me move him over to the sidewalk," Dick shouted over the noise that always accompanied a fire. "Whatever's burning is too hot. This oxygen tank will explode."

Dick put his shoulder under the man's arm and guided him farther away. Digger grabbed the portable oxygen tank and followed him.

"Move the truck back, too!" Dick yelled. All the while he kept a mask over the face of the witness.

"You got here fast from the hospital," Dusty said, appearing out of nowhere. Of course she was here. Chase was here. Dusty hadn't come home last night. They'd been together when Dick called in a panic about Hope.

Hope. Damn, but he hoped she'd be okay alone until Mom got home.

"You know this guy?" Dick asked, checking his patient's pulse and the dilation of his pupils.

"Dick, have you met our new neighbor Ian McEwen? He bought the old Goddard place. His aunt is Mabel Gardiner," Dusty said over the noise and rush of the fire scene.

"Pleased to meet you again. Haven't seen you since that summer we played Little League," Dick said casually, barely taking his attention away from the man's breathing pattern and pulse.

Ian acknowledged him with a nod, still sucking in oxygen through the mask.

"I took him to visit Mabel earlier this afternoon," Dusty continued. "I left him there," she consulted her watch, "a little over an hour ago. He said he'd walk back here to get his truck which was parked in the back of the gym." She couldn't take her eyes away from the horror of the fire.

Another siren approached from uphill. The fire must be

really intense for the chief to call in backup from the county station up by the community college.

"You need to go home, Dusty," Dick said, pointing to the rushing firefighters dragging huge hoses, manipulating them to get the best arc of water to fall on the blaze. He knew from experience how their muscles had begun to ache about now. They'd grow even more tired before this was over. "You'll be in the way."

"I'm not running away, Dick. I need to know if the static parade is doomed. The entire All Hallows Festival might fall to a similar fate." She choked back tears.

Quite a different woman from the baby sister who hid from reality in the basement of her museum as recently as three months ago.

Ian McEwen's breathing became more regular and his pulse settled down, though it was still rather rapid. Adrenaline would do that. "You shouldn't have tried to stamp out the fire," Dick said noting the char marks on his work boots. He held the oxygen mask in place so Ian couldn't respond. "That's a good way to get hurt. Also a good way to get accused of setting the fire." His words came out angry, much more so than the situation called for.

He looked away from his patient and wished he hadn't. Firefighters jumped and jerked about, limbs flailing, backlit shadows against the tendrils of fire reaching to entangle them.

He conjured images from Dante's *Inferno*. Or Mussorgsky's *A Night on Bald Mountain*.

Police Chief Beaumain elbowed his way through the gathering crowd of looky-loos that Chase barely kept at bay. He aimed for Dick and the witness.

"What'd you see?" he barked as soon as he'd finished the formalities of name, address, and phone number. And McEwen's connection to Mabel.

Ian jerked the mask away from Dick who was trying to replace it. "I saw the silhouette of a man running away from the front entrance. He windmilled his arms and stumbled like he was drunk or had MS or something. Then I smelled the smoke."

Dusty caught Dick's gaze with her own. She mouthed

something that might have been "Snapdragon." He couldn't be sure. Didn't want to discuss the prime suspect in public. Still, he had to know.

"Jerky like Saint Vitus' Dance?"

"What's that?" Chief Beaumain asked.

Ian shrugged. "Never heard of that one. Is it something new the kids are doing?" His voice sounded a bit wheezy.

"Never mind." Dick shoved the oxygen mask back over his face. He nodded to Dusty.

"It's getting dark. We'll never find him until sunrise," she said quietly.

"Find who?" Beaumain asked, alert and wary.

"Haywood Wheatland," Dick said. *Otherwise known as Snapdragon.* "I've heard rumors that he caught ergot poisoning while he was incarcerated. The jerky lack of muscle control is indicative of the toxin. Insanity follows close behind."

"Ergot? Isn't that medieval? You get it from moldy rye bread?" Ian asked. "How could that happen in jail? The food is inspected . . ."

"Tight budgets. Cooks save money by serving bread that has sat around too long." Beaumain shrugged in dismissal. "Scrape off most of the green and who's to challenge them?"

"Ergot affects barley and some wheat as well as rye," Dusty added. "It shows up usually during a famine or after floods. The county jail is notoriously damp."

"Serving tainted food is not right," Ian protested.

"It's reality," Dick retorted. "Let's get you in an ambulance."

"I'm fine."

"No, you aren't. Smoke inhalation is sneaky. I want you checked out." Dick pulled Ian up and shoved him toward the waiting ambulance half a block away. He should have summoned a gurney but didn't think it could get through the crowd.

"Did you smell an accelerant?" Beaumain called after them.

"Gasoline." Ian turned and tried to go back. "Maybe more like kerosene, not as sharp or acidic as gas."

Dick kept a firm grip on the man's arm.

An out-of-control Snapdragon. Thistle lost in The Ten Acre Wood. Hope suffering from abandonment issues. He needed this night to be over with so he could settle his problems and get life back to normal, with Thistle and, maybe, his daughter.

"This has got to end. We take care of the fire-fascinated vandal tomorrow at dawn."

"Agreed," Dusty and Chase said together.

Chicory inspected the saucers with spices and herbs heaped in the center of each. Good thing Juliet used fresh in all her cooking. He and Hope had only gone as far as the pantry to find what he needed.

They'd arranged the saucers in a circle in the clear space between Dick's bed and the closet. A squat candle sat in the middle of each container, surrounded by a full mix of the dry ingredients. Once all was in place, he'd sent Hope to bed, and made sure she went there and didn't wait outside eavesdropping. Then he'd waited for Dick to come home.

He just barely made the midnight deadline. More delay came when he'd made Dick take a quick shower. The smell of sweat and smoke and tired male could easily interfere with the magic, if only in Chicory's concentration.

"Are you sure this is going to work?" Dick asked. Now he smelled of soap and damp hair—not noxious and deadly fumes. He turned a box of matches over and over, seemingly reluctant to open it and begin the process.

"No. But it is all I can offer you. Thistle won't listen to you while you are big. You have to be as small as me and have wings to get her attention." Chicory took a pinch of chili powder and mixed it with rosemary and a touch of sage. He hummed the melody of an old song while he pondered the cilantro and thyme. The composer had gotten things right. But would the exotic foreign cilantro work instead of good old-fashioned parsley?

"We have to set this in motion precisely at midnight," Chicory said. Only a few more seconds to wait. "You'll awake at dawn and the transformation will be in place. But it will only last until sunset. If you haven't convinced Thistle to come home by then, you won't get a second chance."

Chicory certainly hoped Dick would be back to normal by sunset. Otherwise, he and his friend would be trapped inside each other's bodies for all eternity, or until one or both of them died.

If the magic worked at all. His memory of the spell was sketchy and full of holes. He'd had to think hard about what to put into saucers.

"I understand. Tell me what to do."

"Water. We need a big glass of water!" Chicory remembered the final ingredient. "The herbs are Earth. I'm Air. You'll light the Fire. We just need Water to bind it all together."

"Fine." Dick reached behind him for the half-full glass on his night table.

Chicory scattered a few drops on each saucer.

"All you have to do now is strike the match, touch it to each candle, and drop it into this saucer at the west side of the circle when I say. Thistle is west of here. Better make that two matches to represent the Fire of your love, which is what this is all about."

Dick nodded. Chicory flew a circle widdershins around and around Dick where he sat cross-legged in the middle of the circle. He wound the spiral tighter and tighter, starting low and working up. All the while he sang his own music, *Dum dum do do dee dee dum.* He made the rhythm as complex as the aromas coming from a garden of mixed flowers, tall and short, robust and delicate. He matched his wingbeats to Dick's heartbeat.

"Now," he shouted in the middle of a phrase and continued his music and his spiral downward. He heard the rasp of the matches striking the brown stripe on the box, watched the red-orange flame flare upward. The candle wicks glowed in succession around the circle, deosil starting at the west.

Dick released his fingers and two matches dropped head first.

The blast of magic combining with chili pepper threw Chicory across the room. Darkness reigned across all his senses.

# Thirty-eight

"**T**HAT WON'T WORK," DUSTY SAID, staring at the assortment of equipment Chase had "borrowed" from the kitchen of his family's diner.

"Why not?" He held up the circular spatula with straining holes in it. The streetlight on the corner sent slanting rays to glint off the shiny metal.

"That is fine for throwing the crushed ice at Pixies." She tapped her mother's large picnic cooler she'd filled with bags of cubes. "Ice is lethal to them. But the fry basket is metal."

"It will trap a Pixie on the ground," he protested.

"It's stainless steel. Steel is made of iron. Even the most deranged Pixie will avoid it. They are hard enough to catch without driving them away with iron."

"So what do you suggest?" Chase threw his box of supplies as well as the cooler into the back of his pickup.

Dusty looked up and down the street for inspiration. She tasted blood as she worried her lip with her teeth. A glimpse of an askew picket fence, much in need of painting caught her attention. Lights shone through the off-balance, broken mini-blinds. "We ask the town Eagle Scout for a butterfly net."

"Huh?"

"Ian McEwen. If anyone in this town has a butterfly net, it will be him." She marched across the street and through the sagging gate, pausing briefly out of habit, as if to ask any resident Pixies for permission to cross their territory.

But no Pixies lived here. The garden could surely use

their attention. The house showed signs of ongoing repairs
new wood on a window frame, a sturdy new door with shiny
locks, glass had replaced cardboard in the small window
above the door.

Dusty rang the bell, surprised when she heard an interio
chime in response.

"Coming!" Half a minute later Ian flipped the deadbol
and opened the door a crack with the security chain still on
"What? Do you know what time it is, Miss Carrick?" He
ran a callused hand through shower damp hair. Shor
strands tried to stand on end but didn't have enough length
to do more than look scattered, like a field of hay afte
someone walked through it.

"Sorry to disturb you so early, Ian, but we were wonder
ing if you had a butterfly net we could borrow?" Dust
asked sweetly.

"What? I haven't even had coffee yet. This is the wrong
season to catch butterflies, or even the dragonflies that in
fest this city." He made to close the door on them.

Chase jammed his booted toe into the crack. "Think
back to your childhood, Ian. Think back to the summers w
played together in The Ten Acre Wood."

"So? We had some good times before . . . that last sum
mer."

"Think back to your aunt's home," Dusty continued, try
ing for a mesmerizing lilt in her voice.

Ian's eyes glazed over a bit as he chased memories a
fleeting as a Pixie.

"No."

"It's true, McEwen," Chase growled. "Look, you don'
have to believe anymore, but if you have a net, could w
borrow it?"

"I suppose. Give me a minute. I think it's in the boxes
haven't unpacked yet in the spare room."

Five long and anxious minutes later he returned an
shoved the net with a worn handle and warped fram
through the crack in the doorway. "This whole city is craz
Sometimes I think I should move back to Portland for m
own sanity."

"Maybe you should stay a little longer and find your sanity here," Dusty whispered.

Hand in hand, she and Chase skipped back to the truck and headed for The Ten Acre Wood.

"Where's Dick?" Chase asked as he unloaded the cooler. "He said he'd meet us here."

Dawn had just begun to swell along the eastern horizon.

Dusty waved the butterfly net around, testing the swish of the flexible mesh. Now all she needed was a Pixie to catch in it. "If Dick said he'd be here, then he'll be here."

"Hey, watch where you swing that thing, lady!" a tiny voice yelled at Dusty.

She looked around for the source.

"Over here. What are you? Blind as a Faery in sunlight?" A skinny yellow-and-green Pixie hovered in front of Dusty's eyes.

"Oh, hello. Who are you?"

"I'm Dandelion Five and Chicory put me in charge of this campaign." He puffed out his chest and threw back his shoulders with pride.

"Pleased to meet you, Dandelion Five." Dusty dipped a curtsy to him, a little hard to accomplish wearing jeans, hiking boots, and a plaid flannel shirt. Then she spotted a dozen other dandelion Pixies looking identical to Five. "Mind if I call you Leo so I know you're the leader?" she whispered.

"Leo, why Leo?" he spluttered.

"It's short for Lion."

"Oh, okay, then. Leo I am."

"Where is Chicory, by the way?"

Leo shrugged. "He didn't tell me. Just put me in charge. About time someone recognized how valuable dandelions are."

"Why, of course, a dandelion is the perfect plant. The greens are good eating—cooked or raw—the flowers provide a lovely yellow dye . . ."

"And make dandelion wine," Chase added.

"Wine, yes. How could I forget?" She grinned at her fiancé. "The roots can be roasted for either a vegetable or dried and ground for a coffee substitute." She grimaced at the remembered taste of one of her mother's experiments.

"The seed pods make a perfect child's toy," she concluded.

"Don't forget a bouquet of flowers to a loved one! And we are the only Pixies who can survive the winter no matter how cold it gets," Leo chortled with pride. Then his face grew serious again. "Who are we here to fight?" He brandished his hawthorn spike as eloquently as the finest rapier.

"Snapdragon," Chase said, butting in to the conversation.

"Oooooh, he's evil. I've fought for him and against him," Leo replied. He swished his thorn around in a complicated circle that was more flourish than weapon.

"But first we have to find him," Chase muttered.

A flutter of red and gold in the elbow of a branch on the Patriarch Oak caught Dusty's attention. "I don't think finding Snapdragon will be the problem."

The sound of big, human-sized voices woke Thistle. She shoved Pixie arms and legs out of her way to peer over the lip of the hollow log they'd made into a bower.

"Wake up, everyone, the cavalry has arrived!" she said as she kicked and pushed awake every Pixie within reach, which was most of the tribe. Her heart swelled that her friends had come, prepared to rescue her and her family from Snapdragon.

But the one person she wanted here had not come. She'd allow herself to cry away the ache—or make it deeper— later. Right now, she needed to be out there organizing the coming battle. If that trumped-up Dandelion Leo would let her.

Quickly she left the nest and tweaked Dusty's hair by way of welcome. "Where's your brother?" She dared not say his name or she'd let loose with all of her tears at once.

"I don't know," Dusty replied. "He said he'd be here."

"And here I am!" Dick said a little breathlessly. His voice sounded different . . . shrunken.

Thistle scanned as she flew a tight circle around Dusty and Chase.

A scatter of Dandelions darted into view, clutching Dick by his hair and an oddly fashioned kilt of flower petals. He had indeed shrunk to Pixie size with wings and everything. "So why aren't you flying?" she asked, amazed at the magic that enveloped him. She tasted Chicory in the air every time he twitched. This was indeed a potent spell. Big enough that Chicory was probably sound asleep and snoring for the rest of the day.

"Dick, you came," Dusty said on a sigh of relief.

"Of course I came. And I can fly now," he called the last to his escort.

Abruptly, they dropped him. He tumbled down three blossom lengths before he caught air and righted himself.

"You can fly?" Thistle asked.

"Yes, I can. I'm just not used to it and got a bit tired. It's a long way here from our house."

"We found him gasping for breath by the back gate. He barely made it out of the house," one of the Dandelions sneered.

"Oh, Dick, I am so happy you came," Thistle cried. She led her love to the flat rock overlooking the pond.

"I came for you. I need to take you back home with me, or stay a Pixie. I don't care as long as I'm with you." He kissed her.

"What about Hope? Are you prepared to leave her?" Thistle asked cautiously.

"I don't want to. But if staying a Pixie is the only way I can have you, then I'll have to trust my mother, and Dusty and Chase, and Chicory and his tribe to take care of Hope for me." He kissed her nose. "Don't we have some work to do first?"

Human-sized tears threatened to choke her. She could tell by his expression that he really did care. He wanted to be human, but he had to give her the choice.

"Thank you, Dick. I love you. You have to trust me that I will come back to you as a human. But I've learned from you and Dusty the importance of responsibility and commitment. I have to take care of Snapdragon and find a leader for my tribe. I owe them."

"Yes, you do. No more running away from the past for either of us. But you don't have to do it alone. I've got your back, Thistle, my love. Now give me a sword and let's go meet the enemy before he comes to meet us."

# Thirty-nine

D ICK FLEXED HIS WINGS. His shoulders protested the work. No worse than a three-hour football practice.

A tiny voice in the back of his head reminded him that he wasn't seventeen anymore. His muscles didn't like working that hard.

*I have to do this,* he reminded himself, *for Thistle, for Hope, and our future.*

New strength flushed through him along with his resolve and commitment. The wing thing got easier as he worked through stiff muscles.

He leaped upward, only half-surprised that he kept going as his wings grabbed air. Thistle leaped ahead of him, flying instinctively. He still had to think about it.

She grabbed an extra sword from a Dandelion and tossed him one, too. Great, he had to fight *AND* fly at the same time. "I can do this. I have to do this."

"Give up, Thistle Down, you can't win against me!" Snapdragon taunted. He thrust his sword forward. Lethal poison dripped from the tip.

But his arm wavered just a bit. The toxins gained potency in his system, robbing him of strength.

The medical portion of Dick's brain noted that the purple-red fungus pockets on Snapdragon's wings had grown to encompass most of the delicate tissue. Hardly any yellow or gold remained.

"Wanna make a bet?" Thistle called back. "Oh, wait a minute, betting is a Faery thing. Of course you'll take a bet.

Before you do, look around you, you crazy mutant. Where's your army? Where are the Faeries you work for? They've abandoned you. All of them. Just like they deserted Pixies when they went underhill. Just like they always do. I have friends. Real friends. They follow me out of love, no magic compulsion. Compulsion is a Faery trick."

Sure enough, the only Pixies behind Snapdragon were a pathetic gaggle of wilted Dandelions. Long past their prime and ready to hibernate.

"Chicory offers a place within his tribe, to any of you who leave Snapdragon before blood is shed," Leo announced.

The wilted troop perked up a bit.

"That's a full place within the tribe, not just drifting around the edges like an outcast weed. We offer a nest *inside* the attic," Dick confirmed.

"Um, Dick, have you discussed this with Chicory?" Dusty whispered. She didn't seem at all surprised to see him shrunk to four inches tall and wearing only a kilt of flower petals.

But then, Dusty had always believed in magic: the magic of Pixies or the magic of a medical miracle that saved her life. It made no difference to her. Indeed, she represented the entire town in that mixture of belief.

"Watch out!" Chase bellowed.

Dick covered his ears and lost air. Something rattled loudly.

Chase drew back his arm and cast a spatula full of ice chunks at Snapdragon. He'd never thrown a better forward pass on the football field.

Snapdragon rose up on his tattered wings and looped around the spreading array of lethal ice.

Thistle darted away to Snapdragon's other side. "Over here, you bully. You can't battle both of us," she sneered, diving in with her own sword pointed at the mutant Pixie's heart.

Dick thrust himself forward at the same time.

Snapdragon dropped toward Dusty's hair. The Dandelions whipped in, making a solid wall between the enemy and his prey.

Dick breathed a bit easier as he watched Dusty twirl away, jumping over rocks and downed branches with the grace and ease of the ballerina she always wanted to be.

Another pelting of ice brought confusion and shrieks. The limp Dandelions deserted the battlefield en masse.

"Rosie threw us out on *his* orders," one of them whispered to Dick as he zoomed out. "No weeds sullying their pure tribe."

"Pure, my wings," Dick retorted. "He's the one tainting the good name and pure blood of Pixie!"

"Incoming!" Chase warned. He shifted his stance for a new style of attack. Something hard and dark flew from his left hand at the same time more ice shot toward Snapdragon.

Dusty followed up with her own fist full of mud. Right left, left right, ice and dirt pelted Snapdragon. The last lingering Dandelions ducked away in every direction, leaving their flagging leader to face the barrage alone.

Still Snapdragon jabbed at Dick or Thistle, whoever ventured closer. His thrusts went wild, easily parried.

Together, Dick and Thistle drove him closer and closer to Chase and Dusty and their lethal ice chest.

A dirt clod struck Snapdragon squarely between the wings.

He halted in midair, gasping.

"What a pitiful sight," Dick mused, half aloud. "Much as I hate to do this to any creature, I need to put you out of your misery. Like a rabid dog or a cat gutted by a raccoon." He dove fast and furious, aiming his sword at his enemy's heart.

"Put him out of *our* misery, you mean," Thistle echoed.

As one, they descended upon the startled Snapdragon. Their swords sank deep into his chest at the same moment, between heartbeats.

Before Dick could grasp the enormity of having killed another sentient being, Dusty lunged beneath them and scooped Snapdragon into her butterfly net. With a deft flick, she deposited the tiny corpse into the ice chest. Chase kicked the lid shut.

And it was over.

"We'll turn him over to animal control so that they can lift the ban on daytime activities." Chase grinned hugely. "Wonder what they'll really see when they do an autopsy?"

Dick almost fell out of the sky, exhausted, winded, triumphant, and sick-at-heart. He had killed someone.

Thistle held out her hand to Dick, settling lightly beside him on a comforting, but cold and wet, tuft. "I never lost your ring. It stayed with me, a constant reminder that we love each other and whatever happened here in Pixie, you and I belong together. I had a job to do. That's the real reason I left. Not because of you and Hope. I want Hope to be a part of our family. A big, important part." She smiled, feeling a bit shy at the possibility that something could still go terribly wrong.

Her awareness of the humans watching and listening faded. She needed to concentrate on Dick and only Dick.

"And I appreciate it. I had a job to do first, to truly find my daughter and learn to love her." He took Thistle's hand and kissed the ring. "Now how do we get back to our human bodies? There are things we have to talk about, decisions we have to make. And I imagine Chicory is looking a bit strange at six feet tall with blue hair and skin." He drew in a deep lungful of air. She watched his exhaustion fade to mere tiredness, saw the moment his heart settled into a steady rhythm.

Thistle giggled. "Chicory will last a bit longer." She looked up, trying to figure out how to reverse the magic that had brought them both to Pixie but must now reject them.

Even as she watched, her tribe crept out of their hiding places. They scurried about, looking to each other for direction. Gradually, Foxglove the younger took control, sending them about their daily forays seeking food and fun.

Thistle smiled. She knew one of them would evolve into leadership without her. She just had to let them do it. Probably, Foxglove had been directing them all along and they only pretended to follow Alder.

She was a sensible one, not terribly aggressive, but practical. She'd see that a treaty got signed and the Patriarch Oak would once again be neutral territory, open to all Pixies.

A broad brown leaf broke loose from the Patriarch Oak and drifted down to land on the pond. It floated in a circle for a moment before the gentle current caught it and dragged it slowly, but relentlessly toward the waterfall where it must tumble from the quiet, timeless peace of the wood into the mortal chaos of humankind below.

"As I climbed the steps from down below," Thistle said slowly, carefully, "I shrank. So maybe we must fall down to grow big." She grinned hugely, anticipating the best of all Pixie magic, a mating flight.

Still holding her hand, Dick looked up at the towering oak. When he turned his attention back to her, he rested his forehead against hers. "Um, I'm more than a bit tired, not used to flying and all. Getting up there would be the end of me. I'd not have enough left to get us down safely."

Thistle placed two fingers into her mouth and blew a long shrieking whistle. A male varied thrush responded with an inquiring chirrup before landing on top of the flat rock. He turned his head right and left, catching them in his strange gaze. The bright stripes of orange and black along his back and wings rippled and fluttered with minute shifts of his wings.

"You should have a net made of vines to hold you while he lifts you to your bower," Dusty said. She crouched beside the rock.

"Not necessary for so short a flight," Thistle said with confidence. "This guy is an old friend. He helped me once before." She laughed again at how eagerly the bird had flown Milkweed in her net on a long and diverse path to her wedding. A wedding that had been delayed so long it never took place. She hoped she hadn't cursed her own wedding with her side trip back into Pixie.

Not wanting to think about that yet, she climbed aboard the bird's back between neck and wing. Dick scrambled up behind her, desperately holding tight around her waist.

A few sharp wingbeats brought them to the upper reaches of the old oak tree. Thistle eagerly jumped free of the bird and grabbed onto a twig that supported one of the last leaves of the season. Dick followed her, more falling than scrambling. She caught his arm and steadied him.

He looked over the edge of their tiny branch. "That's a long way down." He gulped. His transparent wings stilled. His breathing grew rapid and shallow.

"That's why a mating flight is so special," she replied. "It takes courage, commitment, and trust. And calm. Breathe deeply and think about a soft and gentle ending rather than the wild and precipitous beginning."

"That's what getting married is all about." He held her close and kissed her long and hard.

Electric tingles sprang from the diamond-and-amethyst ring up her arms to her head and down to her feet. She shivered in delight.

"Let's do this before I chicken out," he said, looking into her eyes rather than down the great distance of the oak's challenge.

Thistle turned within the circle of his arms, making sure to flatten her wings. "This is all up to you, love. I can't help you. But I trust you. Come what may, we make this flight together. We end it together, joined for all time."

Thistle squeaked as Dick filled her body and her soul with his love.

"Say good-bye to Pixie," she said in wonder as they stepped off the topmost branch into the air.

An updraft caught them, driving them upward. Wisely, Dick let it take them where it would, away from the entrapment of the spreading branches. "Use the lift to steady your wings," she coaxed.

He did.

All too soon, the air released them. They dropped dramatically. Thistle's heart formed a huge lump in her throat. She resisted the urge to break free and save herself. She had to trust him.

Then he remembered to set his wings to working. Their descent slowed. They had a few moments to relish the glory of spiraling flight while joined in the intimacy of mating.

He buried his face in her hair, breathing heavily as he strained to maintain and control their flight.

His wings began to fail and the ground rushed toward them at an alarming rate. But suddenly it didn't seem as far away as it should.

Dick's sweating hands shifted for a better grip. "If we die, we die together," he grunted through clenched teeth.

New sensations of wonder filled Thistle as she realized he'd grabbed hold of her by her swelling breasts. Her Pixie slenderness curved and grew. And so did his.

Complete and fulfilled, they tumbled the last short distance to land abruptly in the mud at the verge of the pond at the feet of Dusty and Chase.

"It . . . that was so beautiful," Dusty gasped in wonder.

"They call it making love for a reason," Chase answered, dropping a kiss on her nose. "With the right person, for the right reasons, love grows exponentially each time."

Thistle breathed deeply, relishing the sensation of soft leaf litter and damp earth beneath her cheek and the warmth of Dick's arms enfolding her naked body against his. "Love. We made love and watched it grow so big Pixie bodies couldn't contain it anymore."

"Ahem," Chase cleared his throat.

Thistle risked opening her eyes enough to see his face flush deep red as he turned around. Dusty followed suit. The two looked at each other with deep longing, then swiveled their heads away. As one, they shed their coats. Dusty's fell atop Thistle. Dick clutched Chase's as he shivered with cold. Now that the afterglow of love faded, Thistle, too, felt the chill of a late October morning.

"You two, take my truck," Chase said, holding his keys out to them, behind his back. "We'll walk." He grabbed Dusty's hand and started off along the path toward the museum.

"Are we really married by Pixie law?" Dick whispered in Thistle's ear. He nuzzled her neck as he spoke.

"Yes," she breathed in satisfaction.

"Good, because I'm never letting you leave me again."

"What about human rituals?"

"We'll deal with that when the time comes. Right now, you and I are together. And we both need to go home and get out of the cold."

"Mabel's house first," she whispered. "We'll have a bit of privacy.

Dreams of a hot bath, together, propelled Thistle upward. She didn't need her wings to right herself. She didn't miss them at all.

# Forty

"**B**ENEDICT! WAKE UP!" Juliet called through the door to her son's room.

Chicory opened one eye warily. Exhaustion nearly drove him back to sleep before he realized where he was, where Dick wasn't, and what he had done.

"Um. Getting a shower now," Chicory called back, to keep Juliet out. He hoped he sounded enough like Dick to stall her.

Then he looked at himself under the sheet and blankets. *Gulp.* He was big. *Really big.* Like big enough to fill the bed nearly end-to-end. Okay, Dick was that tall. So far so good.

He tried flexing his wings and discovered them missing. Panic forced him to sit up. He looked awkwardly over his shoulders. Blank. Nothing. Not even an energy signature like during the few times he'd masqueraded as human to help Mabel and Dusty with special chores last summer. Who was he, what was he, without his wings? He was grounded. Helpless. Immobile.

Was this what Thistle had felt like when she landed in Memorial Fountain last summer?

Nope. Not quite. Alder had stripped her of not only her wings, but her lovely lavender skin and purple hair. She'd become truly human.

Chicory still had blue skin. He reached up and pulled down a forelock while rolling his eyes upward. Yup. He had blue hair as well. And broad, muscled shoulders. He thought maybe he was built stockier than Dick, too.

He was still Chicory, just different.

"Benedict? Are you okay? You sound like you have a cold," Juliet said through the door. "All that sulking. Now get up. I think you have work today, don't you? It's Friday. And you need to talk to Hope, and her mother."

Chicory faked a cough. "Fire last night. Too much smoke. I'm calling in sick." If he could make the phones work.

Oh, he didn't have to. Dick took care of that yesterday when they cooked up this scheme together. The memory of Dick's exact words, postponing several appointments with doctors and clinics popped clear and bright into Chicory's mind. Hm, so this is what it was like to be human and think ahead.

"I don't like the sound of that cough, Benedict," Juliet said at the same time she pushed the door open. "I'll make you some nice chamomile tea with honey."

Chicory flipped the sheet back over his naked body. He'd lived with humans long enough to know how they felt about bare skin, especially certain parts of bare skin.

"Oh!" Juliet squeaked back a scream.

"Hi, Mom," Chicory said and waved to her.

"What . . . what . . . have you done to my son!"

"Not much," Chicory hedged.

"This looks like a lot more than 'not much.' Again, what have you done with my son?" She nudged one of the saucers filled with herbs and candles with her toe.

"Um, please don't do that, Juliet. If you want Dick back, you have to leave the spell circle intact."

"Oh, my God. You've stolen my boy with magic. You've made him a changeling. I'll never see him again."

"No, no, no, no." Chicory really hoped he wasn't lying. "We switched places. Temporarily," Chicory said. He couldn't think of a stall that wasn't an outright lie.

"For . . . for how long?" Juliet staggered to the armchair in the corner where Dick had heaped his clothes for several days. She seemed oblivious to the creases she added to the mess.

"Just until sunset," Chicory replied.

"This sounds dangerous. I think you should bring him back right now." Her chin quivered and her hands shook.

"Sorry. No can do. Once the spell is set, it can't be re-

versed until it runs its course." Chicory smiled, hoping Juliet
would find some humor in the situation. Too bad his tiny
silk cap didn't change size with him. He'd like to doff it to
her as a token of truce.

"I don't care. I want my son back. Now."

"Um, Juliet, aren't you overreacting just a bit?"

"I said, bring my son back!" she shouted, standing tall
and clenching her fists. "Bring him back now, or I'll throw
the lot of you Pixies out into the cold." She tensed her jaw
and thrust it forward belligerently.

"I don't know how." Chicory hung his head. He felt hot
and cold all over. "Not until the spell runs its course."

And he had to pee. He couldn't flit outside or even into
the bathroom without embarrassing Juliet, and therefore
himself. Something had to give. And soon.

"What do you mean you don't know how? This is worse
than the doctors telling us they didn't know for sure if they
could cure Desdemona. I almost lost my daughter. I. Will.
Not. Lose. My son."

"You won't lose him. We have to let the spell run out. Or
Dick finishes what he set out to do. Disrupting it now might
kill us both."

"No. No. I can't lose him. I just can't. I need my boy."
Tears slid down her cheeks, gathering speed and volume.

Panic cramped Chicory's middle. He didn't know what to
do. Except dash to the bathroom and take care of business.

Juliet buried her face in her hands. He took advantage of
her distraction. A few moments later he returned with a
thick towel draped around his hips.

"Desdemona is deserting me, getting married. I almost
lost her to cancer and now I'm losing her to that . . . that
man! She didn't come home last night, or the night before.

> *'Ingratitude, thou marble-hearted fiend,*
> *More hideous, when though show'st thee in a child,*
> *Than a sea-monster.'* "

"Juliet, why does it bother you that your children are
growing up and finding lives of their own, mates of their
own, homes of their own?" He touched her shoulder in

mute sympathy and wondered if he would cross too many boundaries of politeness if he hugged her.

> *" 'How sharper than a serpent's tooth it is*
> *To have a thankless child!'*

I . . . I . . . is that what I'm doing?" She looked at him, truly bewildered. Her tear-ravaged face showed a different Juliet, a vulnerable and lonely woman, middle-aged with huge changes disrupting her ordered life.

"I think so. What happened all those years ago? It made you hold your children so close you smother them; that you have to control everything around you. So you organize, manipulate, and bully people into following your plans."

"Nothing that is your concern." She stiffened her spine and made to stand up.

Chicory pushed her down, keeping his hand firmly on her shoulder. "You're doing it again. Pushing me away rather than facing the truth. Quoting the Bard rather than admitting there is a problem."

"It is none of your concern."

"I'm your friend. I've taken refuge in your home. If you can't tell me, an imaginary Pixie who doesn't exist in your reality, who can you tell?"

"I don't have to tell anyone."

"I think you do. If you don't confront your past, you will have to keep running away from it and never learn to cope with now."

Juliet froze in place, holding her breath.

Chicory counted the long moments until her eyes regained focus and her chest heaved with indrawn air. Her shoulders slumped and a new spate of tears flowed. "Cancer almost killed my child, and I could do nothing about it I couldn't even donate my bone marrow to help cure her Benedict did it and now they are closer to each other than they are to me, their mother," she whispered.

"And so you became obsessed with Shakespeare and quote him rather than admit to anyone, including yourself that you could not control the situation."

She nodded, gulping back her tears.

"You didn't do 'nothing.' You got Dusty the help she needed, you sat by her side and held her hand through the pain, you gave up your career as a teacher to school her at home. You changed your diet to match her needs. You did not do 'nothing.'"

"I've driven my husband away with my obsessions."

"He's not gone for good. Just taking a break." Chicory flashed his cheekiest grin. "He'll be back because he loves you and the children you have together. If he didn't, he'd have divorced you years ago, and taken a mating flight with someone younger and more manageable."

"You think so?"

"Yup. So, Mom, what's for breakfast?"

"Now, I promise you'll only be in skilled nursing care for two weeks," Phelma Jo assured Mabel as she locked the brakes on a hospital wheelchair.

"I can take care of myself." Mabel stubbornly crossed her arms, not moving from the side of her hospital bed. She'd dressed in old slacks and shirt with socks and soft shoes, with the help of a nurse's aide.

"You'll only need to stay at the facility *two* weeks if you behave yourself and don't overdo. If you bring on another heart attack, you'll be right back here. Indefinitely." Phelma Jo gave back stubborn for stubborn.

"It's too expensive," Mabel insisted, eyeing the wheelchair suspiciously. "And I won't use one of them damn things." She kicked at the chair.

"Medicare and your insurance from the police union will cover it all." Phelma Jo gave up her death grip on the chair's handles to slide an arm around Mabel's waist and ease her into her new chariot.

"I hate being dependent," Mabel grumbled. But she did settle into the chair, testing it for comfort and size. She looked like a shrunken doll. A very stubborn shrunken doll, but too tiny and frail to face the world alone anymore.

"Excuse me, but I'm taking Aunt Mabel home with me," Ian McEwen said from the doorway.

"The arrangements have already been made for skilled

nursing care at a facility. I inspected the place myself. It's clean and bright and cheerful with an efficient and friendly staff." She faced Ian with hands on her hips as if he were the enemy and not Mabel's weak and aging heart.

"I've already arranged for daily help to stay with her while I'm at work."

"But your house isn't handicap accessible. You'll have to add a ramp and remodel a bathroom on the ground floor," Phelma Jo reminded him, triumphantly.

"In the works. I'll take her now." They both grabbed the wheelchair handles at the same time, jostling for control.

"Oh, my heart," Mabel groaned and slumped.

"Mabel!" Phelma Jo and Ian shouted at the same time. "Get a nurse! Help me get her back into bed."

"Oh, get over yourselves," Mabel snickered. "Got your attention anyway." Her gaze shifted back and forth between them.

"Don't do that again, Aunt Mabel. You scared us," Ian said on a long exhale.

"I needed you two to stop arguing and work together.

"Hmf." Phelma Jo stepped back, feeling like an intruder in a family argument. Dammit, she'd been more like family to the old woman than Ian, even though they didn't share blood. They shared more, a long history, friendship, conspiracy, and a mission.

"Admit it, both of you, you like each other. A lot."

Phelma Jo risked a brief glance at Ian. Their eyes locked for half a heartbeat, then they both looked away. A guilty flush flamed in her cheeks. The tips of his ears reddened as well.

"So, it looks like I have some work to do with both of you."

Phelma Jo pointedly looked anywhere but at Ian. He examined the walls as if looking for cracks, or mold, or something, anything but look at her or examine his true feelings.

She felt the same way.

"Phelma Jo, take me to your pristine facility for two weeks. *Two weeks* only. While I'm there, you, Nephew Ian, will fix up your house so I can stay there in comfort and ease. You will both visit me at the facility every day. At six PM. No variation. I intend to be busy the rest of the day and evening getting well. This town won't last long without me. Come along now, we've work to do. Together, all three of us. And you two together when I can't go with you."

# Epilogue

"**A**UNT DUSTY, YOU REALLY NEED to do a final walk through the maze before it opens to the public," Hope said. She bounced from foot to foot in eagerness. "It's the professional thing to do."

"I suppose you're right." Dusty watched the girl for signs of an agenda besides the opportunity to be the first one through the maze. She really had two dozen things to do in the next ten minutes, including counting the cash for the admission box, sorting the tickets, making sure the museum had all of its fake (and real) cobwebs in place, that the extra flashlights and light wands were fully charged at the rental table . . .

"Miss Carrick!" M'Velle hailed her coming up the path from the street. Her multiple black braids with beads woven into them chimed and clicked together with each step. She was dressed as a dancehall girl, in opposite colors to Dusty's white-and-green costume. "We really need to talk to you."

"What's wrong?" Dusty gathered the long skirts, ready to run to the rescue. A lacy wool shawl covered her nearly naked shoulders and a long feather bobbed annoyingly in her hair.

"We've got a proposition," Meggie added breathlessly as she joined her friend. Her blonde hair was bound tightly into a bun tonight, and she wore a prim missionary wife's calico gown.

The two girls should have swapped roles if they wanted to fit their personalities. But then they wouldn't really be costumes. And that was the whole point to Halloween!

Dusty wanted to giggle at her observation. She forced herself to soberness to address the girls as an adult and professional.

"Such as?" Dusty eyed her helpers suspiciously.

"You know that we're on the senior prom committee?" M'Velle asked. She bit her lip in unconscious imitation of Dusty's nervous habit.

"Yes."

"We've raised a lot of money so we can have the prom at the Dockside Ballroom on the Columbia River," Meggie said.

"But with the bad economy and all, a lot of kids can't afford the tickets," M'Velle finished.

"So?"

"We thought, and we talked to the rest of the class, that maybe we should hold the prom in the school gym."

"It's supposed to be ready to reopen at the end of April. The smoke damage isn't as bad as we all thought at first. Most of the fire was contained in the front lobby."

"And this concerns me how?"

"We thought that the school really is as much a part of this town and its traditions as the museum, the maze, the parades, and the other festivals. We should make the reopening of the gym a community event."

"The jazz band wants to play swing dances and pop music, so we won't have to hire a DJ."

"We should have torn down the building and built a whole new one," Phelma Jo grumbled from behind Dusty. She seemed to be hiding there as Ian McEwen wandered the grounds inspecting electrical cables and placing fire extinguishers in convenient locations. "The insurance would have paid for most of it, and it's about time this town moved on from the glory days of their high school years. Life really is much better after graduation, but some people will never grow beyond the football field or pompoms."

"I don't know about that," Dusty mused. "Chase's football skills helped a lot yesterday."

"And your childhood dance classes stood you in good stead too, baby sister." Dick dropped a kiss on her hair, batting away the stupid ostrich feather. Then he straightened and turned back to Phelma Jo. "Still running away from your past, Phelma Jo?" He held Thistle's hand, as he'd done almost continuously since that spectacular mating flight yesterday. He also stayed near Hope as much as possible, frequently with an arm thrown around her shoulders, as he did now.

"I've moved onward and upward. I'm not letting memories—bad ones mostly—hold me back." Phelma Jo glared at him smugly. But she also moved around the admissions table, keeping distance and bodies blocking her from having to watch Ian McEwen.

"I think turning the prom into a community celebration of the reopening of the high school front wing is a marvelous idea," Dusty said. "It will be something for this town to look forward to since we lost big chunks of the All Hallows Festival."

"But not the most important part of it. The maze," Chase reminded her. He wore his pioneer sheriff's costume. The big silver star on his chest and the modern gun on his hip served as reminders to one and all that he was back on duty. He'd accept some pranks; it was Halloween after all, but nothing outrageously stupid or dangerous.

"Aunt Dusty!" Hope whined. "You really need to tour the maze. Now. While you can still see . . . things."

"Oh, all right." She stepped onto the gravel path lighted by a string of white LED bulbs.

"Can I come, too, or is this a girl thing?" Chase asked, capturing her hand.

"You are always welcome." Dusty reached for his hand.

"I understand there are a lot of private little nooks and dead ends where couples can step aside," Dick said, looking longingly into Thistle's eyes.

"Go find a tree," Chase muttered.

"Maybe we should, too," Dusty giggled.

"Later," Chase said, raising his eyebrows in speculation.

"This way. Come quickly," Hope beckoned them from the first shadows of the tree canopy. She stayed a few yards ahead of them as she wound through the trees along the barely lighted path.

"Hey, Dick!" Judge John called from his station behind

Dedication:

*This book is dedicated to all those who believe in magic; whether in the miracle of a baby's smile or modern medicine that saves lives every day. May you find Pixies in the park or in your attic or in the eyes of the ones you love.*

a replica gallows. His ghost makeup made his eyes seem to burn in the fading light. He represented the first judge in town who was well known for convicting men and women to hang on the barest of evidence.

"What's up?" Dick replied.

The entire group paused, even the anxious Hope.

"I got your paperwork late last night. Looks like the Bureau of Vital Statistics has approved Thistle's petition. You'll be getting a birth certificate in the mail within the week."

"That is wonderful. We won't have to wait much longer to get married." Dick shook the judge's hand.

Thistle snuggled close to Dick and nibbled on his ear. "But we're already married," she said softly.

At least that's what Dusty thought she said. A clamor of voices at the beginning of the path distorted the words.

"Are you coming or not?" Hope called at the next bend in the path. "We're running out of time."

"What is so important . . . Oh." Dusty paused, hand to her heart. A long white blob drifted from a hanger within a huge cedar tree. In the ghostly light it looked like the headless spirit of a long lost bride.

But it wasn't.

"My wedding dress!" she gasped, realizing that the gown she had longed for, the bias-cut silk that draped and swirled so beautifully on the store mannequin now drifted within the haunted maze, taunting her with its unobtainable beauty.

"Look, there's a note," Hope chortled, holding up a slip of paper hanging from the folds of heavy white silk.

"To Desdemona, from your mother."